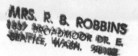

This Week's *Short-Short Stories*

This Week's
Short-
Short
Stories

*Edited, with an Introduction and an Essay
"How to Write a Short-Short Story" by*

STEWART BEACH

 Random House
New York

Contents

Introduction

BY STEWART BEACH

THE MAGAZINE short story has had its ups and downs through-out the last forty years, and just now it is showing a new and healthy vitality. At last, so it seems, this most lively and sensitive literary form is emerging from its partial eclipse in fact-studded periodicals to reassert its claim on the public affection. The short story is once more finding a place of first importance.

In fact, the whole field of fiction is sharing this revival of interest—and excitement. One collateral indication is to be found in the mounting sales of paper-covered reprints and original novels. In 1952, it is estimated, some 250,000,000 copies of these books were sold—about eighty per cent of them devoted to fiction.

It all reminds me of a wise observation which has been made on the frequent complaint that the legitimate theatre is dying. "All the theatre needs," says this comment, "is a few good plays." The fate of the short story, after all, is in the hands of its authors.

It is worth tracing what has happened to the short story in recent years. After a particularly brilliant flowering in the twenties and early thirties, the pall of the depression fell over the gayety and brightness, the piercing reality which had furnished themes for the writers of the prohibition era. In the dark days of the mid-thirties, the laughter became hollow, the words began to sound only shrill, even gangsters lost their false glamour. At a time when it might seem that "escape" in any form would be attractive, the anxieties of plain living apparently absorbed the attention of the public.

Of course, there were great stories written in those years. There are always great stories. But some of the heart went out of magazine fiction while its accustomed practitioners were taking a long look at sociology—at changes in the life around them. And some of them never survived the change.

The magazine short story is the most contemporary of all forms. It sharply reflects the life out of which it is written and is, therefore, peculiarly sensitive to customs, moods and changing currents of thought. From 1941-45, for example, it was unthinkable to read a story about a civilian of service age without looking for the explanation of why he was not in uniform. And it was always there—the physical disability, the concern with some vital form of war work. Even today you will find that most stories about men in their mid-twenties explain that "Jim was back in this country after two years in Korea." Quite unconsciously, but nonetheless dogmatically, the public likes to be assured that its heroes are men of honor who have fulfilled their duty to country.

The war undoubtedly retarded a heady revival of the short story in two ways. It provided a world of action, anxiety, drama and tragedy far more real than one a fiction writer could imagine. The public wanted to learn about this real world. But the war also carried off a whole beginning generation of writers. How many great talents were lost forever we shall never know. It must have been considerable enough to upset the orderly replacement of the writers who flash brilliantly for a time and then drop out or abandon short stories for other forms of writing—novels, plays, Hollywood, the radio and now television.

I frequently hear the complaint that there are no longer many great names in fiction, and those who make the charge are thinking back twenty and twenty-five years to a time when there were literary giants regularly producing short stories. But many of these giants are already dead. Some have ceased writing entirely. And others confine their talents to longer forms. We have had to wait for a new crop to mature. Most of the writers who appear in this collection have long since made their reputations within the profession. But many of them, too, must wait before becoming big names till the great novel or the great play engraves them on the mind of the larger public. Some of these, at least, are the giants of tomorrow.

In making this selection from recent fiction published in *This Week Magazine,* I have confined my choices deliberately to the short-short story—the tale which runs from a thousand to two thousand words. I have tried to make it show the infinite variety which the short-short story possesses today, as well as its new vitality. All of these stories have been written and published since the war, and most of them have appeared in the past two or three years.

What they have in common is a story to tell. Here is narrative in its full sense—the preoccupation of the storyteller with his story. Some of them are sheer entertainment and pretend to nothing more. Some of them plunge far deeper into human emotions. But all of them have that sense of revelation which is the true catalyst of fiction. Many of them churn up some universal truth and draw from it a memorable experience—a story to remember.

In recent years, I think, some critics have tended to forget how good and satisfying a thing is the story with plot, the story that *is* a story. In these last dozen or twenty years there has been a great fuss made over the Chekhov-inspired preoccupation with the "little" story, the story in which action is minimized—the doings of little people whose lives are without drama. I have no quarrel with that kind of story. When it is written with understanding sincerity and the beauty of quiet understatement, it can be a memorable experience. But it can never equal in universal appeal the satisfaction of the more robust, plotted narrative which begins a story—and ends it.

Selecting fiction for a magazine with the vast audience of *This Week* is a challenging task. Its circulation is upward of ten and a half millions, its weekly readership well over double that. Every story in this collection has been read—and liked —by some millions of people. These fifty stories, you might say, without, as the phrase goes, fear of contradiction, are reader-tested. They are all—already—best sellers.

New York City
1953

This Week's | *Short-Short Stories*

1

VICTOR CANNING

The Man Who Hated Time

VICTOR CANNING is an English novelist who enjoys great prestige in his own country and a growing reputation in America. His books are marvels of suspense and exciting plot, set against colorful backgrounds. His occasional short stories, like this one, are unusual in conception, and touched by the element of surprise.

YOU COULD TELL it was coming. The touch, the hard-luck story and, because my own glass was full and his empty, my own suit reasonably respectable and his unreasonably shabby, I was sorry for him. A man's always wondering at such times if he may not come to it himself. Twenty more years and I would have reached his sixty-odd, and a lot can happen in twenty years.

He edged along the seat a little and leaned across the table. From his waistcoat pocket he pulled out a watch and laid it between us. It was a good watch, silver, and with those finely wrought gold hands that they don't put on watches these days.

"It's yours for a couple of quid. Nothing wrong with it and honestly come by."

You could tell he was an old hand at the game by the way he ignored the preliminaries and came right to the heart of the problem at once.

"I don't want it," I said, but because a man's money is his own and he's entitled to be a damned fool with it at times, as I pushed the watch back I passed over a ten-bob note.

While he was recovering from the shock I ordered a beer and a ham sandwich for him from the bar.

"I'd rather you bought the watch square," he said when the attendant had served him.

"Forget it," I said.

He took a sip of the beer to help him, but it had the opposite effect. "I hate the sight of watches," he said suddenly, like a man remembering something he'd forgotten. "They started it all."

"All what?"

"This." He flicked his hand across the front of his shabby suit and bit into his sandwich.

I had half an hour before an appointment, and it was raining outside. He had me, and from the slick way he slid into his routine I knew there was to be no escape.

"Chris Selby was his name," the old man said. "A London theatrical agent, handled quite a few head-of-the-bill names and a great many more nearly as good. Yes, he was doing well for himself was Chris Selby, but he could never resist the temptation to do a little better—even if it meant going outside his own line of business."

He went into the story easily, and you could tell he'd had a lot of practice.

The whole thing took place just after the 1914-18 war—a long time ago, but there are a lot of people who still remember it and who think the Twenties were a pretty good period to live in.

This Chris Selby, it seems, was a Prince Charming with a smile that came on and off like the summer lightning, a voice like butter when he wanted something from you and poison if you got in the way of his fifteen per cent. But on the whole few people did get in his way, and most people liked him because they didn't really know him.

He used to make five or six trips a year to Paris on business picking up acts and vaudeville turns, trying out his smile along the Champs-Elysées and never feeling lonely in the evenings or counting his francs to see if he had enough for another Pernod.

Twice a year he would take his car over.

He always went over Dover to Calais and back that way, and most of the Customs boys knew and liked him because on a ten-minute acquaintance five or six times a year he was the kind of man anyone would like, and also he was generous with complimentary tickets for the London shows.

He never had any trouble with the Customs, and the truth was that, except for the two car trips each year, there was never any need for trouble because he never tried to get away with anything. But when the car went over—that was different. Twice a year he used to bring back about 5,000 watches.

I know it sounds a lot, but it's surprising how many watches you can pack into a car, particularly if your twelve-gallon tank only holds two gallons of petrol and the rest watches, and the floor of the car is a false one. Of course, it means filling up with petrol pretty often, but no one minds that if the gross profit on each trip touches £1,000.

If you or I tried anything like that we'd be as nervous as kittens with a duck for a foster mother and probably give ourselves away. But not Chris Selby. A theatrical agency is pretty good training in putting up a good front. He never felt nervous and he knew his stuff.

Now, that November, so my friend told me, Chris Selby set off from London in his car feeling pretty angry. He wasn't nervous or worried about the watches he was going to bring back; he was just looking forward to seeing the man who supplied him with them in Paris.

There had been certain aspects of the batch he'd taken back in the previous July which had annoyed him and made the trip less profitable than it should have been.

As he drove into the sheds at Dover he showed none of this. He put on his usual agreeable front, handed out a bunch of complimentaries for a new show in town, and in a couple of hours was driving out of Calais on the Paris road, perfectly composed and his anger under control.

In Paris he put up at the Hotel Balzac and that evening he went round to see his supplier. This was a modest little jeweler at the bottom of the Avenue Wagram called Monsieur Audiat, who ran his business with the help of his rather slow-witted brothers.

Monsieur Audiat was careful as well as modest. Chris Selby was his only customer for this kind of work, and he was content with a regular twice-a-year profit rather than more constant business with the risk of publicity.

The day before Chris Selby was due to go home he would leave his car overnight in the garage at the back of the shop and Monsieur Audiat—with the help of his rather slow-witted brothers—would have the watches all packed away in the car by the next morning.

Chris Selby found Audiat and his brothers at the back of the shop and, without wasting time on polite inquiries about their health and with the smile turned off and the butter in his voice gone rancid, he let them have it.

A thousand of the last batch of watches had been duds, most of the others hadn't come up to specification, and the whole lot had been so badly packed into his car that many of them had been broken.

He embroidered on this theme for about fifteen minutes, slipping in frequent references to the personalities of Audiat and his brothers, their parents and the general perfidious nature of the French as a whole. It was the kind of performance he was rather good at.

In the end Audiat could have gladly stuck a knife into his heart—if it hadn't been for the fact that no Frenchman willingly destroys the source of a nice little profit—and even the half-witted brothers got the idea that the *anglais* was angry because he hadn't had watches that worked as well as looking good. However, Audiat finally explained that the batch of watches had been bought by him from Switzerland and he had packed them unexamined into the car and, when Selby quieted down, he promised that there should be no trouble with the next batch, which was arriving the following day.

But the next day the watches hadn't arrived. Nor the morning of the day after that when Selby drove his car around.

Now Selby had hoped the watches would arrive that morning so they could be packed in time for him to make Calais for the last ferry that night. He wanted to be in London the following day for the opening of a new show in which he had an interest. To show how he felt about things Selby examined the genealogy of the Audiat ménage again and swore that if the watches didn't come in time he'd take his business elsewhere in future.

He spent the day clearing up a little unfinished business with a fan and dove dancer he felt he could promote professionally and privately in London, telephoning Audiat now and then to see if the watches had come in.

At six o'clock that evening when he telephoned he learned that the watches had just arrived. He left the dancer to feed her doves and whipped around to Audiat.

He told him exactly how he wanted the watches packed and Audiat promised that his brothers should examine them all and see there were no duds and that the car could be picked up at four in the morning, which would give Selby time to drive to Calais and make the early morning ferry. He'd be in London after lunch and make his new show that evening.

Just after four in the morning he was away, singing to himself, driving fast and practicing his smile on the women at the level-crossing gates. When it was a matter of practice, Selby didn't mind what kind of woman it was.

At Calais it was a raw cold morning and he had no trouble with the French Customs. He saw his car aboard and then went down to the bar and had a coffee laced with brandy. Most of the way over he dozed.

At Dover he went ashore and saw his cases through, telling the officer who was examining them not to be surprised if he shook out any feathers or corn because he had just booked up a fan and dove dancer. Then he went over to clear his car.

The Customs officer on the car was one he knew well, a man about his own age. He gave him the big smile, cracked the feathers and corn joke again, and answered the usual questions. Everything went well, the smile, the joke, the easy manner and the promise of a free seat at the new show if the officer liked to write and remind him some time.

He'd got the all-clear signal and had his hand on the car door about to get in and drive off when all over the place there was a mad wail of sirens for a few seconds and then everything stopped.

Chris Selby didn't have to be told what it was. In those days the First World War wasn't far behind and when the sirens went at eleven o'clock on Armistice Day everybody stopped and there was silence for two minutes. There really was silence. Even the sea gulls stopped bawling their heads off. Chris Selby and the officer stood by the car like wax figures and you could have heard a pin drop.

No one did drop a pin, but Chris and the officer heard something else. From the car, not loud enough for anyone else to hear, it's true, but loud enough to do the damage, came the gentle sound of 5,000 watches ticking off, all carefully wound by the stupid Audiat brothers who wanted to please the *anglais* by making sure that he had watches which were in working order as well as looking good . . .

It was here that my friend stopped his story to finish his ham sandwich and beer. I'd had my ten-bob's worth, all right. But there's always something that drives a man on to get a little more for his money, and I said: "Now tell me that you're Chris Selby and maybe I'll buy the watch for a couple of quid."

But the old boy shook his head. "Selby died years back. No, I'm the Customs officer. With his smile and his ten-minute charm he talked me into a partnership—and two years later we were both caught."

2

ARTHUR GORDON

The Alchemist's Secret

GASLIT PARIS of the nineties is the setting of this unusual story by Arthur Gordon. We liked it for its stark and almost eerie reality as a "Gothic tale" which Edgar Allan Poe might have conceived. Although Mr. Gordon is as American as Savannah, Georgia, where he was born, in this story he has caught the literary flavor of nineteenth-century France.

SITTING QUIETLY IN his little herb shop on a crooked street in the shadow of Notre Dame, Doctor Maximus did not look like a very remarkable man. But he was. Five hundred years before, he might have busied himself changing the baser metals into gold. But in Paris of the nineties, it is said, he worked at a more subtle alchemy. He changed dreams into realities—provided, of course, you could pay.

The man who came into the gaslit shop this early October evening in 1891, was prepared to pay. He stood just inside the door, blotting his forehead with a silk handkerchief although actually the weather was rather cool. He was holding a heart-shaped package tightly under one arm. "You are Monsieur le Docteur Maximus?"

The Doctor bowed respectfully.

"I have a problem," said the visitor nervously. "I am told you might help me with it."

"Indeed?" said the Doctor mildly. "Who told you that?"

The newcomer glanced around uneasily at the dim shelves, the leathery tortoise dangling from a string, the small stuffed crocodile with its dust-filmed eyes. "Last night we had a dinner guest. A foreign diplomat. First secretary of the—"

9

"Ah, yes, Pechkoff. It is true I did him a small service."

"He was not very specific, you understand. But after a few glasses of cognac he talked rather freely. I got the impression . . ."

"Yes?"

"That if it weren't for your—er—assistance he would still be married, most unhappily, to his first wife."

Doctor Maximus took off his glasses and polished the spotless lenses. "She died, I believe, poor woman. Quite suddenly."

"Yes," said the visitor, "she did. So suddenly that there was an autopsy. But they discovered nothing wrong."

"Of course not," said Doctor Maximus, smiling gently.

"My wife," said the visitor with a certain agitation, "is a very beautiful woman. Naturally, she has many admirers. She has always ignored them until recently, but now there is one—I don't know which one—a younger man, no doubt. She admits it! She demands that I make some settlement. I will not—"

Doctor Maximus raised his hand. "The details," he murmured, "do not concern me."

The visitor's face was tight and dangerous. "I am not a man to be made a fool of!"

"No," said the Doctor, "I can see that."

"Madame," said the visitor abruptly, "is very fond of candy." He unwrapped the heart-shaped package and placed it on the counter. It was a box of chocolates. "I thought perhaps you might—ah—improve the candies at your convenience and then post them to her. She would be very pleased. I have even prepared a card to enclose." He took out a small rectangle of cardboard. On it was printed in neat capitals: *From an admirer.*

Doctor Maximus took the card and sighed. "My fees are not inconsiderable."

"I did not expect them to be," the visitor said stiffly. He did not flinch when the price was named. He paid it, in gold coins. He blotted his forehead once more with the silk handkerchief. "Will you be able to send the candy tonight?"

"Perhaps," said the Doctor noncommittally. "We shall see. And where should it be sent?"

"Ah, yes," said the visitor. "Of course." And he gave Madame's name and address.

Doctor Maximus wrote the information on a slip of paper. Then he scribbled three digits on another slip and handed it over. "You, sir, are customer 322. If there are any difficulties, kindly refer to that number. Not," he added, "that there will be any."

With one hand on the doorknob, the visitor hesitated. "It won't be—" he wet his lips—"it won't be painful, will it?"

"Not at all," said Dr. Maximus. He peered over his spectacles in a benign and sympathetic fashion. "You seem rather upset. Do you want me to give you something to make you sleep?"

"No, thank you," said his visitor nervously. "I have my own prescription for insomnia: a hot grog before going to bed."

"Ah, yes," said Dr. Maximus. "An excellent habit."

"Good night," said the visitor, opening the door into the narrow, ill-lit street.

"Good-by," murmured Dr. Maximus.

Taking the box of chocolates in one hand and the slip of paper in the other, he went into the little room at the rear of the shop. From the shelf above his test tubes and retorts he took a big black book, opened it, and looked at the record of the previous transaction. There it was, entered only that afternoon in his spidery handwriting: *Customer 321. Complaint: the usual. Remedy: six drops of the elixir, to be administered in husband's hot grog at bed-time . . .*

Dr. Maximus sighed. Then, being a man who honored his commitments, he opened the box of chocolates and went to work. There was no great rush. He would post the parcel in the morning.

In the herb shop, as in life, you got just about what you paid for. But his motto was, First come, first served.

3

NATHANIEL BENCHLEY

Mrs. Crocker's Mutiny

NATHANIEL BENCHLEY seems to have inherited the rich sense of comedy which always enlivened the writing of his father, the late Robert Benchley. Because he was a naval officer in the last war (Atlantic and Pacific theaters), you might suspect—and you would not be far wrong—that there is a bit of autobiography in this.

"ZIP ME," SAID Ellen Crocker, backing toward her husband.

Martin Crocker held his right forefinger on the half-completed knot of his bow tie, zipped up the back of Ellen's dress with his left hand, and went back to tying his tie. That completed, he put on his dinner jacket, fussed briefly with the breast-pocket handkerchief, and bared his teeth at the mirror. Satisfied, he lit a cigarette and glanced at his watch.

"What's all the rush?" he said. "We're not due at the Graysons' until eight-thirty."

"Martha Gresham and her doctor friend are coming here for a drink first. I told you that this morning. Did you get out the ice?"

"No. I'll do that now. Who's the doc?"

"Somebody she met at a party. She says you'll like him."

"I feel fine."

"No—he's young and nice. There's the bell—answer it, will you?"

Crocker went to the door, opened it, and kissed Martha Gresham lightly on the forehead. He looked at her escort, who was short, had a slightly upturned nose, and close-cut blond hair.

"Mr. Crocker, this is Dr. Campbell," Martha said. "Martin—George." She waved her hand back and forth, and Crocker shook hands with the doctor. "Come in," he said, "and let me fix you something. Are martinis all right?"

Ellen came in while Crocker was mixing the drinks, and Martha introduced her to the doctor. They sat down and Crocker passed them their martinis.

"Let me know if those are all right," he said. "They're four to one."

Martha took a sip of hers and shuddered slightly. "Delicious," she said. "George was just telling me," she continued, "of a fascinating case he had a while ago. A man had backed into an electric fan. George said his scars are going to look like a weather map of the United States."

"Actually, I suppose he's pretty well healed by now," the doctor said. "It happened seven years ago, when I was at St. Albans."

"You mean St. Albans Naval Hospital?" said Crocker.

"Yes," said the doctor. "Why? Were you in the Navy?"

"I should hope to tell you he was," said Ellen dryly.

Crocker laughed. "Don't mind her," he said.

"What branch were you in?" asked the doctor.

"Subchasers. PC's."

"I worked with some PC's once," the doctor said. "I got on a can after St. Albans, and we did some convoy work in the Caribbean with PC's."

"You weren't by any chance on the *Barney*, were you?" asked Crocker.

"That's the one."

"I'll be damned. I worked with the *Barney* for almost a year. It must have been before you came aboard, though. Their doctor was a guy named—named—Pritchard. Yeah—Doc Pritchard. Nice guy."

"Was that the baby crying?" Ellen interrupted.

Crocker listened. "I don't think so," he said.

"Would you be a lamb and look, though? He's been sort of fussy all day."

Crocker got up and left the room, and Ellen then turned to the doctor.

"Tell me, Doctor . . ." she began, hurriedly.

"His name is George," said Martha.

"All right, George. Tell me, what are you doing now?"

"Well, I was lucky. I got a partnership with a pediatrician, and I handle some of his work. I'm slowly building up a practice of my own."

"We may come to you any day now. Our baby has been having a miserable time. I hate to talk shop, but . . ."

"There was nothing wrong," Crocker said, reappearing. "He was quiet as a clam." Ellen took a deep breath and laid her hand on the doctor's arm, but before she could think of something to say Crocker was talking again.

"Was Baldy Moorehead still skipper when you were on the *Barney*?" he said.

"For a while," the doctor said. "He was transferred about four months after I came aboard. The exec took over. Magruder."

"That Magruder was a madman. I'll never forget one night in Guantanamo, when we all closed the Oboe Charlie, Magruder decided he'd get back aboard without the gangway watch seeing him. He crawled on his hands and knees up the gangway," Crocker got down on his hands and knees to illustrate, "then back past the number three gun tub, and finally down into the wardroom, thinking he hadn't been spotted. The next day he looked at the gangway log, ready to chew the watch out for doping off, and saw an entry which said: '0130—Mr. Magruder aboard on hands and knees. No further remarks.' "

They all laughed and Crocker resumed his seat, dusting off his knees.

"Magruder had a rough time later on," the doctor said. "He ran aground in Key West."

"You mean by the degaussing range there?"

"Yes."

"Nastiest channel I've seen."

Ellen moved over next to Martha. "Why didn't you tell me your doctor had been in the Navy?" she whispered.

"Well—I didn't think it mattered," Martha answered.

"Mattered? If you expect to get a civil word out of Martin all evening it matters. I can't figure out why all these people say they hated the Navy so, when all they do is talk about it when they get together."

"Well, next time I'll bring an Army man."

"That wouldn't make much difference. Martin could find something in common with a paratrooper, even if it was only the fact that they were on the same side. You don't know any Germans, do you? Or Japs?"

"I can look," Martha patted her hair back.

"Even then," Ellen said slowly, "I suppose he'd find that one of them had been in the same area he had, and they'd get to clacking about who outsmarted whom. My God, but I hate war." She drained her drink. "Martin, darling," she said, "your guests need some more drinks."

"I'm sorry." Crocker got up and went over to the bar for the shaker.

"Doctor," Ellen said quickly, "maybe you can settle a problem for us. Martin says that mixed drinks are worse for you than highballs, but I claim that you get the same amount of liquor in each, so there's no difference. What is the medical point of view?"

"Sure, you get the same amount of liquor," said the doctor, "but in a highball, you take it more slowly. It's diluted. The only thing that makes a difference is how fast you get what you get. Generally speaking, that is."

Crocker poured the drinks. "That reminds me of the night the war was over," he said, putting the shaker back on the bar. "We were in Leyte and couldn't get any regular liquor, so we used the medicinal alcohol and mixed it with grapefruit juice. What a night *that* was!" He sat down and sipped his martini.

"Oh, were you in Leyte, too?" the doctor said. "I was there for the invasion. That was the first time we really caught the *kamikazes*."

"They were worse off Okinawa," said Crocker.

Ellen sank back in her chair and looked at Martha. "I give up," she said.

As they were waiting for a taxi, Ellen drew Crocker aside. "Listen," she whispered, "will you please try to talk about something besides the Navy at dinner? There are other things going on in the world, you know."

"I'm sorry. You and Martha were talking and I didn't want to interrupt you. The doc and I just found a lot in common, that's all. I'll be good."

"That's a promise?"

"Sure." He patted her gently on the seat.

The taxi drew up and they got in, Ellen and Martha and the doctor in the back seat and Crocker on the folding seat. Crocker gave the driver the address and then turned sideways. "Take in all lines," he said, and as the cab started he added, "Starboard engine ahead one third." He winked at the doctor, and in doing so missed the sudden tightening of his wife's lips . . .

At dinner, Crocker was seated next to a girl whom he knew slightly, and whose main interest was in getting into the theater. Looking at her, Crocker figured that she should have no trouble whatsoever, provided she could act. She was tall, but she was relaxed and graceful, and when she tilted her head back to laugh, her long dark hair just brushed her shoulders. Crocker was telling her the name of an agent he knew, when his wife's voice seeped through the conversation and brought his train of thought to a jarring halt.

". . . and whenever a ship was transferred from Trinidad," he heard her saying, "it flew some funny flag hoist as it went out through the nets. And all the other ships, the ones that hadn't been transferred, answered with . . ."

"Wait a minute," Crocker interrupted, "I don't think that's one to tell here. Not the hoist anyway."

"I don't see why," said Ellen gaily. "That's what makes the story." The conversation died down, as the other guests looked expectantly at Ellen.

"I was just telling Mr. Basker," she said, by now in full command of the room, "of some of the wonderful things that happened to you in the Navy. But you're better than I—you tell him."

"Tell him what, Ellen?" said Crocker, irritated.

"Oh, tell him about the time your gyro compass went out during a hurricane and you got turned around and headed back where you came from and didn't know it until the next morning. That's a very funny story," Ellen added.

"You've already told it," Crocker snapped. "That's all there is to it."

"Well, then, tell him—oh, I know. Tell him what your lookout said when you first sighted Japan."

"I don't remember."

"Of course you do. You told it just the other night. When the Whittakers were over to visit us."

· "It's not so good, really," Crocker grunted.

"Go ahead," said Basker. "I think we're old enough to hear it."

Everybody laughed.

"Well," Crocker stammered, "he just said, 'No wonder so many Japanese come to America.'"

He trailed off, miserably, and someone at the other end of the table groaned loudly.

The doctor coughed, more or less out of sympathy.

Crocker turned to the girl on his left. "Now, this agent I was telling you about," he said. "His name is . . ." For a moment he couldn't think of the name, because Ellen was talking to Basker again.

The general conversation had picked up a little from

the morass in which Crocker had left it, but Ellen's voice was still audible all around the table.

"I think the funniest story of them all," she was saying, "was the time Martin almost hit a tug in New York harbor. The tug started to cross in front of him as Martin was coming in for a landing, and Martin told the quartermaster to blow two honks on the whistle, to show that he would turn right—"

"Left, damn it all—left," growled Crocker.

"Left, then. At any rate, the whistle stuck and made only one honk, so the tug turned left and Martin turned left, and he almost rammed it. The tug pulled up against the dock to get out of Martin's way, and all the crew jumped onto the dock, because they didn't know what Martin was going to do next. But Martin came in and made a very nice landing, using only three bells. Or was it two, dear? I never remember."

"What difference does it make?" growled Crocker.

"Well, I think it's nice to know you could make a good landing after being so rattled and almost ramming a tug. Don't you, Mr. Basker?"

"I think it's fine," said Basker. "Perfectly splendid."

"Martin was really a very good skipper," Ellen continued, "although one time in Panama he ran over a tree and had to—"

"A *tree?*" Basker interrupted. "Did you use the Navy to gather coconuts?" There was general laughter, and Basker seemed pleased with himself.

"This was a floating tree and it was night and he couldn't see it. At any rate, he had to go into drydock because the tree broke a thingummy on his rudder. Do you know how they get a ship in drydock?"

"I can't say that I do," said Basker, looking around the table and smiling.

"Well," Ellen rearranged the table silver, "here's your drydock and here's your ship. Now, you get your lines over here—" she picked up Basker's water glass—"and then you ease her gently . . ."

"I think your wife makes a very good press agent," said Crocker's companion. "If I'd known you were the seagoing type, I'd have worn my sou'wester."

Crocker winced. "All right, all right," he said. "Don't rub it in."

He looked across at Ellen. "I'm sorry," he said, raising his hand. "Really."

4

ELLERY QUEEN

Murder Without Clues

THE NAME of Ellery Queen was devised more than a quarter-century ago by two young mystery writers, Frederic Dannay and Manfred B. Lee. For a long time they kept up the masquerade of Ellery's real identity. But the secret has long since been revealed, and This Week has been fortunate to engage this writing team for a series of short mysteries.

TO THE NORMAL palate the taste of murder is unpleasant. But Ellery is an epicure in these matters and certain of his cases, he deposes, possess a flavor which lingers on the tongue. Among these dangerous delicacies he places high the Case of the Three Widows.

Two of the widows were sisters: Penelope, to whom money was nothing, and Lyra, to whom it was everything; consequently each required large amounts of it. Both having buried thriftless husbands at an early age, they returned to their father's Murray Hill mansion with what everyone suspected was relief, for old Theodore Hood was generously provided with the coin of the republic and he had always been indulgent with his daughters. Shortly after Penelope and Lyra repossessed their maiden beds, however, Theodore Hood took a second wife, a cathedral-like lady of great force of character. Alarmed, the sisters gave battle, which their stepmother grimly joined. Old Theodore, caught in their cross-fire, yearned only for peace. Eventually he found it in death, leaving a household inhabited by widows exclusively.

One evening not long after their father's death Penelope the plump and Lyra the lean were summoned by a servant to the drawing room. They found waiting for them Mr. Strake, the family lawyer.

Mr. Strake's commonest utterance fell like a sentence from the lips of a judge; but tonight, when he pronounced "Will you be seated, ladies?" his tone was so ominous that the crime was obviously a hanging one. The ladies exchanged glances and declined.

In a few moments the tall doors squealed into the Victorian walls, and Sarah Hood came in feebly on the arm of Dr. Benedict, the family physician.

Mrs. Hood surveyed her stepdaughters with a sort of contempt, her head teetering a little. Then she said, "Dr. Benedict and Mr. Strake will speak their pieces; then I'll speak mine."

"Last week," began Dr. Benedict, "your stepmother came to my office for her semi-annual checkup. I gave her the usual thorough examination. Considering her age, I found her in extraordinarily good health. Yet the very next day she came down sick—for the first time, by the way, in eight years. I thought then that she'd picked up an intestinal virus, but Mrs. Hood made a rather different diagnosis. I considered it fantastic. However, she insisted that I make certain tests. I did, and she was right. She had been poisoned."

The plump cheeks of Penelope went slowly pink, and the lean cheeks of Lyra went slowly pale.

"I feel sure," Dr. Benedict went on, addressing a point precisely midway between the sisters, "that you'll understand why I must warn you that from now on I shall examine your stepmother every day."

"Mr. Strake," smiled old Mrs. Hood.

"Under your father's will," said Mr. Strake abruptly, also addressing the equidistant point, "each of you receives a small allowance from the income of the estate. The bulk of that income goes to your stepmother for as long as she shall live. But at Mrs. Hood's demise, you inherit the principal of some two million dollars in equal shares. In other words,

you two are the only persons in the world who will benefit
from your stepmother's death. As I've informed both Mrs.
Hood and Dr. Benedict—if there is a single repetition of
this ghastly business I shall insist on calling in the police."

"Call them now!" cried Penelope.

Lyra said nothing.

"I could call them now, Penny," said Mrs. Hood with the
same faint smile, "but you're both very clever and it might
not settle anything. My strongest protection would be to
throw the two of you out of this house. Unfortunately, your
father's will prevents me. Oh, I understand your impatience
to be rid of me. You have luxurious tastes which aren't
satisfied by my simple way of living. You'd both like to re-
marry, and with the money you could buy second husbands."

The old lady leaned forward a little. "But I have bad
news for you. My mother died at 99, my father at 103. Dr.
Benedict tells me I can live another thirty years, and I have
every intention of doing so." She struggled to her feet, still
smiling. "In fact, I'm taking certain precautions to make
sure of it," she said. And then she went out.

Exactly one week later Ellery was seated beside Mrs. Hood's
great mahogany four-poster, under the anxious eyes of Dr.
Benedict and Mr. Strake.

She had been poisoned again. Fortunately, Dr. Benedict
had caught it in time.

Ellery bent over the old lady's face, which looked more
like plaster than flesh. "These precautions of yours, Mrs.
Hood—"

"I tell you," she whispered, "it was impossible."

"Still," said Ellery cheerfully, "it was done. So let's re-
sume. You had your bedroom windows barred and a new
lock installed on that door, the single key to which you've
kept on your person at all times. You've bought your own
food. You've done your own cooking in this room and you've
eaten here alone. Clearly, then, the poison could not have

been introduced into your food before, during, or after its preparation.

"Further, you tell me you purchased new dishes, have kept them here, and you and you alone have been handling them. Consequently the poison couldn't have been put on or in the cooking utensils, china, glassware, or cutlery involved in your meals. How then was the poison administered?"

"That's the problem," cried Dr. Benedict.

"A problem, Mr. Queen," muttered Mr. Strake, "that I thought—and Dr. Benedict agreed—was more your sort of thing than the police's."

"Well, my sort of thing is always simple," replied Ellery, "provided you see it. Mrs. Hood, I'm going to ask you a great many questions. Is it all right, Doctor?"

Dr. Benedict felt the old lady's pulse and nodded. Ellery began. She replied in whispers, but with great positiveness. She had bought a new toothbrush and fresh tooth paste for her siege. Her teeth were still her own. She had an aversion to medication and took no drugs or palliatives of any kind. She drank nothing but water. She did not smoke, eat sweets, chew gum, use cosmetics . . . The questions went on and on. Ellery asked every one he could think of, and then he shook up his brain to think of more.

Finally, he thanked Mrs. Hood, patted her hand, and went out with Dr. Benedict and Mr. Strake.

"What's your diagnosis, Mr. Queen?" asked Dr. Benedict.

"Your verdict," said Mr. Strake impatiently.

"Gentlemen," said Ellery, "when I eliminated her drinking water by examining the pipes and faucets in her bedroom and finding they hadn't been tampered with, I'd ruled out the last possibility."

"And yet it's being administered orally," snapped Dr. Benedict. "That's my finding, and I've been careful to get medical corroboration."

"If that is a fact, Doctor," said Ellery, "there is only one remaining explanation."

"What's that?"

"Mrs. Hood is poisoning herself. If I were you I would call in a psychiatrist. Good day!"

Ten days later Ellery was back in Sarah Hood's bedroom. The old lady was dead.

She had succumbed to a third poisoning attack.

On being notified, Ellery had promptly said to his father, Inspector Queen, "It is suicide."

But it was not suicide. The most painstaking investigation by police experts, utilizing all the resources of criminological science, failed to turn up a trace of the poison, or of a poison container or other possible source, in Mrs. Hood's bedroom or bath. Scoffing, Ellery went over the premises himself. His smile vanished. He found nothing to contradict either the old lady's previous testimony or the findings of the experts. He grilled the servants. He examined with remorseless efficiency Penelope, who kept weeping, and Lyra, who kept snarling.

Finally, he left.

It was the kind of problem which Ellery's thinking apparatus, against all the protests of his body, cannot let alone. For forty-six hours he lived in his own head, fasting and sleepless, ceaselessly pacing the treadmill of the Queen apartment floor.

In the forty-seventh hour Inspector Queen took his son forcibly by the arm and put him to bed.

"I thought so," said the Inspector. "Over 101. What hurts, son?"

"My whole existence," mumbled Ellery; and he submitted to aspirins, an ice bag, and a rare steak broiled in butter.

In the middle of the steak he howled like a madman and clawed at the telephone.

"Mr. Strake? Ellery Queen! Meet me at the Hood house immediately!—yes, notify Dr. Benedict!—yes, now I know how Mrs. Hood was poisoned!"

> *Editor's Note:* And now you know everything
> that Ellery knows. Can you guess the solution?

And when they were gathered in the cavern of the Hood
drawing room Ellery peered at plump Penelope and lean
Lyra and then he croaked:

"Which one of you is intending to marry Dr. Benedict?"

And then he said, "Oh, yes, it has to be that. Only Penelope
and Lyra benefit from their stepmother's murder, yet the
only person who could physically have committed the murder
is Dr. Benedict . . . Did you ask how, Doctor?" asked Ellery
courteously. "Why, very simply. Mrs. Hood experienced
her first poisoning attack the day after her semi-annual medical checkup—by you, Doctor. And thereafter, you announced,
you would examine Mrs. Hood every day. There is a classic
preliminary to every physician's examination of a patient.
I submit, Dr. Benedict," said Ellery with a smile, "that you
introduced the poison into Mrs. Hood's mouth on the very
thermometer with which you took her temperature!"

5

LEE ROGOW

Laziest Man in Texas

MR. ROGOW is so thoroughly identified as a New Yorker that you might wonder what he was doing in Texas. But he is also a gifted storyteller, which puts no limit to settings for fiction. In New York, besides writing occasional short stories, he spends his time in television, radio and has contributed sketches to Broadway plays.

"THE THING THAT makes me superior to a worthless old desert rat like you," said Jake Vesey, "is stratamagee."

"You mean strategy," I said.

"That's what I said, stratamagee," said Jake Vesey. "Now wash them dishes."

Jake always did have an elegant way of expressing himself. When he got to palavering enthusiastically around a campfire, the coyotes would come down in a circle and squat on their haunches and listen, and the rattlesnakes would stop buzzing under the rocks. I reckon it was that more than anything else that kept Jake and me prospecting together for thirty years, in spite of some of his indifferent traits and attributes, such as being the laziest man in Texas.

"Sure you got stratamagee," I said. "You also got yourself a .38 revolver. If you didn't have that artillery in your fist, your stratamagee wouldn't be worth the horns off a hoptoad."

Jake shifted the field piece in question from his right hand to his left, which didn't signify a thing, since he could pop buttons off your vest with the gun in either hand. "Howsoever," he said, "I have the weapon. You have not. That takes us back to fundamentals. Friend William, you will wash them dishes."

I picked up the tin plates we'd used for supper, and carried them down to the creek they called Surprise Water. Surprise Water was a good name for it, right enough. When Jake and I stopped to fill our canteens from the stream, it was this new stuff, uranium, we were after. We had no more thought of finding gold than we did of finding a ketchup mine.

After thirty years of drifting around the west looking for a big strike, Jake and I had just about given up prospecting. We spent our time sitting in front of the Boone City post office telling lies. But when the government offered ten thousand dollars for any uranium ore find rich enough for economical mining, Jake and I got all fired up again. Jake sent away out of a catalogue for one of those portable dinguses that makes the clicks when you're over radioactive ore, and we scraped together an outfit.

Well, sir, we weren't more than four days out of Boone City when we stopped at Surprise Water. Jake and I were changing off on the camp chores, and it was my turn to wash out the pots. I was giving it a swirl when something bright caught my eye in the sand at the bottom of a pan. Oh, it was color all right. I'd been scratching around for it too long not to know it when it turned up in my own pan.

I yipped for Jake, and he came a-running. Any old-timer will stir his stumps when he hears there's color in the pan. We tried a few more test pans, working along the edges of the creek. The color got stronger, and pretty soon we got to working up a small rise on the other side of the creek. We finally had to quit on account of dark, but we were out of our blankets before sunup and by one o'clock that afternoon we'd struck the pocket.

I rassled up a good supper that night, by way of celebration. After chuck, I built a cigarette and said to Jake, "Your turn on the dishes, I recollect."

"I'm a rich man," said Jake, "and if there's anything I hate and despise more than anything, it's washing dishes."

"My sentiments exactly," I said.

"Tell you what, William," said Jake, in a lazy sort of way, "I'll give you one hundred dollars in gold to wash the dishes for me."

"Jake, you're talking to a plutocrat," I said. "I reckon my share of that little hole in the hill is eighteen, twenty-thousand dollars. It doesn't fit my position to hire out as a common dishwasher."

Jake sighed. "I hate to have to do this, William," he said, "after so many happy years of partnership." His hand snaked behind him and came back filled with a .38 revolver. "Wash them dishes, William," he said. "Cleanliness is next to godliness."

I let my hand wander casual like along the blanket toward my pack. "Never mind feeling around, William," said Jake. "I told you I had superior stratamagee. I already pitched your gun in the creek. Wash them dishes, William. And don't just rinse them. Rub some sand on them. It's more sanitary."

I stood up. "You couldn't pull that trigger," I said. "Not a tub of lard like you. Not after thirty years." I turned and started to walk away from the fire. Next thing I knew I lit flat on my face. I rolled over and saw that Jake had shot out the heel of my right boot. I'll say this for Jake Vesey—he's cute with that .38.

"I won't kill you," said Jake. "But I'll miss awful close. Take the chance if you want to. Or wash them dishes."

I washed the dishes. After I was through, Jake got up and lumbered off into the little stand of woods behind our camp. When he came back, he was without his gun. "Let's get some sleep," he said.

I waited until he was sawing wood inside his bedroll, and I went looking for his gun. He'd hid it too well. I came back and looked at him sleeping and thought I'd bounce a boulder off his skull. But we'd been partners too long for that. And besides, I had to admit to myself that I couldn't help being tickled over the whole thing. It was the kind of stunt that made Jake an interesting feller.

Next morning, when I woke up and rolled out, Jake was sitting there with the .38. I made breakfast and washed the dishes. Jake bunked the gun again, and we spent the day on that pocket. Jake did his share of that part of the work. It was impossible for even a lazy man to keep his hands off that ore.

I guess it must have taken us twelve, fourteen days to clean out that hole in the hill. We had no way of weighing the dust and nuggets exactly, but it figured to run around eleven thousand each. And that would be about all we'd get out of it. Pockets are fine when you find them, but it takes more than one sweet deposit to make it worthwhile to some mining company to start big operations.

When we loaded up the burros and started back to Boone City, Jake was feeling spry as a colt in clover.

"Now that it's over, William," he said, "you got to admit you got more out of this than just that gold. You got a valuable lesson. I ought to charge you tuition."

"If you're talking about washing dishes," I said, "I knew how to do that before I came."

"I'm talking about stratamagee," said Jake.

"Oh, that again," I said. "Yep, I learned something about it. I learned it so firmly that I'm going to use it to make sure I never have to wash dishes again."

"Not eating in restaurants, I hope," said Jake. "Eating in restaurants, your eleven thousand'll melt like fat on a skillet."

"You're underestimating my stratamagee," I said. "I'm referring to the Widow Fletcher."

"I don't believe I know the lady," said Jake.

"Lives in a yellow clapboard house on Piute Street," I said. "Bakes pies that float off the table. Roast beef you can cut with a dull fork. And her coffee—well, if I was poetical, I'd make up a poem about it."

"Bondage," said Jake. "You'll sell yourself into bondage."

"With a smile on my lips," I said. "The Widow Fletcher also has dimples in her elbows." As we trailed into town, I pointed off down one of the four side streets. "There's the yellow clapboard house," I said.

"You hustle on down to the assay office," said Jake. "I got legal business to take care of."

When I came by the Widow Fletcher's two hours later, Jake was sitting on the front porch looking amiable. They were married a week later.

Happens I was over there last Sunday for dinner. The food was good—mighty good. Not as good as what I get over at the Bon-Ton Restaurant, but good. But the food wasn't the most enjoyable part of the dinner. The really enjoyable part happened after dinner, when the ex-Widow Fletcher came out of the kitchen.

"All ready, Jake," she said.

"Now, Cornelia," said Jake, in a sort of whining tone.

The ex-Widow Fletcher put her hands on her hips, and the dimples went out of her elbows. She lifted her voice a mite and the windowpanes rattled up and down the street, and the dogs and cats hid under the porches.

"Jake!" she said. That was all. Just that one word. But the sound of her saying his name had the same effect on Jake that I'd seen it have on Buzz Fletcher, the lady's first husband. Jake seemed to get smaller right there in his chair. Then he stood up and walked into the kitchen. I followed him in, and helped him tie the bow on his apron.

"You might be a little clumsy at first, Jake," I said, "due to lack of practice. But you'll improve with experience, like Buzz Fletcher did. This is like a lot of other things—a question of stratamagee."

It's only my instinctive politeness that prevents me from repeating what Jake Vesey said as he started to wash the dishes.

6

JOHN D. MacDONALD

I Love You (Occasionally)

THE NOVELS of John D. MacDonald have sold over 2,500,000 as paper-cover originals. Unlike the hard, fast-moving books, his short stories are spiced with gentle satire of average men and women. The editors liked this one because it deals pleasantly with the guilty feeling men sometimes have that they are being less than ideal husbands. But see what happened to this poor fellow when he tried to reform.

IT STARTED WITH one of those quizzes in the back of a magazine. Harrison Coombs, riding the commuter train back through the steel-colored dusk of the last working day of the year, sleet whanging away at the window at his elbow, saw the title of the quiz as he leafed by it. "How Good a Husband Are You?"

Three pages beyond, he found that he was feeling mildly defensive and so he turned back to the quiz and took out his pencil. "Show you how good I am," he muttered.

The first question jolted him a bit. "You take home flowers (often) (seldom) (only on anniversaries)." The testee was to underline the proper word, which carried a point score.

In the brokerage profession Harrison Coombs had learned how to achieve a quite impressive objectivity. He knew at once that to underline (seldom) would be hedging a bit. Hunching over the line. With a quick deft line he underlined the last choice.

"You tell her she looks lovely (once a day) (once a week) (once a month) (once a year) (never)."

"Hmm," said Harrison Coombs.

He wavered between once a week and once a month, then with an upsurge of honesty, he underscored (once a month). At least it was not as bad as the two remaining choices.

He finished the test feeling more defensive than when he had started it. He totted up his score and turned to the indicated page. The first paragraph, which started: "Your wife is or should be a divinely happy woman . . ." he skipped rapidly over. That was not for him. His paragraph, for scores of eighteen through twenty-six, was down below the middle.

"You, sir, are not a newlywed. You are complacent. You are taking your wife for granted. Slowly and surely you are starving her for the love and appreciation she needs. It could be that, unless you mend your ways, the marriage you have been accepting so casually may blow up in your face. Whether she admits it to herself or not, she is beginning to resent you. But there is still hope for you. If you change your ways at once, your marriage can be rebuilt."

Harrison Coombs slapped the magazine down on the empty seat beside him. "Balderdash," he said. "Scare psychology. Nothing to it."

There had been a comforting feeling about heading home through this dismal dusk. Now some anonymous quiz-master had robbed him.

"Nothing to it," he mumbled again. "Laura understands me and she knows I love her."

The man in front of him turned around and said, "Of course she does, old man."

Harrison Coombs flushed. "Wise guy," he said.

The train panted to a stop at his station. Harrison got out onto the exposed platform, his shoulders hunched against the bite of the sleet. He spotted his car a hundred feet away and trotted to it. Laura leaned over from behind the wheel and opened the door for him. He clambered in and shut the door against the horrid night. "Foosh," he said.

She leaned toward him and he kissed her. A stabbing kiss. Then he remembered the quiz question about pecks instead of kisses and he took a second shot at her, holding this one a bit longer.

A low whistle came from the back seat. Harrison Coombs turned around and glared at the enthralled faces of his two offspring. "Watch your manners," he growled, scowling fiercely.

"Your father was just trying to get warm," Laura said.

"Yes," said Harrison, "Ha ha."

"Rough day, dear?" Laura asked.

"Average for the end of the year. Everybody trying to get their losses in this year, and push the profits over into next. Your day go all right?"

"Would have had a canasta prize this afternoon if Betty Hedgins hadn't fouled me up. Otherwise no change. Steak sound good to you?"

He made certain animal noises that indicated that a steak was a very good choice. She spun the car expertly into the driveway and he jumped out and boosted the door up. She drove in and he pulled the door down. They went on into the house and he went right upstairs.

He washed up and reached into the closet and had his hand on the flannel shirt, the one with the elbows out, when he remembered another part of the quiz. "Do you ever dress up, just for your wife?" (never)

Harrison went to the bureau and dug around until he found the pearl-gray wool job. Under dry-cleaner's paper he found pale-gray slacks. He dressed carefully, combed his hair and went down the back stairs.

Laura stared blankly at him. "The flannel shirt is in the closet, dear."

"I saw it," he said uncomfortably.

She scowled. "Listen, you! Did you ask anybody to come around tonight?"

He felt obscurely injured. An unjust accusation. "No, I didn't. And if a man can't look decent in his own house, I'd like to know . . ."

She patted his cheek. "You look perfectly sweet. Now go make us a drink. I set out the makings. I'll be along."

He made the drink feeling somewhat moody. The quiz had been quite severe about those snappish little losses of temper. He took the tray with shaker and glasses into the living room. The fire crackling cheerfully in the fireplace dissolved his feeling of insufficiency. He poured a drink for himself, sat by the fire and sighed contentedly.

Yes, it was about time he gave some serious thought to his relationship with Laura. Damn lucky in that department. Lovely girl. Figure was better than the day he married her. Whistle-bait, and that's the truth. Always get a tight feeling in the back of the neck when some joe starts paying too much attention at a party. Time to give the girl a break. Make her feel wanted and appreciated. The job she's got is no cinch.

Thus, when Laura came in for her drink, Harrison Coombs was filled to the brim with the warm self-regard that comes of having decided to be a better husband.

He smiled fondly at her and filled her glass and handed it to her. After she sipped, he said throatily, "You look lovely tonight, darling." (once a day)

Laura jumped as though a small firecracker had gone off under the chair cushion. She looked at him. "What did you say?"

"I said you look lovely," he said.

She looked at him somewhat blankly. "Gee, thanks!"

"Is there anything wrong with my saying that?" he asked stiffly.

"No. No. You can say it if you want to." She stared at him a bit oddly and finished her drink with a great deal more speed than usual. She said:

"You're pretty, too. That shirt and the fire and the drink and that gray at the temples. They'll be after you to go around huckstering whisky."

The children charged in and skidded to a stop. Meg pointed a thumb at Harrison. "Where's he going?" she demanded.

"If it's the movies can we come, can we?" Derek demanded.

"No one is going anywhere," Harrison said, accenting each word.

Their faces fell. Things seemed a bit strained during dinner. Each time Harrison looked up he found the three of them staring at him. It was disconcerting.

After dinner he read the paper, but he had to read some paragraphs quite a few times to get the meaning. The quiz was severe with husbands who hid behind the paper. When Laura came down from putting the children to bed, and after the dishwasher had churned to a damp stop, he put the paper aside and beamed across at her. She looked up from a lapful of socks. "Finish the paper that quick?"

"Well, I just thought we might talk," he said, "or something."

"Harrison Coombs, are you in some kind of trouble?"

"I am not in any kind of trouble, and if a man can't come home and talk to his own wife I don't know what . . ." He stopped and manufactured a warm smile. "Would you like to have me read to you, darling?"

Do you share your evening with her? (often) (occasionally) (seldom) (never)

"Well," she said uneasily, "if you really want to take the trouble . . ."

He dug around in the bookshelves and found something that looked all right. An historical romance. He read until his voice was hoarse. Then he smiled over at her. "There, I'll read it to you bit by bit until we've finished it. Why on earth are you wearing that glazed look?"

She yawned. "Goodness! It's sort of hypnotic, isn't it?"

"Now we can talk," he said jovially. "Just think. Good old nineteen-fifty is about gone."

"And next year is nineteen fifty-one," she said.

"We've had a good time this year in spite of—in spite of the international tension, haven't we, darling? Hasn't it been fun?"

"Dear, are you positive you feel all right?"

"I feel fine!" he snapped.

They went up to bed. He was first in. He lay in his bed with his fingers laced at the nape of his neck and watched her at the dressing table brushing her hair. Lovely girl. None better. Time to appreciate her.

He cleared his throat. "I love you, darling," he said, proud of having achieved what sounded like a Boyer-esque intensity.

She twitched violently. She stood up and came over to his bed and put her hands on her hips and glared down at him. "I'm getting to the bottom of this right now."

"But I . . ."

"Have you gone and gotten yourself all wound up in some tawdry little office affair? Have you? Have you? Who is she?"

He sat up, righteously indignant, "If you have no more faith in me than that . . ."

"What am I supposed to think when you come prancing home and posturing around and acting like somebody in the senior play at Jefferson High?"

"Now you listen to me, my dear!"

"I will not listen to you! Why didn't you do it up brown? Why didn't you come smirking home with flowers or candy or jewelry or something else to . . ."

"Laura, I . . ."

"And if you think that by imitating a garden variety Gregory Peck you can take my mind off what you've been doing—and—and—oh, oh, oh . . ."

The brush thudded to the floor and she crumpled on her bed. He reached out and patted her gingerly and ineffectually on the shoulder.

Laura wrenched away from his touch and increased the tortured tempo of her sobs.

And then he knew how he had to do it. He forgot his slippers. He padded down in his bare feet, turned on the lights, found the magazine on the table where he had put it when they had come back from the station.

He trudged upstairs with it, opened it to the proper page,

shoved it under her arm. He stalked petulantly into the bathroom and slammed the door. After a time the sobbing
stopped abruptly. There was a long period of silence and
then a sound as if she were being slowly strangled. Then that,
too, stopped.

She tapped on the door. Her tone was properly abject.
"Harrison?"

"Go away. Go to bed. Go to sleep."

"Please, Harrison!"

He unlocked the door and opened it cautiously, stared at
her. "Whuff!" he said.

She pirouetted so that the black lace hem swirled around
her ankles. "Remember it? Christmas. Four years ago."

"What were you saving it for?"

"For a time like this, I guess."

"Listen, Laura. If you ever, ever try to kid me about taking
that quiz . . ."

She touched his lips with her finger tips. She looked oddly
solemn, and very young. "I couldn't. That would be like
laughing at what you were trying to do."

He put his arms around her. "Trying, and not much of a
try."

She pushed back and looked up at him. "Don't think I'm
not appreciative, now that I know. I'm a woman and I guess
some part of me likes all those things they said in the test.
But I know you, dear. You can't put on an act. You have your
own ways of telling me, and one of them is that look in your
eye right this minute. When you lose that, I'll really start
fretting."

He frowned. "That quiz didn't give me any grade on a
look."

Laura's nose wrinkled enchantingly as she smiled. "Of
course not, silly! Anybody can see that the person who wrote
that quiz has never been married."

7

PAT FRANK

Those Wily Americans

PAT FRANK has often used his experiences as a foreign correspondent for background in his stories. This one comes straight out of his observation of the Russians at the end of the war. He is the author of the hilarious best seller of a few years back, "Mr. Adam," and has had a more recent success with his serious novel of Korea, "Hold Back the Night."

TO: *Chief, Secret Political Police, Zhitomir.*
FROM: *Inspector Nuhka.*
SUBJECT: *Capitalist propaganda.*

In accordance with the general instructions to check carefully soldiers returned from occupation duties in the West, where they have been exposed to reactionary capitalistic influences, the arrest was made of Ivan Petchana, who lives at 112 Georgievsk Street.

Petchana is a lieutenant who served capably, but without special distinction, in Marshal Konev's armies. At the conclusion of hostilities he was assigned to the 641st Infantry Regiment for occupation duties in Vienna.

The regimental Political Commissar made no adverse report on Petchana except to report that on occasion he fraternized with an American sergeant, and at least twice visited the Weisser Hahn Hotel, where this sergeant was billeted. Before returning to his home, Petchana was sent to the camp at Urulgrad for the usual six months' period of re-

38

indoctrination. There, he displayed no outward evidence of subversive activities.

It was not until he came back to Zhitomir, and resumed his post as assistant Auditor in the Stalin Gas Works, that Ivan Petchana showed his moral and intellectual loyalty had been undermined, and that he had become a tool of the American so-called democracy.

A confidential report was made to me by Anya Krotnick, who is our agent at 112 Georgievsk. The Petchanas occupy two rooms on the second floor, and Anya Krotnick also lives on this floor. She is the best friend of Sophia Petchana, the lieutenant's wife.

Anya Krotnick's report said that Sophia Petchana, and all the other women in the house, had been corrupted by insidious American propaganda. Indeed, the Petchanas kept a propaganda book hidden in their rooms. Anya Krotnick had seen this book, and Sophia Petchana had shown it to the other women. They all talked of it constantly, and the Petchana rooms had become the most popular meeting place in the house.

Having received this information, I began an investigation, first examining Petchana's dossier, and then raiding his apartment. Because of the seriousness of the charge I took with me two of my men. I knocked on the Petchana door at four in the morning, the hour when criminals are most likely to be in bed, with no chance to hide incriminating documents.

Sophia Petchana answered our knock and, perhaps because of a guilty conscience, or perhaps because it has become known that I pay my calls at four, displayed agitation, crying: "I have done nothing. I swear I have done nothing."

"Nobody said you did anything," I told her. I find it best never to indicate to criminals of what they are suspected, until they are well trapped by their own conversation.

Petchana, wearing trousers and an undershirt, then came out of the bedroom. He is a slight, thin-nosed man, wearing spectacles. He is of the quiet, studious type which I have found can be most dangerous, when infected with foreign ideas. "Do you want to talk to me?" he asked. Then he told his wife, "Go back into the bedroom, Sophia."

"No, stay here," I ordered her, wishing to give her no chance to get rid of the book, in case it was in the bedroom. "I simply want to have a little talk with your husband. It is nothing you cannot hear." I turned to him and asked casually: "I only want to know about your friend, the American sergeant—the one with whom you went to the Weisser Hahn Hotel?"

"Oh, him," Petchana burst out, undoubtedly without thinking. "He was a good fellow. He gave me this." Petchana held out his arm, and showed me a wrist watch.

"Gave you that? Why?"

"It was this way. It was in the early days in Vienna, in '45— the crazy days when everybody bought watches. We all had two or three years' back pay in Austrian schillings, and nothing to buy in Vienna until the Americans came. The Americans had watches, and so we bought watches. One day I was in the Karlsplatz, and I saw this American sergeant wearing this watch. As you see, it is a fine watch with a black dial, luminous figures, and a red second hand. I offered him seven thousand schillings for it, which to him was seven hundred dollars. He told me I was crazy. He talked German, as I do."

"This American told you you were crazy?" I said.

"Yes," said Petchana. "The sergeant said that he paid only twelve dollars for it in the United States, and that it was old and didn't keep good time. He said he could get all the watches he wanted in the American Army store. Then he gave me the watch. He said he wouldn't cheat a brave ally."

"Do you expect me to believe that?" I said. "In return for the watch, what did you do? Did you sell your country for a cheap watch?"

"Sell my country? Of course not. He asked nothing,"

Petchana said, realizing for the first time how he had in-criminated himself.

"Didn't he ask you questions about Russia?"

"Yes, he did ask questions. He said he was very much inter-ested in Russia, and sometimes he believed that he didn't get all the facts about Russia in the American papers."

"And you told him things."

"I told him nothing that was secret. He told me of his country, I told him of mine."

At this point I decided to use the shock method. "And then, Petchana," I said, "he gave you the American propaganda book! And you have the book hidden here?"

Sophia Petchana's eyes darted at the china closet. On top of the closet I found the book. It is a very heavy, very thick book, lavishly illustrated, in all the colors.

It must have cost the American Department of Propaganda an enormous sum to print and distribute this literature.

Petchana didn't speak. "Now tell me," I ordered him, "exactly how you came to get this book, and what instructions the sergeant gave you. Also I want his name, and all informa-tion you have about him and his associates."

Petchana said the sergeant's name was Moore, and that his companions called him Slim. He came from a small town in the middle of the United States called Hyannis, Nebraska. "The sergeant said he kept this book," Petchana said, "be-cause it reminded him of home. When I showed interest in the book, he said he would give it to me when he went back to the United States of America."

"And he did give it to you?" I asked.

"Yes."

"Didn't you know everything in this book is lies, and it is dangerous American propaganda?" I asked him.

"I didn't know it was propaganda at all," Petchana said. "I didn't know it was lies, either."

"Did you show it to anyone outside this house?"

"No. I showed it to no one. Perhaps some of my wife's friends saw it. That is all."

I have been through this book thoroughly, and the text has been translated into Russian. It is true that the contents are so preposterous, the claims it makes so exaggerated, that thinking people would not believe it. Anyone who knows anything about the world would know that the peasants who live in the small villages of the United States could not have the luxuries shown in this book.

However, the book may be dangerous among unthinking people, particularly among women, and I recommend that all precautions be taken to halt its circulation. Undoubtedly attempts will be made to infiltrate others into the Soviet Union. It could cause great dissatisfaction if believed.

I feel that Petchana was an innocent dupe of the American propagandist sergeant. In addition, it would not be wise to call attention to this book by a trial. Therefore I recommend he be released. However, all women who have seen this book should receive instruction in a re-indoctrination school. This includes Anya Krotnick.

The book has been sealed. I recommend that it be sent to Moscow to be placed at the disposal of the anti-propaganda division of the Politburo.

The book is called *Mail Order Catalog*.

8

PAUL MARCUS

Tip the Green Earth

A PILOT HIMSELF, Paul Marcus knows something about the emotions aroused by flying a small plane in a fine blue sky. To any writer, this is an interesting piece of construction. It is almost like the climactic ending of a longer story, in which a decision already reached is now to be carried through to tragedy.

ELIZABETH DIDN'T BEHAVE like a girl who has decided to die.

The little yellow plane turned into the final approach, and Elizabeth kept alternating her glance: first over the nose to be sure she was lined up with the runway, then out to the wings to see they were level, and next to the airspeed indicator to hold a steady glide. When she was twenty feet from the ground, she eased back on the stick to flare out, the airplane ballooned a little, and then as it settled she pulled back steadily. But the airplane struck the ground before the stick had come all the way, and went leaping down the field like a startled antelope.

"Give it throttle and go around again!" Bob, her instructor, yelled from the back seat.

She pushed the throttle forward, and when the plane was airborne she held it in level flight a moment and then put it back into a climb.

"Didn't get the stick back fast enough!" Bob yelled.

"I know it!" Elizabeth shouted furiously. "Don't you think I felt those bounces too?"

She kept the plane in a steady climb, for a moment looking

43

over the nose through a mist. When the altimeter showed four hundred feet, she made a level ninety-degree turn to the left and then began climbing again. Anyway, she thought, she was following the traffic pattern all right. But after that landing, he'd never solo her today.

Why couldn't Bob understand? He'd been Jim's friend; they'd flown together in the war. He should understand that a woman who'd known Jim couldn't live without him. Perhaps, she thought bitterly, she should say it: Look, you dumb fool, you don't have to worry about whether I'm safe to solo. My lover died in the air over Germany three years ago, and I've tried to live without him—but I can't. I'm only learning to fly so I can die as he did!

"There's your spot, down there," Bob said, tapping her on the back.

"I see it," Elizabeth said disdainfully. She pulled the throttle back and held the nose up in a glide.

"How about carburetor heat?" Bob said.

She grabbed the carburetor heat knob and yanked it out as though it were Bob's heart.

"That's better," Bob said.

She made a gliding turn to the left, hating him too much to answer. She straightened out, made another turn, and then she was on her final, the grass runway smooth and glistening ahead. She flared out, brought the stick back and bounced again. Only this time, as the plane bounced, she eased the stick forward, then brought it back slowly as the plane settled. She made a good three-point landing.

"Pull off to the right," Bob said to her.

Elizabeth taxied off the runway. She set the parking brake and waited for his lecture. He opened the door. "Let me out of this fire-trap," he said.

"Hey, where're you going?" Elizabeth said.

"You're too dangerous. I'm getting out. Go fly by yourself."

She looked at him and drew a breath.

"I want you to go around the traffic pattern just as we have been doing. After you make your landing, if I wave at you, do it again," said Bob.

"Okay."

"Go fly it the way he did, kid," Bob added gently.

"All right, I'll do it the way he did."

Elizabeth taxied to the end of the field, looked around for traffic, then lined up with the runway. She advanced the throttle.

With Bob's two hundred pounds out of the back seat, the airplane darted down the runway with new power, and was airborne in half the time it had taken before. Elizabeth's breath caught with joy in the sensation of leaping from the earth. It felt as though she herself had taken wing with one strong leap. Where before the plane flew her, now she was flying the plane. It was her will, her cunning and purpose that bore them aloft.

She reached four hundred feet and leveled off. She made a turn, and began climbing again. The altimeter touched eight hundred. She kept on climbing. She looked down at the field, at the two runways outlined with white stones, the small hangar and the line of parked planes. She looked out the other side and below she saw a white house and red barn. As she watched, it suddenly seemed to her that the plane was not climbing, but she, by holding back pressure on the stick, was shrinking the earth and everything on it.

At two thousand feet she leveled off. She thought: why not now? If she were to pull the stick back until the plane stalled and then hold hard rudder, the plane would go spinning down toward earth. She knew that, for she had practiced it with Bob, to learn to recover from spins.

A gentle gust hit the wings, lifting the plane sharply upward. She felt a quick exhilaration as she sensed in her body the wonderfully firm, solid buoyancy of the air. How had she ever thought of the air as "nothing"? It was there to ride upon, strong and secure as the land or water: except that the reality of its strength was subtle, like the strength and reality of the spirit.

She did not pull back on the stick. Instead, she moved both stick and rudder to the right. And then a miracle happened. When she had done that before, the plane had turned to the right. But this time, when she moved the controls the whole big green earth tipped. She straightened up and flew level, her head light with a new sense of strength and grace.

Now she moved the controls to the left. It happened again; the earth tipped. A kind of delirium of joy came over her, and she rocked the controls back and forth. There she was, waving the earth around her like a green banner. Oh, darling, she thought, was it like this for you? Did you shrink the world, did you tip it, did you wave the earth around you like a green banner?

She pushed the stick ahead, and in the swiftness of her descent the earth came up as though she pulled it to her breast like a lover. She pulled back on the stick; the airplane zoomed upward, and the earth fell away as though spurned and found unworthy. It was unworthy, she thought; she would not take the earth, but would have the limitless free sky. She rolled the airplane into a steep bank. The movement through the air was as personal as though her arms were outstretched and the wind was beating against her palms.

Here, in the air, she had been born again.

She knew then that it had been like this for Jim too. He must have rolled in the sky like a lamb on the grass; he must have rubbed his back against the clouds. Sometimes he'd dived and pulled the earth to him like a lover; then he'd spurned it with a pull back on the stick. Death had no part in his flying. He flew for life.

And now that she knew, she would fly it the way he did. . . . She turned the airplane back toward the field, filled with the sense of being new-born.

When the field was beneath her, she glided down into

the traffic pattern. Opposite the spot where she wanted to land, she applied carburetor heat and then cut the throttle.

As she was coming across the base leg she saw Bob, still standing beside the runway. And suddenly she knew that she no longer lived alone. She would tell Bob, and others too who had tipped the earth, and they would understand. For her happiness was as limitless as the air in which she had found her life. It was too big not to be shared.

9

EDWARD ACHESON

The Big Shot

AS A PROFESSOR OF LAW at George Washington
University, Edward Acheson produces few short stories.
But in this one he is at his most amusing best. The scene
is the State Department, where Mr. Acheson's occasional
tours of duty brought such men as Brax under his observation. He is a brother of Dean Acheson, Mr. Truman's Secretary of State.

IT WAS SPRING, and it was spring in Washington. The lo-
cale was important because of the ephemeral and almost
momentary quality of that season along the lower reaches of
the Potomac. From the Appalachians to the Rockies nature
awakes by a series of spaced yawns and interspersed stretches.
In the Capital, winter reigns until the streets simmer. Between slush and perspiration the Lord has provided spring.
And Washingtonians take advantage of all twenty-four
hours.

George James Waton-Braxton was enjoying it to the full
extent of his capabilities. Furthermore, it was Tuesday and
Tuesday was his day to lunch at the Mayflower, at the Men's
Bar to the left of the Connecticut Avenue entrance. From
his office he took the elevator down to the main floor of the
Department. In Washington the Department was and is, of
course, the State Department. There's the Department of
Commerce, of Labor, the Army and Navy Departments. And
the Department. George took the elevator to the main floor
on Tuesdays because of the long flight of stone steps down to
Pennsylvania Avenue. Some divisions of the Department had
been moved with the Secretary to the "New War" Building

on Virginia. But not James Waton-Braxton's division. There
was a certain sweep to those steps.

Halfway down he adjusted his homburg and tucked his
stick under his left arm, frowning slightly. He was thinking
about the gloves he carried. He carried them because of the
incipient hole in the left one, but a pair of late-rising tourists
who noted the frown and the striped trousers felt a renewed
confidence in their country's ability to deal with the Russians. George waited for the light at the corner of Seventeenth and the Avenue, but when he stepped off the curbing
he collided with an individual who had, indecorously, tried
to beat the traffic on Pennsylvania.

"Beg your pardon, Mr. Secretary. Beautiful morning, sir,"
George said, restraining a desire to touch his hat in salute.
He compromised on a smiling bow. The recipient was obviously confused. And for several reasons. The chancery coat
had startled him. He was wondering whether George was
some chargé d'affaires involved in his own present harass-
ment. For this particular Assistant Secretary of State had forgotten to sign an important letter on Saudi Arabian oil. Now
the British, blast them, would pick it up for a song.

"Yes, beautiful song," he said, and rushed illegally across
the street.

George would have sworn he'd said "Beautiful song," and
on second thought considered it quite likely. Assistant secre-
taries were unpredictable and eccentric—for the most part
transitory; a couple of years, four, at most. Like the British
war commissions that conferred the title "temporary gentlemen." Not at all the career-service type. George wondered
momentarily what job this particular jay-walking Assistant
Secretary might be performing. Cultural affairs? Economics?

Perhaps. After all the Department was immense and
intricate, which, together with the nature of its function,
conferred on its members an impenetrable and dignified
anonymity. George smiled to himself trying to picture the
social maelstrom which would engulf the neophyte who

dared ask a foreign-service officer what actually he did. The amused and tolerant smile, the facile absurdity of the explanation—and then ostracism. Yes, the Department has its own peculiar brand of "evasive action."

Because it was spring and Tuesday the Mayflower seemed surprisingly close. The blocks flowed past like vignettes in a travelogue. Seventeenth Street melted into Farragut Circle and Connecticut Avenue took over on the other side with no conscious transition. And there were the three revolving doors all locked open against the season. George walked the length of the lobby down to the main dining room and back again as though looking for someone and then, carefully noting the electrically lighted sign "STEP," he stepped and entered the Men's Bar.

"George, m'boy!"

"Well, Brax. Greetings."

"Hiya, 'Ambassador.' How're all your little Ruskis?"

George smiled generally at the group arranged along the wall at the little tables for two and disposed of his hat, gloves and stick. "Gentlemen," he said, and sat down. Most of the men he knew. Fellow named Cole or Dole who had something to do with non-ferrous metals for the Reconstruction Finance Corporation, a couple of British naval officers, an Australian with the International Bank, a King's Messenger and an American aviator who wore eagles and looked like a sophomore halfback. The one with the carefully pressed suit and the glasses he didn't remember. Dole or Cole made the introductions.

"Brax, want you to meet Mr. Southard, Jack Southard. He's down from New York on some sort of an oil swindle, far as I can see. This is Mr. Waton-Braxton of the State Department, Jack." The two men shook hands gravely.

"Oil?" George asked.

"Lubricants generally," Mr. Southard said. "You've probably heard of American Lubricants, Incorporated. Matter of fact, we have a little matter up with you fellows right now.

Matter of fact, that's what I'm down here on right now, little matter of an Iranian concession."

"Iran?" George inquired, vaguely looking over the cocktail list. He always had a dry martini, but he always looked over the list first.

"Yeah, Iran," Mr. Southard said.

George leaned back and called the waiter, "Whitey—oh, Whitey. Make mine a dry martini and really dry this time. Tell Callahan. He'll know."

Under cover of the ordering, the RFC man said to Southard, "Lay off the Iranian business. You'll never get anywhere that way. He'll clam up on you." Mr. Southard looked a little wild-eyed.

George turned back politely. "Forgive me. You were saying?"

"Nothing," Mr. Southard said.

One of the British officers helped out. "Read the Prime Minister's speech, Brax? If you ask me it's the usual—what do you chaps call it?"

"Eye-wash," the RFC man suggested.

"Hog-wash."

"Malachi."

"Quite," said the British officer. "Usual form."

"One might say, pre-season form," George put in. "Not worth a double blue in my book." The Englishmen and George beamed at their little joke, leaving the Americans to their cocktails.

George finished his martini and ordered a hot chicken sandwich. The conversation shifted to Mr. Gromyko and then to supersonic speeds. The Australian began talking about the balance of power in the Pacific. George listened, nodded at appropriate moments and enjoyed his hot chicken sandwich.

Suddenly Mr. Southard threw discretion out the window. "You handle these oil matters, Mr. Blackstone?"

"Braxton," George said smiling. "Waton-Braxton, with a hyphen for some unintelligible reason."

"Sorry," Mr. Southard said. "But do you? The oil, I mean."

George glanced at the King's Messenger. "We handle what the Secretary in his infinite wisdom throws our way, I suppose you'd say. Oil? Well now, I'd scarcely call myself an expert."

"Brax never heard of oil," the RFC man supplied. "Brax and Rockefeller. They just know what they read in the papers."

"Do you handle it?" Mr. Southard wasn't used to being given a runaround. He liked facts that stayed put.

"It is not, shall we say, my specialty," George told him kindly.

"Well, dammit, whose specialty is it, anyway? I've been batting my head . . ."

"If you're referring to oil imports, I'd suggest Averell . . . I should think the Secretary of Commerce, Mr. Harriman, might be the right channel," George told him.

"I'm not. I'm talking about Iranian oil. The whole thing is a hell of a mess and no one seems to be responsible for it. If you fellows don't take any interest . . ."

George laid down his knife and fork. "I didn't catch your name, Mr.——?"

"Southard, James F. Southard, American Lubricants, Incorporated. And all I've got to say is . . ."

"Mr. Southard," George held him in mid-sentence. "The Iranian matter has not as yet reached my desk. I am wholly uninformed."

The King's Messenger called for Whitey, said he had to be off, "frightfully official business and all that, you know," told a quick story about flying the Atlantic with a cigarette lighter some Ambassador had forgotten, and the gathering relaxed to some extent. Mr. Southard said he really had to be going and went. The remaining members beamed at each other.

"Really frightfully sorry, old boy." The Australian seemed somehow to feel responsible. "Chap was sitting here when I came in. Hardly do to ask him to leave, really."

" 'Snothing," George dismissed the incident.

"Lad really had it in for you fellows," the RFC man said.

George smiled, "Our sins are many at the Department. Perhaps we can bear up under one more." He rose, gathered up his hat, gloves and stick. "Good afternoon, gentlemen. I trust we shall foregather shortly with perhaps less—er—vocal lubricants." In a chorus of rejoinders, good-bys were said, which included Whitey's thanks for the twenty-cent tip which brought the whole check to one sixty-five. But no matter, it was budgeted for.

Spring still waited outside the Mayflower. The gray pigeon still retained his position on the exact front of Admiral Farragut's hat. Out-of-town drivers, turning left, continued to make Seventeenth and the Avenue a gauntlet even for the agile. It was a shame that work had to be done on such a day.

At the Department George greeted the guard, who was surprised into saluting, and took the elevator to the fifth floor. His measured tread carried him down the east side of the building to a large room with a heavily rococo carved ceiling. In rows, old-fashioned wooden lockers were separated by benches. George took off his coat and vest, placed these with his stick, gloves and hat carefully in a locker marked with his name.

He removed from the locker and donned an alpaca office coat and began the task of fitting cardboard around his cuffs, fastening it with elastic bands. Then he rose silently and proceeded down the corridor to a door marked "Foreign Service Personnel . . . Accounts Division . . . Adjustments Section . . . J. J. Oliver, Chief . . . Use other door." George didn't. He used that door, and was greeted by a swarm of clicks and whirrings. None of his colleagues looked up. He circled the room to his desk, the fourth in the third row. An eight-inch pile of papers awaited him. He didn't glance through them. He took the top one and began punching figures into his comptometer. The heading caught his eye and he stopped to read. "Expenses . . . Iranian Mission . . . Jan-Feb . . . Vouchers Attached."

He got to work immediately. The Iranian matter had finally reached his desk.

10

ALEC WAUGH

Wed, My Darling Daughter

ALEC WAUGH spends a good bit of his life in travel—
living happily in places known, and not-so-well-known,
and producing books about them. But he also writes novels
and short stories, most of which find some unusual facet of
human nature to light up. This one will surprise you. Mr.
Waugh is a brother of Evelyn Waugh.

"DARLING, THEY'RE CERTAIN to object; they'll say that
I'm too young; that you're at college still; that we've only
known each other fifteen days. You can guess how Mummy
feels about early marriages, after the way her own turned
out, and my stepfather will back her up. He's been divorced,
too—twice."

He nodded. He had feared as much. She was just nineteen.
He was still taking a post-graduate course.

"Now this is what we've got to do," she said. "Settle for
anything they ask. If they demand a two years' engagement,
we'll say, 'Fine.' If they insist on 'no announcement,' we'll
agree. Play the game their way and then work on them. Get
them on our side first. Then when they see we're serious,
darling, I'm certain they'll have given way within a year."

"They'd better not take longer."

His arm was about her shoulders; his hand gently but with
a deepening pressure was stroking the soft flesh of her upper
arm. She had the sensation of something underneath her
heart going round and over.

She flung her arms about his neck. "Darling, I could wait for you ten years, but I'd hate to do it."

That evening as she broke the news, her mother and stepfather exchanged an understanding glance. So, just as she had thought: they had long foreseen the possibility of this; they had mapped out in advance their defensive strategy.

She could not have been more wrong.

Her stepfather spoke first. "I don't know what your mother thinks but personally I like Stanley very much. He's talented, he's ambitious. His father is well connected. As far as I'm concerned, my dear, you couldn't have made a happier or a wiser choice."

Her mother nodded. "The kind of thing I've always hoped for you."

Her stepfather took over.

"When were you thinking of getting married?"

It was the very last question she had expected. "Well, I don't know, we hadn't really . . ." She checked, looking at him interrogatively. He answered the question for her. "Myself, I don't believe in long engagements. My parents insisted on a year. It was quite a strain, and oh, the boredom of those visits to future aunts-in-law. Let's see now, this is mid-October. Your mother and I thought of wintering in Florida. Why shouldn't you be married about Christmas? You could go to the Virgin Islands for your honeymoon. Then you'd be back in time for the new term— What's wrong with that?"

Wrong. What could be wrong? She was inarticulate with gratitude. Stanley was equally overwhelmed.

"Christmas. What, *this* one? My, that's swell. Yes, sir, it certainly is that . . . this very Christmas." . . .

Within three weeks of meeting Stanley, she was discussing the details of the bridesmaids' dresses with her chief confidante.

"I can't believe it's really happening," she said. "Mummy astonished me. She was so broadminded, so understanding about it all."

The chief bridesmaid-to-be chuckled.

"Have you ever bothered to work out your mother's age?"

"Of course. She's forty-two."

"Born in '09, that's to say. Too young to remember World War I. Read Hemingway at high school. Came out in '28; the last year of the boom, the first years of the depression—hipflasks, speakeasies, John Held Jr. cartoons; that's when she made her first dates. They were tough babies then.

"We always think of our parents as old fogies. The very word parent suggests starched linen. I wish you could have heard your mother discussing it with mine. Modern wasn't the word for it. 'Unless it surprises everyone and lasts, a first marriage is like the measles. Best get it over early.' "

"Mummy said that?" Her face expressed total disbelief.

"That wasn't half. 'Once a girl's married, then she has a status. The men she meets will think of her in terms of marriage. She has a chance of marrying again if the bubble bursts. But once she gets classified as the girl men date, that's where the danger starts.' "

"How modern can you get?"

She said it with a laugh, but her toes curled angrily inside her shoes. So that was how they talked about this miracle that had lit her world. Something like measles, to be got over quickly. What hurt her most was the impressive logic of it all. It all made so much sense. Marriages were breaking up on every side. The fabric of life was so unstable. War after war and threats of war. People stayed young so long. At forty, fifty, sixty even, they were falling in love and breaking homes. How could you at nineteen make out a blueprint for the self that you would become at fifty?

Her heart was heavy that evening as she sat facing Stanley across a table in a booth. Three weeks ago she'd had no idea he even existed. In twenty days not only her whole future but her very nature had been floodlit by him. If that could happen in twenty days, what might not happen in twenty years, in more than twenty . . . thirty, forty years? Her stepfather and her mother made such sense. It was all so reasonable and worldly wise . . . Yes, but even so . . .

"It cheapens everything," she said. "I feel that they're doing their very best to get rid of it all, over and done with, as soon as possible."

"That's just what they *are* doing, I should say. There's a parable, don't you remember, about the seed that's sown on stony ground, that comes up too soon."

She nodded, miserably. An exact parallel. They were being rushed into this, she and Stanley, given no time to put out roots.

"It makes you feel so helpless," she complained.

"Does it? It doesn't me. I feel that I've been dared."

He smiled; there was an easy confidence about his smile; the masterful confidence that comprised in the last analysis, the core of his attraction for her, giving her the sense that he could make up her mind for her, induce her to do things the way he wanted; not for his sake, but for hers, for theirs; a tender, a considerate forcefulness.

"I hit back when I'm dared," he said. "I take up the challenge."

"But in this case, how . . ."

"Refuse their offer. Wait till I'm through college."

She flushed; she had never felt more furious in her life. "If that's all you care about me, you can take your ring back."

Her right hand caught up her left, tugging at her third finger. He stretched across the table, dividing her hands, holding them in his. "Idiot," he said. "You don't need telling surely, that the very first time I danced with you I wanted . . . how shall I put it?—to start off with you, on a honeymoon right away. That's what I want this instant. But surely, you realize too that this is very special."

He paused. His voice had taken on a deeper tone. The pressure of the fingers tightened.

"This isn't just another marriage," he was saying. "This *is* unique. Neither of us can ever say again, 'You are the first.' "

"You mean . . . you, too . . . you can say that . . . not only me."

He nodded, slowly. There was a look of adoration in his eyes. She had a sense of all the good fairies at a christening, tumbling their jewels in her lap. That he should have said just that . . . the thing that she had prayed and hoped but never dared to ask. Oh, yes, but it *was* special, this thing between them now. They must take every chance to protect, preserve it. Whatever else in life came twice, this could not.

"Listen," he was saying. "When I saw you first across that room, something inside me gave a pounce. 'This is it,' I thought. It was. But let me tell you this. Each time I see you, each time I get a letter from you, each time I hear your voice on the telephone . . . well, there's something new, some new 'you' that I fall in love with. Maybe if we let this pile along a little, not for too long but just a little . . . let me find a whole lot more new 'yous' to fall in love with, then when we do get married, say in June, my, that will be the works."

She sighed; a long, slow sigh that came from a deep well of happiness. She felt she had been born to have this said to her. Thank heaven her mother had been so modern. If her mother hadn't been, she might have missed it.

11

INDRO MONTANELLI

A Hero Returns

AN ITALIAN JOURNALIST, Indro Montanelli has had more than his share of hazards. He reported all the wars of the late thirties and forties—Ethiopia, Spain (Franco expelled him), Finland, Poland, Norway, Libya, Greece, Russia. He was condemned to death by the Germans and barely escaped to Switzerland. At war's end, he reports, he stood third on the fascists' list of those condemned to death; tenth on the communists' score.

THE FIRST THING which the inhabitants of Rovato thought of when the American troops drove out the Germans in the summer of 1945 was to put back on its pedestal the statue of the Village Hero. It had been taken down at the beginning of the war to protect it from the dangers of bombardment and had been hidden in a cave on Mount Pisano.

The statue represented a naked man with an eagle on his left shoulder and was not very beautiful. It had been unveiled twenty years before to the memory of Folco Ferrasco, who died in an attempt to cross the Atlantic in an airplane. This had been one of the many unsuccessful attempts which were made before Lindbergh's, and nothing more was ever heard of its protagonist. However, it was through Folco Ferrasco that the name of Rovato, his native village, found a place in history, and it was high time that this happened.

For centuries Rovato had suffered from an inferiority complex with regard to its neighboring villages, each of which had a monument dedicated to some "illustrious citizen." On the hills opposite was Vinci where Leonardo da Vinci was born; on those to the right was the birthplace of Machiavelli; and on the left lay San Miniato, where the poet Carducci had lived. Only at Rovato no important personage to whom a statue could be erected had ever lived or been born until the day on which Folco Ferrasco had made the historic gesture of setting out alone in an airplane for America.

He lost his life, but at last the people of his village found glory. This is how it came about that on the very day the Germans left Rovato and the Americans entered it the inhabitants hurried in a mass to the cave on Mount Pisano and brought the statue back to the village in triumph for a celebration.

Antonio Ferrasco was gazing from a window of his house which looked out on the square where the ceremony was to take place. He was a cousin of Folco and just because of this relationship stood a good chance of being chosen mayor in the next elections. He was thinking about the speech which he was going to make in an hour or two at the reinstatement of the Village Hero on his pedestal when his old butler, Battista, came in to announce that a chaplain of the Allied Forces had called to see him.

"Show him in," answered Antonio and then went himself to meet the visitor.

The chaplain did not belong to the United States Army but to the Brazilian force which had occupied the neighboring village where Machiavelli had been born. He was a tall man with a noble bearing and a great gray beard which grew all round his face.

"My name is Father Cristoforo," he said in good Italian.

"You are welcome!" Antonio answered and, as they walked together into the house, "What can I do for you?"

"Practically speaking, I am afraid there will be nothing you can do," the priest replied. "But," he looked round and added in a low voice, "can we speak freely here and be quite certain that no one will overhear us?"

"Quite certain," Antonio answered, surprised and a little disturbed.

"There used to be a door in this room which led straight through into the servants' quarters."

"It was bricked up some years ago and the servants are no longer here. The only one left is the deaf old man whom you saw," Antonio answered smiling, but on second thought he broke off abruptly and fixed the chaplain with a surprised and questioning look. "How did you know that in this room—"

Father Cristoforo smiled at him indulgently. Then putting his hand in the inside pocket of his jacket he drew out a worn leather photograph holder and handed it to Antonio. It was the portrait of an old lady with two children.

"Granny Francesca!" Antonio exclaimed. "Dear Granny Francesca with me and—"

He raised his eyes toward the chaplain and gave him a look in which incredulity was mixed with amazement and terror. Father Cristoforo still went on smiling. A moment afterward they were in each other's arms.

"And what now?" said Antonio when Folco had finished the story of his adventures.

"What now?"

"I suppose that you will be coming back to—to stay with us here."

Folco scrutinized him intently. It seemed to him that in his cousin's question there was more of fear than hope.

"No," he said after a little, "I don't believe so. You see, I left on that flight without really feeling that I had the vocation of a hero. I was alone in the world. My nearest relation was my uncle, your father, who urged me into the enterprise. Oh, no, I don't mean to reproach him with it. He loved me, in his way, as he loved everyone else in his family, including you and your mother. In his way . . .

"But above all he loved his little Rovato of which he was mayor and he would have done anything to win it a little celebrity and—a monument. He didn't want to get rid of me, for I was no trouble to him. He only wanted to use me for the glory of Rovato. I believe he had always seen me, ever since I was a baby, in the form of a statue. It was only to please him that I undertook such an enterprise, not because I felt myself a hero, and yet I have become one.

"Moreover I have found Faith. I did not have it when those good missionaries picked me up half dead from the wreckage of my crashed machine. I only stayed with them so as not to spoil your father's pleasure in the statue which he had ordered in the meantime, not for my glory but for the glory of Rovato.

"I had not even found Faith when I took my vows two years afterward in Brazil and I only took them because it was the one way to change my name, to ensure that I would be forgotten and to avoid being a cause of sorrow to my uncle. But all the same, without wishing it, I have become a hero; and thus, too, without hoping for it, I have become a believer. I have no intention of abandoning my cloth and my priesthood, and I will not remain among you."

He paused, and Antonio felt extremely embarrassed. Folco was his cousin and the only relation he had left in the world.

"I will only stay with you for a few days," the chaplain continued. "Just long enough to visit old friends who are still alive and the places where we grew up together."

Antonio cleared his throat with a little cough. "Yes, yes," he said quite naturally. "Only, you see, in a little while there is going to be a celebration."

"What celebration?"

"The return of your statue to its pedestal. The whole population has gone in a mass to fetch it from the cave where they have jealously hidden it to keep it safe from bombardment. As you have seen, many houses in the village have been destroyed by bombs. Well, would you believe it—even those who have been left without a roof over their heads

consoled themselves with the thought that you, at least—
that your statue—was safe."

"Do they love me to that extent?" said Father Cristoforo,
smiling.

"Oh, even more! Every day they take flowers to the monument; every Sunday the band goes and plays in front of it
the 'Hymn to Folco,' which was composed in your honor by
poor Maestro Parodi. You remember him? He is still alive
and every time he hears his masterpiece played he weeps with
emotion!"

"For me or for himself?"

"For both, perhaps. They have called the hospital and the
football team Ferrasco, and forty-six per cent of the children
born in the last years have been given the name of Folco,
once exclusive to our family."

"Who knows," said the chaplain, smiling again, "how
happy they might be to see that I am alive and flourishing!"

"Of course, of course," said Antonio. "They would be very
happy, except that—"

"Yes, Antonio?"

"Except that they would have to give up the statue. You
understand. To keep a statue in the square, naked and with
an eagle perched on its arm, when the model is here, without
an eagle, fully clothed, what's more, clothed as a priest . . ."
Antonio raised his arms helplessly and then let them fall.

"They would be happy to learn that you are alive—certainly. But they've become used to the statue. Because of it
they can meet the people of Vinci and San Miniato on
equal terms. And on top of all that they will think that
under fascism they had a statue while now democracy has
taken it away from them. They will be happy, but—why
are you laughing?"

"I am laughing at your embarrassment, my dear cousin,"
said Father Cristoforo rising to his feet and slapping him on
the back, "and at your likeness to your father who was, after

all, a very good fellow. Don't be frightened of anything, my boy. The statue will stay there. It is I who am going away."

An hour later, before an applauding crowd which filled the square, Antonio Ferrasco delivered the awaited speech in honor of the Village Hero, restored again to his pedestal.

The shouting reached to the interior of the cathedral where, kneeling before a crucifix, Father Cristoforo was praying.

"Forgive them, O Lord," he said, sinking his head on to his chest, "and forgive me, too. Thou who readest what is in the heart of Thy creatures, knowest for certain that in mine there is no delight in vanity but only indulgence, that indulgence for men's sins which Thou hast taught me, toward pride and the love of glory . . ."

12

MAX SHULMAN

Chance for Adventure

> HIGH ADVENTURE is something that is very much a matter of proportion, as this story proves. You can find it in far places; it is just as apt to be lurking at home. Max Shulman will be remembered as author of "The Many Loves of Dobie Gillis" and of "Barefoot Boy with Cheek," a short story which came to life as a play on Broadway.

GEORGE ROUNDS, a placid, middle-aged man of Grainbelt City, Minn., and Edna, his placid, middle-aged wife, liked to stay home better than anything. Night after night they sat happily in their snug little bungalow. Their mild blue eyes twinkled behind their bifocals as they looked around them and saw the good, sturdy furniture and the numerous gadgets that made housekeeping simple and living gracious. "Improvements," they called these gadgets, and their greatest pleasure was to install a new improvement. It was a pleasure they experienced often; the local appliance dealer had no better customers than George and Edna.

They loved their home so much that they even spent their vacations there. It was, in fact, during a vacation that they had their windfall.

They were sitting in their living room one night and twinkling. Perspiring just a trifle too, for it was a hot August night. "George," said Edna, "do you think we could afford an air-conditioning unit?"

"I don't know, dear," said George doubtfully. "Not if we're going to get that dishwashing machine, the deep freezer, the electric juicer, the electric floor waxer, the outdoor grill, and the television set."

"That's right," Edna said sadly.

They sat in an absorbed silence dreaming of a house equipped with every conceivable gadget—a house that would be a living representation of the atomic age. A simultaneous wistful sigh was interrupted by the sharp peal of the electric doorbell. George hopped up to open the door and admit a Western Union boy who handed him a telegram for Edna.

"Who in the world would be sending me a telegram?" Edna wondered. She opened the yellow envelope and, in unbelieving tones, read the message: "Archibald Mainwaring died recently. You are sole heir to estate of $5,000. Money waiting for you at my office, 30 Rockefeller Plaza, New York City. Please wire instructions. (Signed) Newman Spears, Attorney."

George could already hear the soft hum of an air-conditioning unit, but he concealed his glee and said sympathetically to his wife, "I'm sorry, dear. Was he a close relative?"

"My Uncle Hardtack," Edna answered. "Really my great-uncle. I haven't seen him since I was a little girl. Maybe thirty-five years."

"Hardtack?" asked George. "You never told me about him."

"I'd forgotten," said Edna. "But it all comes back to me now." A strange, rapt look came into her eyes. "He was a big man, a great big man with red hair and a red beard and anchors tattooed on his arms. He used to come and visit us once a year. He'd swagger into the house, roaring a sea chanty, and he'd empty his sea bag on the table and there would be presents for everyone—silk shawls, ivory bracelets, little jade figures, knives with inlaid handles. Then he'd call for rum and sit there drinking from the bottle and laughing and telling wonderful stories about his experiences in China and India and the South Sea Islands and all over the world."

Edna was smiling and her cheeks were flushed. George felt vaguely disturbed.

"Edna," he said, "I've never seen you like this before."

"He would take us out every night," she continued. "First the theater and then a fine restaurant. He would order a tremendous dinner—steaks and lobsters and squab and bottles and bottles of wine. He'd eat and sing and laugh and yell and then fall asleep at the table and Father would have to carry him out. Then one year he had a fight with two policemen and Father told him he could never come back. I was eight years old then; I never saw him again. . . . Oh, George, he was such a happy man. He enjoyed life, every minute of it. I remember how he used to give me ten-dollar gold pieces and say, 'Here, honey, get a little fun out of life.' "

George glanced uneasily at his wife's ecstatic face. "We better wire the attorney," he said.

"George!" cried Edna. "Let's use the money for fun. Just for fun. You're on a vacation. Let's take a long trip and forget about everything. Just have fun. Let's, George." She seized his arm.

"Well . . ." he said dubiously.

"We've never had a trip, George."

"We never wanted one," he pointed out.

"But this is different, don't you see? Uncle Hardtack would have wanted us to do this. We have to, George. It's our duty to Uncle Hardtack."

"It is?" said George nervously.

"Certainly," said Edna firmly. "Let's go some place gay and mad."

"Yellowstone?" George suggested.

"A sea voyage," said Edna. "We'll go to New York and get the money. Then we'll visit Uncle Hardtack's grave, and then we'll take a cruise to the Indies and the Lesser Antilles and South America. Oh, let's, George!"

Her face was as earnest as a little girl's trying to persuade her parents that she should be taken to the circus. George's resistance suddenly melted. "All right," he said. "We'll fly to New York tomorrow."

"Promise me you'll have fun, George," she begged. "Because if you won't, I won't either."

"I promise," said George.

And truly he tried. He was airsick all the way to New York. The traffic during the cab ride from La Guardia Field terrified him. Manhattan's noise and crowds made him cringe. The elevator ride to the attorney's fifty-eighth floor office almost tore his eyeballs out.

But he kept smiling. "Great," he whispered to Edna at thirty-second intervals. "Never had such fun." The important thing, he figured, was not to spoil Edna's trip.

They collected the legacy, went to the cemetery to place a wreath on the small headstone marking Uncle Hardtack's grave and took a cab back to their hotel.

George was determined to make their evening in New York a success despite his increasing horror at the price of everything. Sixteen dollars a day for their hotel room, he thought, and shuddered.

He gallantly presented Edna with an orchid and fought his way into an ancient tuxedo. Edna slipped gingerly into a diaphanous silk creation which she had been assured was all the rage in sophisticated circles. Edna herself felt that the dress was much too frivolous, indecent, in fact. So did George, but he forced a smile and told her she looked wonderful.

"I wish there was a cape or something," said Edna. "I feel naked."

"Nonsense," said George, blushing at the plump matronly expanse left bare by her decolletage. "You look fine."

They entered the hotel's ornate dining room feeling horribly conspicuous. George, in a valiant attempt to be magnanimous, ordered champagne. Edna's mild blue eyes were incandescent as she lifted her glass and toasted George and their trip.

They drank.

"Sour," said Edna.

"Tastes a little like citrate of magnesia," said George.

They went to bed wearily that night assuring each other that New York was wonderful. George drifted off to sleep thinking wistfully that tonight's $27 check would have covered the first instalment on a television set.

The next morning they went to the steamship office. In the cab, George leaned heavily against the seat, silent and ashen. "George," said Edna, "are you having fun? I mean really?"

He opened his heavy-lidded eyes and jerked upright. "Of course," he said brightly. "This is wonderful."

"You're sure you want to go through with this?"

"Certainly," he said with much heartiness. "Don't you?" he added hopefully.

"Oh, sure," she said quickly. "Sure."

A tiny, wispy old man greeted them at the steamship office. "We want to take a cruise," said Edna, "to the Indies, the Lesser Antilles, and South America."

"My," said the little man cheerfully, "that's quite a trip. Have you made it often?"

"No, this is the first time. But," Edna smiled, "you might say I come from a seafaring family."

"Is that so?"

"Well, one member of the family anyway. My great-uncle —possibly you may have heard of him—Archibald Mainwaring?"

"Hardtack?" cried the little man. "You couldn't mean Hardtack Mainwaring?"

"Why, yes," cried Edna. "Did you know him?"

"Know him!" exclaimed the little man. "I worked with Hardtack for fifty years."

"Do you mean," George asked, "that he used to sail on this company's ships?"

"Bless you, no," replied the little man. "Worked right here in this office, selling tickets at the next window."

"You mean recently," said Edna, "after he stopped going to sea."

The little man chuckled and shook his head. "Hardtack never went any place . . . Oh, except years ago he used to take a day coach to Minnesota on his vacations. But he stopped that about thirty-five years back. After that, he spent his vacations here on the waterfront, talking to sailors and getting tattooed."

George and Edna stood speechless.

"Hardtack would have given anything to be a sailor. But he never could. Hardtack got terrible seasick."

"Pardon us," said Edna and led George away to a nearby bench. They sat without speaking for several minutes.

At length Edna turned to her husband. "George, are you having a good time?"

"Are you?"

"Terrible."

"Me too."

"Let's go home."

He leaped to his feet. "We'll buy the air-conditioning unit," he said eagerly, "and there'll be plenty of money left for the dishwasher and the deep freezer and the electric juicer and all kinds of other stuff."

"No," said Edna. "We'll buy the air-conditioning unit and nothing else."

"But what will we do with the rest of the money?"

"We will get a marker for Uncle Hardtack's grave," said Edna. "A big marble marker. Shaped like an anchor."

13

COREY FORD

A Man of His Own

COREY FORD'S English setter, Cider, often finds his way into the author's writing. This story, Ford confides, is a fictionalized version of the way Cider got his man. Corey Ford's writing runs all the way from nonsense to the most serious studies of World War II and Air Force policy. He is a Colonel in the Air Force Reserve.

HE'D ALWAYS WANTED a man of his own. His father had a man that he hunted with, and slept on the floor beside at night, and always referred to as the Boss; but his father's man was considerably older than he personally had in mind. Obviously his father didn't think his man was so old, but they had belonged to each other ever since his father was a puppy, and probably his father didn't realize that there was a little gray in the man's hair now, and he didn't jump over stone walls or run up a steep hill as fast as he used to. The Boss was all right for his father, but what he wanted was somebody more his own age, somebody he could grow up with and have all his life.

He used to plan what he'd do with this man when he found him. He would take him wherever he went, of course, and let him sleep in the same room with him, and in the fall they would go hunting together. He was not quite sure what hunting was, because he was only six months old and his father had never let him come along; but he had seen his father and the Boss getting into the car, and the Boss would have a gun, and they would both be grinning, and his father would be making a funny little whining sound in his throat as if he were about to burst with excitement; so he knew that hunting would be fun. He used to dream at night how it would be when he owned somebody he could take hunting with him. He would dream about it so hard that his paws would twitch in his sleep, and scratch on the kennel-floor and his litter-brother, the big one with the black patch, would growl at him and wake him up.

He knew his man the moment he saw him. You can always tell, a thing like that. It was a warm afternoon and he was standing in the kennel yard in the sun, watching a big orange-and-black butterfly moving in lazy circles through the air. Now and then the butterfly would flutter near him, and for some reason that he did not understand he would begin to tremble a little. The butterfly landed at last on the grass just outside the wire, and he began to move toward it cautiously, lifting his paws one by one and setting them down again, feeling that strange trembling inside him. And then somebody moved between him and the butterfly, and he looked up, and a boy was standing on the other side of the wire.

He was young and gangling, just like himself, and his cheeks were smooth and his forearms had not begun to feather out yet with shaggy hair like the Boss'. But his hands were big enough to handle a gun. His back was long and he carried himself very straight, with his head high, and something about him made you know that he was used to being in the woods, just the easy way he moved. This was his man, he knew at a glance. He did not have to look any further.

The boy was with an older man, about the same age as the Boss. Evidently the older man and the Boss knew each other, because the Boss came hurrying out of the house and shook the older man's hand, and then shook hands with the boy. "I heard you had this new litter, Earl," the older man said to the Boss, "so I brought the youngster over. I want him to have a good hunting dog."

"They're all good," the Boss smiled. "They're by old Duke, that I've hunted with for over six years."

The boy was standing so near that he could almost touch him, and he braced his paws against the wire and tried to catch the boy's eye. If he could catch the boy's eye and tell him, then the boy would know, too. Once the boy almost looked at him, but just then the older man spoke to him, and he turned.

"Which one do you like, son?" the older man asked.

The boy's eyes moved slowly over the other pups in the yard, and finally came to him, and stopped. He looked expectantly at the boy, thinking of all the things they were going to do together. He could see them reflected clearly in his eyes, like looking at himself in a pan of water. He saw them getting into a car together, and the boy had a gun, and they were both grinning, and he began to make a funny whining sound in his throat, and then, because he could not contain himself any longer, he barked out loud. His father had told him never to bark, men didn't like dogs that barked and made a nuisance of themselves, but this was his man and he had to tell him. Of course it was wrong, because the Boss yelled "Hey!" at him, and the older man said: "He's noisy, isn't he, that little white one?"

He knew he had done the wrong thing. The boy wasn't even looking at him now. "I don't know," he hesitated. "I like them all."

"That big one with the black patch looks like the pick of the litter to me," the older man said. "How about him?"

He was trying to catch the boy's eye, but the boy was looking at his litter-brother instead. "Yes," he said at last, "I like him."

"Well, then," the Boss smiled, "that settles it, I guess."

He could not even bark because it was wrong to bark. He stood with his paws braced against the wire, wagging his tail a little to keep his courage up. He saw the Boss lift his litter-brother over the wire. and carry him toward the car, the older man and the boy following. He waited, but the boy did not look back. His ears lowered, and his paws dropped heavily to the ground. It was all over. The other pups had begun to play again, and the sun was shining, and overhead the orange-and-black butterfly was still soaring, circling nearer and nearer . . .

The butterfly lighted on the dirt inside the yard, a few feet in front of him; and suddenly everything inside him seemed to go tight, so tight that he began to tremble all over. His eyes were fixed on the butterfly, and slowly his neck stretched out toward it, and his tail stiffened, and his right forepaw drew up beneath him. He stood there motionless, frozen by some instinct he did not understand, feeling the most delicious excitement he had ever known.

He heard the boy call sharply: "Hey, Dad! Look!"

"Say, Earl, you've been holding out on us," the older man exclaimed. "There's a hunting dog!"

He could not take his eyes from the butterfly, but somewhere far off he heard the boy ask: "Would it be all right if I changed my mind?" and the Boss said: "It's your dog." He heard the boy's feet pounding across the grass toward him, and a shadow fell across the dirt, and the butterfly darted away. He would have to teach the boy not to run up on a point like that. There was a lot to learn about hunting, but they would learn it together. He had his man, and that was all that mattered now.

14

CYRIL HARE

Amazing Lady

CYRIL HARE is the pseudonym of an English judge
who doubles successfully as a writer of mystery stories.
Out of a busy life he has managed to write several full-
length novels based on crime, as well as a number of short
stories. Here's a brief bit of drama whose "shock" shows the
surprise of his extraordinary talent. Read it and see!

WHEN RICHARD ARMSTRONG, explorer and mountaineer, disappeared in a blizzard in the Karakoram, his only daughter
Hermione was just turned twenty. He bequeathed her a
good deal of unusual experience gathered in remote parts of
the world, but very little else.

For more tangible aids to living she had to look to her
uncle Paul, who was in a position to supply them on a very
lavish scale. Paul Armstrong had confined his explorations to
the square mile of the earth's surface lying east of London's
Temple Bar and found them extremely fruitful.

Hermione was a slender, fragile creature with observant
blue eyes, a determined chin and a small mouth that remained closed unless speech was absolutely necessary. She
gave her aging uncle and aunt no sort of trouble, submitted
quietly to the horseplay which passed for humor with her
tall, athletic cousins, Johnny and Susan, and kept her own
counsel. In that cheerful, noisy household she passed almost
unobserved.

In the following winter Susan Armstrong was killed by a fall
in the hunting field. Six months later, Johnny, playing a

ridiculous game of leap frog with Hermione on the spring-board of his parents' swimming pool, slipped, crashed into the side of the pool and broke his neck.

Paul and his wife had worshiped their children with uncritical adoration. The double blow deprived them of all motive for living, and when, shortly afterwards, they fell victims to an influenza epidemic they made not the slightest resistance. Though Hermione herself insisted on ministering to them, refusing the doctor's suggestion that professional nurses be engaged, their end was but briefly delayed.

Even with death duties at their present level, Hermione was a considerable heiress. With the calm deliberation that had always characterized her she set about to look for a husband suitable to her station in life. After carefully considering the many applicants for the post she finally selected Freddy Fitzhugh.

It was an altogether admirable choice. Freddy was well-to-do, well connected, good-looking and no fool. Their courtship was unexciting but satisfactory, the engagement was announced, and on a fine spring morning they went to Bond Street to choose a ring.

Freddy took her to Garland's, those aristocrats among jewelers, and the great Mr. Garland himself received them in his private room behind the shop. Hermione examined the gems which he showed her with dispassionate care and discussed them with an expertise that astonished Freddy as much as it delighted Mr. Garland. She ended by choosing a diamond as superior to the rest as Freddy had been to his rival suitors, and they took their leave.

Meanwhile, the shop itself had not been idle. Shortly after Freddy and his beloved had passed through the door of Mr. Garland's private room, two thick-set men entered and asked the assistant at the counter to show them some diamond bracelets. They proved to be almost as difficult to please as Hermione, without displaying her knowledge of precious stones, and before long there were some thousands of pounds worth of brilliants on the counter for their inspection.

To the bored assistant it began to seem as though they would never come to a decision. Then, just as Mr. Garland was bowing Freddy and Hermione out of the shop, everything began to happen at once. A large limousine slowed down in the street outside, and paused with its engine running. At the same moment one of the men with lightning speed scooped up half a dozen bracelets and made for the door, while his companion sent the doorkeeper flying with a vicious blow to the stomach.

Freddy, who had stopped to exchange a few words with Mr. Garland, looked round and saw to his horror that Hermione was standing alone in front of the doorway, directly in the path of the man. She made no attempt to avoid him as he bore down upon her. It flashed across Freddy's mind that she was too paralyzed by fear to move. Hopelessly, he started to run forward as the man crashed an enormous fist into Hermione's face.

The blow never reached its mark. With a faintly superior smile, Hermione shifted her position slightly at the last moment. An instant later the raider was flying through the air to land with a splintering of glass, head first against the showcase. The whole affair had only occupied a few seconds of time.

"You never told me you could do ju-jitsu, Hermione," said Freddy, when they eventually left the shop.

"Judo," Hermione corrected him. "My father had me taught by an expert. It comes in handy sometimes. Of course, I'm rather out of practice."

"I see," said Freddy. "You know, Hermione, there are quite a few things about you I didn't know."

They parted. Hermione had an appointment with her hairdresser. Freddy went for a quiet stroll in the Park. Then he took a taxi to Fleet Street, where he spent most of the afternoon browsing in the files of various newspapers.

They met again at dinner that evening. Freddy came straight to the point.

"I've been looking at the reports of the inquest on your cousin Johnny," he said.

"Yes?" said Hermione with polite interest.

"It was very odd the way that he shot off the springboard onto the edge of the pool. How exactly did it happen?"

"I explained it all to the Coroner. I just happened to move at the critical moment and he cannoned off me."

"Hard luck on Johnny."

"Very."

"Hard luck on that chap this morning that you just happened to move at the critical moment. I don't think you told the Coroner that you could do this judo stuff?"

"Of course not."

"Hard luck on Susan, too, taking that fall out hunting."

"*That*," said Hermione flatly, "was *pure* accident. I told her she couldn't hold the horse."

Freddy sighed. "I'll have to give you the benefit of the doubt over that one," he said. "But I'm afraid the engagement's off."

Hermione looked at the diamond on her finger and screwed her hand into a tight little fist.

"I can't stop you breaking it off, Freddy," she said. "But you'll find it very expensive."

He did. Very expensive indeed. But he thought it well worth the money. As has been said, Freddy was no fool.

15

MacKINLAY KANTOR

Papa Pierre's Pipe

SUCH BOOKS as "Long Remember," a novel of Gettys-
burg, and "The Voice of Bugle Ann" have given Mr.
Kantor a sure place among American writers. In this story
he has gone far afield from native themes to produce a tale
which might have been told by Daudet, if Daudet had lived
so long. It is in the great French story tradition.

ST. AMAND LE BON was as far as the Nazis went in their 1940
drive to the south. That far, and no farther: as far as the big
dun walls of the *pensionnat*.

At that point the invaders had to reckon with Papa Pierre
and with an illusive, distorted, thin-worn substance which
sentimental people (provided there are any left in this
world) might characterize as the "spirit of France."

It all began long ago, when the armies of Bismarck came
swarming far to the north and east of St. Amand le Bon, and
a stupid youth named Pierre was captured by them. While
les Allemands held him in durance, Papa Pierre, then known
only as Pierre the Fat, manufactured his masterpiece. It was
a pipe.

Various materials went into the construction of Pierre's
pipe. A broken stem of amber—dropped by some officer who
visited the prison, perhaps; a smooth cherry twig; a pilfered
block of brier root. After time had performed its proper
seasoning, after his fumbling fingers and horn-handled knife
had done their work, Pierre sported the largest pipe in the
captive army.

With peace, Pierre came puffing grandly back to St.

Amand le Bon. He stood enveloped in clouds of acrid smoke
and told horrific tales about his campaign. Every village the
world over has its butt—its hopeless, doltish jester.

Pierre's daily bread and wine were earned at the hostelry
of M. Georges and Mme Manille. They conducted a hotel of
sorts, directly opposite a crumbling hulk of sodden stone
where medieval monks had enjoyed ecstasies and tribula-
tions.

Papa Pierre—he was forever "Papa" because of his girth
and whiskers, though he boasted no children—performed
the duties of gardener, hostler, scullion, garbage collector,
and more menial offices of the chambers.

Occasionally there came reward in the shape of copper
coins and, rarely, silver francs when travelers strayed that
way. These perquisites served to stoke Papa Pierre's pipe
with tobacco; there was a village joke, purely legendary, in
which the mayor rose screaming from his bed to summon
volunteer firemen—the hotel was ablaze—women and children must be saved—it was only Papa Pierre's pipe, after all!

By the time Papa Pierre stood within his sixties, *circa*
1914, he was as much a part of the village scenery as the
crumbling walls of the monastery—though rather less
decorative.

In that year the monks were ghosts. Their brown habits
were supplanted by the black overalls of the little boys who
squealed or chanted or fought behind the lichened walls;
the building had become a *pensionnat* and a cheap one at
that.

Papa Pierre stood at its gates to watch the first column of
poilus as they moved toward the front. He waved his pipe,
and shouted threats against the Germans, and told loud lies.

The infantrymen were not impressed. "And did you kill
ninety—*morbleu!* I should think it would have been a
hundred!"

"Did he kill them with his belly?"

"No, he must have eaten them. That is the reason he is so fat."

"The pipe—the great pipe!" another soldier cried. "He must have killed them with that!"

Papa Pierre blustered, and tried to explain just how he had made the pipe—and in a German prison, too. But the school-boys took up this jesting with ready voices. They pursued Papa Pierre with raillery through all the months and years of the First Great War. His was a dangerous pipe, they said; it had killed so many men.

"Non, non!" poor Papa Pierre would shriek. "Allow me to explain, *mes enfants!* I did not kill Germans with this pipe. . . ."

The postwar years brought amazing improvements to St. Amand le Bon. The highway was widened and paved: a glass-and-metal tree grew in front of the inn door; it bore a liquid fruit called *essence* on which the automobiles were fed. Papa Pierre undertook the office of hostler once more, but Mlle Annette, daughter and heir of the earlier innkeepers, sniffed her disapproval.

"You and your big pipe," said Mlle Annette. "We'll not have you near the automobiles! Why, half the time flames and sparks are spouting from your pipe. Do you not know that *essence* will explode?"

Papa Pierre coughed and muttered. Papa Pierre was grow-ing very old.

Increasing motor traffic flowed down the years from Paris and Fontainebleau. Pierre's hands grew more fumbling; his dirty chins collapsed within their flesh. The human relics who had known the days of monks in St. Amand le Bon fell away and left Papa Pierre alone.

But he swore and threatened, in 1939, in the days of mobilization. His moldy voice incited the young men who trooped to the station, suitcases in hand.

"The dogs!" wheezed Papa Pierre. "Let me tell you, children, if I were young I would never permit *les Allemands* to enter France again. I would blow them up!"

The gayety of 1914 was lacking in this modern war. Men who went into the army went with grim jaws and set faces.

"How would you blow the Germans up?" asked one of Papa Pierre. "With your pipe?"

The North was overrun in May and early June; troubled Paris burst her bonds; her populace came pouring south through Souppes and Montargis, through Sens and Joigny. And of this fleeing torrent, the village of St. Amand le Bon received its share. People tramped and limped and perspired. They pushed their gasping cars, fairly beneath the shutter encasing Papa Pierre's stable window. But Papa Pierre stayed behind when the rest of the village ran away.

"Why," he screeched, "should I run! I did not run in 1870!"

Finally, since Mlle Annette had run away with the rest, the aged Pierre shuffled into the inn's public room and helped himself to tobacco. He heard the exhausted tramp and rattle of other hordes outside the window. These were not civilian hordes; they were military, and they seemed running, too. Papa Pierre put his head out of the window to speak with a weary rear guard.

"I did not run from them," scolded the old man.

An officer smiled, "Neither will we, *grandpère*. See, our soldiers have taken up a position in the *pensionnat*. They have machine guns, and those walls are thick. . . . Out of there, old man! We have orders to evacuate all citizens who have remained."

An airplane chose that moment to sweep close, hammering the crooked street, and Pierre fell back from the window in fright. When he looked again, the lieutenant and the other soldiers were past caring whether Papa Pierre was evacuated or not.

The old man muttered about this for a time, and then,

growing hungry, he crept to the kitchen for food and back into the public room for fresh tobacco.

Germans appeared, beneath the clouds of late afternoon; they upset themselves from their motorcycles and described strange postures in the street, and stayed that way. When the French machine-guns in the boarding school had ceased their more earnest staccato, Papa Pierre took an observation: these first Germans were surely dead. But more appeared on the outskirts of the village. More motorcycles, more trucks with armored sides.

The *pensionnat* still stood; an angry trickle of bullets came from its battlements. But the Germans were trying something new. They brought forward, under the shelter of houses, a kind of armored water tank; they trailed a snake of hose. Soldiers in strange suits and masks—they crept like a fire brigade, bearing the nozzle forward.

Papa Pierre smelled the juice they were employing. It was an odor he knew well enough. *"Essence!"* he hissed. "They would drench our brave soldiers with gasoline, and burn them to a crisp!"

They would soak the wall and windows of the boarding school, and then someone would throw a match or fire bomb. It was just the same as lighting a fuse to a powder barrel.

The German hose burst. For a moment it coiled and twisted angrily, spurting gasoline over all and sundry until the flow was shut off . . . It had sprayed the walls of the hotel; *essence* dripped in puddles across the window sill. Papa Pierre was soaked through the shutter.

Slowly, incompetent hands fumbled with the catch; Papa Pierre swung the shutter ajar. He looked out upon the street of St. Amand le Bon. There was little of importance to be seen excepting Nazis and gasoline . . . the liquid had not yet saturated the *pensionnat*.

But the Germans were yanking up a fresh hose. Angry officers beside the great tank were cursing their men to the task. A car screamed to a halt; from all the heel-clicking which ensued even the blinking eyes of Papa Pierre could discern the importance of these new arrivals.

Essence everywhere, but not yet washing the wall behind which the French lay fortified. Papa Pierre began to laugh. He saw the hose, the asbestos-clad men who tended it—the way back to the great reservoir. He saw generals beside the tank, and all the other gray-green invaders who clustered along the roadway.

"A fuse!" cackled Papa Pierre. "A fuse leading to a powder barrel!" He flapped the shutters wide, and dozens of the enemy saw him. They shouted warningly. Their desperate bullets began to rap against the window where he stood; but all unheeding, Papa Pierre puffed the blazing sparks of his great glowing pipe fairly into the nearest puddle of gasoline.

16

ELIZABETH CRAWFORD AND HERBERT DALMAS

Rush-Hour Romance

NEW YORK'S SUBWAY SYSTEM seems an unlikely place for love to burgeon, but to this determined young man and equally determined young woman it took on the importance of a lifeline. Mr. Dalmas is a veteran at writing stories, screen plays and articles, and has tried his hand at producing pictures. Miss Crawford, New York editor and writer, has collaborated with him on a number of stories.

AT 8:45 ON A drizzly late winter morning a girl in a long cashmere coat walked onto the subway station platform at Seventy-seventh Street. She was an extremely pretty girl, with short brown hair and naturally shadowed gray eyes, the kind of eyes they say in Ireland are "put in with a sooty finger."

Some half dozen people away, a tall, thin young man wearing a light raincoat did his best not to stare, but he could not conceal his appreciation of what the girl did for those drab surroundings. He tried repeatedly to look elsewhere, but his expression of grave approval, intensified by a pair of horn-rimmed glasses, kept coming back to her.

When the local roared in, he got on the same car she did. It was crowded, but there was still air-space between passengers.

After a moment, he said, "I beg your pardon. Did you drop this?" He held out a small gold pin, fashioned like a feather.

Startled, the girl said, "Thank you." She took the pin and smiled at the young man. He returned the smile benevolently.

But as the train pulled into the next station, a puzzled frown came to her face.

"I think you made a mistake," she said. She gave him the pin. "This isn't mine. I have one like it, but I'm sure I didn't wear it today."

"I know," the young man said gently. "I merely asked *if* you had dropped it." He saw a flash of astonishment in the gray eyes.

"I can explain," he added quickly. "For two months, ever since the first time I saw you up there at Seventy-seventh Street, I've been trying to find a way to speak to you— properly.

"One day—February 15, it was—I noticed this pin. You were wearing it on a black wool suit. It took me till three days ago to find one like it. This is the first time you haven't worn yours. I knew," he explained, "you'd realize this wasn't yours—and then you'd probably speak to *me*."

"And I did, didn't I?" she said. She looked at him appraisingly.

He said earnestly, "I don't want you to think I go around trying to talk to girls on the subway. My name is Sanford Ormes—if you think of it as Sandy, it's simpler. I'm with Miller and Bothwell—law firm. I just happen," he said, producing a folded paper, "to have this with me. A letter the dean at law school wrote when I took the job. It says my character is all right."

He handed it to her. She looked surprised, then laughed. "I'm sure it does," she said.

"You might look it over today," Sandy said. "I'd like to think it would be all right to speak to you tonight on the train home. I've noticed," he said, "that you usually take the subway about five minutes to five."

She said, "I'll be typing a market report this afternoon. I'll probably work late."

"About six-thirty?" he suggested, and she nodded. He frowned with displeasure. "That's awfully late to have to work," he said. "You won't get any dinner."

"Yes, I will," she said.

"I can imagine," he said skeptically. "A chopped egg sand-wich, probably, and a cup of coffee—sent in. Wouldn't you have dinner with me? You've got to have a decent meal after the kind of day you put in."

She thought about that a moment. "I'd like to," she said, "but I've promised to have dinner with my grandfather—at home."

The train pulled into Grand Central then. They crossed the platform to take the express amid the usual indescribable chaos on the subway at rush hour. They were wedged to-gether immovably all the way downtown, but Sandy seemed rather happy.

As they crossed Broadway at Wall Street, the girl said, "I always feel as if I've done a day's work by the time I get to the office after that ride."

Sandy nodded. "You'll miss the rush-hour tonight anyway," he said. "You know, I hate it as much as you do, but the thought of being able to talk to you in the morning and at night makes the subway seem like—well, like a much better place. Do you think we might go to the movies some night? Could you leave your grandfather all right?"

"I think so," she said. She stopped at the Broadway entrance of Number One Wall Street. "Maybe I ought to tell you my name, too," she said. "I don't talk to just anybody on the subway either."

"Good heavens!" Sandy burst out. "I know that. You didn't think I meant—"

"I know you didn't," she said gently. "It's Sarah Chandler."

She went into the building, and Sandy walked on. From time to time, he repeated "Sarah Chandler" to himself in a pleased undertone . . .

At 6:45 that evening, the cab driver said, "It's your business, Mister, but the clock's got eighty cents on it already."

"She'll be along," said Sandy, dripping in the steady drizzle.

"It's always risky," the driver pointed out, "waiting for a dame."

"Not this one," said Sandy. "Cabs are tough to get down here this time of night, and I don't want her to have to ride home in the subway—"

At that moment he saw her coming through the door of the building. He crossed the sidewalk quickly.

"Hello," he said and stopped. There was a man in the next section of the revolving door—a man perhaps an inch shorter than Sarah and somewhat kewpielike in appearance, though his white hair, pince-nez, black Homburg and stick gave him a distinguished air.

"Hello," Sarah said in surprise to Sandy. To the white-haired gentleman she said. "Darling, this is Mr. Ormes." And to Sandy again, "Mr. Chandler, my grandfather."

"How do you do, Mr. Ormes," said Mr. Chandler, offering his hand. "Bad night." He gestured with his stick.

Sandy turned. A glittering town car—very long and very black—was purring to a stop behind the cab. Sandy, through the fog that is the first stage of shock, realized that Mr. Chandler was waiting by the open door of the town car.

"Can't we give you a lift uptown, Mr. Ormes?" he said.

"No, thank you," Sandy mumbled. "No—I just happened to be passing by."

Mr. Chandler got in; Sarah waved, and the town car murmured away through the rain.

Sandy watched it go. Then he paid the cab driver, who was shaking his head in a disillusioned manner, and walked numbly down the subway steps, trying to adjust himself to a collapsing world.

He had had it planned so clearly. Of course, for a time they would both have gone on working. But he was making enough money now to make him believe there would sometime be a period when he would be the only one to fight the battle of the rush-hour every day. The phrase "taking her away from all this" had been in his mind—but how do you take a girl away from a million dollars?

Next morning, Sarah came through the turnstile at Seventy-seventh Street just as the local clattered along the platform. Her eyes found Sandy in the crowd, and she smiled.

"Good morning," she said, as they got on.

"Good morning," he said.

For some moments that looked like the end of the conversation. Then she said, "I'm sorry about last night."

"Nothing to be sorry about," Sandy said.

"Well," she said, "I should have told you who my grandfather was. But I didn't expect to see you. Then I looked back and realized about the cab—" Sandy, his face a delicate pink, said nothing. "It was an awfully thoughtful thing to do," Sarah said.

"I had the picture pretty well figured out," Sandy said. "The poor little working girl. All that talk about movies—" He shook his head. "It was a little naïve," he said.

"I don't know why," Sarah objected. "I like movies. And I really am a secretary, even if I do work at my grandfather's firm."

"Hiram Chandler," observed Sandy, "is a pretty famous name around Wall Street."

"Sometimes I wish it weren't," Sarah said. "He's got pretty strong ideas about how people ought to work for their living —and he wants me to learn about securities and things. But he won't let me work any place else down there for fear I'll get special privileges on account of him. I don't get any special privileges at Chandler and Grasse."

"No—" Sandy agreed. His manner was preoccupied.

"I don't mean I don't like the work," she said. "It's interesting. I might even enjoy it quite a lot if it weren't for the rush-hour twice a day."

The train pulled into Grand Central.

They rode downtown in the morning and home at night

together for two weeks, and they talked as well as two people can when breathing itself is a task. But in all that time Sandy didn't mention movies again.

Then one evening, as they were crossing the platform at Grand Central, someone tapped him on the shoulder. He turned and saw that it was Hiram Chandler, complete with Homburg, pince-nez and stick. He was rumpled but his poise was undiminished.

He said, "Young man, I want to speak to you. Alone."

Since the crowd was churning thickly in every possible direction the word had to be interpreted loosely. Sandy glanced quickly at the local across the platform. Sarah was inside, and the doors were closing.

"I got on the car behind you," Mr. Chandler said, "so she wouldn't see me."

He battled constantly for position. Sandy, with the seasoned instinct of a veteran, remained rooted like a reed in the wind.

"Gene Bothwell's an old friend of mine," said Mr. Chandler. "He says you have a great future in his firm."

"Thank you, sir," Sandy said.

Mr. Chandler dismissed the topic with a gesture.

"From what Sarah told me," he said, "I gathered that you had indicated a certain interest in her. In my day—" he fought briefly and victoriously with a flying wedge of people headed for the stairs—"in my day, we didn't think well of a young man who led a young lady to believe he was interested in her and then did nothing about it."

"I am not a fortune hunter," Sandy said with dignity.

"Don't be a snob," advised Mr. Chandler.

"I merely mean," said Sandy, "that I have nothing to offer her."

"You've offered her a movie," Mr. Chandler said, "which, incidentally, I'm good and tired of hearing about. That's why I'm here."

"She lives in a different world—" Sandy began.

"A woman's world," said Mr. Chandler, "is where she wants to be. That's the world she lives in, no matter what her physical surroundings may be. A man can save himself a lot of time and trouble, you'll find, by learning that early."

"I think it's quite plain where Sarah wants to be," Sandy said. "She wouldn't subject herself to this daily routine—this rush-hour business can be pretty exhausting, you know—if she didn't want to make a success of what you want her to do in Wall Street."

Mr. Chandler was hit solidly on two sides at once. He snatched his flying pince-nez from mid-air and struggled back to face Sandy.

"Let me tell you something," he said irritably. "The day after you invited my granddaughter to the movies, her work at the office began to go to pieces. It got worse—till she just wasn't worth anything—"

"Did it ever occur to you," Sandy interrupted, "that she might be tired? The work you make her do—"

"I don't make her do any work!" Mr. Chandler broke in, raising his voice exasperatedly. "That's what I'm trying to tell you. I don't know what she does all day between these rush-hours, but she doesn't come near the office. I fired her ten days ago."

17

VICTOR CANNING

The Smuggler

MODERN CLASSICS, we predict, will want to include "The Smuggler." In this story, Victor Canning has expressed his own particular genius. It is a tense study of two characters—a dictator and a common fisherman, daringly placed alone in a room—and at odds. Either could kill the other. This is the stuff of which drama is made.

THE GREAT MAN stood at the window of the Winter Palace. Across the paved courtyard, beyond the long sweep of ornamental railings and the still line of gray-uniformed guards, lay the wide bowl of the only harbor the island possessed. He raised a hand and scratched the back of his neck and the movement made the early morning April sun, reflected from the blue of the Adriatic, glint on the gilt oak leaves of his epaulettes.

A respectful three paces behind him the Chief of Police stirred uncomfortably and said, "That's his boat coming in now. For a year this has been going on, and until now we have never known which of the many fishermen it might be. This time our information is reliable."

"Denunciation?" The word was harsh and bitter.

"Yes."

"Anonymous?"

"Yes."

"You have suspected him?"

"He and every other fisherman on the island, but until now I would have said that he was the last man . . ."

The figure at the window turned and a pair of cold, brown

eyes regarded the Chief of Police shrewdly. They were eyes which missed nothing.

"You sound almost regretful. You like him?"

"Everyone on the island likes Tasso."

The Great Man walked past the Chief of Police towards his desk and from the shadow of the curtains at the window rose the brown and black length of his great Alsatian. As his master sat down the dog dropped heavily to the floor at the side of the desk.

"Your men are waiting for him?"

"Everything is ready."

"Go down yourself and arrest him and bring him here. Do not question him. Say nothing to him. Bring him here."

The face of the Chief of Police showed his surprise. A large hand with a thick gold ring waved at him, and the ghost of a smile passed across the face of the Great Man. "Bring him here. For once I have time on my hands. I am curious to talk to a man who has found a soft corner in the heart of a Chief of Police. Such men are rare."

The Chief of Police would have spoken again but the cold, brown eyes had grown colder and the ghost of a smile had gone. The Chief of Police saluted and left the room.

The Great Man lit a cigarette, eased his short powerful bulk back into the wide chair, and his left hand dropped to the neck of the Alsatian, the squat fingers teasing at the dog's thick fur. After a while there was the clatter of heavy boots on the wide marble stairway outside the room and then the door was opened. Tasso stood on the threshold, behind him two armed guards and behind them the Chief of Police. The Great Man eyed them in silence for a while and, in the long pause, the cries of the stall holders from the market along the quay front seeped faintly into the gilt and velvet stretches of the room.

"Let him come in alone," he said suddenly.

The doors closed behind Tasso, and the fisherman came slowly down the room. The dog by the chair side stirred, beginning to rise, but the firm fingers tapped its head gently and the animal relaxed.

Tasso stood before the polished desk. He was a short, powerful man, much like the other in build. His eyes were brown, but with a warmth in them, his face tanned and creased with years of the sea, and about the wide lips clung a subdued smile. He showed no fear, nor embarrassment, though he knew well the identity of the man before him, had seen him resplendent at ceremonial parades and known those cold, brown eyes from a thousand photographs in a thousand public places. He stood there with his shabby blue jacket swung open to show a dirty red shirt, his trousers flaked with fish scales. In the lapel of his jacket he wore a half-opened yellow rose.

"Your name?"

"Tasso Susvid."

"Age?"

"Fifty-three."

"Occupation?"

"Fisherman."

"And smuggler."

"No man willingly puts his initials on a bullet." The frank brown eyes watched the plume of smoke rising from the other's cigarette.

"You have been denounced."

"The innocent as well as the guilty are often denounced."

The Great Man stirred comfortably and the ghost of a smile came back. "Let us assume that you are a smuggler for the moment."

Tasso shrugged. "Why not? I have time on my hands. My fish are caught and my wife will sell them."

"Why do you smuggle? It is against the interests of our country."

"If I do it—and we merely pass time with this game—it is to make myself more money. The better off the citizens of a country are, the better off the country."

96

"There are times when you smuggle out enemies of our country. A man who does that merits death."

"Why not a reward? Surely a country is healthier without its enemies?"

The lips of the Great Man tightened and for a moment his eyes narrowed. Then he laughed gently. "What do you bring in so valuable that it outweighs the risk of death?"

"Cigarettes."

"We make our own."

"But the one you smoke now is American."

"What else?"

"Whisky."

"I prefer our own rakia."

"I agree, but there are people in the capital who think differently. There are also nylons and perfumes."

"For the women in the capital?"

Tasso smiled and shook his head. "For any woman. Every goat girl on this island covets a pair of nylons, and if you tend goats you have need of perfumes."

The Great Man smiled, almost openly now, and said, "And all these things you bring from over there?" He nodded toward the sea.

"If I were a smuggler I should bring them from there, yes."

"How long would it take—in your boat?"

"Ten hours across, four hours there, and ten hours back. Twenty-four hours."

"When did you go out on this fishing trip?"

"At nine o'clock yesterday morning."

The Great Man glanced at a clock on the wall. "It is now half-past nine. It's odd—your trip lasted exactly twenty-four hours."

"I ran into bad weather last night and we had to heave-to."

"We?"

"My son works the boat with me."

"Your boat is being searched now."

"They will find nothing."

"You have a radio? Maybe someone warned you . . ."

"There is no radio. No one warned me. Remember, we are only pretending that I am a smuggler."

"It is a game not without its dangers. During the war, you were a partisan?"

"Yes, I fought. Later, because I know the coast, I was a pilot for the Allied naval forces."

"You like the English?"

"They understand the sea, and they keep their heads in an emergency. Both qualities I admire."

"Who doesn't? But even so, everything is passing from their grasp. In politics, in art, in commerce and in sport they are being swallowed up."

Tasso shrugged his shoulders. "In all these things, perhaps. But I like them still because of all these the one thing they will really care about is sport. Only being able to draw with our National football team yesterday—they will find that hard to swallow."

"You are interested in football?"

"Every man on this island is. My son is captain of the town team."

"He will be proud when you are shot for smuggling."

"The bullet has yet to be marked. Remember this is a private game between us."

"You are denounced. The game is finished."

"Denounced by whom?"

"I don't know, but I should say your wife."

"Why?"

"She is a woman. Women notice small things . . ." A large hand rubbed gently across a broad jowl for a moment and the thick gold ring caught the light from the wide windows. "Four hours over there is not long, but it is long enough for a man to forget his wife. You wear a fresh rose in your lapel. A man who lands from sea after twenty-four hours with a fresh rose in his coat gives himself away. After a ten-hour trip from over there it would be fresh. Maybe your wife has noticed it and grown jealous of the one who pins a flower to your coat before you leave. Jealousy makes all women dangerous. Yes, I think it was your wife who denounced you."

Tasso smiled and raised his hand to the rose. "I am fifty-three. At thirty-three my wife was often jealous, but those years have gone. We are still playing our game. Look—" Tasso tossed the rose on to the desk. The movement made the Alsatian rise quickly, but a broad hand went out to restrain it. The Great Man picked up the rose and saw that it was artificial, made of wax-coated silk.

Tasso said, "It was the gift of an American nurse during the war. Ask any man in this town and he will tell you that I always wear it. After six years it is still fresh."

The Great Man was silent for a moment, turning the rose over in his hand. Then he looked up and smiled.

"A man who holds my power can resent the mistakes he makes. Out of hurt vanity I might take revenge and none would question my right. A snap of my fingers and our friend here . . ." he nodded to the Alsatian, "would tear your throat out. I should let him, for you are too frank and your tongue too ready."

But the smile still played about Tasso's mouth and he slowly raised his hand to the back of his neck, saying, "If you should try—there would be two throats cut. The dog's and your own." From the back of his coat he pulled a knife and placed it on the desk. "The Chief of Police is a conscientious man, but your presence here flusters him. He was so anxious to get me up here that he made a bad job of searching me."

The Great Man picked up the knife and gently tried the edge of the blade on his thumb. Then he said reflectively, "There are a thousand men who would have liked the chance you've just thrown away."

"I am a fisherman, not an assassin."

"And also a smuggler. Some instinct told you to jettison your goods before coming in."

"I am a fisherman."

"No. I may have been mistaken about your wife, but not over the smuggling. Yesterday evening you were over there."

"I was at sea—hove-to."

The Great Man went on, turning the knife in his hands as he spoke. "You left this island yesterday morning with your son. According to you, you have been twenty-four hours at sea, seeing no one and without a radio."

"That is what I said."

"And you landed here a little less than half an hour ago and were brought straight up to me without a chance to talk to anyone?"

"That is so."

"And yet you knew that our National football team had drawn with the English team? The game was played in London yesterday afternoon, after you left here. You heard the result over there when you landed. Both you and your son would be interested in the result. If you had been at sea twenty-four hours without a radio you could not have known the result. It is forbidden to go over there, but you went as you have so often gone."

Tasso's face never altered. For a moment the two men stared at one another. Then Tasso nodded slowly. "The game it seems is finished."

But the Great Man smiled and shook his head. "No, I have enjoyed the game too much to have it finish this way." He stood up. "You are free to go. What I know I shall keep to myself, and you will have no trouble with the Chief of Police."

"Why do you do this?" Tasso's face showed his surprise.

The other put his hand for a moment on Tasso's shoulder. "You made a mistake, one mistake that could have meant death. That can happen to the bravest and cleverest of men. It might happen to me one day. If it does, I shall know I have a friend on this island with a boat. A man can never have too many friends."

18

RODERICK LULL

The Dog That Sounded
Like a Fire Siren

RODERICK LULL lives in Portland, Oregon, and the
Northwest serves as background for many of the stories,
novelettes and serials he contributes to the magazines. But
this tale of an accomplished terrier has nothing to do with
the Northwest. Mr. Lull asserts that it was inspired by a
genius dog he once owned.

IT WOULD NOT be correct to say that my low standing in the
eyes of Mr. and Mrs. Brown was due entirely to the fact that
I've helped Uncle Cash's dog, Speed, develop his amazing
talent.

Even before that they had, to understate the case, been cool
toward me. Of course, Sally Brown said it was just that they
were sour on everything, not only me, because their variety
store was doing badly.

Anyway, the Speed episode sewed the business up. Mr.
Brown said that he meant to see Sally married to the right
man if it was the last thing he ever did. "Furthermore," he
said, "the right man is not a dim-wit of a soda jerk who has
nothing better to do than teach a dog how to make a noise
like a fire engine."

"Sir," I said, "it is true that I am at the Kumin Pharmacy.
But I am taking a course in accounting and I have straight
A's so far."

"Scram," Mr. Brown said.

That night Sally sneaked out of the Browns' living quarters, which were above the variety store, and slipped into my old wreck of a car. That was the way it was—she had to act like a thief in the night to see me at all.

She is a very beautiful girl, if you happen to like a redhead with a skin like country cream, and a figure that belongs in next year's French bathing suit, and eyes you want to swim in, they are so blue.

"Darling," I said. "I was thinking that—"

A little way off a fire siren wailed. And at once, from the Browns' apartment, Speed let go. I shuddered as he put his all into his work and got louder and louder. "If I ever live my life over," I said, "I will have nothing to do with dogs."

"I understand, darling. But they—"

Just then Mr. Brown slammed a window up. "Sally!" he shouted. "If you're with that scrawny, four-flushing counter-jumper I'll—"

"I think he wants me to come in," Sally said. "Good night, precious."

But I should explain about Uncle Cash and Speed.

Uncle Cash is Mrs. Brown's uncle. He is a retired railroad man with a pension and a taste for cigars and whisky. He lives with the Browns and pays well for his room and board.

Speed is a very gentle, liver-and-white dog with a great fondness for eating and sleeping. He has a remarkable gift. He can make a noise like a siren.

I became involved with Speed when we got in the habit of taking walks together, just Speed and I.

One day a fire engine came by us, its siren going full blast. Without warning, Speed let loose. He made his mouth round, and lifted his head, and his eyes got bright. There he was, a living siren.

So, just for the hell of it, I developed his talent. It was quite a job and it took weeks. But finally he got it. He'd make the siren noise each and every time he heard a fire engine. And besides, he'd let her go when you gave him the command, "Fire, Speed, fire!"

Uncle Cash thought it was wonderful and that, as matters turned out, put me even deeper into trouble with the Browns. Every time Uncle Cash came home feeling happy he'd yell "Fire!" at Speed and the result drove the Browns nuts. On top of that, cruising police cars responded to Speed's siren on two occasions.

As usual, Mr. Brown was most explicit. "I am told, Baker, that you are responsible for that damn dog making that—"

"Only partly, sir. You see—"

"Shut up, Baker. I have only one more word for you. My daughter is not going to have anything to do with an animal trainer. Period."

The heat was really on. They watched Sally like Scotland Yard operatives assigned to a murder suspect.

As for Sally—well, she pretended it was nothing on the rare occasions when we were able to meet for a few minutes. She tried to act her usual cheerful self but she was as transparent as glass. Half the time she was on the verge of tears.

"It's their store," she said. "They've got a big stock and a million bills, and not enough trade to keep a mouse alive. If the sale goes over maybe—just maybe—"

"Sale?" I said.

"They're going to have a sale, darling, to raise cash."

There had been a piece on sales in my correspondence course. You had to do something unusual if you were going to get the crowds. I told Sally that. And then I kissed her.

She pushed me away. "Don't do that again," she said. "Anyway, not till I have time to think. What could we do that's unusual?"

All of a sudden it came to me. I said, "Make it a kind of lottery. For instance, every person whose sales slip number has a zero at the end gets a free prize. Those with two zeros get a better prize and so on. Most of the prizes can be small. Just have a few good ones, like electric mixers and radios. That'll bring 'em in."

I kissed her once more and was given full co-operation. "I

like the idea," she said. "But perhaps I shouldn't say it came from you, not just yet. Let me sort of cast around and see what happens."

She reached for the car door. "You can't go yet," I said. "I love you, Sally."

She was so close to crying that it really hurt. "I love you too," she said.

Well, they used my idea for the sale. The neighborhood paper came out with a whopping big ad about how they were not only offering the greatest bargains ever heard of but were giving away free—absolutely free!—valuable merchandise to the people whose sales slip numbers ended in zeros. They put a banner clear across the store front that said: "Of Course We're Crazy—You Take Advantage Of It."

The sale was on a Saturday and I spent my lunch hour standing in a doorway near the store. It was going over big.

I came back when I got through work at six and walked slowly by. Business was still good and the shelves were looking bare. If anything would mellow the Browns—which I doubted—this should be it. I saw Sally helping wrap packages and I'd have given an arm just to be able to help. But I didn't dare go inside.

A big man strolled by, glanced inside and kept on going. I'd never seen him before, so I figured he must be a newcomer to the neighborhood.

I hung around till eight, when they finally closed. Then I went home.

But something was preying on my mind—something besides that worry about Sally that was always there. The Browns had taken in a lot of money today. They'd have to keep it on hand overnight, and then—

I don't pretend I'm extra bright. I just acted on a hunch. I went back and parked near the store. It was dark and lonely there now, with hardly anyone around. I'd been there a long time when I heard the sound of a door being slammed. It came from the general direction of the Browns' quarters. I sat up.

After a moment a big man, carrying a metal box under his arm, came hurrying up the street. Back of him a low-hung shape trotted along. It was Speed, who loved everybody and always enjoyed making new acquaintances.

Then there was a terrible yell in Mr. Brown's voice. "Help!" it said. "Thieves! Burglars! Thieves! Help!"

I piled out of the car and now it was my turn to yell. "Fire!" I hollered. "Fire, Speed, *Fire!*" Speed was on the ball. He started down low, and moved up the scale, and when he hit the absolute top he sort of let it die away, just like a real siren, and then he took hold of it again and repeated. It was wonderful.

The man with the money box said something unprintable. I started for him. Off in the distance another siren started to moan—I heard it while Speed was gulping a fresh lungful of air. "Keep it up, Speed," I called. "Fire! Fire!" Then I nailed the guy with a flying tackle just as Sally's father burst out of the store.

The thug was no bowl of cherries. He came down on top of me and let me have the edge of his hand in the neck. I thought, *Sally, I love you. My last thoughts are of you.*

But I hung onto him. Speed was still going all-out, and in the background I heard the other siren, getting louder all the time. Finally there was the screech of brakes at the curb and people running.

And then, at long last, I heard a tough, strange voice. A cop's voice. It said, "Just relax, pal, unless you want me to blow you in half." It was the prettiest voice I'd ever heard. Except for Sally's, of course.

When everything had settled down I was in the Browns' living room. The yegg had been taken away in the paddy wagon, the cash box was safe and sound on the table, and Mr. Brown was thanking me in a stiff sort of way. Mrs. Brown, who is a very fat woman, looked as if she didn't know what to think.

Uncle Cash said, "If Johnny hadn't taught Speed to make that siren noise on command, where would you be now? I ask you."

"Well," Mr. Brown said, "it certainly is funny how things can turn out."

Sally sat up straighter. No one ever looked so beautiful and proud as she did right now.

She said, "And, as I was trying to tell you just before we got held up, it was Johnny who suggested how to run that sale. Why, we got rid of practically everything!"

"So we did." Mr. Brown acted as if he didn't quite believe it. I have to confess that I was a little surprised things had gone so well.

"If nobody has any objection," I said, "Sally and I can just catch the late show at the Rivoli."

Mr. Brown shifted slightly. "Well," he said. Then he looked at the money box. "Well, have a good time."

"Don't stay out too late," Mrs. Brown said, but I don't think her heart was really in it.

"If you're ready, Sally," I said. "Nobody seems to have any objection."

"Am I ready!" Sally said.

It was a very nice wedding—small but select. It took place two weeks after I was promoted to bookkeeper and assistant manager of the Kumin Pharmacy. We had one rather unusual guest—Speed. We put him right up front, where he could see it all, and he behaved perfectly. In fact, he went to sleep on us and snored gently through the service.

We told Uncle Cash that we'd strangle him if he hollered "Fire!" and he did hold back, until the ceremony was over. Then he yelled "Fire! It's a fire, Speed!" and Speed was up to the occasion. It seemed to upset the minister, who was not used to our ways.

19

Q. PATRICK

This Looks Like Murder

> Q. PATRICK, like Ellery Queen, is the pseudonym of
> a writing team which also uses the name of Patrick Quentin
> for book-length mysteries. The Q. Patrick detective is
> Lieutenant Trant, a personable and susceptible Princeton
> alumnus who is happily attached to the Homicide Bureau
> of the New York Police Department.

LIEUTENANT TRANT OF THE New York Homicide
Bureau picked up the insisting phone in the squad room.

"Police!" gasped a woman's voice. "This is Marian Alberts
—640 East Seventy-eighth. Come—come quickly. He shot
me."

Trant blinked. "Who shot you?"

"George. George Willis. He's escaping on the express to
San Francisco. Get him. But, oh, come quickly. I think I'm
dy . . ."

There was a choking sob followed by the clatter of a
dropped receiver. Then, faint and playful from the other end
of the wire, came the surprising tinkle of a Strauss waltz.

Tum-ti-*tum*. Tum-ti-*tum*.

Stung by the urgency of this most unorthodox call, Trant
shouted to Sergeant Riley: "Get to Grand Central and pick
up a George Willis off the express." Leaving rapid instructions, he sped in a police car to Seventy-eighth Street. Mrs.
Marian Alberts was listed for the fourth floor. He ran upstairs
and rang. There was no reply. He was about to force an entry
when a cool girl's voice behind him said:

"If you must beat down doors, pick someone else's. My
aunt hates drafts."

He turned. A slim blonde in mink with very blue eyes stood clasping a package of unromantic groceries. He explained the call. Shakily she opened the door with a key and dumped her groceries next to a pigskin hatbox in the hall.

They both hurried into a large living room. Sprawled across a flowered carpet, with a telephone receiver dangling above her, lay a middle-aged woman.

"Aunt Marian!" cried the girl.

Together they dropped to the woman's side. Trant's trained eye surveyed the wound just above the heart. She was clearly dead. He scanned the floor for a gun. None was visible. He rose. On the table, beside the phone, a carved wooden cigarette box and a radio, stood a small aquarium of tropical fish. Something gleamed dully across the smashed water weed at the tank's bottom. Lifting the lid, he reached through scurrying fish and pulled out a small pistol.

The girl was clutching a cigarette like a lifeline. Trant held a match to her sympathetically. "Smoke. It'll help. You're her niece?"

"Yes. Cordelia Ash." She gave a faint, grateful smile. "I live here. I've just come back from work. I'm a model."

"Recognize this gun?"

"Yes. It's Aunt Marian's. She's—was nervous of burglars."

"Who's George Willis?"

"George? How do you know his name?"

"Just be an answering machine, Miss Ash. You'll find it'll keep the shock back."

"He's Aunt's latest protégé, her partner. He's starting a business—fabrics. Aunt put up the capital."

"How much?"

"All she had. There's a paper. A sort of contract."

"And a will?"

"Not that I know of. Just some insurance policies. Unless she's changed them, I'm the beneficiary."

"Can I see them?"

The cigarette in her lips, the girl moved dazedly to a Vic-

torian painting of a benevolent greyhound and opened it like
a door. From the safe beyond she brought Trant some documents.

He glanced through the insurance policies which had been
taken out a year before and, at Mrs. Alberts' death, brought
her niece twenty thousand dollars. He then studied a much
more interesting paper—a brief legal statement in which
Marian Alberts invested one hundred thousand dollars in
Willis' Fabrics, with the added stipulation that, in the event
of her death, the capital remained in the full possession of
George Willis.

Trant whistled. "Why was she so enthusiastic about Willis'
Fabrics?"

The girl looked embarrassed. "She was in love with him.
He was much younger. It was a mess. But, poor Aunt Marian
—ever since her husband's death she's been terribly confused.
A couple of years ago she even had to go for a while to one
of those institutions. It always took this form—falling for very
young men."

"And getting killed by them," Trant said.

In spite of its sensational prologue, this seemed a dis-
appointingly open and shut case. George Willis not only inherited one hundred thousand dollars by the death of the
pathetically romantic Mrs. Alberts; he had even been denounced by his dying victim. George Willis—a thoroughly
commonplace murderer.

Then, suddenly, a Viennese waltz began to dance in Trant's
memory, each note shimmering like a tropical fish. His interest soared. A commonplace murderer—indeed!

Soon the apartment was swarming with his men and later
a ruffled Sergeant Riley arrived with George Willis.

"I got him just before the train started."

George Willis was a young man with exasperated eyes. He
barked: "Heaven knows, I'm sorry for poor Marian. But I
insist—"

"I know." Trant studied him thoughtfully. "You didn't

kill her. You just stopped in to tell her you were walking out
on her. The capital for Willis' Fabrics seemed like a fine idea,
but the emotional demands that went with it were a little too
much. Right?"

George Willis gaped. "How on earth did you know? I explained I couldn't go through with it. It wasn't fair to her. I
told her to tear up the agreement. I . . ."

"In her way," mused Trant, "Mrs. Alberts must have been
a rather remarkable woman. She knew she'd lost you, but she
didn't tear up the agreement. She shot herself instead—so
you could have the money without strings."

"Shot herself!" shouted Sergeant Riley. "With the gun in
the fishtank?"

"Ah. That brings us into a different field." Trant turned
almost sadly to Cordelia Ash. "They tell me that models, for
some mysterious reason, always carry hatboxes to and from
work. You came in without a hatbox but there's a charming
one in the hall. The groceries were a good casual prop, but
that entrance with me was your second entrance, wasn't it?
You'd come back earlier, found your aunt dead and done a
little restaging. The gun, for example, out of her hand into
the closed fishtank to make suicide impossible."

She puffed at a cigarette in icy silence.

"I see your problem, of course," continued Trant. "Those
insurance policies were taken out last year—after your aunt
had spent some time in a mental home. No company insures
against suicide when someone has been institutionalized. You
tried to salvage a desperate situation. It was quite a bright
idea. If you'd managed to get Mr. Willis convicted of murder,
you'd have got the insurance payments and the hundred
thousand dollars, too—as next of kin."

Sergeant Riley's thick neck was red. "But you're nuts,
Trant. This Alberts dame accused Willis herself over the
phone."

"Oh, no, she didn't." Trant crossed to the hand-carved

cigarette box. Smiling ruefully at Cordelia Ash, he opened its lid. Instantly came the tinkling melody of a Strauss waltz.

"A woman called me at police headquarters, yes, but it was a woman who, after she'd dramatically claimed to be dying, opened this musical box for a cigarette. I heard the waltz myself. A dying woman isn't apt to reach for a cigarette—not even in a tobacco ad."

He watched Cordelia Ash. No, she was too cool, too goddesslike. Not really the type he admired.

"Imitating your dead aunt's voice, cheating insurance companies, framing a man for murder! Nice if you can get away with it, Miss Ash, but—" He leaned toward her and gently removed the cigarette from her lips—"I'm afraid you're the classic example of the girl who smokes too much."

20

ARTHUR GORDON

A Kiss for the Lieutenant

THIS HAUNTING STORY, slight as its plot is, had
a solemn impact when it was published not long after hostilities started in Korea. Behind its innocent prank was the
shocking reality that boys too young for World War II
were about to face death in alien skies, and that an Air
Force widow, still very young herself, could be almost a
mother to them.

SHE WAS UNDENIABLY a very beautiful girl, and they were
fighter pilots enjoying what might be—for all they knew—
their last afternoon of leisure for a long, long time. And so . . .

"Go ahead," hissed Lieutenant McElwain in his friend's
reluctant ear. "Go ahead, speak to her. I dare you!"

"Yeah," echoed Red Brubaker, tilting his cap forward.
"You're always telling us what a wolf you are. Well, prove it!"

"Get going, Johnny," said Sid Greenberg, the sardonic
one. "You won't find anything like that where you're going,
I'm telling you."

"Aw, fellers," said Johnny Bascombe, "lay off, will you?"

But he kept looking at the girl. She was sitting in an old
convertible with the top down, her face turned up to the sun,
her eyes closed. She was wearing a strapless sundress, and her
shoulders looked warm and golden, and the line of her throat
was something to see.

Beyond the convertible the waters of the little lake
sparkled in the sunlight and children played on the strip of
sand. The beach was less than a mile from the air-base, and
every few minutes a jet fighter would streak like a meteor into
the sky. Sometimes a flight of four would roar across the lake

in a shattering crescendo of sound. But members of the little
summer colony were used to them now. They seldom glanced
up.

Sandy McElwain nudged his friend again. "A buck says
you're afraid to speak to her. Five bucks says you don't dare
ask her to the Saturday night dance. And ten bucks says you'll
get a royal brush-off if you do!"

"Better grab it, Johnny," Red Brubaker said. "Easy money,
for a man of your matchless charm."

"Don't say you haven't got time," Sid Greenberg chuckled.
"The bus from the base won't pick us up for at least ten
minutes."

Johnny Bascombe stared from one mocking face to another. "All right, wise guys," he said to his squadron mates.
"All right, I will!"

He moved across the intervening space, a neat, slender
figure in his summer suntans. On his collar, the silver bar
winked in the sunlight. His eyes were a good-humored blue;
his hair, still damp from his swim, was an unruly black. He
was not more than twenty-two, but he was an officer in the
Air Force of the United States of America. In the air he flew
an F-84 jet fighter, and on the ground he walked like a king
of the earth.

At least he did until he came near the convertible. Then
his courage failed him. He looked once over his shoulder. In
the shade of the trees his friends were urging him on with
wild, unmistakable gestures.

He was trapped, and he knew it. He said, in a surprisingly
small voice, "Excuse me . . . "

The girl straightened up slowly and looked at him. She
did not seem startled; she kept her hands folded in her lap.
She said, in a perfectly friendly voice, "Hello, Lieutenant."

And Johnny Bascombe, squadron wolf, found himself
completely at a loss. He could not simply blurt out an invita-
tion to the Saturday night dance—it was too ridiculous. And
for the life of him, he could think of nothing else to say. He

simply gazed into the girl's eyes with an agonized and hopeless plea for understanding—and uttered no sound.

The girl looked over his shoulder at the convulsed figures under the trees—Brubaker was actually rolling on the ground —and when her eyes came back to Johnny's face there was an amused comprehension in them. "It's a bet, isn't it?" She said. "A bet, or a dare. Or both."

Johnny gulped. His face felt as if it were on fire. "That's right," he managed to say. "How did you know?"

The girl smiled a little. "I know soldiers pretty well. You're from the base, aren't you?"

Johnny nodded. Why, she's wonderful, he was thinking; she's not even angry! Maybe she would come on Saturday if I asked her. Maybe . . .

"Tell me," the girl said, "have they still got that sign hanging over the gate? The one that says, 'Through these portals pass the best damn pilots in the world'?"

"Why, yes." He was surprised. "You've been there, then?"

The girl did not answer. A sturdy, diminutive figure was trudging toward the car. It was a small boy of five or thereabouts, a towel wrapped around his wet swim suit. "Okay," he said briskly, climbing into the convertible. "We can go, now."

Johnny stared at the youngster. There was a definite resemblance. He said, tentatively, "Your kid brother?"

The girl put her hands on the wheel, and for the first time he saw the narrow band of gold.

"This is my son," she said proudly. "Butch, say hello to the Lieutenant."

"Hello," said Butch. He looked at Johnny's silver wings. "My daddy was a flier," he said matter-of-factly. "Not jets. Mustangs. That's all they had in those days."

Johnny Bascombe wet his lips with his tongue. He looked at the girl. "Was a flier?"

She nodded. "He was stationed here in 1944. I was eighteen, that summer. We got married; he went overseas . . ." An

F-84 split the sky over her head and drowned the rest of her words.

Butch looked after it thoughtfully. "He didn't come back, you know," he said. "I guess he did the war too hard."

Johnny Bascombe said, in a kind of gasp, "I'm sorry."

"It's all right," the girl said. "We get along, don't we, Butch?"

"Sure," said Butch. "We get along."

The girl looked over Johnny's shoulder. "Your friends are waiting. We mustn't disappoint them. Come a little closer; that's right." She put her arms around his neck and kissed him. "Good luck, Lieutenant. God keep you safe."

The engine caught. The convertible moved away.

21

JACLAND MARMUR

Mad Island

JACLAND MARMUR knows the sea as few writers do, from following it for eight years. His first stories were written on the kind of ships which often serve as background for his stories and novels. But with success, he "swallowed the anchor" and went ashore to devote himself to writing. He lives across the Bay from San Francisco.

IN THE PILOT BOOK, where its insignificance affords it no more than two terse lines, it is called Friendly Island. Because a grateful skipper, miles off trade route, after a hurricane one dawn, first discovered it looming off his lee bow; and he found sweet water there for his sea-spoiled casks.

But all the copra boomers and schooner men of the Archipelago refer to it, if at all, by a different name. To them it is Mad Island, for all its look of paradise. It took Johnny Trevort some time to find out why.

Johnny was second mate of the foundered brig *Ripana*: he reached that place unconscious, lashed to a rolling spar that battered him over the reef, floated him across a purple lagoon, and disdainfully deposited him, a black inanimate speck, on a beach of pure white sand. When at last his salt-crusted eyes opened in haggard sockets, the first thing they noticed was a violence going on under a twisting of ragged canvas still fast to the other end of his spar. Fascinated, he watched while a large tawny cat dragged itself from under, weak and bedraggled but miraculously alive. The instant it saw the supine man it crouched, belly-flat, green eyes baleful, its wet tail slowly fanning. It spat, lashed out with one fore-

paw, and dragged itself miserably away. A bitterness crossed
Johnny's lips. Sole survivors: the second mate and Lucifer,
the ship's cat. "What did I ever do to you," he mumbled to
that slinking thing, "that you should hate me so?"

But Johnny was young and tough: he recovered quickly.
And there was plain evidence of prior castaway habitation.
In a copse of coco palms he discovered a spring bubbling
into a rocky basin of cool sweet water; beside it the remains
of a lean-to clearly built by sailor hands. He unearthed a
mullet net, a bird snare, a disintegrating box containing a
rusty nail and a piece of flint someone must have used to
fashion fire. "Why," said Johnny gratefully, "this is as easy
as eating pie!"

It was. Fish were plentiful; sea crab in every crevice of tide
rock; birds and eggs in abundance; coconut, breadfruit and
the little red island berries. But it was desperately lonely, and
after a while there was practically nothing to do. It got so it
bothered Johnny, who had intelligence: but it didn't bother
Lucifer, the cat, who hadn't. The cat simply reverted to wild
savagery, its hate of the man more intense than ever. Johnny
knew.

He set out tempting food for his fellow castaway, patiently
inviting friendship. It was no good. The cat's hate was im-
placable. It slithered up for water when he wasn't there and,
if discovered, sprang instantly for cover to crouch spitting,
fur up, tail fanning, perpendicular pupils narrow black slits
of hate in the green bale of its eyes. Till that day Johnny
Trevort leaped up, furious, hurling a stick with all his
strength.

"You . . . !" He was screaming, wild and disheveled under
a burning vault of empty blue. "Everyone in the *Ripana* was
my friend! Why couldn't it be one of them instead of you,
you slinking beast!" The cat sprang away, a tawny streak of
light. So Johnny staggered down the beach. He sat with his
head in his hands till the sun on his head and neck was a
searing flame. Then, wild-eyed, he looked up across the

ocean waste. "Lord knows how long I'll be here before I raise a passing ship," he told emptiness in a loud dull voice. Then he got up slowly to bathe his fever out in the warm blue sea. . . .

It was Sammy Fanning's topsail schooner, taking a passage for Biltangi no one but shrewd old Sammy knew, that sighted a fluttering signal rag on Mad Island. Proust, the surgeon from Government House, was with him, making the Archipelago rounds; and Sam, his scorched brown face polished by the westing sun, told the doctor what he thought in a flat, hard voice. "Find no one there," he said. "I know: I been four times. Cut one fella down from a leather thong on a coco palm. The others—they just walk out in the sea one night, I guess." He shook his head. "Place must be haunted; they all go nuts. An' it's easy livin' there."

"Too easy, Sam." Doctor Proust pulled at his small, brown philosopher's beard. "There's nothing for them to resist. Even the rain is warm and sweet. A man's mind washes away when it's too friendly and easy like that. Nations and civilizations, too, Sammy. I'll get my satchel, though."

It seemed the skipper was right. When the frightened brown boys pulled the small boat across the flat lagoon, the beach was deserted. There was nothing on that stretch of sand except an odd thing made of slatted sapling wood. It looked like a home-made goal cage for a hockey game, except there seemed to be a trap door open above on a coco-fiber hinge. Captain Fanning frowned, making to wade ashore and investigate.

But he stopped. Abruptly. And he pointed, sorrowfully shaking his head.

Distantly, in the lush growth, they made out a tall, weathered man with a youthful, vigorous face, his only clothing a loin piece of woven coconut husk, a thin stick in his hand. He was beating the brush occasionally in an intent and insane way. Sammy, looking at the doctor, reached for his rifle.

"Crazy as a wild March hare! We may have to tie him up. Have that piece of line handy."

They watched the man's movements in a fascinated sort of horror. He made lightning-swift rushes, first in one direction, then in another, his stick outstretched now and then. But he kept working slowly toward that cage on the beach. Till the doctor, leaping up with sudden violence, seized the skipper's arm. "It's a cat! He's stalking a cat the way a sheep dog does a wild ram!"

That's what Johnny Trevort was doing with the consummate skill, the patience of many months of heartbreaking effort. He had the cat in the open now.

It wheeled and sprang, crouched for instants spitting its hate, its up-furred tail in ceaseless motion.

Johnny never touched it once. But every move he made forced the infuriated feline steadily toward the open sapling cage. Until, while sun-bitten Captain Fanning and Doctor Proust watched in fascinated astonishment, the animal was forced inside the trap. It could go no other place. Reaching forward instantly with his stick, Johnny released the catch and the trapdoor dropped, locking the spitting cat inside.

He had some trouble reaching through the slats to seize it by the scruff and loop some fiber line around its clawing paws. Then he deposited it in the stern sheets of the boat where its baleful eyes glowed with hate. "Thank you for waiting, Captain." Johnny's breathing wasn't much disturbed. "I couldn't leave without my friend."

Sam Fanning, frowning suspiciously, still had his rifle ready. "Put up your gun, Sam," the doctor told him quietly. "The man's all right."

Johnny Trevort smiled faintly, knowing what the skipper thought. "I tried to make a friend of Lucifer for the sake of companionship. But he always hated me. Then I almost killed him, he enraged me so. If I had, I'd be . . ." Johnny hesitated; then went on with quietness. "I kept my wits sharpened and sound against his hate. It took me four months to catch him that way, first time I tried. When it got too easy with this large cage, I made smaller ones . . . I'm glad you came."

Captain Fanning lowered his rifle slowly: the brown boys launched the boat. As they pulled toward the schooner, dipping her nose in the purple sunset swell, Johnny Trevort eyed her with a still, deep longing. Then he looked down at Lucifer, the tawny cat who thought him an enemy. Sammy looked, too, at the snarling, spitting thing. "Friendly!" he growled acidly, pulling his teakwood cheek. "Looks more . . ."

"I didn't say he was friendly," Johnny Trevort explained with the greatest simplicity. "I said he was my friend."

22

WILLIAM BRANDON

College Queen

A TRANSPLANTED VERMONTER, William Bran-
don has never found that California, where he lives, could
dim his memories of the Green Mountains. But California
provides him with themes and backgrounds for his stories,
which he finds in the studios, the cities and, as here, in a
college. This is a charming little invention with a "you-
never-can-tell" ending.

DR. TODENTANZ ELEVATED HIMSELF a time or two on his
toes and fixed his eyes on the paneled ceiling in his favorite
lecture-room attitude. He said, "To the superior intellect the
mass man is always utterly predictable. That is one of the
basic principles of my teaching."

The class opened notebooks and thirty sweatered backs
bent to scribble.

Dr. Todentanz was thinking, as he often did, that the
undergraduates before him represented the mass man and he
himself, naturally, the superior intellect. He was entertaining
himself by establishing, even this early in the term, the utter
predictability of each of them. The two boys and the blonde
girl in the center of the front row, for example: there was a
pattern to be read at a glance.

The girl was extraordinarily pretty. She had a nice smile
and sea-blue eyes (in which, Dr. Todentanz thought poet-
ically, Ariel would be wont to sparkle). Her casual skirt and
cardigan had probably cost more than an associate professor
made in six weeks. She was the young who would inherit the
earth and find it delightful. Dr. Todentanz thought of her,

120

almost without irony, as The Girl Who Would Always Have Everything.

The young man on her right was clearly a big-man-on-the-campus type, fraternity president, varsity halfback, and the owner of a yellow convertible. Dr. Todentanz mentally named him Big Pupil. It was plain that Big Pupil was actively interested in promoting a close acquaintance with The Girl Who Would Always Have Everything. It was utterly predictable that, being Big Pupil, he would manage this small matter with ease and dispatch.

The lanky student on the left of The Girl Who Would Always Have Everything was also deep in dreams of her, Dr. Todentanz had observed, but in his case prediction need not hesitate in awarding a quick blank. A grim lad, grinding out the last year of his GI degree, he was hopelessly distant from the Greek-letter life of Big Pupil and The Girl Who Would Always Have Everything. He was certain to remain a disappointed worshiper from afar.

He was traveling under the added handicap, Dr. Todentanz happened to know, of a war orphan he had quixotically adopted in France, a little girl who was now nine years old and attending the elementary school operated by the university in connection with the College of Education. To support this rather absurd responsibility he worked several hours a day in the faculty restaurant and several hours a night in a local laundry. Dr. Todentanz gave him the title of Earnest Quixote.

Earnest Quixote would sooner or later attempt some stumbling overture toward The Girl Who Would Always Have Everything, but it would fail. It would win him nothing but embarrassment, and afterward Big Pupil and The Girl Who Would Always Have Everything would laugh about it together and then forget the incident completely.

As the first weeks of the term passed, Dr. Todentanz was pleased to see his predictions working out with their usual accuracy.

Big Pupil seized his opportunity to shine in the eyes of The Girl Who Would Always Have Everything on an occasion when the professor had turned some remark of hers with a particularly witty reply. The class guffawed, and Dr. Todentanz got lost for a time in a lengthy pause of self-appreciation, for he enjoyed savoring these small triumphs. The silence had stretched into a minute or so when Big Pupil said impulsively, "Am I writing too fast for you, Professor?"

Dr. Todentanz was able to forgive him because he understood Big Pupil's intention of presenting himself, by that wisecrack, as the gallant defender of The Girl Who Would Always Have Everything. He was not surprised to see them later that day walking under the elms holding hands.

Earnest Quixote was some time longer in building up to his forlorn pitch. It was an extravagant gesture, dramatic in a desperate way and unhappily corny, much as Dr. Todentanz had anticipated.

It took place on the afternoon that Psychology 108 spent in the college elementary school, studying the children there. A fourth-grade teacher, asking her charges to tell the people what they wanted most in all the world, called upon the dark-eyed little girl, Jeanne, who was Earnest Quixote's child of charity. It developed that Jeanne did not want a puppy dog or a kitty cat or even a bicycle, which last Dr. Todentanz knew to be a red-hot lie, as Jeanne had admired his own bike with wistful longing on more than one occasion.

The teacher said, "Then won't you tell us what it is you do want, dear? There must be something you secretly wish for above everything else."

"I want a mother to go with my father," Jeanne said. She pointed at Earnest Quixote. "That's my father there, only not really, but he's sort of my father, and he's very nice."

Earnest Quixote turned red.

"I see," the teacher said. "And you want a mother, too."

"I want one awfully bad," Jeanne said. "But I want a nice one. Maybe one like her." This time Jeanne pointed at The Girl Who Would Always Have Everything.

The class giggled and Big Pupil grinned patronizingly and Earnest Quixote turned white.

"She looks like she'd go good with my father," Jeanne said. "I think she'd go very well with him."

The class howled happily, the teacher dismissed Jeanne, and Dr. Todentanz declared the day's session at an end.

Earnest Quixote, wretched with embarrassment, went to The Girl Who Would Always Have Everything and said, "Look, can I drop dead or something?"

The Girl Who Would Always Have Everything smiled and said, "Well, no, but it's nice of you to offer." She was not captivated or offended, but only amused, all as Dr. Todentanz had foreseen.

But the professor was intrigued enough by the little girl's part in this patently put-up job to look for her later on the school grounds. He found her starting to ride away on a shiny new bicycle.

"Ah," Dr. Todentanz said, "a present!"

"I just got it today," Jeanne said. "That's why I said I didn't want a bicycle, because now I've got one."

Not far away, Dr. Todentanz saw Earnest Quixote and The Girl Who Would Always Have Everything on a bench. Earnest Quixote was talking with great seriousness. Now the lame apology, Dr. Todentanz thought, the embarrassed silence, and the next stop would be his swift consignment to outer darkness, as far as the girl was concerned.

"Could it be," Dr. Todentanz suggested craftily, "that somebody gave you that bicycle for saying what you said today about wanting a mother?"

"I'm not supposed to tell," Jeanne said.

"But it was a gift from someone, eh?"

"Well, yes."

Dr. Todentanz indicated Earnest Quixote on the bench. "Him?"

"Oh, goodness no," Jeanne said, astonished at his unworldliness. "Her."

23

LORD DUNSANY

The Memory Machine

FOR FIFTY YEARS, Lord Dunsany has been spinning tales of a fantastic world which he has created. An Irishman, he lives just south of London in the rolling fields of Kent. Jorkens, the uninhibited raconteur who appears here, has been one of Lord Dunsany's great characters, spinning stories of his adventures in far places. But this one—and one of his most fascinating—took place in London itself.

ONE DAY AT the Club we were talking of crooks, if I remember right, when Jorkens joined in with the remark, "I knew a man who made a point of keeping the law. Quite right too, of course. But he made all the money he wanted."

"How did he make it?" said someone.

"He made it out of a curious discovery," said Jorkens. "Something he picked up in conversation, probably quite by chance. I'll tell you what he used to do. I won't give you his name, because he did all his work along a rather narrow line, rather like that line that they have at Eton for football, going either way from the goalposts; one side of the line was perfectly legal, and on the other side was prison.

"Of course he always kept to the legal side of it, but he was a bit close to the line; and, in case he ever strayed an inch or two over it, I don't usually give his name. So I will call him Jones, and I am sure you will understand.

"I think we do," said someone.

"Very well," said Jorkens. "Jones would find a woman who had plenty of money; he didn't care how much; he didn't ferret out details. All he cared about was that she had plenty to spare. Of course there were several people who were able

124

to tell him all about that. Men like Jones easily find them. And then he was in with a watchmaker. Well, he put together a machine with hundreds of cogwheels and lots of little wires and screws, and I think a crystal or two, a very elaborate affair. Then he would take it round to the house where the wealthy lady lived, and ask to be allowed to show it to her."

"And was he allowed in?" asked Terbut, who was listening to Jorkens as usual. Though why he listens I don't know, because he detests Jorkens!

"Jones wasn't the kind of man," said Jorkens, "who couldn't get into houses. That was the most important part of his work."

"What arguments did he use?" asked Terbut.

"The old argument," said Jorkens.

"And what argument is that?" asked Terbut.

"He just asked the butler if he had any use for a five-pound note," replied Jorkens. "Because, if he had, Jones used to explain, he happened to have one in his pocket that was no particular use to him at the moment. Then he put down in the hall the big box that held his machine, and was shown up by the butler, and hurriedly apologized for taking up the lady's time, and explained as quick as he could that he had a machine of the nature of wireless, that could overtake any words said by anybody during the last fifty years. And then, whatever the lady had intended to do, she listened.

"All sounds ever uttered, he used to explain to her, were still in the air, though naturally growing fainter; but any words uttered in the last fifty years were echoing louder than the sound of a man breathing in Paris would be in the North of Scotland; yet wireless was able to make such breathing extremely audible in the Highlands.

"He then admitted with considerable frankness that his invention was not nearly so wonderful as Marconi's, and he began to explain it to her, for which purpose he used scientific and technical terms that were very impressive. When he got her thoroughly muddled he asked to be allowed to show her his machine, and she would send for it and it would be brought into the drawing room, and its mass of cogs and wires naturally muddled her more.

"Jones used to stand silent for a bit, while she looked at the machine, so as to give the muddle time to sink in, and then he would explain how it was sensitive as whatever kind of wireless he saw in her house, could overtake echoes of old words, amplify them and reproduce them for the ear of any-one listening today; say them again in fact.

"Was it necessary, she would probably ask then, to take the machine to the place where the words were said?

"No, he would explain; that could be done by turning the dial, a kind of direction-finder, while another dial was turned till it got the right date, and the right time of day.

"Like a great many businesses, it was all in the talk. Get that wrong, and you couldn't sell the best champagne at cost price; get it right, and you can sell any cheap wine mixed with quinine, at a pound a bottle. His machine merely picked up the dwindling echoes of those old words, he said, as a wireless receiving set picks up inaudible whispers in the air and brings them down to our ears; and he explained, if explained is quite the right word, how his silly little wheels with all their cogs multiplied the dwindling echoes till it brought them back to the exact audibility of the original words.

"How much of those explanations he made I do not know, but he gave them the right amount, whatever it was, and when they had had it he came to the price, which he used to say was a thousand pounds."

"A thousand pounds?" said Terbut.

"Yes," said Jorkens. "Sometimes more."

"And did he get it?" asked Terbut.

"He wasn't after it," said Jorkens. "In fact, if he thought there was any risk of its being paid, he would make it con-siderably higher. I will explain. His demand for so large a sum would lead to haggling, and after a bit of that Jones would take his leave and say that he would think it over and come back next day.

"And then the deal would take a curious turn: for before he actually left the room Jones would explain that he was not asking for any money to be paid to him yet, because his marvelous invention was not yet actually completed. Moreover all his work, and all his calculations even, were in those cogs and wheels, which had taken him ten years to make, so that if anything happened to his contraption, or whatever is the right word for it, it would be impossible for him to make another, at any rate for ten years, so that the world would either never have his invention, or would at best have to do without it for that time.

"And so, this solitary machine being of such enormous importance, might he leave it with the lady in her big house, where he knew that it would be safe, rather than expose it once more to the terrible risks of a taxi and his own little lodgings? And he would complete it finally and make it workable in a very few weeks.

"Sometimes a lady would be a little reluctant at first to let him leave the logophone, as he called it, with her; but to any of those that are accustomed to get things of value from other people it is comparatively easy to leave something of value with them; and the value of this box, as he used to explain to them, was something very special.

"And then with a final warning of the deprivation it would be to the human race, if his invention was not guarded with the utmost care, and all its fragile wheels protected from accident, he would leave the house.

"Next day, or perhaps the day after, he would come back, usually the day after, so as to give them plenty of time. He would come back and the lady would be full of apologies; either the butler, overcome by the weight of the box, had dropped it from the top of the back-stairs onto the stone floor at the bottom, or a fire had broken out, or a young housemaid, frightened by the logophone's odd appearance, had thrown it out of the window; whatever it was, in every case the invention was smashed to pieces.

"Then Jones used to weep. He was very good at weeping. And that had an odd effect on the women, because a man does not usually weep. It was to them like a tiger singing. They didn't expect it, you see. Well, then they began to talk about compensation. Jones usually got round about two hundred pounds."

"But why ever did they all smash the machines?" asked Terbut.

"Oh, I don't know that," said Jorkens. "But if you were a woman, how would you like to feel that some of the things you said ten or twenty or thirty years ago might be overheard by somebody today and reported to the wrong people? Anyway, and whatever the reason, Jones tells me the women who got their hands on his machines always smashed them. It never failed once, Jones says."

24

GEOFFREY COTTERELL

The Delicate Warning

GEOFFREY COTTERELL is considered one of the
best of the young English novelists, just emerging to an
American reputation. Before the war he was a prodigious
short-story writer. During his service as an artillery officer,
and later, he concentrated on novels. He assures the editors
that this is the first story he has written since 1939.

DOLLY HASELDENE CAME HURRYING on to the lawn
behind her pretty, twentieth-century Tudor house, her plump
middle-aged face glowing with excitement. She crossed the
grass to where her sister sat in a deck chair, with one hand
holding a cup of tea in mid-air and the other supporting on
her lap a book about prisons, of which she had been an ardent
reformer for nearly thirty years.

"Becky, Sybil Watson's just been on the telephone—they
live about two miles away—terribly rich—it was about her
bazaar—but who do you think is staying with them?"

"Well, who?"

"Ian Fordham!" Dolly announced, watching intently for
her sister's reaction. It seemed negligible, though there was
a sip at the tea which might mean something. In any case
Becky was never prone to exhibit her emotions. "Wouldn't
it be fascinating to see him again?" she went on eagerly. "I
mean—if we could get him here! The only thing is—Becky,
dear—would you mind very much seeing him?"

"Of course not. Why should I?"

The reply was given in the brisk, rather hearty manner
which years of hard work and living alone had developed in
her. Dolly smiled in immense relief.

"Thank goodness! Because he's coming. I've invited him."

"Does he know I'm here?" This was not so casual.

"Yes! I didn't speak to him myself but I made sure Sybil told him Becky Spencer was here for the week end, so he'll know you're not married, by the way—and the message was that he'd be delighted to drive over for an hour. I couldn't help doing it. I'm beside myself with curiosity to see what he's like!"

"So am I."

"Becky, dear." Dolly touched her hand. "After all this time can't you tell me why you did it? You were never in love with anyone else. He certainly wasn't—at least he's never married."

Becky was silent, and her sister looked searchingly at her pleasant, good-natured face. She wore her fifty years lightly. But Dolly almost shuddered to think how desolate her own life would have been without her two boys now at Oxford and her husband who was out on the neighboring golf course. Why Becky had chosen to break her engagement had been a problem which had bothered her for years.

"There was a good reason," Becky said after a moment, and Dolly at once had a feeling that she was doubtful about it. "I can't explain it any more than I could then. Perhaps I was wrong. I don't know."

"If only—!" Dolly began, but checked herself. It would be wise to say no more and hope. "Anyway, I'm going in to change."

She was delighted to see that Becky had the same idea. The two sisters went into the house, arm in arm.

When she reached her bedroom Dolly went at once to a drawer in which she kept old curios and after some rummaging pulled out a faded postcard. It was addressed to Becky, and on the back was a photograph of Ian.

He stood leaning against a photographer's prop table, a pleasant young man with a suit and haircut of the early

Twenties. It had been sent from Switzerland, where, Dolly remembered, he was spending a few days with his parents. She had kept it sentimentally because it had arrived on the day Becky made her decision.

She could still see her sister looking a little pale when the family were all together for luncheon and how she had put down her spoon into her untasted soup and said in that curious, thin voice, "I can't marry him."

The amazing thing was that they had seemed such a perfect couple. Becky had been an extremely pretty girl, Ian a good-looking young captain at the Staff College. He was clever but modest, and everyone liked him. Dolly had met him first and invited him to their Hampstead home for Sunday tennis, but as soon as he saw Becky he was spellbound.

And she lost the appraising look which had disposed of several followers. She went about blissfully for months. The families met, and the engagement was announced in the "Times." They seemed wonderfully in love. But back had gone the ring, as soon as Ian returned from Switzerland.

Nobody knew why, then or since. Becky added nothing to her lunch-time statement. After a while she settled down to her study of prison conditions, and had seemed happy. Ian, of course, had had the distinguished career that everyone expected. During the war he had commanded an army. If only Becky had married him, she would be Lady Fordham now. Perhaps she still would be.

Dolly gazed mistily at the postcard but inside she was tingling. She was still in the bedroom when her husband came home from golf. She told him the news excitedly.

"Of course she's trying to be calm, but I know she isn't. You must change your suit, Philip. After all, he's a general and very eminent. I expect she's always been in love with him really. Goodness knows why she ever chucked him. But if only she could marry him now and make up a little for all she's missed—"

"My dear girl," Mr. Haseldene said unromantically, "I suppose you've decided where they'll go for their honeymoon?"

"You'll see," Dolly told him.

By the time the guest drove up in a rather weather-beaten Rolls Royce, she had brought herself to a pitch of expectation. She could hardly bear to wait for the meeting of the old lovers. The sisters remained in the drawing room while Mr. Haseldene went out to welcome him. Becky, as if trying to look undisturbed, was still reading her book. But Dolly could see that she was quite pale.

Mr. Haseldene came back, shepherding in a thickset, bald-headed man. Dolly advanced with heroically summoned graciousness. The general took her hand.

"Why, hullo, Dolly. How well you look."

"Do I? Thank you!" Almost trembling she indicated her sister. He was already moving toward her.

"Becky. You look just the same."

"Well, Ian," Becky said. "How are you?"

In a strange, wonderful way it seemed to Dolly that her voice was high and young again.

"What will you drink?" Mr. Haseldene asked, mechanically breaking the spell of the moment.

"Whisky, if I may."

The general settled down as easily as if the years had rolled backward and he was paying one of his calls at Hampstead. His conversation was light but full of interest, he gave them several titbits about the war, the government, a new story about Mr. Churchill.

A thrill went through Dolly as she observed the fascinated way Becky was looking at him. For her he was probably as smooth faced and youthful as ever. It looked as if things were shaping splendidly.

After a while, however, she began to feel restless. The guest was relating one celebrity anecdote after another, and he himself seemed to be the leading figure of each. "Monty said to me—" "So I told the Prime Minister—" Mr. Hasel-

dene made a few attempts at conversation, but the mono-
logue continued relentlessly.

Dolly had to remind herself that it was an honor to hear
all these things at first hand, but the feeling at last became
overpowering that this was the most insufferably conceited
man she had ever met. She glanced at her husband. He was
beginning to look impatient. Even Becky's eyes now seemed
glazed. Dolly's earlier romantic hopes had gone for good. No
one could live with a man like this.

The general's voice went on, "I pointed out to Ike—"

At last he got up.

"I've enjoyed this enormously," he told them. Luckily
there was no suggestion that they might meet again. His
hand lingered a little in Becky's, but it was clear that he
meant it merely as a kindly gesture.

They watched the car disappear down the road. Mr. Haseldene said drily, "Well, he's a wonderful chap, all right, but
he certainly knows it."

He went inside, and the sisters stared at each other. Dolly
could not contain herself. "I would never have dreamt—he
used to be such a quiet, modest boy!"

"Yes, everyone thought so."

Dolly seized her arm. "This afternoon you said there was a
reason—surely you can tell me now?"

Becky nodded slowly.

"Do you remember him going to Switzerland with his
parents?" she asked. "He sent me a postcard from Montreux,
where they were staying. It was a full length picture of himself—in the usual studio pose, leaning against something and
trying to look casual. You know the kind of thing."

Dolly heard her in astonishment. She certainly knew, for
there was no doubt that the postcard was the one upstairs.

"When I saw it first at breakfast time I loved it," Becky
went on. "Then I took it to my room to look at by myself
and suddenly I began to feel uneasy. After all, it was the
first time he'd ever been there, and you know how beautiful

Montreux is, with that marvelous blue lake and the mountains at the back? The more I thought about it, the more I
knew I couldn't marry him."

Dolly looked at her sister closely. "But what was wrong?"

"Well!" Becky smiled. "Don't you see there was something impossible about a quiet, modest young man who went
to a lovely place like that, with postcard views of it on sale
at every other shop, and who could only think of sending
me his own portrait?"

25

The King

MAX BRAND is one of the many names by which Frederick Faust wrote himself into the hearts of Americans. His most famous title was probably "Destry Rides Again." His greatest wish was to serve his country when war came. Because of a heart condition, no service would take him. So, as a war correspondent, he went to battle and was killed at Anzio. This story was found among his papers after his death.

IT WAS A big day when Rudy Zandor consented to dine with me at Chasen's because those were the years when he was astonishing Hollywood with a series of super productions. He was another Sampson whose strength lay not in his long hair but in his perfect self-confidence.

The country he loved, the flag he followed, the God he worshipped was Rudy Zandor. So I put in the whole day working on my plot and reached the restaurant rather full of hope.

Zandor was hardly an hour late, which seemed a good sign, and then he came in with a yes-man named Gregg and Jimmy Jones, whose real name is Jonascsky. Zandor raised quite a buzz with his entrance because he always dressed for public appearances. This time he wore corduroy trousers, a riding coat buttoned high around the throat, and four days' whiskers. His friends were in dinner jackets for contrast.

Rudy was almost at my table when another murmur started. All eyes left him, and in came Raymond Vincent Etherton in his black coat and white stock like an eighteenth-century ghost. It was rather hard on Zandor to have his entrance messed up like that for he was completely forgotten as the old man went by, looking straight ahead and failing to see the people who spoke to him. He went to his usual corner, waited for his coffee and cognac, and contemplated the dignity of space.

When Dave Chasen in person brought the brandy, Etherton became gently and kindly aware of him, for he was really abstracted, not merely high hat. Thirty years before, when he consented to be King Arthur for D. W. Griffith he must have been a glorious man.

Some of the glory hung about him as Henri Quatre in *Ivry* or as Richard the Lion-Hearted in *The Talisman*. He never was cast except as a king and he moved through his parts without the slightest acting, merely lending his presence, as it were. The whisper had it that there *was* a dash of real royalty in his blood but no one, even in Hollywood, dared to suggest the bar-sinister to Etherton.

Even Hollywood was surprised by the appearance of such a man on the screen. He was more a rare legend than a fact. That was why Chasen's buzzed so this evening.

Zandor, in eclipse, looked pretty sour.

"That man," he said, pointing at Etherton. "Who is he?"

Jimmy Jones winked at me. It was the yes-man who gave the answer. A celebrity in Hollywood can't help accumulating them as the north side of a tree gathers moss.

"That's Raymond Vincent Etherton," said Gregg.

"I want him. He has a hungry look. I want him to play Shylock," said Zandor.

"The *Merchant of Venice* after the big western?" I asked.

"Before," said Zandor. "I'm not doing the western."

My hopes went crash; and at the same moment I heard Gregg ordering caviar.

Jimmy said: "You can't buy an Etherton, Rudy. He doesn't need money but he acts now and then to raise the level of the screen and show the world what royalty should be."

Zandor waved his hand at Jones. "You bother me," he said. "Go away."

Jimmy Jones went away.

"Now get Etherton. Offer him twenty-five thousand," directed Zandor.

His Number Two boy went over to Etherton and I felt a little sick about Zandor and about myself for being with him.

Etherton was sipping his brandy when the yes-man leaned over his table and started talking. The old fellow showed no sign that he heard a syllable. Presently he laid a bill on the table, stood up, and walked through the Number Two boy as though the fellow were a thin mist. He passed out of Chasen's, and Gregg came back to Zandor, astonished.

"Nothing could stop him—not even *your* name, Rudy," he said.

"Why didn't you raise the bid?" asked Zandor, furious. "I don't care what sort of blood he has in him; *nobody* walks out on me. Why didn't you offer him fifty thousand?"

"But I didn't have the authority," said the yes-man.

Zandor looked him over from his chin to the sleek of his hair and turned his shoulder; it was plain that there was one parasite less in his life.

It was a rotten dinner. I tried to be bright for a while but gave it up after Zandor had snarled a few times. The great man was preoccupied. In the middle of his chicken *cacciatore* he jumped up and left the tableware jingling.

"Show me where this Etherton lives," he commanded.

I paid the bill and took him to Etherton's house, small, sedate, withdrawn from the vulgar world behind a formal Italian garden. The California moon, for we have a special variety out here, was laying cool silver over everything and the fountain statue left a perfect shadow on the pool.

The door of the house was open. I don't know why this shocked me so much. It was like seeing the great Etherton with his mouth agape. Zandor leaned on the bell. It made a thin chime of music far inside and we had no other answer. Zandor went in.

"You'd better not do that," I protested. "The old man won't stand intrusions."

"Look!" said Zandor. "I knew it—hungry!"

I followed him a step and saw him pointing to the living room; there was enough slanting moonshine to show that it was empty. The waxed floor shone like water but there was not a stick of furniture.

Zandor strode through the open door beyond and into the kitchen. There was a rusted gas stove. Something scurried away on a shelf and I saw a bit of nibbled cheese rind and cracker crumbs. But Zandor was moving on through a naked dining room and into a bed chamber that was furnished with box springs on the floor, a pier glass, and a big, gilded chair in front of the mirror. In the chair sat Etherton wrapped in a black cloak with his white head thrown back and his right hand at his breast, supported by something.

He looked at us with deeply veiled eyes of contempt and seemed about to make a gesture of silent dismissal. It needed another glance to see that all his gesturing had ended, for what supported his hand was the hilt of the little medieval dagger he had driven through his heart.

I looked away from him to the three big photographs which hung on the walls and showed me Etherton as the Lion-Hearted in heavy chain mail, as Henri Quatre with the famous white plume in his helmet, as King Arthur bearded like a saint.

Understanding grew in me. Those rare appearances of Etherton on the screen had not been a casual amusement but the nerve center of his whole life. His parts never had been large but they had made him a king and with a child's pitiful sincerity he had enclosed himself within a dream. Rather than step outside it, he had starved. I could imagine with what care he dressed himself this evening, borrowed the last possible dollar from a pawnbroker and went out for the final time to see if Hollywood once more would give him a shadowy throne. Instead, it preferred to see in him the wicked money lender, so he came home and erased himself from the page.

Zandor was triumphant.

"You see? You see?" he roared at me. "I was right. I *did* spot the hunger in him. He's been on a throne for thirty years but when he got the Shylock offer, he knew that I'd seen the starvation in his face. The twenty-five thousand scared him. He was tempted and he almost fell. The fifty thousand would have bought him, lock, stock and barrel. But that fool of a Gregg didn't know how to bargain."

I got out into the garden. It was a warm June night but I was shivering. Zandor followed me. The bigness of his voice made the fountain pool tremble.

"He wanted to be a king or nothing, you see?" roared Zandor.

"So he came home and ended his reign. You get it? It's big stuff. It's new. It's a picture. And it's mine."

26

ELLERY QUEEN

The Sound of Blackmail

THE METHOD of the Ellery Queen stories is unique in mystery writing. They are always written *by* Ellery Queen in the third person, but *with* Ellery Queen as the protagonist. This one, in the series done for This Week, the editors particularly liked. It shows how clues, so skillfully planted by the author that they pass unnoticed by the reader, are used in the ending to unmask the culprit.

BLACKMAIL SPEAKS ITS own peculiar dialect, but it has this advantage over other forms of expression: It is the universal language, understood by all.

Including the Sicilian. Mrs. Alfredo had heard its hissed accents, and she wept.

Ellery thought he had never seen a less likely victim. Mrs. Alfredo was as broad as a *gnoccho*, her skin had a time-grated Parmesan look, and her hands had been marinated in the Chianti of hard work. It seemed that she ran a very modest boarding house in the West Fifties which sagged under a mortgage. How, then, blackmail?

But then he heard about Mrs. Alfredo's daughter Lucia, and Lucia's Tosca, and how encouraging the Metropolitan Opera people had been about Lucia's voice, and Ellery thought he detected the sibilant accent, too.

Lucia's career was in jeopardy.

"On what ground, Mrs. Alfredo?" he asked.

The ground was foreign. In her youth Mrs. Alfredo had been a cook. One summer an employer had taken her to England; in England she had met an Englishman, and the Englishman had married her. Perfidious Albion! Within a month Alfred had vanished with her life's savings. What was worse, although eventually she recovered most of her money, the glamorous Alfred was discovered to possess another wife who claimed, and proved, priority.

And what was worst, in inexorable course the poor woman found herself about to have Alfred's baby. Mrs. Alfredo, as she had begun to call herself, fled Bloomsbury for her adopted land, posing as a widow and never telling anyone her bigamous secret except Lucia; and in the prehistoric days when a house could be bought with the widow's mite she had purchased the ancient property in the West Fifties which was now her livelihood and the hope of Lucia's operatic career.

"Long time I scared that Lucia's secret come out," she wept to Ellery, "but then a friend from Bloomsbury write me that Alfred die, so Lucia and I forget our shame. Until now, *Signor*. Now it comes out. If I do not pay the money."

The crudely lettered note had been pushed under her bedroom door. Five thousand dollars was demanded for silence about her daughter's illegal state. "How do they know, *Signor* Queen? Never do we tell anyone—"

The money was to be placed under the loose newel post on the second-floor landing.

"A boarder," said Ellery grimly. "How many boarders do you have, Mrs. Alfredo?"

"Three. Mist' Collins, Mist'—"

"Do you have five thousand dollars?"

"*Si*. I do not pay off the mortgage—I save for Lucia's voice lesson. But if now I pay this money, Maestro Zaggiore give no more lesson! And if I do not pay, it will be known about me, about Lucia. It break Lucia's heart, *Signor*. Ruin her career. Already she is cry and cry over this."

"Young hearts take a heap of breaking, and careers with real talent behind them don't ruin easily. Take my advice. Don't pay."

"No," agreed Mrs. Alfredo with a certain cunning. " 'Cause you catch him quick, hey?"

The next morning Mrs. Alfredo's newest boarder awakened in one of her feather beds to the enchantment of strains from "Madame Butterfly." *"Un bel di,"* sang Cho-Cho-San in Italian, *"vedremo levarsi un fil di fumo. . ."* The piano sounded as if it had served aboard the U. S. Gunboat *Abraham Lincoln* along with Lieutenant Pinkerton, but the voice coming through the aged walls rang as sweet and rich as a newly minted coin. And Ellery rose, and dressed like a struggling writer just in from Kansas City, and went downstairs to Mrs. Alfredo's dining room, determined that Lucia should have her chance.

At breakfast he met Lucia, who was beautiful, and the three boarders, who were not. Mr. Arnold was small, thin, pedantic, and looked like a clerk in a secondhand bookshop, which was exactly what he was; Mr. Bordelaux was medium-sized, fat, garrulous, and looked like a French wine salesman, which was exactly what *he* was; and Mr. Collins was large, powerful, and slangy and if he had not turned out to be a taxicab driver Ellery would have turned in his honorary police badge.

They were all three amiable, they took turns ogling Lucia and praising Mrs. Alfredo's *uovi con peperoni,* and they departed—Mr. Arnold for his Cooper Square bookshop, Mr. Bordelaux for his vinous rounds, and Mr. Collins for his battered taxi—in a perfect corona of innocence.

The next three days were incidental. Ellery ransacked Mr. Arnold's room and Mr. Bordelaux' room and Mr. Collins' room. In the evenings and in the mornings he studied his ABCs, as he privately called the three boarders, discussing books with Mr. Arnold, wines with Mr. Bordelaux, and nags and dames with Mr. Collins.

He tried to reassure Lucia, who was tragically desperate. He tried to get Mrs. Alfredo's permission to take the note and her story to the police, for their assistance along certain lines he had in mind; Mrs. Alfredo became hysterical. He advised her to deliver a note to the loose newel post saying that it would take a few days to raise the money. This she consented to do, and Ellery carefully refrained from insomnia that night, merely making sure that entry from outside the building would leave traces. In the morning the note was gone and there were no traces. . .

Ellery did all the things one does in such cases, and what he gathered for his pains was the knowledge that the blackmailer was Mr. Arnold the book clerk, or Mr. Bordelaux the wine drummer, or Mr. Collins the taxi driver, and he had known that from the beginning.

But the fourth morning dawned with a bang. The emotional hand of Mrs. Alfredo was on his bedroom door, and its owner cried:

"My Lucia! She lock herself in her room! She does not answer! She is at least dead!"

Ellery soothed the frantic woman and hurried into the hall. From three doorways three heads protruded. "Something wrong?" exclaimed Mr. Arnold. . . "Is it that there is a fire?" cried Mr. Bordelaux. . . "What gives?" growled Mr. Collins.

Ellery tried Lucia's door. It was latched from inside. He knocked. No answer. He listened. He heard nothing.

"Dr. Santelli!" moaned Mrs. Alfredo. "I get il dottore!"

"Do that," said Ellery. "Collins, help me break this door in."

"Lemme at it," said the powerful Mr. Collins. But the old door was like iron.

"The ax of the fire," howled Mr. Bordelaux; and he flew down the stairs after Mrs. Alfredo, carpet slippers flapping.

"Here," panted Mr. Arnold, appearing with a chair. "Let's have a look through that fanlight." He scrambled onto the chair and peered through the transom above the door. "She's on the bed. She's been sick—"

"Any blood?" asked Ellery anxiously.

"No. . . But there's a box of sweets. And a tin of something—"

"Oh, no," groaned Ellery. "Can you make out the label?"

Mr. Arnold's Adam's crabapple bobbed before the little rectangular window above the door. "It looks like . . . rat poison."

At which Mr. Bordelaux appeared with the fire ax and Mrs. Alfredo with an excited gentleman in his undershirt who looked like Arturo Toscanini. They all tumbled in to find that Lucia had attempted to commit suicide by filling some chocolates with rat poison and bravely swallowing them.

"*Molto, molto,*" said Dr. Santelli happily. "Her tummy rejects. All to go out!" And later, the doctor called Mrs. Alfredo and Ellery in, and he said: "Lucia. *Cara.* Open the eye."

"Mama," quavered Lucia.

"'*Bina,*" wept Mama.

But Ellery set Mama firmly to one side. "Lucia, the Met needs you—believe me! You're never to do such a foolish thing again. Anyway, you won't have to. Now I know who the blackmailer is."

> *Editor's Note*: And now you know everything that Ellery knows. Can you guess the solution?

"My clients will press no charge," Ellery said later to the silent man holding the suitcase, "so long as you're smart enough to keep their secret. I might add, before you go, that you're much too careless to make a successful blackmailer."

"Careless?" said the man with the suitcase.

"Oh, criminally. Mrs. Alfredo and Lucia had never told anyone about the illegal marriage. So the blackmailer must have learned about it from the bigamist himself. But since Alfred was an Englishman who had lived—and died—in England, the great likelihood was that the blackmailer was English, too, you see.

"You've tried very hard to conceal it, but in the excitement of this morning's events you slipped. Only an Englishman would have called a rectangular transom a 'fanlight,' chocolates 'sweets,' and a can of poison a 'tin.' So if you're ever tempted to try a scoundrelly stunt like this again—watch your language, Mr. Arnold!"

27

BUDD SCHULBERG

All the Town's Talking

BUDD SCHULBERG set the nation talking with "What Makes Sammy Run?" which has sold more than a million copies. His more recent thinly disguised novel about F. Scott Fitzgerald, "The Disenchanted," had a phenomenal reception. And here is one of his rare short stories, in a suburban setting, calculated to challenge and make you wonder.

YOU KNOW HOW married couples get after a while if they're not careful. A couple like the Johnstons, say, who used to hold hands in high school and went steady all through college and got married as soon as George was making enough money in the law office.

Oh, sure, George and Deborah loved each other. That is— they would never look seriously at anybody else, they would grow into middle age together, and watch their children develop, and keep on going, each pulling an oar, right on to the end.

But you might say the fires of passion were pretty well banked and, like the thermostat in the living room of their $14,600 suburban house in Laurel Heights, could be sent up or down with a brush of their hand but were usually set at a comfortable 68°.

And the Johnstons weren't the only ones. Their whole crowd had slid gradually, imperceptibly into that passive apprenticeship for middle age that sneaks up on couples ten years wed and—according to insurance figures on longevity —half dead.

There were the usual Saturday night get-togethers when, invariably, the "boys" would gravitate to the den to talk business and sports while the "girls" lightly complained of their husbands' foibles, exchanged ideas on child upbringing and agreed that television might not be so bad if it weren't for those inane commercials. Once in a while one of the boys would get a special glint in his eye for somebody else's wife, providing outraged telephone conversations for almost a week, and there was the time Charley Griffin was found in the pantry bussing Emily Stever—but, after all, that night everybody had had a little too much to drink, it being the Johnstons' anniversary.

But by and large, their crowd was well-behaved and—well, stylized, you might call it, the years having worked them all into a pattern that was commonly if mutely acknowledged. It might have been a little dull, but it was not unpleasant. At least everyone knew what to expect, which made for a certain poise and confidence, if not excitement, in the group.

Then one day another couple was added to the crowd, and not only that but another element. It started one afternoon when George called Deborah from the office and said, "Honey, guess who blew into town this afternoon!"—Deborah said just a minute, she would have to turn the washing machine off, the darn thing was noisier than ever—"Old man Springer himself!" George disclosed. Jack Springer was George's college roommate and their best man, a gay boy and perennial bachelor. "And guess what—the fair sex caught up with Jack at last! Hold onto your chair now—he's married. Yep! As it must to all men, old Springer's a benedict. Haven't seen the lucky girl yet but I hear she's real whistle stuff. Name's Charlene—how d'ya like that—Charlene. Looks like glamour has come to Laurel Heights at last. They're going to settle here. Jack'll be branch manager for Chase 'n' Ward."

"How nice," Deborah said, at the same time calling to

someone at the back door, "Just-a-minute-I'll-be-right-there
. . . 'Bout time our crowd had a little new blood."

That next Saturday evening was unlike any they could
remember since their crowd first started getting together.
The Springers were something special all right. Charlene was
sleek and long-legged with blue-black hair and velvet eyes
smoldering in a pale, oval face they recognized from innumer-
able perfume ads in the "New Yorker."

Jack's forehead was a little higher than they had remembered it but he still looked more like a movie actor than a
branch manager. They were a honey of a pair all right, everyone agreed, the most attractive couple that ever settled down
in Laurel Heights.

But it wasn't just their beauty that charged the atmosphere
with a special new excitement. It was the way they responded
to each other. "Not like married folks a-tall," Emily Stever
put it into words for all of them, "but like—well, like *lovers.*"

The first thing Jack Springer did was to break up the
circles of man's talk and hen huddles. "No sir, you don't keep
me away from my baby all evening, just to tell me how you
would have had an 84 if only you hadn't sliced on the 17th."
As Jack brushed the boys aside, Charlene came up and
nuzzled into his neck approvingly. "That's my lover boy!"
They would touch each other's fingers in such a way that
everyone in the room could feel it.

"Say, how long've you two love birds been married, anyway?" Charley Griffin's tone had meant to be sardonic, but
the envy showed through.

Jack laughed. "Let's see, we'll have our fifth month anniversary next Friday at 5:37—won't we, kitten?" Jack and
Charlene Springer looked at each other as if there was no
one else in the room, and their eyes brightened with a special
secret for each other.

"Five months!" George said. "Looks more like five
minutes."

"It's love love love," Jack Springer sang, and he and

Charlene laughed. Everyone was a little embarrassed, and, yet, each had to admit it, titillated, looking at wife or husband wonderingly, all with the same dull ache of memory and regret.

The Springers were the first to leave that night. For half an hour it had been obvious that they merely had been waiting for the polite moment to make their getaway. Charlene hadn't so much as acknowledged the admiring glances of the other males. Jack hadn't taken his eyes or his hands away from Charlene all evening. Deborah was watching from the porch door as Jack went around and opened the car for Charlene, the way George used to in their courtship days. An involuntary sigh became a little stifled yawn when Jack kissed Charlene as he helped her in.

"Well, there isn't much doubt about those two being in love." Deborah had turned back to her husband with an ambiguous smile.

"I think it's a little gooey, myself," George grumbled. "They should be able to keep their hands off each other in public."

"I don't know, I think it's rather sweet," Deborah said. And she wanted to add, How long has it been since we held hands across the table or pressed our knees together in that exquisite conspiracy of lovers, while dining out with friends? It had been nice—reassuring. Why had it stopped? What day—what minute?

George and Deborah went on arguing about it in the weeks to come, carefully feeling their way around the edges of it, for fear of upsetting the balance of their own union, their own comfortable, loyal, tired, tenth-year love.

When they all dined out together it was traditional to separate wives and husbands, but in the case of the Springers this courtesy had had to be jettisoned. "What God has brought together let no dinner party split asunder," Jack had laughed and squeezed Charlene's hand.

When the crowd was too large to drive to the movies in one car it had become standard practice for married couples to split up, amidst the usual banter about "not trusting that wolf with my wife." But Jack always made sure it was Charlene who snuggled into his lap, and there were even shrill, unwifely cries of "Jack, stop it!" that brought George and Deborah back to their college days of double dates.

George kept saying it was all pretty revolting, especially when, at the Griffins' party, Jack and Charlene were discovered in the arbor necking like a couple of youngsters. "That's the last straw," George insisted. "Why, they've been married almost a year now—why don't they relax?"

"But that's just the point, dear," Deborah said.

She and Emily Stever had had lunch with Charlene that day, and Charlene had fascinated them with a new book she had just read—"Marriage: Life Sentence or Prolonged Love Affair?"

"Once you think of yourself as just a housewife and your husband as just the breadwinner, you're finished," Charlene had advised these two women who between them represented 17 years of contented married life. "To keep your marriage *alive*, you must try just as hard to please your husband, charm him, yes, girls, and *excite* him, as before you were married." It had seemed to Deborah, over a third martini that was three times her luncheon quota, terribly wise and adult advice.

It made her wonder, for the first time in years, about her own marriage. What a drab, matter-of-fact thing it had become. Why, when she came to think of it, George probably didn't even love her at all. She was just—a convenience, a habit. In the ladies' room she gave her cheeks a desperate little dab of rouge and regarded, more critically than usual, the somewhat tacky figure staring out at her from the mirror. She could never have been a dream-boat like Charlene, of course. But she had let herself go. There was that complacent what-does-it-matter-I've-got-my-man look.

At Charlene's suggestion, in fact with Charlene along as mentor, she had had her hair cropped short in the new poodle cut that had looked so adorable on Mary Martin. Then Charlene picked out a sheer pastel nightgown and a richer shade of lipstick that would "do more for you, Deborah darling."

On their next Saturday night Deborah clung to George, even curled up kittenishly in his lap and, when they got home that night, after an uncommonly long time in her dressing nook she slunk in and wound her arms around George's back. George pulled away and stared at her as if she had lost her mind. "What the devil are you made up for, Debbie—Theda Bara in 'Three Nights in a Harem'?"

Deborah threw herself on the bed, not at all exotically, with tears smearing the new make-up job that Charlene had taught her. George stamped off and slept in the den. Deborah went sniffing off to sleep tormented by vivid images of "Marriage—Prolonged Love Affair" as only Jack and Charlene Springer could know and enjoy.

Deborah was strangely quiet for the next few days. She made his breakfast, handed him his mail, answered him with um-hums, and that was about all. Maybe she and George had worn this marriage out. Wouldn't it be wiser, more modern to do something about it now than to let it drag on to its weary, listless end? Or wait until George found himself a newer, fresher love?

Oh, *damn* Charlene and Jack and all their talk of living-every-moment-for-love. Why did they have to come to Laurel Heights anyway? She and George had been perfectly happy and contented, until . . .

Deborah was supposed to be vacuuming the living room, but she had just been standing there staring into her troubled dreams when the phone rang. "George—" he never called in the middle of the day like this—"is something wrong?"

"No, honey, I just thought I'd better tell you Jack and Charlene won't be coming for dinner Saturday night."

"Oh—I'm sorry." She had been counting on that little

dinner party. They say sometimes these things are infectious. "We could make it for Sunday."

"No—Deb—they're definitely separating. Jack says the marriage is finee. Charlene's leaving for New York this afternoon."

"But Jack—Charlene—why it's impossible! They were so crazy about each other. Why, only last Saturday night they—"

"Beats me. Jack says he'll tell me all about it sometime. Says—here's the funny thing—says he could see the handwriting on the wall after the first three months. Says they used to go home and fight something awful. Well, what'll we do Sa'day night, ask the Griffins and the Lanes?"

"Darling," Deborah said, and she said it exactly like herself and not at all like Charlene, "Why don't we just have dinner alone, you and me, and then after dinner, well—" she smiled to herself—"we'll see."

"Swell. Well, I gotta get back to work. S'long, Deb. See ya, honey."

Yes, my darling, you'll see me, this year, and next year, and next, and next. As she turned from the phone, she noticed on the end table the book on "Marriage: Life Sentence or Prolonged Love Affair?" that Charlene had forgotten. "Of all the nonsense," she thought, and suddenly she was profoundly, explosively happy. "Of all the naïve, immature nonsense."

Then she couldn't help worrying about Charlene and feeling a little sorry for her as she started getting dinner ready: stuffed pork chops, a lot of work but worth it just to hear George say they were even better than last time. She turned on her favorite soap opera and listened to it as she worked. It was pretty silly, she knew, to enjoy a corny soap opera so much, but there it was, every day, so much the same and yet each day just a little different, on and on and on. . . .

28

VLADIMIR PETROV

"Get a Horse, Comrade"

VLADIMIR PETROV, who now teaches Russian to graduate students in Yale, spent six years in the dread Kolyma region of Siberia as a slave laborer. He has written two books about his experiences in Russia, and how he managed to escape. With all the horror he has lived through, Petrov maintains a lively sense of humor, as you will see in this story of the Russia he has known—and doesn't want to revisit.

EACH ONE OF us used to have ambitious dreams of some sort in childhood. I, for instance, wanted to be a Minister of Foreign Affairs. It didn't matter in what country, but it had to be a Minister and it had to be Foreign Affairs. My friend Vanya wanted to be the director of a chocolate factory, and little blonde Sonya wanted to be Stalin's wife.

We were often inconsistent in our ambitions. Vanya forgot about his chocolate factory when the icebreaker *Cheliuskin* sank in the Arctic Ocean and its crew waited to be rescued for a month on the ice. After this Vanya wanted to be a polar explorer. He even ran away from home and spent more than twenty-four hours on the ice of a small river near by. He caught cold and was beaten by his conservative father, but only after the mill in our town burned down did he change his plans. Then he decided to become a fireman.

The only consistent one was our mutual friend, Kolya. At a very early age he decided to acquire his own car and nothing could shake his desire. It was useless to explain to him that only cabinet ministers and the Chairmen of City Soviets have cars, and that their cars are not even owned by them but

by the State. It didn't help to remind him that when they are
put in jail, the cars are inherited by their successors in office.

Kolya remained true to his ideal and, since he was a practical man, he tried to acquire his own car by every possible
means.

Actually there was only one practical method—to win it in
the State lottery. There was a very small chance—one in a
hundred million. But Kolya did not lose hope, and doggedly
collected tickets. When he grew up and became a bookkeeper, nothing could keep him from spending money on
the tickets.

Kolya was practical, and he preferred to get his tickets
secondhand, at one quarter the price, since the citizens on
whom these tickets had been forced by Party organizers were
glad to get back even a quarter of their wasted money.

Then the unbelievable happened: Kolya won a car! To
appreciate the meaning of this event, it is enough to state
that in our city only the Chairman of the City Soviet, the
Secretary of the City Committee of the Communist Party and
the head of MVD had cars.

Kolya rushed into our office, panting. Dragging me out
into the corridor, he whispered: "I won, do you understand?
I won!"

"Won what?"

"A car! A new one! All my own!"

"Impossible! This is some sort of a fraud."

"No, it's absolutely true—here's the list of winners and
here's the ticket."

I checked the figures. It was a fact: Ticket No. 886,224 had
won an automobile. . . .

"Perhaps this is a winning ticket," they told us, "but we'll
have to send it to Moscow so they can make sure that it isn't
counterfeit. When they have checked the ticket, they'll send
you a car—if there are any available, that is . . ."

Kolya lost his high spirits and became sad. I tried to comfort him as well as I could: "You see? You shouldn't have got

all excited. Your ticket will definitely turn out to be a fake. And even if it's real, you still won't get the car because the State needs cars more than you do. You'll get 10,000 rubles. Of course, they'll let you buy a Government bond with 5,000."

However, Kolya continued to worry. He was annoyed with us and shared his feeling only with his friend Sonya, the same Sonya who had once wanted to be Stalin's wife but had since changed her mind. But we, Kolya's friends, were proved wrong. In about a year a car was actually sent to him. When all of us, armed with bottles of gasoline, went to the station to get the car, we were amazed. New, black and shiny, it sparkled with the light of a long-standing impossible dream.

"What are we going to do now? Who's going to drive it?" I asked.

"I'm going to," Kolya said majestically.

"But do you know how?"

"I do, and I have for a long time."

Sonya laughed happily.

"Aren't you surprised?" she asked us.

We were astonished. It turned out that Kolya had learned to drive in the School for Chauffeurs where there was an old instructor with a wooden leg and a car which, everyone said, was the first one that Henry Ford had ever ridden in. Kolya had taken his driving lessons in strictest secrecy. Only Sonya had been told about them.

While bumping in and out of the ruts, as we drove slowly through the streets of the city, we understood the strength and persistence with which Kolya had gone after his happiness. He sat behind the wheel with Sonya next to him. The four of us, his old friends, sat in the rear.

In the center of town a policeman stopped us at the corner: "Show me your license, Citizen!" he said sternly to Kolya. Kolya, still excited, took a paper out of his pocket and proudly handed it to the policeman.

But the policeman was not satisfied.

"Why are there so many people in the car?" he asked severely.

"The laws of traffic do not forbid it," said Kolya with assurance.

"Are you sure?" said the policeman doubtfully.

"Quite sure!"

"Well, I'll check on it. You may go ahead."

Until evening there was a crowd around the car, which stood by Kolya's house. Little boys were in the majority, but there were some adults too. Kolya polished the car with a businesslike air, while we scattered out through the city in search of gasoline.

This was not an easy quest. It is true that gasoline could be bought from the tradesmen at the bazaar, but, first, the price was very high—ten rubles a bottle, and, second, the tradesmen, to make a bigger profit, diluted it with water, and the car worked badly on this mixture.

Therefore we had to look for gas in garages and factories, a completely thankless task.

However, we did manage to acquire some, and Kolya started to drive to work, picking all of us up on the way. In the evening he took little drives with Sonya.

Then an unpleasant incident occurred. Kolya was summoned by his director, who said: "Very bad, young man, very bad."

"What's the matter?" asked Kolya.

"You go to work in a car, while I, your director, have to walk. This shows a lack of respect for your superiors."

"But I won the car," said Kolya timidly. "It's mine, legally . . ."

"That doesn't interest me. I know that you are undermining my authority in the eyes of the whole organization. You can walk just as well as I can; you have only a half hour's walk. If someone is to ride I should be the one. After all, I am the director. In any case, you can sell the car to the Trust, and it will pay you 3,000 rubles."

"Three thousand? But I could have received 10,000 instead of the car!" said Kolya indignantly.

"That doesn't interest me," said the director very coldly. "I have already checked with Moscow and found that only 3,000 rubles can be spent to buy a car for me. So think about it . . ."

Kolya was forced to go to work on foot. Frankly, we were just as glad. We did not have to find as much gasoline, and walking was something we were used to. Also, the roads were in such bad condition that after a short ride we felt as if we had crossed the ocean in rough weather. Only Sonya and Kolya himself didn't get car sick.

But even their rides soon ceased. Once, as we came back from work with Kolya, we noticed that the car, which was standing in front of his house, had become strangely low on one side. We ran up to it quickly and saw that it had only three wheels. No one knew who had taken the other wheel.

There were three other cars of that model in the city, and the driver of each was capable of stealing. But the other three cars belonged to such high personages that Kolya could not dare even to think of instituting a search. He was very upset, poor Kolya, and even Sonya could not comfort him.

The next day the starter and spark plugs disappeared, and Kolya had to spend all day Sunday taking all the detachable parts from the car and putting them in the house. We all helped him and the atmosphere was solemn, almost like a funeral. Only Sonya cheered us. "Don't be sad. We lived well before we had the car. We'll live even better after it's gone."

"It's all right for you," said Kolya. "But the car cost 10,000 rubles, and now . . ."

"But you didn't pay that for it," said Sonya wisely.

"Not much less," grunted Kolya, rolling a wheel under the bed. "You know very well that I bought those damned lottery tickets for ten years."

In spite of our combined efforts, we did not finish disassembling the car on Sunday and Kolya had to spend every night in it all week until the next Sunday. But still some little boys broke two windows, so that Kolya caught cold from the draft.

At last he drew a calmer breath. The automobile's parts, it is true, were piled up in his room and very much in the way, but there was nothing more to steal outside. In place of the windows, Kolya put pieces of plywood, so that the boys could not climb into the car.

Sonya settled the matter. They were supposed to be married just before the New Year, but Sonya absolutely refused to move into a room where one was constantly tripping over automobile remains. So Kolya was faced with a choice: either the automobile parts, or Sonya!

Strangely enough, Kolya reacted quite calmly to this protest of Sonya's. Much later he admitted that he had thought that Sonya would stop loving him if he no longer had a car. He made his decision. He went to the director and said: "Do you remember last summer you offered me 3,000 rubles for my car? I am ready to sell it, but without one wheel and the starter, which have been stolen."

"Do you suspect anyone?" asked the director sternly.

"Oh, no, absolutely no one," Kolya said quickly.

"Well, all right, in its present condition, I'll buy the car for 2,500 rubles."

"It's a deal," said Kolya happily, "but I'll need three days to put it together."

"All right," said the director with generosity, "you have three days' leave, without pay . . ."

Kolya spent three days putting the car together. Then the director's new chauffeur arrived, bringing a wheel and a starter. The transfer took place and Kolya received the money. Kolya and Sonya decided to get married the next Sunday.

At closing time on Saturday, the director's secretary came

to Kolya and said, in strictest confidence: "You should hear what's happened! An inspector arrived from Moscow to look over our office. He saw the car, which he liked very much, and then he found out from someone that it had a stolen wheel. He was furious and threatened to bring the director to trial. The director got frightened, and, as a result, the inspector took the car back to Moscow with him."

Thus our city now had one less car, but we did not grieve over this. Kolya and Sonya were about to be married.

As they sat at the table after their wedding, happy and satisfied, Sonya said:

"You can't imagine how happy I am with the successful ending of the automobile adventure. Kolya should have known that the desire for private ownership is a hangover from the bourgeois past and the result of the corrupting influence of the western imperialists . . ."

"That's not correct!" exclaimed Kolya.

"What do you mean 'not correct'?" We were horrified.

"It's very simple. I am still a property owner. But instead of a miserable little car, the best wife in the city belongs to me!"

He was right, too.

29

DICK PEARCE

A Touch of Sun Tan

NEWSPAPERMEN quite often combine their factual reporting in office hours with off-hours fiction, but not many manage it as successfully as Dick Pearce. A San Francisco reporter, he takes time to do serials and—now and then—a short story. This one is as light as air. It might have happened on the Pacific, or the Atlantic, or the lake you know.

NANCY'S DIFFICULTY WAS one that many a rich girl before her has known. Whereas Nancy summered at the resort of her family's choice from June to September, the young men came for only two-week periods. A change of males every two weeks has certain advantages, true, but variety can jade too.

That was the state of affairs at Marlowe-by-the-Sea on this Monday when the pallid stranger showed up at the beach. He caught Nancy's eye firstly because she scanned the beach every Monday to check on the new crop, secondly because he stayed out of the sun, and lastly because he stayed away from her.

Nancy's suitors at the moment were three, all in their second week and slightly desperate, made that way either by her slim loveliness or her fat income, or both. Two she called Mike and Ike. Not because those were their names but because they looked like each other and like a million other young men—tall, muscular, toasty brown and unoriginal. The third was Jed, an old man of thirty-five who dried and curled as he tanned. He was an interior decorator, and had a lead of sorts over the other two because he could explain Existentialism.

When opportunity presented itself Nancy slipped away from all three and made her way past the beach umbrella of the pale stranger. Her left ankle, as strong as it was trim, nevertheless oddly turned under her, with the result that she kicked sand on his book.

"Oh," she said. "I'm awf'ly sorry."

He looked up, smiled, blew the sand off his book and said, "Forget it." His gaze returned to his book, but after a moment it transferred thoughtfully to the offending ankle. Nancy limped away, cataloguing him to herself as twenty-six, underweight and the mental type. She liked his alert eyes.

During the rest of the day he did not once offer up his whiteness to the sun's rays. And he was under his umbrella again the next, or Tuesday morning. Nancy was mystified. That a man would dare hold on to his natural color amidst hundreds of be-browned, be-blackened and be-oiled people —was it moral courage or just an allergy to sunlight?

She waited until Mike and Ike raced into the ocean and Jed rolled on his stomach. Then she floated her golden tan past the stranger, stopping when she saw his eyes moving from his book to the ankle again.

"It's better," she said.

"It's perfect," he said.

"Aren't you ever going to lie in the sun?"

He asked gravely, "Why should I?"

"Why? Because—well, everybody does. It's good for you."

"Who says so?"

This was disconcerting. She said defiantly, "The doctors. You need sunshine vitamins and things."

"Dr. Joshua Chandler doesn't say so. It's his opinion that the damage to the epithelial layer of the skin is greater than the benefit the body derives from ultra-violet radiation."

Nancy gasped. "Who's Dr. Joshua Chandler?"

"The famous pediatrician. That's a baby doctor. He's also an authority on ankles that turn but don't swell."

"I know what pediatrician means," she said sharply. She caught a glimpse of the cover of his book. It was *Chemotherapy and* . . . She couldn't make out the last word, but a suspicion began forming. "What's your name?"

"Josh Chandler. What's yours?" He was squinting at her ankle again.

"Nancy Woods. And you can keep on looking like an albino fish out of Mammoth Cave for all of me, Doctor Chandler!"

"Thank you, Nancy. Your three hounds are becoming unhappy without their leash." It was true. Mike and Ike and Jed were all watching anxiously, and at no great distance. Nancy flounced toward them, briefly grateful for their devotion. . . .

When she hit the beach Wednesday he was drowsing beneath his umbrella. Mike diverted her attention. This was the day Mike had chosen to make his big pitch, to show his undoubted superiority over his two rivals. He fetched spear and flippers and underwater goggles, and dived like a dolphin, while Ike and Jed watched disdainfully.

Presently Mike surfaced with a small fish impaled on the tines of his spear, came ashore and laid it at Nancy's feet.

"Kelp bass," he said proudly.

"Wonderful, Mike," said Nancy. "And so big!"

Mike plunged joyously into the deeps again, giving his foot fins a gallant flip that promised her a barracuda at the least. He did not surface for a very long time. When he did he was limp, floating face down and fighting the water feebly.

Ike and Jed and Nancy ran in and dragged him ashore, to find Josh Chandler hurrying toward them. They were relieved to hand the unconscious Mike into his crisp care. In a few minutes he had the water out of Mike's lungs and some of the ruddiness back in Mike's cheeks.

"He'll be all right," said young Doctor Chandler. "Just forgot that fins on his feet doesn't mean he has gills behind his ears, too." He looked accusingly at Nancy. "But I guess I'd better see him home."

"Careful you don't get sunstroke," snapped Nancy.

Thursday morning he was really deep asleep in his shade, and he was snoring gently. Nancy thought that a little of the weariness was gone from his face. She also thought, spitefully, that he was skinnier than Jed without any of Jed's charm to compensate for it.

Mike failed to show up. But a nervous Jed sat beside her while Ike made his big play. Ike was a master of the surf board. He skimmed in on the combers with acrobatic daring, risking his neck with that studied nonchalance found in the male only when the female is also present.

It was a wonderful show until Ike challenged a big breaker that saw him coming and laid for him. It tossed him up gaily, sucked his surf board out from under him, caught him beneath tons of water when he came down, spun him heels over appetite and flung him headlong into the sand. He lay there until Nancy and Jed dragged him up on the beach. Nancy was not at all surprised to find Doctor Josh Chandler waiting.

After a brief examination he said, "Mild concussion. And no skin left on his nose. I'll take him to a drugstore and fix him up." He got Ike to his feet, then frowned at Nancy. "It would be statistically interesting to know your total summer casualty rate."

"That's gratitude. After all I'm doing for your profession."

Friday was clear and hot. And Jed, alone with her for the first time, was hotly eager. He broiled and perspired and spoke eloquently of love and Jean-Paul Sartre.

Nancy gave him rapt attention with her face, but her mind was busy with the fact that young Doctor Chandler had apparently had his sleep out. He was sitting up beneath his umbrella, shooting frequent glances toward them and smoking too many cigarettes. Presently he arose and sauntered over.

"Heat prostration can be a dangerous thing," he said down to Jed. "You've dehydrated to the danger point. Go home and take a salt pill. And stay indoors the rest of the week."

Jed came belligerently to his feet. But to his own surprise he swayed a little. Doctor Chandler steadied him. "Take two salt pills," he said.

Jed went. Nancy quoted bitterly, ". . . and then there was none."

Josh said, "Now I can get some rest."

"And what have you been doing all week?"

"Resting." He unbent a little. He even sat down beside her. In the full sun. "I don't mind tanning. But lying in the sun heats your body, and heat burns energy. I didn't have any left to burn. That's why I stayed in the shade."

"Go on back to your shade."

He paid no attention. "I really am a pediatrician," he said. "Or will be in a year. Interning now. On call day and night. Dammit, Nancy, a man has to rest some time."

"Then go rest. I won't disturb you again." She looked about her and added sadly, "I've run out of men to disturb you with."

"It's too late. Now my peace of mind is gone."

Nancy said, "You mean I . . ."

"Yes, you. My mind is harassed and confused and"—he looked into Nancy's eyes and couldn't look away—"and bewitched."

"Mine too. It's terrible." She put her hand where he had no trouble finding it. He found her other hand too. Nancy sighed. She said, "Thank goodness we have another whole week for it to get really, fatally bad."

"No, we don't. I've got to be back at the hospital Sunday night."

"Oh, Josh," she cried. But she had expended three men to get the one she wanted. There was no stopping her now. She jumped to her feet. "Come on. Let's run for the shade!"

30

RICHARD STERN

Present for Minna

MR. STERN is a Californian with the wanderlust. He has lived in the Caribbean, France, Spain, and was heard from last winter snowed in somewhere around Brenner Pass. This, confided Mr. Stern, was bad for skiing, but as good a means as any of keeping him at his typewriter. Unlike this one, most of his stories are about sophisticated people and settings.

ANDY SAT ON the edge of his bunk, his big feet set wide and his thick hands clasped and his face furrowed with thought, with worry. And four or five of the crew sat around watching him, waiting for Carl to start it up again on this, the last night out. Carl was leaning against the bulkhead smiling a little in his sharp way. "You got it figured out yet?" he said. "Got the arithmetic all straight?"

Andy opened his hands. He studied their palms. He closed them again. He said nothing. He smiled in a helpless sort of way.

"A case of brandy you got," Carl said. "Good French brandy. Cost you twenty bucks in Marseilles. A bargain, you said. You an' the missus like brandy, a little nip after dinner." He waited until the laughter died. "You got any idea what the duty'll be?"

"Well," Andy said. He shook his head slowly. "Not much, maybe." He sat there like a great bear at the baiting, taking his punishment, wishing it would stop, knowing no way in which to avoid it. "Maybe not much," he said again.

"The stuff sells for six, seven bucks a bottle," Carl said.

"You paid less than two. The difference is duty. Say five bucks on twelve bottles, sixty bucks. You got sixty bucks for that?"

Andy was thinking of the little apartment out in Brooklyn, of Minna, of money in the savings account, of a television set some day, a real good one, with a large clear picture so that Minna, on the long lonely nights when he was at sea, could watch and listen, maybe laugh and forget for a time that she was alone.

And maybe a small sip of the brandy at bedtime, just a sip, to lie pleasantly on the stomach in the empty darkness. They understood one another, he and Minna, and waiting, he knew, is the hard part of life, and small things help, small things like brandy, and television, and the other things he had managed to bring to her. But he had had no idea that on twenty dollars' worth of brandy—

Carl said, "You got sixty bucks so's the missus can have her snort after dinner?"

"No," Andy said, and he listened to the laughter again.

"I tell you," Carl said. "I'll give you an idea." The laughter died down. Andy lifted his head and watched and waited. "I've been thinkin'," Carl said, "an' I got the answer." He paused. He smiled. "Smuggle it through Customs, that's all you have to do. Just smuggle the case right through. Then you won't have to pay nothin'!"

He had thought of it, of course. He smiled at Carl and shook his great head slowly. "That wouldn't be honest," he said. "If they got a law—" the laughter smothered the rest of it, and he sat there patiently waiting for it to die. His thick hands were clasped again. There was no use trying to explain.

"Wouldn't be honest!" Carl was saying. "That's the only reason! You hear him? Wouldn't be honest! I'll tell you what I'll do. I'll lay you ten to one you couldn't get that case through Customs if you tried. How's that? Ten to one. You think it over."

Andy sat alone on the edge of his bunk, and stared down

at his hands, at his feet, at the deck itself. And two of the many ship's cats came in and saw him and eyed one another warily and climbed up onto his great knees and sat there singing at him. He rubbed them idly and spoke to them in a low voice, taking pleasure from their companionship, while his mind walked slowly around and around his problem, thinking of Minna, of brandy, of Customs, of Carl and of Carl's bet.

And the cats, his friends, sang on, as if they were talking to him, telling him something, telling him— His big hands stopped in their stroking. He stared at the cats. They sang on, and Andy was smiling, and his mind was at last at rest . . .

They docked in the morning. They finished their jobs. In the fo'c's'le, Carl cornered him again, and the rest of the crew gathered around, grinning. "Gonna take my bet?" Carl said. "Ten to one? And some of the other guys want in, too. How 'bout it?"

"Well," Andy said. His hands were deep in his pockets. He looked at Carl and he looked at the others, and he looked at the case of brandy on his bunk. Slowly he nodded. He pulled out a small leather purse. "I got fifty dollars," he said.

The bosun held the stakes. Ashore, in the bar across the street from the Customs shed. And they all crowded against the window to watch Andy, with sea bag and suitcase, in shore clothes, come ponderously down for his inspection. And they waited, hearing nothing of the talk.

The Customs man went through the sea bag. He patted Andy. He reached for the suitcase. Andy said, "I can't open that."

"So?" The Customs man was smiling.

"Well," Andy said, "it's full of cats." His big face was crinkled with the effort of explanation. "I mean, we got too many on board, an' the skipper says get rid of some of them."

"Good story," the Customs man said. "One of the best I've heard."

"It's true," Andy said. "The crew, they wanted to toss them over the side. But I like cats, an' I thought if I could take them ashore maybe I could find homes for them." He was sweating; his big face shone.

"I like cats," he said again. "Don't open it, please." His voice shook.

"Look, Mac," the Customs man said. He was undoing the straps. "It won't work, see? It's a good try, but it won't work." He undid the latch and opened the case.

There were six cats, although it seemed like quite a few more. They came out in a rush, clawing and snarling and spitting with rage. They circled the Customs shed, gathering speed, and then they streaked back out the wharf and up the gangplank and disappeared onto the ship.

Andy closed the empty suitcase. He strapped it carefully. He gave the Customs man one long, mournful look. Then he plodded back aboard ship.

In the bar, the bosun was laughing so hard he cried into his drink. And the crew was laughing, too. All but Carl. Carl said, "He can't get away with it! Not that big dumb—"

"You made a bet," the bosun said. "An' that's how it goes."

It was forty minutes before Andy was back to the Customs shed again. He had the suitcase in his hand, and he leaned a little against its weight. He set it down at the Customs man's feet. He wiped his broad face. "You want to open it this time?" he said. "They was awful hard to catch again."

The Customs man stared at the suitcase. He stared at Andy. He opened his mouth and then he closed it again, and Andy waited, quivering inside. "Go on," the Customs man said. "Get the hell outa here."

So there it was. Andy's face showed nothing. "Yes, sir," he said, and he picked up the suitcase and his sea bag and walked slowly across the street and into the bar. He was thinking of Minna, and of a television set, and maybe, although he didn't know what such things cost, of one of those mechanical washing machines that took clothes and a little soap and did everything, all by itself. Minna, he thought, would like that; she could sip her brandy, and laugh at the television screen and listen to the machine doing her work for her. The concept pleasured him.

He let the prospect of these simple delights curl inside him and warm the smile with which he greeted his crew-mates. They crowded around him, pummeling his shoulders. All, that is, except Carl, who sourly watched the bosun take out a sheaf of bills.

Andy stood among them, massive and solid, smiling his helpless sort of smile, while the bosun counted the money into his hand. From time to time the bosun stopped his counting to wipe his eyes. "Them cats," he said. "Squallin' an' snortin' through that shed!"

"Well," Andy said. "I fed them real good when I went back on board. I don't hardly think they mind any more." Minna would like that part of it; Minna liked cats, just as he did. He folded the money and put it carefully into his purse. He smiled at everybody, including Carl. He picked up his sea bag. "Well," he said.

"How about a drink?" the bosun said.

Andy shook his head. "I got to go."

"The old lady?" the bosun said. "She'd never know."

Andy shook his head again. "It wouldn't be honest."

Carl snorted. "Honest!" he slapped the suitcase with his open hand. It gurgled gently. "Honest, he says!"

Andy nodded. "An' I got to tell the man, too."

"What man?" the bosun said. "Tell him what?"

"Why," Andy said, "the Customs man. I got to tell him I got this brandy here. For my wife." And he pulled out the small purse. "An' I got money to pay duty on it." He paused there. "The way the law says."

31

HUGH B. CAVE

Peril of the River

ADVENTURE STORIES are very much in Mr. Cave's blood, and a tour of duty as a war correspondent in the Pacific has provided him with a good variety of background. His stories and serials appear frequently in the big magazines, while he goes foraging for more settings to write from. Most recently he has been exploring Haiti.

BY THE WEEK's end Carling knew his recruiting trip was a failure. The bush natives simply would not listen to him. They preferred to starve in their miserable little river villages rather than work in his tobacco fields, where he could feed and house them decently while teaching them to better themselves.

They had dealt with white men before; that was the trouble. The occasional white man who poked about here in New Guinea's "back of beyond" was usually a fortune-hunter, utterly unscrupulous.

And now it was raining again, mercilessly. He must start back down river to the plantation at once, even with darkness coming on. Already the river was rampant.

He gathered up his things, said good-by to the village headman and made his way past the wretched nipa shacks to the stream's edge, where his boys were waiting. They studied his face anxiously, dreading his decision. The stream was a swift brown flood, tearing at its muddy shores. Out in the midst of it a huge sago palm rushed past, roots upthrust like the hands of a drowning swimmer.

"We'll try it," Carling said. He had to get back! To the

natives, the river was a god of some sort, a thing to be feared. When the angry flood swept into the plantation compound, his people would desert. His wife, left alone, would be terrified.

He stepped into the boat. "We'll go as far as we can, then take to the trail."

His wife. Queer how his despairing thoughts fastened on her as the clumsy dugout bore him downstream through the dangerous dark. He knew what the river would do; its moods were dependable. But he did not know how his wife would react to nature's unpredictability.

Six months ago he had married her in Melbourne, on one of his rare trips outside. Elena, perhaps, had thought it glamorous to be the wife of a man whose life was devoted to helping New Guinea's half-starved, superstitious bush people. She was young, lovely—and she had come to New Guinea like a princess on a holiday, with trunks packed full of ridiculous, exquisite clothes. He had thought it amusing.

"Mahster . . . !"

The fuzzy-haired boy in the bow turned a face contorted with fear, eyes gleaming like cowry shells in the dark. "River him one bad fella!"

"Not yet," said Carling curtly. Then he thought:

Silk dresses. She hadn't worn them, of course, after the first few evenings. He remembered the look on her face as she heeded his gentle advice and returned them to the trunks. She hadn't complained—but her sigh had been a dream expiring as she turned to him with what she thought was a smile, and kissed him to show that she didn't care.

How often since then had she secretly opened those trunks and lifted out their precious contents, just to touch them, hold them, and lay them away again? Twice he had caught her at it, retreating barely in time to conceal the fact that he knew her secret.

She hated the plantation, he supposed. Hated the poor native-built house they lived in, the heat, the insects, the un-

ending loneliness. Even her beloved dresses were slowly disintegrating.

And she feared the river. Above all else, she feared this
treacherous brown jungle stream which tonight was wilder
than he had known it in the whole six years of his fighting it.

"Mahster . . . !"

He stared ahead, aware that the sullen roar was like continuous thunder. To go farther would be suicide. "All right.
Make for shore!" The rest of the way he would have to walk
—a nightmare journey along a trail that by now would be
a morass.

His boys could not, or would not, keep up with him as he
trudged on through the dripping night. Never mind; he
knew the way as well as they did, and the hazards too. But the
river puzzled him. No amount of rain could altogether explain the sprawling surge of water at the hungry edge of
which he traveled. Why was it so high?

He had reached the outskirts of the plantation—was
hurrying past the tobacco fields—when the first light of
dawn showed him the answer and shook him with its implica-
tions. He remembered the huge sago palm rushing past the
upstream village. Here, where the stream was normally narrow and the high banks a tangle of naked roots, more than a
dozen uprooted jungle giants had jammed together. Tons of
debris were piled against the barrier.

The thing was a monstrous dam, partially checking the
stream's flow, forcing the turbulent waters back upon themselves. Even now he walked in soft ooze, as the impounded
river reached out furiously to inundate the fields.

With strange cold calm he surveyed the situation. Unless
the dam broke soon, he would lose the fields—six years of
patient labor. In any case the compound, a quarter mile
downstream, was certain to be swept away when the river
burst its chains. Not that he cared about the house—it was a
miserable thing, needed replacing. Whole compound needed
rebuilding. But Elena would be there, probably left to her

fate by terrified natives—frantic, not knowing what to do.
He ran.

The first thing he saw when he raced up the rickety veranda steps and flung himself through the doorway was the
open closet where she kept her trunks. The closet was empty.
He needed to be told no more. She was gone.

Gone with all her finery. What a child she was! He ran
through the compound, shouting her name. Useless. No one
was here. Native cook, houseboy, plantation workers, all
were gone. The place was abandoned. Some of them she must
have taken with her—impossible to carry her ridiculous possessions otherwise. The rest had deserted.

He hurried down the path to the river, saw the native
boats tugging at the almost drowned landing. The biggest
one, the one she would have taken, was not among them. She
was on the stream then, fighting her way down to the village
at its mouth, probably unaware of the huge reservoir of destruction straining to burst its bonds behind her.

For a moment Carling was tempted to leap into one of the
smaller boats and risk the same destruction in an effort to
overtake her. Sanity stopped him. He looked at the path and
bit his lip. Eight miles. Eight ugly miles through the jungle,
over a trail that twice crossed the stream on flimsy native
bridges. He was already dog-tired, feverish, drenched to the
skin.

The jungle shut like a door behind him. The air thick-
ened. Mosquitoes caught up, massed about him. Doggedly
he trotted along, seeking to conserve his strength.

He needed that strength at the first crossing. The black
earth at the river bank, unstable as jelly, trembled with the
stream's fury. The same giant hand shook the trees from
which the precarious bridge dangled. He crossed like a spider
on sagging strands, not daring to look down. And then on
again—on and on—through muck and morass, over uprooted trees which only yesterday must have been standing
brave at the river's edge. Mile after mile . . .

What would he find when he got there? His wife sitting
among her trunks at the home of the District Officer, probably—if the river were merciful. Sitting there waiting, waiting for the once-a-month mail boat to take her back to civili-
zation, out of his life. He had been insane to hope for anything else! It wasn't a question of love. She loved him. She
would have endured reasonable discomforts for him. But a
plantation in the bush, miles from the nearest white neigh-
bor—he must have been mad to dream of such a partnership.

He crossed the second bridge, more than halfway there.
Time had no meaning now; he measured it by the torment
of fever rising within him, by the numbness of his muscles.

The rain fell steadily, swelling the stream, piling up the
pressure behind the great natural barrier at the plantation.
He would hear the flood when it came—hear trees crashing,
and a noise like a rushing train. The ground would shake
and he would turn from the trail and plunge into the jungle,
blindly. . . . But now there was another sound. A sound of
singing.

He dragged to a halt, unable to credit his senses. But the
sound was real. It came from the opposite bank, where the
ground was higher, where he had not known a trail existed.
So many things a white man never learned about this land of
mystery. Rigid, he stared.

Natives—trudging single file, on their way upstream. Bush
people, probably; in the rain he could not be sure. Their
dress was peculiar . . .

Then he saw, and his heart turned to stone. A sob louder
than the river's roar swelled against his throat and shook
him. He was staring at his wife's treasured dresses, draped on
the black bodies of natives. The silk and lace she had so long
hoarded, had loved to lift from her trunks and look at—
they were sodden rags now, covering the nakedness of
savages. Savages who must have fished her trunks from the
river. . . .

He was too late.

He sat on the wet ground and watched them with anguished eyes until they had disappeared. When at last he pushed himself erect, he plodded on mechanically, no longer trying to hurry. Step by slow step, heartbroken. It took him an hour to complete the last miles of his journey. He would not have cared if the flood had swept down on him.

It was his fault for bringing her here. . . .

He made his way through the village, climbed the hill to the high ground where stood the residence of the District Officer. He hardly knew what he said when the D.O. took him by the hand and led him, as one leads a sleepwalker, to a chair on the veranda overlooking the sea.

"I want—want some of your natives to go upstream—clear the obstruction in the river. Plantation lost, otherwise. Fields washed away. Got to save the fields. Spent years clearing them . . ."

The D.O. looked at him curiously. "Carling . . ."

"Don't tell me they won't go. They've got to! Got to!" Carling roared.

"As a matter of fact"—the D.O. was obviously amused—"every able-bodied man and woman in the village has already gone up river to your place. Your wife, Carling. She persuaded 'em."

Carling sat up, wild-eyed. "Don't joke!"

"No joke about it. She's here, friend—asleep just now, tuckered out. But she did it. Did what you and I have never been able to do." The D.O. was chuckling now—he couldn't have known the agony of Carling's thoughts.

"And you know how she did it, Carling? With a boatload of pretty clothes! Silks and laces, Carling! She stood here on this very veranda, as determined as you please, and traded her past to insure your future." He tugged a heavy gold watch from his pocket and broke into a grin. "They'll be up there by now. Your fields are safe. Come see your wife, man."

But Carling, flushed with more than fever, was already at the doorway.

32

LEE ROGOW

That Certain Flavor

HELL HATH NO FURY like the perfect cook scorned
is the theme of this story by Lee Rogow. For writers it has
a particular interest, since it is an almost perfect example of
short-short story construction. For this reason it has been
chosen for the thorough analysis of structure which you will
find beginning on page 298.

POLLY KINGSLEY HAD a kitchen range with an array of dials
and controls like the instrument panel of a Lockheed Constellation. Polly Kingsley had a card index of tested recipes
as big as a radio writer's gag file. Polly Kingsley had the
assistant manager of Holschweig's butcher shop in thrall; no
woman in Manhattan's middle Seventies ever got such cuts
of meat, or had them weighed with the butcher's hands so
scrupulously behind his back.

Polly Kingsley had all these things, and she also had a
husband who had liked his mother's cooking.

Each evening Larry Kingsley would come home from the
industrial designing office where he worked and kiss Polly
very thoroughly and satisfactorily. Then he would go into
the bathroom and wash his good-looking mug, making
sounds in there as if he were wrestling an octopus. He would
emerge from the bathroom with his face shining, seat himself at the dinner table, and look hopefully at the door of the
kitchen.

In a few moments Polly would appear with his dinner,
over which she had spent from one to three hours of her
afternoon. Sometimes she would present Larry with lamb

176

chops, broiled to the split-second of perfection on the Stove of Tomorrow. Sometimes the feature would be stuffed peppers, oozing succulent rice and savory meat. Sometimes she devised salads, with mounds of tuna fish which somehow managed to be creamy and flaky at the same time.

One typical evening, in the eighth month of their marriage, Polly served her lord and master a stew, with big chunks of beef swimming in rich gravy, and golden carrot rings peeping hopefully from behind enormous mushrooms. She placed it on the table before her man and watched him, her hazel eyes serious and intent, her fresh skin flushed with cooking and concentration.

Larry spooned a generous portion onto his plate, speared a piece of beef, and lifted it to his mouth.

"How is it?" asked Polly.

"Pretty good," said Larry.

"Only pretty good?"

"I mean it's wonderful."

"How wonderful?"

"If you served it to a maharajah, he'd probably send you around a trunkful of rubies in the morning."

"Is that all?"

"Oh, darling, do we have to go through that again?"

"Yes," said Polly. "We have to go through that again."

"Look," said Larry, "you wouldn't respect me if I told lies, would you? I mean, it wouldn't be much of a marriage if a woman couldn't depend on her husband to be truthful in little things, would it? I mean, you want to respect me, don't you?"

"We can skip the acrobatics," said Polly. "You don't think the stew is as good as your mother's, do you?"

"Let me put it this way, dear heart," said Larry. "It's good, extremely good. But Mother's things had a certain definite flavor that this lacks."

"I don't understand it," wailed Polly. "I buy the finest ingredients. I toil in the kitchen for hours. I have the latest equipment. What *could* that woman have done to food that I don't?"

"Search me," said Larry. "All I know is I haven't tasted food like hers since she died. Why don't we just skip it, dear? I like your cooking well enough. Cooks like Mother are a once-in-a-generation phenomenon, like Albert Einstein or Joe Louis."

"I won't forget it," said Polly. "I won't, I won't, I won't! I want to be the best thing for you that ever was. I can't stand it that anybody, even your sainted mother, should have done something better for you than I can."

"I'd be glad to say you've succeeded," said Larry, "but you want to be able to respect me, don't you?"

"Oh, eat your stew before it gets cold," said Polly.

And so it went for months. Polly spent more and more hours in the kitchen, basting, tasting, planning, experimenting with herbs and seasoning. Sometimes, as for example when a thunderstorm collapsed a soufflé, she cried tears of frustration, which would drop off her nose and sizzle into salty steam on the Stove of Tomorrow.

The food she produced would have tempted a strong-willed yogi to break a fast. Larry ate heartily enough, but he always insisted her productions lacked that certain definite flavor.

Polly grew morose. Once she even snapped at the assistant manager of Holschweig's meat market, who promptly overcharged her five cents a pound on a rib roast. Polly noticed, of course, but she was past caring and she left the shop without so much as a word.

When a woman's morale is at that low an ebb, what she needs more than anything else in the world is somebody to tell about it.

So when Polly met Min Frobisher coming out of the supermarket one afternoon, and Min said where had she been keeping herself, and Polly said she'd been working hard in the kitchen, and Min said she never thought Larry Kingsley

was the sort of man who would make a household drudge
of a woman, but you couldn't ever tell by appearances, could
you, and Polly said it really wasn't Larry's fault, and Min
said nonsense, Polly was just protecting him, and she wasn't
due at the hairdresser's for forty-five minutes yet and why
didn't they drop into the Town Lounge and have a cocktail
and talk about it, and Polly said she wouldn't dare, she
looked a perfect fright, and Min said not to be silly, she just
wished a simple little daytime dress looked as well on her as
it did on Polly, Polly said well, she really shouldn't, but seeing as how she saw Min so seldom, well, all right.

Polly Kingsley got home at twenty minutes after six with
her hat on the side of her head, a box of spaghetti and a ten-
cent can of tomato sauce under her arm, and a dangerous
look in her eye. When she went into the bathroom to wash
her face she noticed Larry's robe draped negligently over the
clothes hamper.

Wasn't that just like him, Polly thought. Min Frobisher
was absolutely right. A woman was a fool to make a slave out
of herself for a man who not only didn't appreciate it, but
who figured out ways to make extra work for her.

Polly was ferociously breaking the spaghetti into a pot of
boiling water when Larry came in. "Hello, dear," said Larry.
"I've been trying to get you on the phone all afternoon."

"I was out."

"Out where?"

"Just out. Would you like a minute-by-minute account of
where I was?"

"Certainly not," said Larry, startled. He kissed her. Then
he drew back and looked at her strangely.

"Cooking sherry," said Polly defiantly. "You have to taste
it every so often to make sure it isn't going sour."

Polly slapped two settings down on the dinner table and
went back into the kitchen. The flame under her saucepan
had been up too high: the tomato sauce for the spaghetti had
been scorched. Polly took a spoon and grimly scraped the

burned mixture out of the pan and dumped it on the pale, stringy spaghetti.

She kicked open the kitchen door and placed the platter on the table before her husband.

Then she stood and watched him, her arms crossed.

One word, she said to herself. Just let him speak one word. She'd put on her hat and go right over to Min Frobisher's. Min had a lawyer who had handled both her divorces and was simply wonderful on those things.

Larry twisted some of the spaghetti up on the fork and carried it to his mouth. Just one word, said Polly to herself. One syllable, even.

Larry chewed silently for a moment. Then a strange expression began to appear on his face.

"Polly!" he said. "Polly Kingsley!"

"Anything wrong?" she snarled.

"Wrong?" shouted Larry. "I don't know what you've done, genius girl, but this is *it*!"

"Hah?" said Polly.

"This spaghetti is just like Mother's!" said Larry. "That flavor, that certain definite flavor, it's all there!"

Polly blinked. Then she got her hat off the hall table, and went and put it in the closet. Then she went over and sat on her husband's lap and put her arms around his neck.

She could fix herself a snack in the late afternoons, she decided, and burn Larry's food afterwards.

It would be a dirty trick to play on the Stove of Tomorrow, but it was little enough to do for the man she loved.

33

BETTY KJELGAARD

The Age of Love

SHEER ROMANCE is something that is not easy to handle. There is always the danger that it will become sloppy, sentimental. But that is because the real thing is always so close to just those distortions when it is observed by others. The editors thought Betty Kjelgaard, who writes such things beautifully, had skirted the dangers here.

GORDON TURNED INTO the bar ten minutes before the appointed time. Her note had said four-thirty, but she might be early and he didn't want her sitting alone in any bar. Not at nineteen. Not at any age.

The headwaiter greeted him with a smile. "Good afternoon, Mr. Tyler."

Gordon nodded pleasantly. "I'll go back to a table," he said. "A lady is coming."

She was there almost before he had settled himself. He saw the uncertainty as she stepped inside, and then she spied Gordon and was coming toward him on her quicksilver feet. In the haze of the room she was splendid and fresh. The men lounging at the bar turned, their eyes in casual male measuring as she swept by them, and Gordon wanted to shout with ugly harshness, Don't look at her—

He rose. "So," he said. "Skipping school, Mary."

She slipped into the chair across from him. "School," she said with enormous disdain, and took off her gloves. Her hands shook slightly.

Gordon saw that and thought: There's a purpose here important to her. Then he felt the waiter at his elbow. He glanced up. "Two glasses of milk, please," he said gravely.

181

The waiter's eyes looked their approval, and for just an instant the two men had each other's blessed thoughts about the girl sitting there, obviously out of her element, obviously reaching hard for a woman's sureness. The waiter's mouth quirked as he moved away.

Gordon spoke with gaiety. "Now let me guess why you have asked me to meet you here. One—you've overdrawn your allowance and you want me to fix it before Papa finds out. Two—the newest male devastation in your life has asked you to a fraternity brawl and—"

"Stop it, Gordon," Mary said.

Gordon. Not Uncle Gordon. He lit a cigarette carefully. "What, then, Mary?" he said.

She looked at him with her gray-pearl eyes. "I'm in love with you, Gordon," she said.

Shock went chiseling through him, distorting his calm lawyer's mind. What should he do? Laugh? Crack some half-baked joke? Why, he'd known this child all her life, remembered her as a baby because he'd always known her parents. When he grew up, they'd made her call him "Uncle Gordon." *Uncle* Gordon. "You don't know what you're say-ing," he said.

She caught fire all at once, burning, glowing. "Oh, but I do," she cried, low. "It happened at my birthday party two months ago, the night you kissed me when I handed you a piece of cake. I didn't sleep all that night. I couldn't. I just sat in bed and shook and knew I'd never been kissed before to mean anything. And toward morning I got up and looked in the mirror to see if it was me—"

"Mary," Gordon begged. "Look, child—listen—"

"And it was," she said. "It comes like that sometimes, doesn't it? You wonder how you ever existed before, and everything not connected with love seems futile and washed out. I kept it to myself until I couldn't keep it any longer. That's why I wrote you the note last night. And I chose this place because you come here often. It seemed—nicer that way." Her fair head lifted back, her eyes loved the intimate obliqueness of the room as if a part of him was everywhere in it.

"Mary," Gordon said. "I'm all but engaged—remember? To Janice."

"Darling," Mary said. "Darling, darling, darling, darling."

Beautiful awareness, that tender henchman of love, sprang from her voice, shone from her face. Gordon felt beaten by it; hopelessly he poked among the ruins of his own thoughts, trying to salvage some profundity.

"I'm old enough to be your father," he said.

Her laughter came, running through the stale room like a taste of rain to parched meadow. "Ten years' difference. Can you be a father at ten years old? I ask you."

Gordon looked at her . . . "I'm going on thirty—" he said. "You're only nineteen."

She touched his mouth with her forefinger, smiling. "Darling. Gordon darling."

"Janice's old man gave me my start in law seven years ago," Gordon said. "J. B. Fowler himself. You don't forget things like that."

"Were you as handsome then as you are now, my beloved?" Mary said.

"He picked me up, a green kid just out of school and let me work in his office. When he died last year, I felt as though I'd lost all my fingers."

"I love you," Mary said. "Did I tell you?"

The waiter put the glasses of milk on the table. "Drink your milk," Gordon said. "Every child needs milk. Every infant. Bambina. Chitling. Brat."

She leaned forward and her whole clean redolence was as potent as an embrace. "I hope the boy of the family will look like you," she said. "Have your nose, the cleft in your chin."

"What do they do to kids nowadays when they skip school?" Gordon said. "When I was young, we had to chop kindling for a week."

"Imagine two men with cleft chins in one family," Mary said, and the silver bell song of her laughter sparkled again.

Gordon picked up the ash tray and balanced it on top of his milk glass and squinted at it. "In ten more years my bones will be like old peanut brittle. They'll snap every time I move."

"I'll take such good care of you then," Mary said. "And love you twice as terribly because of your old bones."

The ash tray fell off the milk glass with a bright noise. "I have the beginnings of asthma," Gordon said. "I sniff all the time. How do you think you'd feel, going out in your crowd escorted by an antiquated guy who sniffed like a horse?"

She was very lovely sitting there, bringing her gift of love to him. "I'd lift my head," she said, "and look around and say, 'I'll bet none of you can do that!'"

He thought: Get this kid off your neck. This baby with the angel's mind and the heart framed in her eyes. He said, "I'm having dinner with Janice tonight. I had dinner with her last night. Does that mean anything to you?"

"It means you got stuck with her two nights in a row, poor dear."

"And Friday night we're going to the civic concert. She and J.B. never used to miss a one."

"Remember the time you ran and hid in the hills because your mother wanted you to go to the civic concert?"

"No," he said in exasperation, "I don't."

"I do," Mary said. "Can Janice swim? Can she belly bust into the water?"

"Janice," Gordon said, "does not care for swimming. That's nothing against her."

"Remember how you used to let me go swimming with you when I was twelve, because I was the only one of the kids who could keep up with you out to the raft?"

"No," Gordon said.

"Does Janice ride?"

"She's allergic to horses. Her nose gets stuffed up."

"Remember Sweet and Genevieve, your ponies?" Mary's eyes were dreamy. "You always said you'd never be without a horse."

"She's all alone out there in that big house now," Gordon said. "J.B. never wanted her to be alone."

"She ought to get a good big watch dog," Mary said.

"Janice—"

"—does not care for dogs," Mary said.

Gordon's face reddened. "Look. You're still not too old to have your seat warmed, young lady."

"What color are her eyes?" Mary said.

Gordon lit another cigarette, startled. The lighter flame wavered roughly.

"Finish your milk," he said. "I'll buy you a lollipop and one of the better comic books." Well, so what? he thought. The color of a girl's eyes isn't important. I know her hair is dark.

Mary obediently picked up the glass of milk and took a sip and put it down again. Gordon saw the part in her hair, the long tassel of eyelashes on each cheek.

"Gordon," she said then.

"Yes."

"How did you feel when you fell in love?"

He said evenly, "Why I suppose like any man who has reached that particular ultimate. You search a long, long time for love; one day you find it, just like that. A woman's smile, maybe, the way she walks, the touch of her lips. Whatever it is, you know the search is over."

She was studying him. He had the sensation of looking into forest pools of the most exquisite clarity. "The touch of her lips," she said.

"What?"

"Your words," she whispered.

Pins—with dangerous little points were sticking him all over his chest with orderly timing.

"I don't know what you're talking about," he said. "If

you're not going to drink up, let's go. I'll tell your mother what an undisciplined urchin she's raised."

Mary did not move. "Gordon—do you know when you started rushing Janice?"

His voice was stiff. "I've been seeing Janice for almost a year."

She shook her head, and the gesture was somehow sure and powerful. "I don't mean that way. You began giving her the big rush the night after my birthday party."

His heart was doing a fandango. He swallowed. Had he—had he? "Listen, Mary—"

"I didn't mind then," Mary said. "A lot of men are afraid of love in the beginning. But I thought two months was long enough to let it run. That's why I'm here."

He sweated. "Maybe you misunderstood me. I go with Janice. I'm going to be married."

"You can't marry a ghost, my dearest," Mary said sweetly.

".What?"

"J.B."

"What?" he said again, his forehead wrinkled.

"You're a loyal knight on a shining white horse. You loved J.B. Not Janice. But you felt sorry for her, and you've tried to make your sorriness act like love."

Through clenched teeth he said, "And I suppose you're trying to tell me I'm in love with *you*."

Mary gazed at him and the glow went from her eyes and they burned with a bright sadness. "No," she said quietly. "That's not for me to tell you, Gordon. That's for you to tell me—if you ever want to. Just wait until I get my gloves on and I'll go." She made a movement under the table.

He had his moment's astonishment while the incredulous thought went through him: This isn't the child I've always known. And realized, then, that he was looking at a woman who had just spoken truth, a woman whose search had ended identically with his at a birthday party two months ago. He saw the flurry of motion under the table and panic hit him. She was going—

"Mary, wait!"

He felt light and wild and joyous then, partly because his next words were very important, but mostly because he knew now how long he had been waiting to say them.

"I love you, Mary. I love you."

Her face, her eyes, shone. And on her lap the gloves lay, still secure and untouched in their golden bracelet attached to her purse.

34

MARC BRANDEL

The Hasty Act

THIS COULD HAPPEN to almost anyone—a case of
the quick flush of righteous indignation leading a young
man into a horrible predicament. Mr. Brandel is chiefly
known as a novelist and has four books to his credit which
have had high critical acclaim. His latest were "The Bar-
riers" and "The Choice."

I WANT TO MAKE this clear right away: I didn't get mixed
up in this thing on purpose. I'm not one of those slick, hard-
boiled characters mystery authors like to write about. As a
matter of fact I'm timid. I'm not ashamed to admit it.

Until today I had never been mixed up in anything more
far-fetched than the Quartermaster Corps back in Forty-
three.

Until an hour ago I had never worried about anything
more serious than losing my job.

And now I'm sitting here sweating. It's cold in the apartment, too—I think that new superintendent drinks—it's just
nervousness that's making me perspire. I'm bewildered and
scared and confused and I don't know what to do. There
doesn't seem to be anything I can do except wait. Wait for the
phone or the doorbell to ring. Wait for whoever he is.

And yet I can't see how I deserved to get into this mess. I
can't see how it was really my fault. It could have happened
to anyone . . .

It all started this morning, or rather at lunch time, and all
because it was raining. If it hadn't been raining I'd have had
lunch as usual at Chester's Restaurant. The hot roast-beef

sandwich is very good there. But it's five blocks to Chester's from the advertising agency where I work, so I put on my raincoat and dashed across the street to Pierre's instead.

Pierre's is one of those shiny places with tables around the walls and a man who meets you in the lobby. It isn't the kind of place I can afford very often, so I thought I might as well make an occasion of it and have a cocktail before lunch.

I checked my raincoat at the little box in the hall, followed the manager to a table near the kitchen and ordered a martini. I had two of them. That was my real mistake, I suppose. It probably had quite a lot to do with what happened next, because the martinis didn't make me hungry the way they're supposed to. In fact, I had a very light lunch and even after the coffee I still felt sort of free and not reckless exactly but not at all timid either.

That's when I first saw her, as I was finishing my coffee. She must have been eating in the other room or I would have noticed her before. She was very noticeable. She was the kind of girl who might have been an assistant editor on a chic fashion magazine—she had on one of those coy hats and those long white gloves people on fashion magazines wear—except that she was just a little too spectacular. Her hair was too blond, her complexion too perfect, her clothes too expensive.

The funny thing was she was walking straight toward me and she was smiling the way my boss does when he's meeting a new client.

"Why, hullo," she called when she was still a yard or two away. "Where have you been hiding yourself?"

I glanced over my shoulder. There was nothing behind me but the wall. She was talking to me. I stood up.

"Hullo," I said. She was even more breath-taking close to. I fumbled with the chair beside me, and she sat down.

"I can only stay a moment," she said. "But it's so wonderful to see you again." She took my hand and squeezed it in her cool white gloves.

I'd never seen her in my life. I should have told her so at

once, of course. But you know how it is. You go along through
life meeting the kind of girls you're naturally cut out for,
and then one day you have two martinis before lunch and
something like this happens to you . . . I squeezed her hand
back.

"Peter's with me," she said, sort of wrinkling her eyes.

I looked up. She was right. There was a young man standing right behind her.

"Peter," she said. "You remember Jim."

That startled me even more than the young man's sudden
appearance had. Because the strange thing is that although
my name's Charles there had been a time years ago in school
when several people *had* called me Jim.

"Sure," the young man said. "Sure. How are you, Jim?"
He held out his hand in a friendly way, and I took it. I didn't
like him a bit. He was a large young man in a gray tweed suit.
He looked as though he might have played football for one
of the big Eastern colleges, except that there was something
vaguely phony about him. He looked too much like that. His
suit was too tweedy, his hair too crew cut, his tie too loose.

"Hi," I said.

He leaned a little over the table. "I'm afraid we'd better be
getting along, Alice," he told her. And then turning to me:
"We've got to get back to the Gosling and pack. We're leaving
for the Coast tonight."

It struck me then that that was exactly what I meant about
him. He didn't have to tell me he could afford to stay at the
Gosling. He could have said "the hotel" and left it at that.

I stood up, too. "Well, it was nice seeing you both," I
began, trying to edge away. But when I'd got clear of the
table I found I was still with them. Peter put his hand on my
shoulder as we started for the door.

"Where you been keeping yourself, Jim?"

"Oh, around." The martinis were beginning to wear off.
I just wanted to get away before they found out I wasn't

Jim after all. Not their Jim anyway. I got my coat check out of my pocket.

"Here. Let me." He took the coat check out of my hand before I could stop him. I was left standing in the lobby with Alice while he got the coats. I watched him give the checks to the girl behind the barrier.

"I almost wish we weren't going now." Alice was wrinkling her eyes again.

"So do I." I stood smiling uneasily at her until Peter got back with my raincoat and his own expensive topcoat. He started to help me on with mine, but I took it out of his hands and tossed it over my arm.

"Well, so long," I said. "It was certainly swell seeing you."

It had stopped raining when I got outside, so I just carried my raincoat back to the office over my arm and hung it in its usual place on the stand behind my door.

It wasn't, consequently, until I was leaving at six that I had it on again and even then I was half way down in the elevator before I noticed the package in the pocket.

It was a long manila envelope. It felt as though it was filled with papers. I took it out and looked at it, wondering where it had come from. There was no name or address on it. And then I saw that it wasn't stuck down, just fastened with the clip. I opened the flap and looked inside.

I almost fainted, right there in the elevator. It wasn't paper it was filled with. It was money. Great wads of bills. I closed the envelope's flap fast and took the next elevator back up to my office. Then I locked the door, took out the money and counted it. I counted it twice. Two thousand three hundred and sixty-five dollars, it added up to.

It didn't take me long to decide what to do next. I remembered Peter getting my coat from the check room. I didn't know what their racket was, or why they had slipped all that money into my pocket, or what I was supposed to do with it. I didn't care. All I knew was that I didn't want any part of it.

I got a cab and went straight to the Gosling.

It took me quite a while to find the number of their room. I didn't know their last names, only their first, but I could describe them pretty accurately, and they were neither of them hard to describe. I was afraid they might have checked out already, too. But they hadn't. They were both of them in the room when I walked in. There were suitcases all over the floor, and Peter was putting some shirts into another one on the bed.

He looked up and smiled when he saw me.

"Well, look who's come to see us off," he said. "Hi, Jim."

I didn't smile back. "I don't know what your racket is," I said. "And I don't want to. But in case you made some kind of mistake about who I was, I never saw either of you before in my life. Here." And I threw the envelope onto the bed.

He hardly seemed to glance at it. He just stood there looking at me with a frozen smile on his face, his large hands hanging loosely at his sides. He was a lot bigger than I am.

I turned and walked out of the room as fast as I could. I almost ran down the hall to the elevator.

I felt pretty good. I felt I had done the best thing possible and got myself out of what might have been a thoroughly nasty business very well.

I stopped and had a good dinner at a place on Third Avenue and then walked slowly home.

I felt pretty good until just about an hour ago.

I had run out of cigarettes and I happened to remember that there was a half pack in my raincoat. I went to the closet and began to feel through the pockets, looking for it.

There weren't any cigarettes in the coat, or anything else. But that didn't bother me for long. I stopped even thinking about cigarettes as soon as I got to the inside pocket and saw the store label stitched on it.

It wasn't my coat.

Yes, of course I called the hotel. They'd checked out a couple of hours before. They must have checked out as soon as they looked in the envelope. And they didn't leave anything at the desk either. No messages. No package. No forwarding address.

So what do I do now? What can I do—except sit here and worry. And wait. Wait to see what happens next. And I know what that'll be.

I keep getting up and looking at the raincoat again, thinking maybe it might be mine after all. But I'm just trying to kid myself, doing that. I know it isn't mine. Somebody else has got mine. And he must know it by now. He couldn't help it.

Mine had my name in it.

35

ARTHUR GORDON

The Devil and Father Francisco

ON THE MEXICAN BORDER, Arthur Gordon was
doing a series of articles about the aliens who flow back and
forth over our borders without benefit of passport or permit. Into this experience walked Father Francisco. And
Father Francisco provides us with a perfect short-short story
with the twist at the end which adds the final bit of satisfaction.

IN THE LITTLE house at the Customs barrier on the American
side of the river, the discussion—like the weather—was quite
heated. Father Francisco heard it from afar as, cassock flapping dustily, he came down the hill. He had had an excellent
lunch with his American colleague, Father Cahill—a luxury
he permitted himself once a week—and now he was on his
way back to his own grubby parishioners on the Mexican
side.

Crossing the border bridge always made Father Francisco a
little pensive. The all-important line in the middle of the
muddy river was quite invisible, but it was definitely there.
Rather like the invisible but all-important line separating the
good life from the bad. Father Francisco had preached more
than one sermon on this topic, his angular face with its hint
of Aztec blood shining with sincerity and sweat. People, he
was firmly convinced, were all fundamentally good. It was
only the devil who sometimes got into them and made them
seem bad.

He poked his head into the little house where Customs
Inspectors Hansen and Cohn were now shouting rudely at
each other. At once the argument ceased.

194

"Hi, padre," said Hansen, a big blond ox of a man. "Come in for a minute and settle this for us, will you?" He turned to his partner. "Will you let the padre settle it?"

Cohn nodded his sharp face. "Absolutely!"

The little priest came in and eased himself carefully onto the corner of a desk. He said, in his careful English, "What is the problem, my friends?"

"We have been informed," Hansen began, "that one Pedro Gonzales, a collector and seller of poisonous reptiles—"

"Is also a willful and consistent smuggler," Cohn finished.

Father Francisco looked unhappily at his toes, as he always did when he heard of wrongdoing. "I do not think I know this Gonzales." He glanced up hopefully. "Just a bottle of tequila, perhaps, now and then?"

"Not tequila," said Inspector Cohn. "Not Mexican silver, either. Narcotics, padre. Opium. Maybe heroin."

"Oh," said Father Francisco, frowning. "That is very bad. But maybe—" his face brightened again—"your information is wrong."

Hansen shook his head grimly. "This informer is usually right. And anyway, look at the setup! Every Friday afternoon about this time Pedro Gonzales comes across the line with a box full of snakes. Rattlers, moccasins, fer-de-lance, coral snakes, all poisonous as hell—beg your pardon, padre!"

"Why not say—poisonous as the devil?" Father Francisco suggested gently.

"Okay—poisonous as the devil. He sells these critters to Jim Moncrief up at the drugstore, and Jim sells 'em—at quite a nice profit—to a pharmaceutical outfit that makes anti-venom serum. Well, now, you known darn well nobody's going to do a very thorough inspection job on a box full of live rattlesnakes!"

"And so," said Cohn gloomily, "we figure he just tapes a few ounces of heroin or a pound of opium under the lid, or somewhere inside the box, and walks right through!" He glanced at his watch. "Should be along any minute, now; he's overdue."

"And the—er—problem you heard us discussing," Hansen went on, "was as to—ah—*which* of us shall make the examination of the snake-box!"

"Ah, yes," said Father Francisco, "that *might* be a problem!"

Inspectors Hansen and Cohn spoke rapidly and simultaneously: "As a man whose heart is none too good . . ." "As a married man with two small children . . ."

"Gentlemen, please!" said Father Francisco. "There is clearly only one way to settle this matter." From under his cassock he drew a silver coin. "You call it," he said to Inspector Hansen, who did call it—wrong, and turned noticeably pale.

"Here he comes now," said the abruptly joyful Inspector Cohn.

Across the Bridge, a sight commonplace enough along the Rio Grande, came a sombrero'd Mexican driving a sleepy burro. On the burro's back was a large wooden box complete with air holes and inside, if you cared to listen, was a sibilant writhing and hissing most unpleasant to hear.

The Mexican stood, sullen under his sombrero, while Inspector Hansen made certain preparations which involved stout rubber boots, heavy gloves, and a large tin garbage pail into which to empty the snakes. Sweating visibly, he took this paraphernalia and the snake box into a small bathroom. Inspector Cohn hastily closed the door and leaned against it.

While they waited, Father Francisco regarded the snake vendor thoughtfully. At last he said, *"Es catolico, Pedro?"*

"Si, padre!" was the instant reply.

But this profession of faith did not seem to please Father Francisco unduly. He stared unhappily at his toes.

Out from the bathroom at last, apparently unbitten, but with a red and angry face, stalked Inspector Hansen. He put his hissing burden on the floor and wiped his forehead.

"Couldn't find a thing! No false bottom—nothing!" He strode up to the Mexican, ran his hands quickly over his clothing. "Okay, so we're wrong! Get going—pronto!"

The Mexican took his box of snakes, turned toward the door.

"*Un momentito,*" said Father Francisco. He slipped off the desk, approached the Mexican, in one quick motion pulled off the wide sombrero and handed it to Cohn. "Perhaps you had better examine this, Inspector."

"But, padre," said the amazed Hansen a few minutes later, "how did you *know* he had the stuff in the crown of his hat?"

Father Francisco sighed. "On our side of the river, all *catolicos* take off their hats when they talk to a padre. But you see, in this case, the devil would not let him."

He walked a little sadly out into the blessed white sunshine. What this Pedro had tried to do was very wrong. A bad man, clearly. Doubtless the *Americanos* would punish him.

But as he neared the middle of the river, a thought came to Father Francisco. He remembered, suddenly, the fragment of Scripture which said plainly: "And the serpent tempted them . . ."

Why, of course, said Father Francisco to himself. Poor Pedro is not really such a bad man. He had too much to do with serpents.

And, faith restored, he stepped briskly across the international boundary that lay before him, fixed and invisible, like the eternal line that divides evil from good.

36

OLIVER LA FARGE

No, My Darling Daughter

OLIVER LA FARGE won a Pulitzer Prize for "Laughing Boy," but this story is a long way from the setting of that novel among the Indians of the Southwest. Mr. La Farge is an archeologist of renown, with expeditions in the Southwest and Central America to his credit. But again, this story has nothing to do with those. It is just fun, and we hope you will enjoy it.

ELIZABETH JANE PENDERSLEEVE GRADUATED FROM Bryn Mawr at the head of her class as well as with assorted extra-curricular honors. Mothers of other Main Line girls envied Elizabeth Jane's mother, for the girl had everything. Her mother was a Stowell, but unfortunately not one of the Chestnut Hill Stowells, and it may have been this slight flaw in her background which made her so ambitious for her daughter.

Most mothers would have been content with the fortune and the position which were Elizabeth Jane's by inheritance, and concerned themselves only lest their child make an unsuitable match, but Mrs. Pendersleeve was determined that her daughter should go yet higher.

Perhaps Elizabeth Jane herself incited her mother's ambitions. She was intelligent, charming and extremely pretty, and she had been all these from an early age. She was also docile, a quality which her mother cultivated assiduously. Only twice had Elizabeth Jane shown any signs of wilfulness, at least as far as the opposite sex was concerned.

The first time was a dreadful attachment to a boy from Brooklyn in the summer of her seventeenth year. It was a harrowing experience for her mother, but it worked out all for the best, for the creature got publicly drunk at a party which Elizabeth Jane had helped him to crash, and he put her through a thoroughly unpleasant experience. Mrs. Pendersleeve felt that it was a lesson to the child that Mother really knew best.

A similar lamentable interest in a quite impossible person occurred in the course of Elizabeth Jane's senior year. This time it was a young man from Texas who was doing postgraduate work at the University of Pennsylvania. His father, one gathered, owned a ranch about the size of Ohio, which produced registered cattle, blooded horses, and large quantities of oil.

Inevitably, he was invited to many too many parties. It was upsetting to see how the young people seemed to enjoy his company, his primitive humor, his odd manner of speech, and his irreverent ideas. By the time of the mid-year examinations, when Elizabeth Jane spent more than a week at home, her mother began to see that she was not only enjoying these attributes, but was attracted by the fellow's good looks. Vulgar good looks, Mrs. Pendersleeve felt, but even physically, and especially in regard to his stature, this young man was unrestrained.

Happily, the fellow was removed shortly after mid-years for riding a horse furiously around the campus late one night on a bet. He disappeared into the wilds of Texas whence he had come, and that was that. Even had he stayed, Mrs. Pendersleeve told herself, while Elizabeth Jane might have persisted in an unfortunate association, she was much too much of a Pendersleeve ever to have considered a more serious relationship with a person from so far south or so far west.

When they went to Newport that summer, Mrs. Pendersleeve had a feeling that this was to be the season of her triumph, a fitting final achievement after her daughter's outstanding success at Bryn Mawr. The feeling proved to be prophetic, for within a week after their arrival there appeared a perfectly delightful Baron Nicholas Jelacic who immediately was attracted to Elizabeth Jane.

Baron Jelacic was tall, although not as tall as the Texan, slender, moderately dark with liquid brown eyes, and an excellent tennis player. He was witty and well read. He was even a direct descendant of Baron Joseph Jelacic, the noble Croat. He professed to ignore the fact that now in 1948 he was in actuality a Yugoslav.

The fact that his family had too little money was, if anything, in his favor. Mrs. Pendersleeve held that an American girl was so much more *secure* in a Continental marriage if she controlled the purse strings. On the whole, Mrs. Pendersleeve thought that next to an actual member of a royal family a Baron was ideal. She gave her daughter certain indications and even at one point spoke to her rather firmly for her own good, and watched the progress of the courtship with deep satisfaction.

It was rainy and chilly that summer. The first time that Baron Jelacic paid special attention to Elizabeth Jane was one afternoon at Bailey's Beach, and unfortunately that afternoon it rained. Elizabeth Jane, who was very seldom in ill health, caught a cold. The cold lingered on.

Sometimes it almost disappeared, but unfailingly it came back again. By the malevolence of fate, her sniffles always seemed to be at their worst when she had a date with the Baron.

Despite a red nose, reddened eyes, and the necessity of using up dozens of tissues a day, Elizabeth Jane seemed to retain her charm for the Baron. He saw her more and more steadily, asked her everywhere, and kept her amused. His kindness and his attentions at times when she knew that she was a mess affected her favorably. It was not yet the end of July when he proposed, and after some hesitation and a long, intimate talk with her mother, Elizabeth Jane accepted him.

Baron Jelacic had been the bachelor of the year. The announcement of the engagement was a sensation. As he had to

return to Yugoslavia in September, there would be a short
engagement, and a wedding to be remembered on the Labor
Day week-end. Special cars would run from Philadelphia,
and Tom Thursby's yacht would bring the guests from
Southampton. Everything was as Mrs. Pendersleeve might
have dreamed it, except that now, when above all times she
wanted her daughter at her most radiant, that dreadful cold
in the head continued to get worse than ever.

Elizabeth Jane gave up swimming entirely, but it did no
good. She took all the treatments her doctor, her mother, two
aunts, old Mrs. Delacourt, and her mother's maid who had
been with them for years prescribed, but none helped at all.
Then the doctor tested her for allergies until several areas of
her anatomy were covered with scratches, but all to no avail.
By the end of August three other doctors had been called in
consultation, and they were making scratches on the calf of
her leg to test her for goldfish, peppermint candy, and champagne.

On the last day of August the committee of doctors sent
for the Baron and were closeted with him for several hours.
They asked him to recall every item of his hours with Elizabeth Jane, with special reference to date and times.

Since the Baron kept a diary with meticulous thorough-
ness, he was able to give an accurate, detailed account. This
information was carefully collated with the rather full record
of the case which the family physician had kept ever since, in
the end of July, this ailment threatened to become an international matter. The Baron was dismissed and the doctors
consulted. Then they sent for Elizabeth Jane and made one
last incision, this time on her forearm.

At eleven o'clock in the morning of September first, with
the wedding just two days away, the committee of physicians
called upon the Pendersleeves. They examined the last test
incision, and found it swollen and angry.

The doctors looked at each other. They nodded solemnly.
One of them said, "Beautiful." Another said, "Nice work,

MacPherson," and that distinguished specialist bowed. He said with solemnity, "The prettiest case of angio-neurotic edema I have ever witnessed."

Then the family physician turned to Mrs. Pendersleeve and said gravely, "Mrs. Pendersleeve, I am very sorry to have to tell you that your daughter is suffering from a psychogenic disturbance. In short, she is allergic to the Baron."

Mrs. Pendersleeve fainted, thus occupying the doctors. Elizabeth Jane rushed from the room. She ran up the staircase and into her own room, slamming the door behind her. She fell into the armchair beside her telephone extension. She blew her nose and caught her breath, then, sniffling slightly, she put in a long distance call to Texas.

37

MATT TAYLOR

McGarry Joins the Easter Parade

McGARRY is a character for whom the editors confess great affection, since McGarry, the plain-clothes cop, with his mouse, Kitty, was born and lives in the pages of This Week. He has been appearing now and then since 1940, and has also been on radio. Mr. Taylor, his biographer, is a well-known writer of fiction.

"I'LL SUE THE darn city!" cries out Dan McGarry, red in the face and pounding the heel of his hand into the arm of the chair. "I'm a plain-clothes cop. It ain't right for them to make me a fancy pants."

He might just as well be talking to himself. His mouse Kitty has a dreamy look in her eyes. "You'll have to get me a corsage of orchids," she says happily. "Shell pink, I think."

And now it's Dan's turn not to listen. "I don't mind dressing up in my best suit on Easter," he growls, "but when it comes to renting striped trousers and cutaway and a high silk hat . . . "

"Hat," interrupts Kitty, sighing and shaking her head. "I suppose it'll cost forty dollars at the very least for a halfway decent one."

"Not for me, it won't," says Dan.

"Of course, not for you," replies Kitty. "For me. Do you think I can wear just anything in the Easter parade?"

"Look," says Dan patiently. "I guess you didn't hear it right. I am the one that marches in the Easter parade. It's the

Commissioner's idea. Me and some other cops got to climb into fancy clothes and mingle with the dressed-up mob as though we belong, and keep an eye peeled for pickpockets, because a lot of high-powered jewelry will be strolling the Avenue on Easter morning."

"I know all that," says Kitty calmly. "But who ever heard of a lone man marching in the Easter parade? Why, you would be spotted as a detective right away if you weren't escorting a lady."

"A cop can't work with a dame tagging along," argues Dan.

"Don't be silly," says Kitty. "I'll be part of your disguise. And now do you want to come along and help me pick out a hat?" She has that feverish, all-aquiver look girls get when they talk about clothes. "I wish I could afford an exclusive model from Madame Renaldi's," she sighs wistfully.

And so Dan starts his tour of duty on Easter morning with his mouse Kitty hanging on his arm. This is usually enough to make him very happy indeed, especially on a sunshiny spring day. But right now he feels pretty glum, because his rented silk topper is too big and it keeps sliding down over his ears, and his high collar cuts into his chin, and his rod bulges uncomfortably in the hip pocket of his tight-fitting striped trousers. But Kitty, with a new sage green suit and green hat and twenty dollars worth of orchids, is enjoying herself in a big way.

She keeps saying look at that outrageous sky-blue hat with the pink feathers and that absurd kelly-green helmet with the pompon until Dan has to remind her he's on duty and color blind to everything except pickpockets on the loose. "I wish," he says, "I was on my own like the other cops assigned to this job."

But this is where he guesses wrong. Because along comes plain-clothesman Fingleman, also in trick clothes, and hanging onto his arm is a dame wearing twenty dollars worth of gardenias. "Meet the missus," says Fingleman sadly. "She thought she'd come along with me for the walk."

"Meet my mouse Kitty," replies Dan. "She had the same idea."

"I just passed the Sergeant and his wife," says Fingleman.

"Hmm," Dan says. "So he's stuck, too?"

"The Sergeant tells me that there's enough ice floating up and down the Avenue to keep a herd of polar bears happy. So we'd better . . ."

"Just look at that enormous yellow cartwheel on that woman!" cries Kitty. "What a monstrosity!"

"And that ridiculous purple turban with the silver balls!" says Mrs. Fingleman.

Fingleman sighs. "All dames," he confides to Dan in a low voice, "go slightly hat happy at Easter. Good luck, McGarry. Keep a sharp watch for any of our better-known dips."

Dan and Kitty stroll on. The crowd gets thicker and the colors brighter and the hats sillier, and Kitty laughs and gushes, and Dan doesn't say anything until he sees a short dark guy and a fancy blonde coming toward him. Then he says to Kitty, "Wait here," and he steps forward and taps the guy on the shoulder.

"You wouldn't be getting into trouble around here, would you, Touchy?" he says.

Touchy Toomey, one of the smoothest dips that ever lifts a wallet, grins at him. "Make sense, McGarry," he says. "Do you think I would dress up in these trick clothes if my dame didn't make me? I am not here on business today. It is strictly for my girl Lilybelle's pleasure. She likes hats."

"Maybe," says Dan. "But with all this ice in easy reach . . ."

"The ice is very tempting," admits Touchy. "But the Avenue is lousy with you cops and you are easy to spot even if you are dressed up like minstrel end men. I am here to give Lilybelle a good time and let her make fun of hats that are only half as silly as the one she is wearing. So . . ."

There is a sudden commotion a few yards down the street. A woman is screaming. Dan can understand enough of what she says. She's crying out, "I've been robbed! It was stolen, I tell you!"

Dan runs forward and pushes his way through the crowd around a weepy old dame. He recognizes her right away. He's seen her at the police balls and in the reviewing stand watching the police parade. She's the Commissioner's wife and she's wearing a bright lilac suit and a hat that looks like an umbrella stand with pink icing on it. "I'm a police officer," Dan tells her. "Who stole what, ma'am?"

"Find them!" moans the old dame, clutching at her throat. "Find the couple that passed a minute ago—a fuzzy blonde. The man was short and dark . . ."

"Touchy!" cries Dan. "You wait here!"

He races back and, of course, Touchy is gone. So is his fuzzy blonde Lilybelle. And so is Kitty. Dan keeps going, dodging through the crowd as best he can. And at the next corner he sees Touchy walking rapidly down a side street. Dan puts on speed and when he can jerk his rod out of his hip pocket he fires twice into the air.

This is enough for Touchy. He stops and waits. "Okay, copper," he says. "But for what? I'm clean. I saw the rhubarb start and I took a walk. I do not like rhubarbs."

"Maybe you're clean," Dan says, "but the Commissioner's wife thinks different."

The old dame is still there when Dan comes up with Touchy. "Here he is, ma'am," Dan says proudly. "I am glad to be of service. And if the Commissioner should ask, the name is McGarry. We'll take this guy to Headquarters, search him and get back your jewels."

"What jewels?" says the Commissioner's wife sharply. "Where's the girl, you ninny?"

Dan gapes. "Girl?"

"Where's the blonde girl who was wearing a duplicate of my hat!" snaps the old dame. "I remember her perfectly. She's a stock clerk at Madame Renaldi's. She saw me buy this divine exclusive model for a hundred dollars. She copied it, the little thief! Oh, that this should happen to me—in the Easter parade! I *never* wear anything that isn't exclusive!"

"Is this what you want?" says a voice behind Dan. He turns and here is Kitty. She is holding out a hat which is a twin of the old dame's umbrella stand with the pink icing.

"I thought there was something wrong when I saw these two hats," Kitty explains. "I was looking around at Madame Renaldi's last week and I noticed your hat. I knew it was meant to be an exclusive. So I caught up with that blonde girl. I told her I'd report her to Madame. I said she might even be prosecuted. I talked her into giving it to me."

The Commissioner's wife takes the umbrella stand from Kitty. She squashes it between her hands like an accordion, drops it to the sidewalk and kicks it into the street. "Thank you, young woman," she says. "You've saved my reputation. You've made life worth living again." She turns to Dan and gives him a withering eye. "Lucky for you this young lady was here to save the situation," she says.

Then she smiles at Kitty. "You must come and see me, my dear," she says. "I'll take you to Madame Renaldi's and buy *you* an exclusive model."

The crowd breaks up. Dan and Kitty are left alone. Kitty's smile is small but triumphant. "Shall we stroll?" she says. "Or don't you want to be stuck with me?"

"I—huh—we—ugh . . ."

She puts her arm through his. "Look at that perfectly outlandish black hat with the orange feather!" she cries.

"Okay," says Dan humbly. "I'll look."

38

OSCAR SCHISGALL

"Take Over, Bos'n!"

OSCAR SCHISGALL has written countless short-short
stories. He is one of today's foremost practitioners of the
form. So this is one—neatly made, but on a theme of high
drama. Here is a story of the meaning of responsibility, and
Mr. Schisgall has pointed it up to a moment of dynamic
importance.

HOUR AFTER HOUR I kept the gun pointed at the other nine
men. From the lifeboat's stern, where I'd sat most of the
twenty days of our drifting, I could keep them all covered.
If I had to shoot at such close quarters, I wouldn't miss. They
realized that. Nobody jumped at me. But in the way they all
glared I could see how they'd come to hate my guts.

Especially Barrett, who'd been bos'n's mate; Barrett said in
his harsh, cracked voice, "You're a dope, Snyder. Y-you can't
hold out forever! You're half asleep now!"

I didn't answer. He was right. How long can a man stay
awake? I hadn't dared shut my eyes in maybe seventy-two
hours. Very soon now I'd doze off, and the instant that happened they'd pounce on the little water that was left.

The last canteen lay under my legs. There wasn't much in
it after twenty days. Maybe a pint. Enough to give each of
them a few drops. Yet I could see in their bloodshot eyes that
they'd gladly kill me for those few drops. As a man I didn't
count any more. I was no longer third officer of the wrecked
Montala. I was just a gun that kept them away from the
water they craved. And with their tongues swollen and their
cheeks sunken, they were half crazy. . . .

The way I judged it, we must be some two hundred miles east of Ascension. Now that the storms were over, the Atlantic swells were long and easy, and the morning sun was hot— so hot it scorched your skin. My own tongue was thick enough to clog my throat. I'd have given the rest of my life for a single gulp of water.

But I was the man with the gun—the only authority in the boat—and I knew this: once the water was gone we'd have nothing to look forward to but death. As long as we could look forward to getting a drink later, there was something to live for. We had to make it last as long as possible. If I'd given in to the curses and growls, if I hadn't brandished the gun, we'd have emptied the last canteen days ago. By now we'd all be dead.

The men weren't pulling on the oars. They'd stopped that long ago, too weak to go on. The nine of them facing me were a pack of bearded, ragged, half-naked animals, and I probably looked as bad as the rest. Some sprawled over the gunwales, dozing. The rest watched me as Barrett did, ready to spring the instant I relaxed.

When they weren't looking at my face they looked at the canteen under my legs.

Jeff Barrett was the nearest one. A constant threat. The bos'n's mate was a heavy man, bald, with a scarred and brutal face. He'd been in a hundred fights, and they'd left their marks on him. Barrett had been able to sleep—in fact, he'd slept through most of the night—and I envied him that. His eyes wouldn't close. They kept watching me, narrow and dangerous.

Every now and then he taunted me in that hoarse, broken voice:

"Why don't you quit? You can't hold out!"

"Tonight," I said. "We'll ration the rest of the water tonight."

"By tonight some of us'll be dead! We want it now!"

"Tonight," I said.

Couldn't he understand that if we waited until night the few drops wouldn't be sweated out of us so fast? But Barrett was beyond all reasoning. His mind had already cracked with thirst. I saw him begin to rise, a calculating look in his eyes. I aimed the gun at his chest—and he sat down again.

I'd grabbed my Luger on instinct, twenty days ago, just before running for the lifeboat. Nothing else would have kept Barrett and the rest away from the water.

These fools—couldn't they see I wanted a drink as badly as any of them? But I was in command here—that was the difference. I was the man with the gun, the man who had to think. Each of the others could afford to think only of himself; I had to think of them all.

Barrett's eyes kept watching me, waiting. I hated him. I hated him all the more because he'd slept. He had that advantage now. He wouldn't keel over.

And long before noon I knew I couldn't fight any more. My eyelids were too heavy to lift. As the boat rose and fell on the long swells, I could feel sleep creeping over me like paralysis. It bent my head. It filled my brain like a cloud. I was going, going . . .

Barrett stood over me, and I couldn't even lift the gun. In a vague way I could guess what would happen. He'd grab the water first and take his gulp. By that time the others would be screaming and tearing at him, and he'd have to yield the canteen. Well, there was nothing more I could do about it.

I whispered, "Take over, bos'n."

Then I fell face down in the bottom of the boat. I was asleep before I stopped moving. . . .

When a hand shook my shoulder, I could hardly raise my head. Jeff Barrett's hoarse voice said, "Here! Take your share o' the water!"

Somehow I propped myself up on my arms, dizzy and weak. I looked at the men, and I thought my eyes were going. Their figures were dim, shadowy; but then I realized it wasn't because of my eyes. It was night. The sea was black; there were stars overhead. I'd slept the day away.

So we were in our twenty-first night adrift—the night in which the tramp *Groton* finally picked us up—but now, as I turned my head to Barrett there was no sign of any ship. He knelt beside me, holding out the canteen, his other hand with the gun steady on the men.

I stared at the canteen as if it were a mirage. Hadn't they finished that pint of water this morning? When I looked up at Barrett's ugly face, it was grim. He must have guessed my thoughts.

"You said, 'Take over, bos'n,' didn't you?" he growled. "I been holdin' off these apes all day." He hefted the Luger in his hand. "When you're boss-man," he added, "in command and responsible for the rest—you—you sure get to see things different, don't you?"

39

PAUL SCHUBERT

The White Elk

MR. SCHUBERT, a former foreign correspondent and radio commentator, is happiest and most at home, both literally and figuratively, in the West where he now lives. This haunting Christmas story is one that has been remembered affectionately. Since its appearance, people have written us, they read it to their children on Christmas Eve.

CHRISTMAS EVE WAS bitter cold out in the Big Horn Basin. As dark came down, squally scud drove across the moon and there were fierce snow flurries. Nine-year-old Sally Grant kept watch at the cabin window. Cliff, her father, had trouble getting Sally to come to supper, and faced frank mutiny when he mentioned bed. If Cliff Grant had had the gumption to take that job wrangling up at the T-bar-T Dude Ranch, he wouldn't have been here playing nursemaid to a youngster. But Cliff didn't have much gumption any more—or any job. Or much hope.

He knew what Sally was waiting for. It was his own doing and he regretted it bitterly. The White Elk! How silly he had been to dream up that mythical creature. He was always like that. Instead of coming out with the truth and telling her times were awful this year and she wouldn't have any Christmas, he had taken refuge in a lie. Told her that Santa Claus didn't come to Western kids, told her not to expect a Christmas tree—all that, he said, was for little Easterners. Dudes.

Then when he saw the look in her eyes, the pang, and heard her slow question: "You mean because I'm Western I

212

don't get any presents?" he had told her about the White
Elk.

"The White Elk lives up in the highest Rockies," he had
said, "and nobody ever sees him except on Christmas Eve.
He's the finest animal that ever lived, tall and noble—all
pure white. He's the one that brings presents to Western
kids. But honey, I don't know if he'll get around to the Big
Horn Basin or not. With so many kids in the world, and
the West as big as it is, you can see that he doesn't get to
visit all of them every year. Don't be surprised if he doesn't
show up."

"He'll come," said Sally raptly. "I know he'll come."

And on Christmas Eve she stood there at the window waiting for him.

"I'm the worst father in the world," Cliff thought with
easy self-pity. "Improvident, brainless, incompetent." Not
much left of the man who used to be a confident, devil-may-
care buckaroo—good enough to ride a name bucker at Madison Square Garden—and be bucked off, of course. Sally's
mother, seeing Cliff go downhill, hadn't been able to take it.
On this first motherless Christmas, Sally hadn't come any
closer to fancy trees and fine presents than glimpses seen
through the windows of Crossley's T-bar-T Dude Ranch,
where the skiing dudes were celebrating. The kid had ridden
up there that afternoon, barebacked, on old Shorty, Cliff's
cow pony.

The White Elk—Sally looked pretty forlorn, standing
there at the window, waiting and hoping, looking across the
sage to the timeless mountains under the timeless stars.

Suddenly Sally called from her lookout at the window.
"Pop! He's coming!" It was twenty minutes to eight.

A cold chill gripped Cliff Grant's bowels. He had been
prepared for disappointment, for weariness and grief—not
for the lift of realization and faith in his daughter's voice.
"What?" he asked lamely.

"Turn out the light!" Sally commanded in a loud whisper. "Come over here and see him!"

Standing behind her small body, looking over her head, Cliff saw an elk walk slowly across the plain through the sage—tall, majestic, with towering antlers—white in the moonlight, white as snow. The whole world was white and virgin with winter. . . .

Straight toward the house the White Elk made his way, picking his steps warily, deliberately.

"You told me he'd come, Pop!" said Sally.

So Cliff, who had created the White Elk, faced his dilemma. In that moment he realized the difference between what he saw, and what Sally saw. Cliff saw an elk, snow-covered, moonlit, moving toward the corral in the hope of getting some of Shorty's baled hay. Nothing unusual about that—deer and elk came down to the Basin every winter. A snow squall had powdered the creature white.

But Sally saw a miracle. "Come on, Pop," she whispered. "Let's open the door. How can he leave our presents if the door is shut?"

As the child opened the door, letting the blast of winter cold into the cabin, the elk looked toward her long and fearlessly, then turned and bounded off to the north.

What a time Cliff had with his daughter, getting her to bed and to sleep. The excitement, the sense of good fortune within the Grant cottage was such that it filled the father as well as the child. Sitting at the table after she was asleep at last, Cliff felt as he had not felt since his own childhood the promise of the morrow.

"Wait till morning," he had told Sally. "No presents until Christmas day."

And he had known, as he said it, that somehow, somewhere, he, Clifford Grant, would find the presents, before tomorrow morning, that would satisfy this child and keep alive her faith in the miracle she had seen. This was the showdown—there could be no failure this time, except at the price of shattering his own last reserves of faith.

To give Sally presents, he must make them out of his own resources. What could he make?

He started with a doll. Between 9:30 and 11:30 that night Cliff Grant made a doll with a head of wood and a rag body —a papoose doll, dressed in fringed leather from some old scraps he found.

But there must be more. Sally the brave, Sally the one who believed the White Elk would come, the uncomplaining, the Western girl—Sally deserved more than a doll.

Cliff was nearly finished with the doll before he remembered something. Hadn't looked at it for years. It was tucked away in the loft, out of sight so that it would be out of mind. Once his most cherished possession. His saddle. Sally was old enough to own a saddle.

He had been using it the night he was bucked off at Madison Square Garden. The night, really, that he began being afraid. He got the saddle down, put it on the table, and sat looking at it under the lamp light. It had been a fine one, hand-tooled and silver mounted, a man's saddle—a saddle to be proud of.

Always brought him luck, too. Funny, to remember that he had once believed in his luck.

He could remember that night, though. The roar of the crowd.

The oppressive smell inside Madison Square Garden.

The lights—the dust of the arena. Himself on a savage, raging horse—bucking out of the chute, across the Garden— fighting the horse, raking him with his spurs . . .

Bucked off. He had been bucked off before, but never like this.

Never this wild fling through the air, the crashing descent —the sight of the horse bucking around trying to come back and kill him—the running men coming to his rescue. The ambulance . . .

Cliff sat at the table, rubbing the old saddle with saddle-soap, shortening the stirrup-straps to fit a child, and realized that for nearly ten years he had been afraid—always afraid. Afraid of life, of work, of marriage, of paternity, of people—afraid of himself.

It was still a fine saddle. A saddle to take a man—or a child—out into life, to the arena, the struggle.

The victory?

Yes, there was still victory, if you ever reached the end of the long retreat and had your back to the wall and started to fight back. Funny thing, to have your fight take the turn of making Christmas presents for a kid—a kid willing to believe in a White Elk.

Sally would be willing to believe in a man, too, wouldn't she? And the man would have to live up to her belief, even if it meant making the most fantastic dreams come true.

At 2:30 Cliff Grant put his head on his arms beside the Christmas presents he had prepared for his daughter, and slept the deep untroubled sleep of a man at peace with himself, and unafraid.

Sally woke him after daybreak, tugging at his arm and yelling: "Presents! From the White Elk!"

Cliff Grant grinned.

"Don't look like much to me. Western presents. Maybe you'd sooner have something else?" he said.

Sally looked at her father reproachfully. "They're beautiful!" she said. "Merry Christmas, Pop!"

"Merry Christmas, honey," said Cliff Grant. He was going to add "and a happy New Year." But he decided he'd let that wait until after he'd been up to the T-bar-T and gone after the job. From now on he was done with promises. Whatever life demanded, he would do.

Cliff Grant had found himself.

40

EUSTACE COCKRELL

The Keyhole Artist

USING LETTERS as the means of telling a story is a
risky business, unless they are quick to arouse curiosity and
suspense. We thought Mr. Cockrell had managed the trick
here and produced a bright, entertaining, humorous story.
The author, who is also an editor, lives on the West Coast.

August 1st, 1948

Mr. Bryan Moriarity,
The Eye in the Sky Detective Agency
New York City

Dear Chief:

Pursuant to your directive I have obtained work in the
household of subject (M. Donnelly) as maid. This first step
was easily accomplished by bribing former maid with week's
pay and appearing next day at door with story she had sent
me to substitute for her until further notice. It may be ger-
mane that subject accepted this rather obvious device in
perfect good faith revealing a truly bucolic naïveté.

Now, as I understand this assignment, I am to make general character analysis of subject, determine former social
stratum, if any, family background and acquire any other
data that a man with the enormous wealth of Mr. Horace
Cavendish (our employer) might find of interest about the
man affianced to his daughter Gertrude. In brief, I am to
find out if the guy is a fortune hunter.

Kathleen O'Brien (Agent No. 14)

P. S. I enclose receipted bill for three maid's uniforms.
Please remit.

August 7th, 1948

Dear Chief:

This is discouraging. I have yet to find anything wrong with this character. Subject was born in a small town in the Middle West, second son of a minister, regularly sends substantial sums of money home to his mother (father deceased). Worked his way through college and law school, admitted to bar in 1937 and practiced in Kansas City until outbreak of war. Enlisted in Marine Corps December 11th, 1941, discharged October 14th, 1945. Rank, Major. (Silver Star) Thirty-two months overseas. This is confirmed by perusal of home-town paper to which subject subscribes and reading of subject's old mail. Credit and professional rating AA. Was spoken of—off the record—by Judge Linshaw as "most brilliant young attorney in New York."

Personally I find him modest, jolly, a fine sense of humor. He is kind (will make more detailed report in person on splinter in finger and burnt asparagus incidents), and why did Mr. Horace Cavendish hire us anyway?

Entertained daughter of employer, Miss Gertrude Cavendish, last night here at dinner. Personally, I thought Miss Cavendish rather cold and superficial and unduly snoopy about subject's background, though subject seemed to evince no reticence in discussing same.

K. O'B. (Agt. No. 14)

P.S. Did you get receipted bill for three maid's uniforms? If so please remit.

August 8th, 1948

Dear Chief:

Miss Cavendish appeared today and questioned me exhaustively as to subject's personal habits, outside interests in general. I gave guardedly favorable replies to questions but naturally refused specific information on basis of domestic ethics. Subject's well-ordered life caused Miss Cavendish some distress and in course of conversation she spoke wistfully of indigent polo player named Sonny McGuire. I found Miss Cavendish less cold and superficial after show of emotion resulting from mention of Mr. Sonny McGuire. But seems parental pressure favors subject.

I waited in (subject had outside dinner engagement and had told me to go home early), suspecting him of having cold and fixed him some hot lemonade. Had interesting discussion of economic theories of Mr. Thorstein Veblen. Subject very sound on works of Mr. V.

K. O'B. (Agt. No. 14)

August 13th, 1948

Dear Chief:

Subject had cold which turned into alarming case of grippe (temp. almost 100) and I am *very* busy. Have arranged to sleep down hall with Mrs. Gibbon's maid so can give full attention to subject without causing gossip.

K. O'B. (Agt. No. 14)

August 14th, 1948

Dear Chief:

Subject's temperature now 100.2! And *I* am in shock. Subject underwent violent moral disintegration with mounting temperature.

A true case of schi . . . Dr. Jekyll and Mr. Hyde and Mr. Hyde has been in ascendancy ever since our discussion about Mr. Thorstein Veblen (whoever in aitch Mr. V is). This morning subject felt hotter to touch and also felt badly. Apparently was enough to cause reversion to true character.

First thing he did was call office to say he would not be in, then after crafty closing of bedroom door (I listened at keyhole), subject phoned one he called Muscles McGill.

I report these snatches of conversation:

". . . have hooks in rich broad . . ."

". . . old man's bankroll thick as his head . . ."

". . . quick wedding before Horace tumbles . . ."

". . . richer than Ernestine in Kaysee and you remember what we took her for . . ."

Also additional random words and phrases. "Old man's blood pressure. Won't be long . . . gilt edged . . . fronting for this mob . . ."

Took subject breakfast, subject snarled, cursed and threatened me with bodily injury due to condition of egg. Subject refused to shave.

The next morning subject's apartment was littered with empty highball glasses, lipstick smudges, cigarettes. For man in subject's weakened physical condition feel that subject's keeping late houris (pardon pun) shows definite schiz . . . definite irrational behavior.

                                        K. O'B. (Agt. No. 14)

P.S. Due to startling nature of this report have sent report in triplicate to Mr. Horace Cavendish and daughter Gertrude.

The Eye in the Sky
Detective Agency
New York City

August 16th, 1948

Kathleen:

Case closed this A.M. with elopement of Miss Gertrude Cavendish and Sonny McGuire. Please report this A.M. to explain:

1. *Your* "violent moral disintegration," evidenced by unethical, dishonest, shysterish trick of sending fantastic reports to our ex-employer, Horace Cavendish and daughter.

2. Why contents of said report are at strict variance with all preliminary investigations, including your own?

3. How a nice young girl with your upbringing could do such a thing?

                                        Bryan Moriarity

August 16th, 1948

Bryan Moriarity, Esq.
The Eye in the Sky Detective Agency
New York City

Dear Sir:

I herewith submit resignation effective this date. I am being married in the morning.

Yours truly,

Kathleen O'Brien

P.S. Please make check for three maid's uniforms payable to Mrs. Marshall H. Donnelly.

41

EDWARD FIELDING

The Fountain of Youth

LOVE AT FORTY, editors often say, is something that will interest *no*body. But here is a story about a woman of forty-two which has already interested several million readers, and we present it as a tale which *most* people will love whatever their age. Mr. Fielding writes a good many short stories, but this is one of our favorites.

MYRA NEWCOMB STRETCHED in the bed and yawned, not delicately but with honest gusto. She was a smartly angular blonde woman, long-limbed and gracefully rangy, with a soft humorous mouth and a practical look in her gray eyes. The sunlight in the room looked ten-ish, and her first emotion of the day was a feeling of guilt. Jim, the old darling, had let her sleep again, getting his own breakfast and going forth to plan the architectural future of a greater New York without so much as a kiss of encouragement. The Shape of Things to Come.

The phrase struck a vaguely disturbing note in her sleepy mind, and she sat up, trying to place her apprehension. The Fear swept down on her then, jumping into her chest, and sitting there like a nervous little monster taking up its position for the day. Suddenly, unsparingly, she had found out two weeks ago that she was getting old.

It had happened at the Trefts' anniversary party. She had smiled at some unknown young man, wanting to make him feel more comfortable, and he had given her that "go-away-granny" look. Just as if she had been trying to flirt with him! "At your age," his eyes had said; and ever since then she'd

222

been deviled with the not-too-admirable urge to peek in a mirror every time she passed one. The peeking had turned up unpleasant truths about her face.

She got out of bed, noticing her figure in its pale lavender nightdress as she passed the mirrored back of the closet door. "Thank God for small blessings," she said. She yawned again, ruffling her shoulder-length blonde hair with her fingers. "You're old," she told herself. "A great big forty-two. It's too bad." Leaning down, she surveyed her face in the vanity mirror. Annoyed that she was peering again, she stuck out her tongue at her reflection and began to dress.

When she was clothed in a trim black suit, she studied herself in the full-length mirror across the room. "You're all right from a distance, baby," she said drily. "But don't get any closer."

She started her day in high gear, as if by hurrying she could outrun the discomfort of her anxiety. There was a letter to Jack, her seventeen-year-old son, to be written. He was at the Cape, running his Uncle Ty's schooner for him and enjoying his first love affair. There was a package of clothes to be wrapped for mailing to France—a family Jim had befriended during the war. Hazel Trefts, Myra's oldest and best friend, phoned, wanting Myra to meet her at one for lunch.

By eleven, the aging Mrs. Newcomb was in a saffron-walled booth of the near-by beauty shop getting a facial. This, too, was something new for her, and she hated her sudden dependence on these discreet but overbearing women. But this was Science, come to save her. Magic in a jar of cream, rejuvenation in the march of skillful fingers across her cheeks.

The whole genteel ritual struck her as somehow ridiculous; but she sat there dutifully, laughing within herself yet at the same time feeling a tragic sense of decline and not liking her twinges of self-pity one little bit.

At lunch, Hazel pointed across the table at the small package Myra was holding.

"What have you got there?" she asked, amused.

"Just some face lotion. Why?"

"Well, you're clutching it so possessively. No one will steal it, darling, if you put it down by your purse."

Myra felt herself flushing. "To lose that, would be to lose all. The beauty operator said it would do wonders for me. Look at my face, Hazel." She leaned forward. "I'm getting old."

"Aren't we all?" Hazel was obviously not in a mood to take anything seriously. "It's a nice face. It could still launch a ship or two."

"Barges only, I'm afraid. Honestly, I came across an old picture of Jim and me—taken in the Poconos, I think, when you and Brent were visiting us, and the change, Hazel. Not in Jim, but in me. It's appalling!"

"Why not in Jim?" Hazel said pleasantly. "It seems to me his hairline has been creeping up and tummy creeping out."

"Oh, Jim hasn't changed a fraction since we've been married," Myra said with conviction.

Hazel smiled in gentle tolerance. "True love must be slightly near-sighted or something. But, darling, don't be so morose. You can't look a bride all your life. What if you are picking up a few wrinkles? You've sown your wild oats, made your conquests, and ensnared the man of your heart."

"But will he stay ensnared?"

"Myra, put that old-fashioned down! It's going to your head." Hazel still found Myra's plight amusing. "Look at me, for heaven's sake! I don't worry, and I'm not a fifth as attractive as you. But Brent thinks I'm passable, and that's what counts."

"Your skin's as smooth as a baby's," Myra pointed out. "You're not the kind that ever wrinkles."

Hazel sobered. "Why, I think you are worried. You don't sound like you at all."

"I don't feel like me—peering in mirrors all the time and running to get facials. My self-concern is disgusting; and yet

I can't seem to help it." She smiled all at once. "Maybe it's just a phase that goes along with one's forty-second year." She laughed and touched the package. "This will save me, anyway," she said. "The plasma of youth."

"Well, thank the Lord you haven't lost your sense of humor."

"I can't find me funny," Myra said.

After lunch, another disheartening thing happened. A man collided with her just as she turned to look in a bookstore window. He was quite a distinguished-looking older man. The bottle of face lotion was sent flying from her hands to shatter on the sidewalk and she herself was staggered in a way that would have been funny if it hadn't hurt. The man steadied her, touched his hat, and walked off abruptly, leaving the valiant, forgiving smile she had summoned to her face to dry on her lips. He hadn't even looked at her. It was just as if he had bumped into another man, and not a very prepossessing one at that.

"Well, I'll be damned," she said under her breath; and then she marched home, a queer kind of humiliation burning her cheeks.

As she was dressing for dinner, Jim let himself into the apartment. He came into the bedroom holding a deep, square box and looking immensely pleased with himself. "I've bought you something," he said.

"Well, aren't you the sweet one." She smiled and went to kiss him.

"I saw it in a window," he said, undoing the box with sly ceremony, "and I thought, What the hell, I know it'll look good on Myra, so why don't I buy it?"

He was holding up something—a hat. The youngest and most frivolous of hats. Words like frou-frou and chi-chi went zipping through Myra's head. She shut her mouth, then said, "Why Jim!" in a tone she hoped sounded like reverent surprise.

"I knew you'd think it was something out of this world."

He was grinning all over himself and rotating the hat proudly on one hand. "Let's try it on."

It froze her to think of putting on such a hat. Nothing could have been more cleverly designed to accentuate her age. Was this his way of pointing out that she was letting herself go? She swallowed and said, "Wait until I slip into a dress."

She went to the closet and took down her youngest print, got into it. Then, as if going to the stake, she reached for the hat and walked to the mirror with it.

She took an inordinate amount of time to pin it on, feeling all the while like a grandmother putting a little girl's ribbon in her hair. Finally she ran out of adjustments and turned to face him.

"Well, here I am," she said in a quiet, abject voice.

"Gosh! You look great!"

She shifted her gaze to the picture on the wastebasket; she felt like weeping. Now that he saw the incongruity, he was putting up a show.

"It's a trifle gay for me, don't you think?" She managed a quick, fearful glance at him.

"You bet it's gay. It's wonderful! Perfect. I showed the girl this picture of you"—he was fishing in his wallet—"and she said you were made for the hat."

"Jim," she said flatly, despairingly, "that picture was taken ten years ago." And suddenly she was crying. She snatched off the hat, held it up. "How can you pretend that I can wear this? It's chic and gay and youthful and I'm none of those things!"

"Why, Myra . . ." He was shocked, knocked off balance. "What are you talking about? Put the hat on, for goodness' sake."

"No, no, I can't!" Her voice was rising. "Jim, I've aged. Can't you see? Look at me!"

"Aged?" He was still nonplussed. "For heaven's sake, Myra. What a thing to say!" And then all at once he was laughing, as if the joke had gone far enough. He sat on the bed. "The lengths a woman will go to to spare a man's feelings. All right. You don't like the darned thing. Let's put it back in its box and forget it."

"Jim, I'm old," she insisted.

"Stop fishing, Myra," he said.

"I'm not fishing," she returned heatedly. "The lengths a man will go to to protect a woman's vanity!"

This time his mouth came open. "You've got your nerve saying a thing like that when I'm the one who's gotten fat and fortyish. You haven't changed a mite since the day I married you, and it isn't fair to keep talking about age when I haven't held up."

He actually meant it!

She sat on the bed beside him and took his hand. "You mean I haven't really changed for you?" she asked in the hushed voice of one confronted with a miracle.

"You know darned well you haven't."

"Jim," she said earnestly. "You've got it wrong. You're the one who hasn't changed."

"Really?" He smiled. "You mean for you?"

She looked around the room in a daze. Age, too, it seemed, was in the eye of the beholder. You went on seeing those you loved with the eyes that had first found them lovable. It was like possessing eternal youth, or a reasonable facsimile thereof. She tightened her hand on his. "I don't know what got into me," she said, smiling. "It's a beautiful hat—the loveliest one I've ever owned."

"Well, it seemed just right to me. You look like a million dollars in it." He turned to her affectionately and persuasively. "Come on. Let's try it on again."

She did feel a little bridelike as she went to the mirror this time. Love, as Hazel had put it, was wonderfully nearsighted.

42

Q. PATRICK

Town Blonde, Country Blonde

LIEUTENANT TRANT has always admitted to a weakness for attractive murderesses, and in this case there are two to choose from—both ornamental blondes. This story turns on an old fiction writer's trick—the insignificant clue which points to the culprit. But see with what style and spirit the story is dressed.

LIEUTENANT TRANT STUDIED the two blondes warily. They were both extravagantly beautiful; and one of them was a murderess.

There was no doubt at all about that.

One of them had just shot Joseph C. Cook III dead in his own living room with his own small automatic.

Trant should have been in his element. He had an unorthodox weakness for murderesses. But he was disconcerted, because he still hadn't the faintest notion which of them was guilty.

He'd already labeled them in his mind—these two discarded girl friends of the amatory Mr. Cook. The Town Blonde, Evelyn Darrell, was a fugitive from Hollywood with lush curves, red camellia mouth, champagne shoulder-length bob. Ingeborg Lindquist, Mr. Cook's Country Blonde, personally imported by yacht from Scandinavia, was athletic, burnt-sugar brown, gorgeously independent of make-up, stirring visions of summer sailboats and romance beneath a midnight sun.

It would have been a privilege, thought Trant, to be shot by either of them.

But which? They both carried gloves, so there'd be no fingerprints. And both had known where Cook kept his gun.

"It would help me a lot, ladies," he suggested sadly, "if one of you could seem just a tiny bit innocent."

"I do not kill him," said Country.

"Neither did I," said Town.

At seven, Lieutenant Trant and his Homicide Squad had reached Joseph Cook's Park Avenue apartment to find Dr. Bourne, the elevator boy and the Country Blonde.

Dr. Bourne said, "Mr. Cook came to my office on the ground floor at a quarter of six to have his sinuses washed out and a penicillin shot. I'm sure of the time because he was very fussy about his health and always punctual. He left at six-fifteen."

"And I brought him right up here," broke in the elevator boy. "Around six twenty-five Miss Darrell showed. Only stayed a couple of minutes, though. Just as I took her down again, this lady arrived." He nodded to the Country Blonde.

"I knock," announced Country. "There is no answer. I hear a moan. Quick I ring for the elevator boy. Together we go in. We find him dead."

"Shot!" whistled the boy.

Trant turned to him. "Know where Miss Darrell lives?"

"Right here in this building."

"Get her."

Later, the Medical Examiner turned from the body. "It's murder." He tossed Trant a paper. "And if you're looking for motives . . ."

Trant read a front-page headline: JOSEPH COOK, MILLIONAIRE PLAYBOY, ANNOUNCES SURPRISE ENGAGEMENT TO TEXAS HEIRESS.

"Surprise is right." The M.E. nodded from the Country Blonde to the Town Blonde who had just made a spectacular entrance. "Guess either of them might be pretty sore."

Trant now had the living room and the two blondes to himself. Nothing had been touched. On a coffee table, a single fluted cocktail glass, with the dregs of a martini, and a shaker, where melting ice still floated, stood in crystal transparency. Next to them, in a careless heap, lay strewn a diamond clip, two diamond rings and a diamond bracelet.

The Country Blonde was standing by the window, frostily ignoring the Town Blonde who lounged on a pink divan.

Trant wished they weren't quite so attractive. "Well, ladies, suppose we hear those interesting stories again. Miss Darrell?"

Town pouted the red camellia lips. "I read about Joe's engagement. Sure I was mad, hopping mad. And when I'm mad I do pixie things. What I did this time was to grab up all the junk the jerk had ever given me and come running over here." She pointed an elegant toe toward the heaped jewels. "When he let me in, I threw them straight in his sinus—and scrammed."

"You're sure he was alive when you left?"

"It doesn't kill you," drawled Town, "to get a load of diamonds in the kisser."

Trant picked up the diamond bracelet.

"And you, Miss Lindquist, arrived only a few seconds after Miss Darrell left?"

"Yes. I too read the paper and am much surprised. I telephone Mr. Cook and he asks me for a drink at six-thirty to explain, he say. I knock. He does not answer. Always he is punctual so I wait perhaps five minutes, thinking he come. Then I hear the moan. I call quick for the elevator boy and his key."

"Unshot when Miss Darrell left; shot before Miss Lindquist arrived." Trant shook his head. "One of you, I'm afraid, is telling a wicked, wicked lie."

And then, suddenly, as he let the bracelet drop on the coffee table, his self-assurance was back. Because he knew. Very calm now, he took out a cigarette case and offered it. Country accepted abstractedly. Town shook her head. "No minor vices."

Trant lit Country's cigarette and turned with an odd smile to Town. "No minor vices? Then perhaps—would you get up?" Town rose. "Here." Trant beckoned. "Nearer."

Dubiously she moved closer. Trant kissed her full on the mouth.

"Hey!" Town broke away, slapping hard.

But Trant, beaming, had turned to a tall mirror and was surveying his own reflected mouth, grotesquely smeared with camellia red.

"Thank you, Miss Darrell. A very pleasant way of getting a solution. And here it is." He moved to the coffee table and picked up the fluted cocktail glass from beside the shaker. "Someone drank this martini recently. Dregs in the glass; ice in the shaker. Now Miss Darrell sheds her lipstick as freely as she sheds her jewels. Witness my mouth."

He raised the glass to the light. "Not a trace of lipstick. She didn't have time to clean it. Takes too long to wipe lipstick off fluted glass." He paused. "But if Miss Lindquist had drunk it . . ."

Deftly he flicked the half-smoked cigarette from Country's hand and held it up. Its end was completely unstained. "See? No shedding."

"But I never come in here!"

"I know, Miss Lindquist, but perhaps that is the wicked, wicked lie. Perhaps you knocked and Mr. Cook let you in. Perhaps you asked him to mix you a martini to give yourself time to sneak out his gun. Perhaps, as he put the shaker down, you shot him. Perhaps you gulped the martini to fortify yourself—and then ran for the elevator boy."

"But is crazy. It is Mr. Cook who drinks the martini himself! He did. He did!"

"Oh, no, he didn't, he didn't." Trant looked at her ruefully. "Mr. Cook was fussy about his health. He would never have dreamed of drinking liquor just after a sinus treatment and a penicillin shot. And if he didn't drink it and Miss Darrell didn't . . ."

Trant sighed. He never really enjoyed out-maneuvering an attractive murderess.

"I can almost sympathize, Ingeborg," he murmured. "That long trip from Scandinavia—and then a Texas heiress. American dollars marrying American dollars. So inconsiderate!"

43

JEROME WEIDMAN

The Man Inside

NOVELS, travel books, screen plays and short stories
keep Mr. Weidman pretty well occupied. His books have
been on the best-seller lists, and continue to sell prodigiously
in paper-back reprints—remember "I Can Get It For You
Wholesale"? This story has a bigness of theme, and an
irony in the telling, which you'll find memorable.

"THIS IS THE only taxi in this town, and I own it," the fat
man said. "If you want me to take you, you'll have to wait,
like I say."

Neither his tone nor his glance was hostile. Nobody, however, not even a far less shrewd judge of his fellow men than
Pritchard prided himself on being, would have mistaken the
attitude of the fat man for friendship.

"All right," Pritchard said pleasantly. "Suit yourself."

The fat man walked across the wooden platform and disappeared into the tiny station. Pritchard set down his bag
and turned to look at the town of Haven in which, after an
overnight trip from New York, he had just alighted. There
was not much to see.

Pritchard had never before been in this part of Ohio but
he could tell, from books he had read and from newsreels he
had seen and from his recollections of the extensive traveling
he had done in his youth for the law firm of which he was
now a senior partner, that there was almost nothing visible
to the naked eye that might serve to distinguish Haven from
hundreds of other somnolent little towns—dozing, at this
very moment and in this same hot sunlight, across all of this
section of the country.

Somehow that simple fact, Haven's complete lack of physical distinction, gave to Pritchard's mission an added fillip of excitement. It was like being presented at court in a foreign land and finding, when you were ushered into the throne room, that the reigning monarch was wearing an old bathrobe and a pair of worn carpet slippers. The door of the tiny station opened. Pritchard turned back. The fat man, crossing the wooden platform, moved with a new spring in his step.

"Okay," he said. "Hop in."

Pritchard hopped in.

"I could have told you I was expected," he said carefully as he settled himself on the rear seat and put his feet up on the suitcase. "It would have saved you the trouble of making that phone call."

The taxi driver's startled glance, shooting up into the mirror over the windshield, caused Pritchard to chuckle inwardly. The accusation of arrogance, a vice Pritchard was certain he detested, would have left him stunned.

Yet it was true that he prided himself on his ability to read character. To it he attributed much of his success which, for a man of forty-one, was considerable. He knew that he owed his senior partnership not to his knowledge of the law, because he was impatient with the part of his profession that demanded the studious concentration of the library, but to his personality and brilliance as a trial lawyer.

And Pritchard knew that his brilliance as a trial lawyer was due to his skill in reading, at a glance and with accuracy, beneath the surface of men into the inner workings of their minds.

If it were not for this skill he would not be here now, in a battered taxi rolling out of Haven's single paved street into the dusty road that led up into the low hills north of the town, on his way to a triumph that had been denied, for almost a decade and a half, to the most distinguished members of his profession in all parts of the world.

Pritchard smiled, with a touch of smugness that he would

have denied indignantly if it had been called to his attention, at the taxi driver's glance in the windshield mirror.

"I didn't mean no disrespect, or anything by making that phone call," the fat man said sheepishly. "It's just that things have changed a lot since fifteen years ago, when the Judge first retired from that Supreme Court bench down there in Washington and he come back here to his home town to spend his last years." The taxi driver shook his head.

"Back there in those days, seemed like every time the train stopped here in Haven, it was some ambassador or a general or a governor, somebody like that, they'd get off and they'd say, 'Take me out to the Judge's house.' Why, once, I remember it was an Indian, not an Indian like we have here in this country.

"I mean one of these Indians with a towel around his head, what they call a turban. Some sort of professor of law or something from Bombay, he was, the way I recall. Came all the way from India, he did, just to ask the Judge some big law question." The taxi driver shook his head again. "The Judge is an old man now, though. Eighty-seven, his last birthday. He won't let nobody come to see him any more, no matter who. Why, the last twelve years or more, he won't even let those reporters come interview him and take his picture on his birthday. They keep running that old one they took on his seventy-second birthday, when he quit Washington.

"He's really retired, all right, Judge Cowper is, and us folks here in Haven, we like to respect his wishes. That's why I called the house from the station, just to make sure you were expected." The fat man's glance in the mirror over the windshield took on a hint of slyness.

"The way I figured," he said, "I figured it must be something mighty important that could get the Judge to break his rule and give somebody permission to come out here from New York to see him—that's the way I figured it."

"You may have figured it right," Pritchard said pleasantly. "Is this it?"

"Yes, sir," the driver said. "This is it."

He stopped the taxi. Pritchard took his bag, climbed out, and paid the driver. He paused for a moment to look up at the lovely white house with the tall columns.

It was such a perfect reproduction of what he had pictured in his mind as the place in which a man like Judge Cowper, whom he had never seen, would choose to spend his last years, that Pritchard found himself torn between a faint feeling of awe and a somewhat more pronounced feeling of self-congratulation on his perspicacity.

With a sense of mounting excitement, he climbed the steps and rang the bell. The door opened. A tall, spare, white-haired man waited for him to speak.

"Mr. Pritchard?"

"Yes," Pritchard said. "I . . ."

"Come in, sir. Come in. Here, let me take that."

"No, please," Pritchard said, swinging the bag out of his reach. The man fitted so much more perfectly than the house into the picture in Pritchard's mind that, for a moment and for the first time in his life, he felt both shy and awkward.

Greatness was a word used so often and so carelessly, even by people like Pritchard, who prided themselves on their precision in these matters, that to be faced with it was an unsettling experience. "I'll just leave it here," Pritchard said. "That is, if I may?"

"Of course. Won't you come into the library? I think you'll find it a bit cooler."

The voice was low and vibrant and, for a man of eighty-seven, it hummed with remarkable vitality. Pritchard, who had been a youngster in law school when Judge Cowper was nearing the end of his long career, could almost hear that extraordinary voice dictating those precise, measured, and yet deeply moving decisions that had added a new dimension to the humanities of the law.

Following that tall, lean, gentle and yet soldierly figure out of the hall and into the high, book-lined library, Pritchard's sense of triumph in his accomplishment, his success in gaining access to this cloistered sanctum from which all the rest of the world had been excluded for almost a decade and a half, gave way before a puzzling emotion that was entirely new to him.

"Now, if you will allow me to get you something to drink? You must be feeling a bit dusty after your long journey."

"Thanks very much, sir," Pritchard said. "I don't want anything, really." He paused, struggling with this entirely new emotion that assailed him. The old man, his beautifully shaped head inclined slightly to one side, seemed to be waiting. A shaft of sunlight from a shuttered window struck the high, white forehead, lighting up the serene face on which the skin was drawn so tightly across the delicate bones that the head seemed to have been hewn from marble. The handsome mouth, thin and ascetic but touched with the fullness of warmth, was parted in a small, gentle, inquiring smile. Pritchard hesitated.

He found himself calling on all his flashy skill as a trial lawyer to help him out of a predicament in which it had never occurred to him he would find himself, but that shrewd knowledge of character, that knack for reading the minds of his fellow men that had been responsible for his success, and had never before failed him, failed him now.

Pritchard knew that he was in the presence of a man who, because there was not even the hint of guile in him, was far shrewder than Pritchard. He knew that this was a man from whom he could conceal nothing because nothing to this man was a mystery, and all at once he recognized the new emotion inside himself for what it was: for the first time in his life, Pritchard felt a little ashamed of himself. "I'm afraid, sir," Pritchard said in a low voice, "I've come here under false pretenses."

The old man's thick white eyebrows went up a trifle. The faint smile around his lips changed just a little. "I beg your pardon?"

"I don't mean that I misrepresented or concealed anything in the series of letters in which I managed finally to persuade you to allow me to come out here to visit you," Pritchard said. "There *is* an important point involving a new interpretation of the doctrine of *res ipsa loquitur* that I've been working with in a recent case, a point that I know you'll be interested in, and that only you can clear up, because it deals with a rule laid down in two of your most famous decisions, a point that I still feel could not be covered adequately in correspondence. That's not what I mean, sir, by coming here under false pretenses. What I mean is . . ."

Pritchard paused again. It was hard to explain something he had not clearly understood until this moment, when he had found himself in the actual presence of this great interpreter of the human side of the law.

It would have been difficult for any man, and it was especially difficult for a man like Pritchard, to explain that it was not his passion for adding a new interpretation to the doctrine of *res ipsa loquitur* that had brought him here, but rather the desire to show to advantage among his colleagues as the one man who had been allowed to pierce the walls of Judge Cowper's retirement. Just the same, it was an explanation that had to be made.

He could see, in those deep, understanding eyes, in the beautifully shaped head, in the mouth at once relentlessly just and gently sympathetic, the lifetime devoted selflessly to work in dusty libraries for the purpose of extracting, from dead words impaled on paper, the warmth of living, the depths of meaning for all his fellows. This was a man who had made of his life a yardstick for other men. Pritchard felt the compulsion to try, however inadequately, to measure up.

"What I mean, sir, is that I owe you an apology," Pritchard said.

It was true that he had come to sit humbly at the feet of a great man, but, in the actual presence of greatness, he knew now that his humility had been dictated by selfish motives.

He had to make that clear. "I want you to understand, sir, that I . . ."

Out in the hall, the doorbell rang.

"If you will excuse me," the old man said. "I think the Judge will understand more clearly than I do."

"The Judge?" Pritchard said.

"Why, yes," the old man said. "That will be His Honor at the door now, sir. He's been out taking his constitutional." The thin ascetic lips parted in the small, warm smile. "I'm Robert, sir," the old man said. "His Honor's valet."

44

VICTOR CANNING

Never Trust a Lady

THE CRIME STORY may seem to be one of the easiest to write, when actually it is deceivingly difficult unless the author has a surprise in store. See how Victor Canning has given it freshness here: His burglar is an upright citizen who steals only to satisfy his love for rare books. And he is surprised at his crime by an intruder who might have confused even a man of tougher fibre.

EVERYONE WHO KNEW Horace Denby thought that he was an honest, decent, respectable citizen. In business he gave a square deal and a reasonable discount, and he was always good for a subscription to the choral society and the boys' club.

He was a bachelor, somewhere in the early fifties, and lived with a shriveled-up housekeeper who thought the world of him and worried over his health, especially his hay fever which he got badly during June and July.

Usually, however, he looked the picture of health, pink-faced, a little plump, a gentle spring to his walk and warm glow to his eyes. He was an ironmonger and locksmith and prosperous enough to employ two assistants. A decent, respectable citizen—but not entirely honest.

It was fifteen years since the prison chaplain—when Horace had served his first and only sentence for a jewel robbery—had tried to straighten Horace out. He liked Horace, everyone did, and wanted to help him, but Horace was unconcerned about his dishonesty. He was only concerned with handling it in such a way that it never got him into trouble again.

Horace had not liked prison. The food disagreed with him.

He didn't get enough exercise, and the books in the prison library were uninteresting and dog-eared. It was this last that turned Horace's stomach. For the reason he broke open a safe once a year was to have money to buy expensive first editions. He had a mania for rare books, but he bought them discreetly through an agent and financed his purchases with an annual robbery which—after his one disagreeable experience of prison—he planned very carefully indeed.

As he walked now in the bright July sunshine up the country lane that led to Shotover Grange he felt confident, for everything this year had, as usual, been meticulously planned. For two weeks—his annual holiday—he had been walking the country around the Grange and he knew everything about the house, its electrical wiring layout, its drainage, and the furnishings and disposition of all the rooms.

The two servants, Ethel and Mrs. Crimp, were alone in the house while the family were in London. This afternoon—strictly against orders—they had taken the local bus to go to the cinema. All this Horace knew, and he felt remarkably happy, though the scent from the new-cut hay made his nose tickle a little. The weight of the rucksack on his back was a pleasurable burden since it contained all his tools.

There was about £15,000 worth of jewels in the Grange safe —quite a reasonably safe safe, Horace thought, except for a man like himself—and broken down he would get about five thousand for the lot . . . Enough to make him happy for another year. There was an edition of Rabelais, printed at Lyons by Jean Martin in 1558, in first-class condition, which was coming up for sale this autumn and two illuminated French Books of Hours which he wanted.

He took the field path to the house and found the key to the kitchen door. Mrs. Crimp had left it suspended on a string inside the water tank. He wiped the key dry on his handkerchief, pulled on a pair of gloves and opened the door. Fingerprints for a man with a conviction were fatal. One of his rare fears was of walking in his sleep and suddenly waking to find himself working on a safe without gloves.

There was a spaniel curled up in Mrs. Crimp's chair in the kitchen. It stirred, gave him a panting laugh and thumped its stub of a tail.

"All right, Sherry . . ."

Horace scratched the dog's head as he passed. Dogs, he thought, were easy. Just give them their right name and a little love. A quotation from Piers Plowman came into his mind, "As courteous as a dog in a kitchen." One day, maybe, he would have enough money to collect the really old Anglo-Saxon stuff.

The safe was in the drawing room, concealed behind a not very good copy of a Rouault. Horace lifted it down and found himself regretting momentarily that he could not collect pictures. They took up so much room. Books were handier in a small house.

It was a nice drawing room, very elegant with Regency furniture and bright with sunshine that flooded in through windows that overlooked a formal rose garden. The air was full of the scent of a great bowl of roses on the table, and Horace felt his nose twitch and tickle. He gave a little sneeze and then slipped off his rucksack. He took his time, arranging his tools deliberately. It would be four hours before the servants returned.

As he had thought, the safe was not likely to give him any trouble. He had lived with locks and safes all his life. They were like human beings. They all had some weakness which could be exploited profitably. The burglar alarm running from the safe had been put in badly. He went into the hallway to disconnect it. Not that it mattered much for the bell could have rung its head off and no one would have heard, but he liked to be methodical. He came back and sneezed loudly as the rose scent hit him again.

People with valuable possessions, mused Horace, as he stood in front of the safe, deciding his method of attack, were so injudicious. Vanity was their downfall. There had been an illustrated article in a magazine of this house, giving a plan of the whole layout and pictures of the main rooms. The writer had even mentioned the picture masking the safe.

Horace shook his head sadly and turned back for his tools. As he bent down for them he found himself sneezing again. He straightened up, burying his face in his handkerchief. Then, as the fit passed, he heard a voice say quietly from the doorway, "What is it? A cold or hay fever?"

Horace turned round in surprise and, before he could stop himself, had said—"Hay fever," and then found himself sneezing again.

When he had finished the voice went on, "You can cure it with injections, you know—especially if you find out what your particular allergy is. I'd recommend you to do that if you're serious about your profession. I heard you from the top of the house just now."

It was a quiet, humorous voice, but not without a firmness which, given cause, could drive out the humor, and it came from a woman standing in the doorway with the spaniel, Sherry, fawning beside her. She was young, quite pretty and dressed in a red suit.

She walked across the room to the mantel-shelf and straightened one of the ornaments. The spaniel went after her, jumping up excitedly.

"Down, Sherry," she said. "Anyone would think I had been away a month." She turned and smiled at Horace, and went on, "However, it seems I've come back at the right moment. I didn't expect to meet a burglar."

There was a twinkle in her eyes that gave Horace some hope. If he handled things properly, he thought, he might yet avoid trouble. He gave her a tentative smile and said, "And I didn't expect to meet a householder."

She nodded. "I can see how annoying it is for you. What are you going to do?"

"My first thought was to run for it," Horace confessed.

"You could, of course. But I should telephone the police and give them your description. They'd pick you up very quickly."

Horace rubbed his chin and then said blandly, "I should,

of course, disconnect the telephone first and then—" he hesitated before going on, a broad smile on his face—"make sure that you'd be in no position to do anything for some time. A few hours grace would be enough."

For a moment she eyed him seriously.

"You'd use violence?"

Horace paused for a while before replying and then he said, "Perhaps I was trying to frighten you."

"You haven't succeeded."

Horace shrugged his shoulders. "It would be nicer," he said, "if you would forget the whole thing. Just let me pack up and go."

"Why should I?" The voice was suddenly sharp and humorless. "You were going to rob me. If I let you go you'll only rob someone else. Society must be protected against men like you."

Horace smiled faintly. "I must admit," he said, "that I'd never seen myself as a menace to society. I only steal from those who can afford it."

"A modern Robin Hood!" There was a sardonic twist to her mouth, but the good humor was back in her voice.

"That's it," Horace agreed eagerly. "I assure you I steal only in a good cause. And I do so hate the thought of prison."

She laughed outright, and Horace pressed his advantage. "Look, I know I've no right to ask anything from you . . . but I'm up against it. Let me go and I promise never to do this kind of thing again. I really mean it."

She was silent for a while, watching him closely. Then she said quietly, "You really are scared of going to prison, aren't you?"

She stood up abruptly and came over to him, shaking her head.

"The trouble with me," she said, "is that I always like the wrong kind of people." She picked up a silver box from the table beside her and took a cigarette. Horace, eager to please, seeing that she was disposed to help him, whipped off his gloves and brought out his lighter.

"You'll let me go?" He held the flame toward her.

"Yes—but only if you'll do something for me."

"Anything you say."

"I'm in trouble with my husband. Before we went away I promised to take my jewels to our London bank, but I left them here in the safe. I've got to wear them tonight at a party so I came down to fetch them, but like a fool—"

Horace waved a hand gallantly, smiling. "But like a woman you've forgotten the combination, haven't you?"

"Yes."

"A pleasure. Leave it to me and you shall have them within an hour. I shall make a mess of your safe, though."

"Don't bother about that. My husband won't be back here for a month, and I'll have it repaired."

And within an hour Horace had handed the jewels to her and hiked happily away.

For just two days Horace contemplated keeping his word to her. But on the morning of the third day the thought of the books he still wanted was too strong. He knew he would have to look for another safe.

He never got a chance. At lunch time he had visitors, a detective-inspector and a constable. Horace was arrested for the jewel robbery at Shotover Grange.

His fingerprints—for he had worked without gloves in his virtuous enthusiasm—were all over the safe, and no one believed his story of the wife of the owner of the house asking him to open the safe for her. The wife herself—a gray-haired, sharp-featured woman of sixty—testified that the tale was nonsense.

Horace is working out his sentence as assistant prison librarian. He often thinks of the charming, quick-witted young lady who was in the same profession as himself and who took advantage of him. It makes him really mad when anyone talks about honor among thieves.

45

CHARLES RAWLINGS

Flash of Lightning

CHARLES RAWLINGS lives in Maine where the sea is his great love. But in this story he has gone inland a bit to produce a story that has the authentic taste of New England soil. His short fiction is always deeply revealing, sharply observed. During the war he was a correspondent in the Pacific, and what he wrote about the First Cavalry Division is still remembered for this same fine quality of reality and of observation.

HE TURNED OFF the radio and stood in the dusk of his kitchen. He had made up his mind about the deer and his tendergreen beans. The deer was just like the chickadees and juncos he put suet out for in the winter.

Still no rain for Maine, the man on the radio had just said. The woods were drier than last year. Not a drop of rain for thirty-eight days. Tomorrow would be thirty-nine. It would be another Class-4 day, which was forestry talk, measuring fire danger. The radio had not said anything about what class day it was for farmers, or the way they were having to barn-feed pastured stock and haul water from the pond up into the fields, or how the wild things were starving.

He moved to the door and stood on his stoop. It was a small stoop on a small wizened salt-box house needing paint. He and the house looked somewhat alike. He was a small wizened man needing paint too. He lived alone, hiring out by the day weeding or taking wood away from the saw in cord-wood time when he needed cash money. He did not need much.

Down in the cove the summer people were having sport

swimming. They were in the cottages every summer now—
Connecticut people. This long dry spell was good weather for
them. Their big cars came and went and the rich people in
them waved, and he waved back when he could not get out
of it. When they had first come four years ago, he had visited
down at the cove the way a man should with his neighbors.
The first time he had seen them in swimming he had made
them laugh.

"There you was," he had said, "mustered in the water with
suits made a-puppuse."

When they laughed and asked him to say it over again so
they could remember it and said it was quaint, he had stayed
out his visit as if nothing had happened but he had never
gone back again. They were different people. What they
thought about, how they felt about anything he did not
know.

That was too bad, for it is a blessing to have close, friendly
neighbors.

He strolled out on the road and over the far shoulder and
down a steep lane to his lower garden. Only the quarter-acre
patch of tendergreen beans was left; a late planting after
peas. The peas and the tendergreens were the two crops the
drought had let him make. The peas were in his cellar now;
neat, green pint jars all in a row. He had planned on canning the tendergreens next week and thanking his lower
patch of ground for giving him enough to vegetable him
through the winter.

It was a strong little piece of ground that drained well
enough to make peas in the early season and yet, watered by
some underground spring, could also grow beans in drought,
in late August.

He stood in the edge of the bean patch and let the smell
of green life come up around him. It was like stepping into
a cooled room. The lower end was where the deer had eaten
last night. The stems stood white and stark in the starlight,
cropped as even as if a scythe had cut them. When he dis-

covered the damage at noon, coming down to cultivate, he had thought at first it had been two deer, so much had been eaten, but it had been only one—a big buck. He struck a match and squatted, studying the track again. A gigantic buck! He spread his fingers and measured the track. Two fingers lay easily in one cloven hoof, two more in the other with an inch gap between. The hoof had sunk so deeply that there were two round indentations in the soft ground where the dewclaws had touched.

"You're hungrier for them, I guess," he said softly to the track, "than I'll ever be."

Still squatting he looked up to the edge of the road. It was in clear view in the bright, starlit night, fifty yards away. The voices of the Connecticut people down the hill were loud and laughing.

"This is a reckless place," he warned as if the deer could hear him, "for a deer. You better be careful."

Just before dawn he stealthily closed the door behind him, stuck his finger in his mouth and held it aloft. Southeast drift. The air had a close hot feel, warmer than it had been in early evening.

Maybe the radio was wrong. There was a smell of rain in the air.

The parked automobile was closer than he had expected to find it. Lying awake he had heard it come up and slow to a stop, but he was used to the sound of louder, older cars and thought it had gone further down the road. It had a gray Connecticut license tag. He tried the door handle on the driver's side and felt it start, then let it turn back.

The little man stood for a long moment looking down the hill toward his bean patch, then moved to the lane and went down.

He headed for the spot where he would go if he wanted to kill the deer. He moved toward it without the slightest sound as he could because he had been stalking wild things since he was barely six. He had walked so many times where his shoes were silently pressing now that he knew where every twig and pebble and tuft of dry whispering grass lay. There was no one in the place when he got there.

For ten minutes he felt that the car was out of gas and whoever had left it had gone on down the road quietly to Johnson's who had a big barn and looked like people who would have gasoline. But at the end of that time he knew that was not so. Connecticut, whoever he was, had seen the deer yesterday morning and he was down thirty feet and a little off to the left sitting on a large granite boulder. He was only a darker smear in the darkness but he could feel him with his eyes.

There was no face or hands to him yet, but on the rock waiting to kill a deer in the tendergreens, there were only a few places where hands could be. If he watched in the right place he could see the gleam of rifle metal. He could see it now if the stars had not misted over.

Now was the time for him to say something. Yell out good and loud so it would scare the deer away if he was in the pitch and scare Connecticut, too. He debated what he would say. "Mister, you don't feed a deer and then kill it." . . . "The law's on, mister, you got no right." . . . "Those are my beans. The deer can . . ."

Why he debated what he would say instead of just shouting out something, he did not know. He was mad deep inside, resentful, but it would not boil up and make him reckless for some reason. He was not a reckless man. He had said the wrong thing once to these people.

The sound of the deer chomping began, a startling sound out of the stillness. Connecticut moved at the sound and he could see metal gleam. He had better be shouting if he was ever going to. Connecticut's weapon was coming up. He opened his mouth.

The crack of thunder aloft was so sudden and unexpected he did not know for sure whether he had shouted or not. The deer, head and neck reared stark against a streak of blood-red dawn, was staring at the sky. He was a magnificent buck. He was like some great noble Moses of the woods listening to God's word. Another sudden flash of light, a strange flash without thunder like the light that enveloped Moses came then. It turned the deer's eyes to red coals and made the tendergreens more verdant than they ever were in brightest sun. Loud-spoken came the voice of the Connecticut man.

"Beautiful!" he said. "Oh, you beautiful!"

The buck swung as if the exultant voice was a stinging whip and in two great bounds he was away.

The little man, because he was higher up the hill, had only to wait for the other to come to him. He stepped in beside him on the lane. The man made one quick dart of his eyes to show surprise and then smiled. He was a big sandy man heavily freckled. A camera hung from his neck.

"You saw him, too?" he said. "What a shot! Say . . ." he stopped in the path. "I figured I'd have to get up early to beat you down there with your gun, saving your beans. Where's your gun?"

The little man shook his head.

"Well, what do you think of that!" the big man said. "Say —I'm going to give you an enlargement—this big. You got a place to hang a picture that big? I'll put it in a bleached cedar frame. We'll call it—what'll we call it? 'The Coming Rain.' "

"Across from the stove, there's a place," the little man said. "There's some coffee on the stove. Come in and see."

"My camera case is in the car," the big man said. "I'd better run up my windows. It's going to rain. I'll be right in."

46

CHARLES CARVER

Twenty Floors Up

DOUBLE TALK seems an improbable basis for a short-short story, where everything has to be crystal clear, but it works out as a pretty useful ingredient here in a frightening situation. Mr. Carver concentrates on the short ones with notable success. His stories are always distinctive, with a rather special flair for unusual backgrounds and situations to commend them.

I GUESS THAT'S WHY the elevator doors at radio studios are automatic—to keep actors like Jay Byrd and me, who have wound up as a television flop, from ending it all by just jumping down the shaft.

I should explain here that Jay Byrd and I are a double-talk team on the radio. We do our best to leave our listeners in a state of helpless confusion. It works this way: The Jay mangles the syllables. I play the bewildered pal. Sort of the poor man's Abbott and Costello. We had been rocking along at the local radio station twice a week with our two-man forum on various matters.

For instance, I would ask him about the record of the present Congress, and Jay might answer, with a little throb in his voice, "Why, yes, the record strikes me as well under alimony and pepsic every single bill in contraction of the long-term pull. Galloping the mandature from the fram block, that is. And I certainly think they are!"

Funny, but we got to be quite a habit with a dozen or so listeners. They said we made better sense than most.

Maybe the whole idea of getting our act televised was dreamy, but we thought it was worth a try. Never let well

enough alone, that's our motto. So we decided to make a stab
at video, and that's how we learned about Mr. Reagan, pro-
gram director for television station WLBN. It seemed to us
he had practiced all his life just to keep people from seeing
him. But we made it. After three long months and a whole
ball of string pulling, we got a test.

And we flopped. Period.

"Fellows," Mr. Reagan said after the test, "this television
is still just a baby."

"You mean we wait till it grows up?"

He looked pained. Came the pursed lips and troubled eye.
"No, not exactly. What I mean is we're working hard to bring
the baby up right. Often an idea that clicks for radio just
won't do for video."

"Make baby sick, huh?" What did I have to lose? He had
written us off.

He smiled thinly. "We simply want to start it off well,
that's all. We want to give it all the fresh appeal we can." He
cleared his throat. "A routine like yours is fine—but only for
listening. Television requires something more substantial,
some plot and movement." I must have looked stupid. "Your
routine needs form," he explained carefully. "It needs a
base." He sounded so earnest that I almost forgot he was no
doubt dishing out Treatment C for the fiftieth time that
week. "Base and form," I repeated, looking owlishly at the
Jay. "We'll remember, Mr. Reagan."

"Fine," he said. "If you work up anything, come back. I'll
be right here."

So here we stood, waiting for the elevator, surrounded by
a crowd of tourists who kept staring at what was left of our
television make-up. I tried to look like an off-duty character
actor, but my heart wasn't in it.

Mr. Reagan had let us down as gently as he could, but I
figured it would take a lot more than just sharpening the
routine to get our act into the best bars. The pursed lips and
troubled eye treatment he gave us after the tryout was en-

couraging enough to keep Jay hoping. However, I have played straight man long enough to recognize such comedy.

So here we were outward bound, you might say. Jay was muttering thoughtfully to himself in his private language. I turned to him. "What kind of sharpening do you suggest, Mr. Bones?"

"We gotta get in some base," he replied, and murmured in a sheer flight of double-talk, "Antlers is the domestic if we want to culvert the thing. It's an upward pagoda."

"It sure is, boy." I nudged him sharply. "Act happy. Here comes the professor."

Mr. Reagan joined our group waiting for the elevator. He nodded pleasantly enough to Jay and me, and we all stood silently, thinking our own thoughts. Mine were bitter. If we hadn't worked so hard to get the test and counted so heavily on it, Reagan's evasiveness wouldn't have cut so deep. But I hated to see three solid months of hope put casually away with that pious line about the infant industry.

"Mr. Reagan," I said softly, "could you explain more specifically what you meant about the routine needing a base?" I was hoping he had left executive tact back in his office and would give us a blunt verdict. I should have known better.

"Your act doesn't lead anywhere," he said gravely. "It isn't well rounded. No nub or gimmick. Work in some action and story."

He sounded just like the Jay. Then the elevator doors slid open and the group got in. It was an express to the ground floor, so I knew Reagan's lecture was about over. But at the same time I had a feeling that he was making sense, and that if I dug around hard enough I might discover the key. I was sorry I hadn't listened sooner. We started down. Thirty floors to go. Twenty-nine—twenty-eight—faster and faster —twenty-five . . .

"Mr. Reagan, could we maybe . . ." Suddenly there was a trembling underfoot, like we were standing on Jello. The car

shuddered to a stop around the twentieth floor, and something just overhead gave a sickening little sigh. Everyone
froze. For a split second not a single heart beat in that elevator. No one blinked or drew a breath. We just hung there.

The elevator girl pushed a red button over and over, but
nothing happened. Panic crouched among us, ready to claw
and scream with ten white faces and twenty hysterical hands.

There was a large woman near me. She had a feather in
her hat. She stood rigid as stone, mouth clamped tight, while
drops of water glistened on her forehead. The elevator girl
began jabbing the button with her fist.

The floor gave—not more than an inch—but the drop
burned the nerves like a charge of electricity. The bulky
woman opened her mouth wide to cry out. Everyone tensed
for the brutal senseless struggle. We were frantic animals
masquerading as human beings.

"Relax, folks," Jay Byrd's voice filled the cage. "That jolt
was only the ratchets gripping the funicular bar. It's okay,
now."

The big woman's mouth half closed. She exhaled a little.
It sounded like a whimper.

"And if the ratchets don't link, they've got six junction
cogs at each loop, plus an extra spandrel. Those spandrels
sure do the business, all right." He nudged me.

"You've been an inspector for some time now, haven't
you?" I said shakily. But it was what he wanted.

"Eleven years," he replied firmly. "And it's just this kind
of butterick that bruffles the customers. Why only yesterday
a skeptible shackle jammed across the street. Naturally the
spandrel took care of it. They're automatic."

Jay was superb. Pretty soon the girl was once more push-
ing the controls calmly, the whimpering woman was mop-
ping her face, and the horrible feeling of hysteria was lifted.

Then we heard a gentle click, and as the elevator moved
downward again, the Jay concluded with simple dignity,
"You see, now it's back on pemmican control."

At the ground floor we got out, feeling a trifle lightheaded. My knees were spongy and I was making the kind of resolutions customarily reserved for New Year's Day. "There is a small bar near here," I suggested.

Someone tapped my shoulder. It was Reagan's ghost. "May I join you?"

We found a handy place and ordered doubles. They brought the color back to our cheeks.

"I didn't get to answer your question back there," explained Reagan, "as fully as I should have." He reordered for all three.

"The gimmick might be, now that I think about it, to have your double-talk session actually solve a situation."

"You mean, like in an elevator, maybe?"

He nodded. "It would give your routine a base, a plot with action."

I looked speechlessly at the Jay. For once I could think of no line to feed him. But he did all right.

"I understand," he said quietly. "We glue the situation maybe once a week and standard the action. Baby might like us, huh?"

"Precisely," said Mr. Reagan.

47

ERIC HATCH

Channel 10

THE SUPERNATURAL is something that isn't often mixed up with television, but it comes in here—on channel 10. Mr. Hatch is an old hand at fiction—novels, serials, short stories. He is an old Hollywood and a new television hand, too. From the Hollywood days, you surely remember "My Man Godfrey." That was only one of his successes.

NOW, LATE AT night, in the dangerous privacy of their bedroom, the quarrel was almost over. It could only have taken place between a man and a woman who for a long time had loved each other with deep sincerity and growing misunderstanding. They were willing now, after endless, acrid hours, to let it be over because each of them felt in their hurt that their marriage was over. It was just a question of ending it— like ending a play.

Either one of them might, in the next moment, say the words admitting it and so bring on the end. The husband— Don Harding, who was a writer and the more articulate, finally spoke them. Sitting upright in the big four-poster bed, he looked at his pretty wife with her sleek midnight hair, and in his bitterness, wondered for a moment how he could ever have found her beautiful.

"It's a shame, Anne—it was beautiful—for so long—us, I mean . . ." He paused and looked closely at his wife who was sitting very still and pale, her yellow silk negligee wrapped close about her.

Anne saw a mistiness dim the hardness in his eyes for a second.

Then the inevitable words of release. "It's perfectly obvious that you can't stand living here with me." Don made the sighing sound of a man lifting a heavy weight. "I think you'd better go to Boston—and visit your mother—pay her a long visit."

Anne got up off the bed, moved to take a cigarette from the many-mirrored dressing table, so that looking at her in the mirrors he saw not only one wife but many of them. The mirrors magnified the unhappiness in her face until he thought that no one woman could be as unhappy as she seemed.

He considered saying this, but it was too late. It was a cold war now. She lighted the cigarette and turned to him.

"I think your suggestion is very good, Don," she said with deadly politeness. "Sally-Anne and I will leave for Mother's tomorrow morning."

She started for the guest room, but as she passed the bed, he caught her wrist, held it so tightly it hurt.

"No," he said, "Sally-Anne stays here. Out in the country where it's healthy—where she belongs." He took a deep breath. "It won't hurt her to be alone with me—she doesn't think I'm a heel because I let a lot of bills pile up while I got going again after the war. She doesn't try to make me think I'm a failure by practicing petty economies.

"She doesn't think I'm a heel because I spent a thousand bucks of my advance on a television set—because I'm working so damn hard to finish the book in a hurry I've got to have some escape."

He waited a moment. "But then, of course," he said softly, "*she*'s only seven years old—and she doesn't know that maybe she ought to feel trapped and unhappy—and—dominated."

He released her hand and she stood for a second, rubbing the red bracelet of bruised skin on her wrist. Tears stood in her eyes.

"Good-by, Don," she said. "I—I won't be seeing you before I leave in the morning. Mother's lawyer can talk to you about Sally-Anne and—and about . . ." She hesitated, even now the word that in some homes is part of everyday language but in this home had always been unthought of, stuck. She made an effort. "About a divorce. Good-by, Don."

"Good night, Anne."

Anne had to force herself to walk through the bedroom door into the hall, to perform the simple yet frighteningly symbolic act of closing the door after her. She started into the guest room, but that seemed symbolic too.

"I guess I'm pretty shaken," she murmured. "I guess I'll go downstairs and fix a drink or something." She looked at the closed bedroom door. "How absurd!" she thought aloud. "Don's in there—sitting bolt upright with his face twisted and tortured looking, the way I've seen him look a thousand times when he was fighting a story."

She counted quickly, "I've seen him sitting up in bed more than a thousand—eight times three hundred and sixty-five—that's two thousand nine hundred and twenty times—less exactly four hundred and fifty while he was away in the war—that's two thousand four hundred and seventy times we've—and now I'll never again—I've said *good-by* to him! It's . . ."

For a second Anne thought of going back into the room. Then she said, "No! I'd be crawling back—like—a—a tame *hausfrau*—the classic, domestic wife. I wouldn't ever have any individuality again. There'd be nothing—absolutely *nothing* left of me! He had no right to buy that thing when we owe so much. . . . Why should *he* have to have an escape? *I* don't."

Then, holding her head proudly, she went into the living room and sat down on the sofa. Across from her, its blank white screen staring at her like a blind eye, stood the television set. The *casus belli* that had wrecked her marriage . . . She glared at it.

"I hate you," she said to it.

It stared back at her, unwinking. She crossed to it, tried to turn it away, but it was too heavy. Then suddenly exasperated, she cried:

"All right! Play something if you like—but stop sitting there leering at me!"

One after the other she began turning the row of knobs under the screen. Don had talked about channels—channel two, channel five. She found a knob that had numbers on it, at random selected channel ten. The screen lighted up, became filled with white lines racing across it so it looked less like an eye and more like a football field.

She turned more knobs and the lines disappeared, dissolving into millions of swirling dots of light and shadow that looked as if at any second they might evolve into a picture, but couldn't quite make it. A low humming sound came from the loudspeaker.

She went back to the sofa, took up her drink and stared at the flashing, whirling dots. It had the fascination of watching fast water running in a stream, or waves breaking. She began to feel calmer and then, gradually, to stop feeling entirely, as though she were under an anesthetic.

As she watched, the dots seemed to tremble, then to take form as a misty, shadowy picture emerged and the humming noise became music—organ music.

Anne stared at the picture. She saw, gradually, hazily emerging, the inside of a church crowded with people and a young man and a girl in a bridal gown with a long veil, standing together at the altar and, facing them, a minister. The minister was white-haired and reminded her vaguely of her father and vaguely of some religious portrait she had seen somewhere. The organ music faded . . .

"Why!" she cried. "This must be one of those bride-and-groom programs like they have on the radio where for being married on the air the bride gets six refrigerators, four convertibles, a fitted bag and a wedding trip—all for free!"

She smiled, amused, then the smile went away and her face

grew thoughtful as the words of the service came to her—
words—promises—that she herself had spoken—eight years
ago.

"To love, honor and obey—I, Anne—take thee, Donald—
to cherish—in sickness and in health—for richer, for
poorer."

That one struck home. She winced. Those were promises
she had made—to Don and to God, and now . . . The service
went on, the bride and groom kneeled, the minister prayed,
then he looked up and suddenly his head filled the screen—
seemed to fill the whole room—staring directly at her.

"Those whom God hath joined together"—the music of
his voice was solemn, inspiring music—"let no man put
asunder!"

The screen went dark, brightened again with meaningless
dots and flashes. Thoughtfully, she crossed the room and
turned off the switch, stood for a little, leaning on the cabinet.

Presently, in a strangely wondering way, the strength of
the minister's words came through to her.

Then she smiled. "I can't lose anything by trying," she
said. "The other way I can lose—I can lose . . ."

Her voice trailed off, as on fast, light steps, she hurried up
the stairs and into the now darkened bedroom. She bent over
her husband.

"Don?" she whispered. "Don, darling?" He stirred, and she
knew he was awake. "Don, it's been awful for you, hasn't it,
awful—working so hard to pay off all those debts and finish
your book and me misunderstanding you. Thinking you
were bolstering your beaten-up self respect by ordering me
around and going out and buying something expensive when
all the time you really just wanted me to understand how
hard things were for you. And you wanted something—somebody—to play with. Oh—Don—Don, I do love you so!"

His arms reached up around her and a great happiness that
was different from anything she had ever felt, surged over

her body. A long time later, speaking aloud, but to herself, really, she said, "The man was right—he was absolutely right."

"What man?"

"The minister on the television, darling. While I was downstairs, I watched it and saw one of those wedding programs—the minister was wonderful—he looked right at me and said about those whom God has joined together. It—it changed my mind about—a lot of things."

She heard his soft, amused laugh.

"Television at this hour of the night, Anne? What channel did you have it on?"

"Why, channel ten. It was wonderful—pictures of flowers and things and a church and . . ." She broke off, even in the darkness she could feel him staring at her, feel a queer, almost eerie, tenseness in the room. "Don—what is it?"

"Anne," he said slowly, "there is no station on channel ten in this area. There's nothing—nothing at all."

She heard his voice, now awed, trembling. "You must have tuned in on—Anne—all the time you were gone I was—you believe in God, don't you?"

He broke off. She nodded. They sat for a moment, hand in hand, silent in the warm darkness, thinking.

Then she said softly, "Of course, Don, staring at all those spots I could have sort of hypnotized myself."

"Yes," he said. "You could have. That *could* be the answer."

But neither of them in that enlightened moment of new closeness, believed for an instant that it was.

48

WILLIAM BRANDON

A Party to Blackmail

THE VARIETY an author displays in his writing is the
quality which keeps him fresh. Compare this story with
"College Queen," earlier in this collection, and you will see
what we mean. Mr. Brandon spends a quarter of his time
writing what he calls experiments—stuff he doesn't expect
to sell. We wouldn't call this an experiment—just a good,
fresh story with nice style in the writing.

MY FRIEND, IRELAND, pointed with his thumb to a lean, dark
man at the end of the bar who looked like a cavalry colonel
in mufti.

He said, "His name is Findlay Vindabel. He was mixed up
in the Glinka Diary blackmail case a few years ago."

Ireland is a private detective, and such things are his business. I said, "The *what* blackmail case? I never heard of it."

"Glinka. It wasn't in the papers till the crack-up came.
You may have missed the connection when it finally broke.
Vindabel was influential in keeping it out of the news. He's
a pretty important and a pretty shrewd lawyer."

"Who was Glinka?"

"Madame Glinka, an astrologer. She had wealthy clients
who told her various things about their lives that they should
have kept to themselves. She put all these stories down in a
journal, or diary. Later the diary was lost or stolen, and
blackmail of some of her clients followed after."

"Madame Glinka was behind the blackmail herself?"

"No, she had an air-tight alibi: she died. Several of Vindabel's old friends and clients were victimized by the black-

261

mailer, so he knew about it, but as I say, he never let the story get out and he promised his friends he'd be on the alert for any information that might help reveal the blackmailer's identity."

We ordered another Martini, and Ireland told me the story. It seems that Vindabel was a curious sort in those days. He was about forty then but he gave the impression of being older. He behaved like a lawyer of the old school. That is to say, he was didactic, opinionated, cantankerous, and a brass-bound, rock-ribbed conservative. It was against the rules in this firm for any young lawyer, on the hottest days to work at his desk without his coat.

But on one night a week, on Monday night, when his chess club met, Vindabel underwent a kind of transmutation. It wasn't anything visible. Outwardly he was the same iron mask at the chess board that he was in his office downtown. But in the style of chess he played, Vindabel completely reversed his personality. His game, instead of being a solid conventional, unbending product similar to what seemed to be the man himself, was like a wild gypsy dance, abandoned to radical innovations and daring hyper-modernism, brilliant with wit. Rather than follow a dull, plodding, familiar line of play Vindabel preferred to lose the game, although he seldom did. He was the champion of his chess club year after year.

The runner-up at the club, the man who would have been champion if he could have beaten Vindabel, was Dr. Timothy Shay. He taught academic psychology at the University but he was independently well to do, and was something of a man about town.

In the course of one of the annual club championship tournaments, Dr. Shay got an inspiration. If he couldn't beat Vindabel at chess, maybe he could defeat him with psychology. You've got to understand a chess player to realize how desperately Dr. Shay wanted to whip Vindabel and win that championship. A second-best game of chess is a terrible affliction. Indeed—acutely painful. Dr. Shay explained his idea to a friend of his, a woman, an actress. She was a rather good actress, and her name was Cathy Jordan.

Dr. Shay hoped to marry her. He said that as a psychologist he thought the striking difference between Vindabel himself and the style of chess he played indicated something in Vindabel's past that had been violently repressed and only came to the surface in his game. Dr. Shay thought it could have been some sort of romantic experience, years before. He knew Vindabel had never married.

Cathy Jordan was no psychologist, but she said she thought it might only mean the man was shy, and the real warmth of his nature came out in his chess.

But Dr. Shay was convinced the anomaly indicated something more concrete. Concrete enough, he said, that if it was well enough shaken up it would crack Vindabel's chess game right down the middle.

He asked Cathy Jordan to help him in an experiment. On the next Monday evening, when he was scheduled to play Vindabel the game that would decide the club championship, Cathy was to meet Vindabel accidentally on the sidewalk as he entered the club and speak to him, as if she were an old friend. She was to say, "Why, Jasper! Hello!" Dr. Shay had learned that Findlay Vindabel's first name had originally been Jasper.

He had completely dropped the name, not even retained the initial, and Dr. Shay thought that was significant too.

It seemed to Cathy Jordan that anyone might reasonably drop the first name of Jasper, and Findlay Vindabel was certainly enough name in itself without making it J. Findlay Vindabel, but Dr. Shay succeeded in interesting her in wondering what might happen, so she went along with the experiment.

Only someone who had known Vindabel very well indeed would know him by the name of Jasper, Dr. Shay reasoned, and the use of the name by an attractive woman whom he couldn't place would shock him into a search of his memories, and his forgotten past would rise up and overwhelm him during the game of chess, and Dr. Shay would win.

Cathy thought Vindabel would be somewhat embarrassed at not being able to recognize her, but would forget the incident in five minutes.

On the night of the game the experiment went as planned. Cathy spoke to Vindabel, called him Jasper, gave him both her hands like an old friend, and talked to him for a while, and then walked on. Vindabel was thoroughly startled, and as embarrassed as Cathy had predicted. When he came in to the chess game he was preoccupied and lost his queen in seven moves and resigned. Dr. Shay won the championship.

"So," I said, as Ireland paused, "another triumph for science. But what does all this have to do with the Glinka blackmail case?" I added.

"Well, after Cathy Jordan spoke to him, Vindabel called his chauffeur and told him to follow her. After the game he was able to find her again, and she eventually told him the whole story of the experiment. The police searched Dr. Shay's apartment that night and found the Glinka diary in a wall safe.

"Dr. Shay was convicted of blackmail and sent up the stream for a lengthy jolt, where incidentally, he still is."

"You mean Cathy Jordan was his accomplice, and Vindabel somehow recognized her as being involved in the case?"

"She didn't know anything about Dr. Shay's extra-curricular activities in blackmail. It was the Jasper that tipped Vindabel off.

"The stuff in the Glinka diary concerned a set of wealthy people, most of whom had known each other for years, and in that group Vindabel had been known since a child as Jasper. He knew he was mentioned in the diary as Jasper, although there didn't happen to be anything in his own strict background that could make him blackmail bait.

"However, his name of Jasper was absolutely unknown out-side the small circle of his closest friends. When Cathy Jordan explained about Dr. Shay's experiment Vindabel realized that Dr. Shay must have got the name from the Glinka diary. It turned out that Dr. Shay had been a silent partner of Madame Glinka's.

"That was why Madame had been successful as an astrolo-ger and a consultant on personal problems: she had had a trained psychologist helping her. When she died, Dr. Shay had come into possession of her confidential journal, that named names, and rich names, too rich for Dr. Shay to resist the temptation of blackmail."

I said:

"Vindabel was a fast man with a deduction, to connect Cathy Jordan's Jasper with the Glinka diary while she was saying hello to him."

"Not that fast," Ireland said. "His notion about Dr. Shay and the Glinka diary came later. He told us at the Bureau that at first he only wanted to find her again because he was curious as to who she was . . . There she is now," Ireland said. "She's a very beautiful woman."

I looked. She was. Vindabel's face lighted up when she met him at the bar. She put her arm through his and they went away together.

Ireland said, "They were married later."

I said, "What happened to his chess?"

"He plays bridge now. Not too well, but a solid game."

49

OSCAR SCHISGALL

Eyes in the Dark

THE SHORT-SHORT STORY is at its best when it deals with a theme in which the revelation of some profound truth is its basic theme. That is the case here. There is a tingling sense of an experience shared, of a surprising realization that through a strange set of circumstances a man can actually *see* with the eyes of the blind.

WHEN I GOT off the train at Walford Junction I hunched against wind and downpour and ran with my grip for the shelter of the station. In the darkness I almost fell over somebody's baggage. Not a single electric bulb was lit anywhere, and when I finally pushed into the door I heard a man call, "Whole town's been without lights since the hurricane hit last night!" A couple of obliging taxis focused their headlights on the station windows, and that helped.

I found a phone booth with a directory, and thumbed through it with the aid of a match until I found John Larcher's number. Presently a woman's voice answered—a pleasant voice, easy and friendly. I said, "This is George Willcox. I . . ."

"*George!*" You could hear delight leap into her tones. "Oh, at last! This is Irene. We got your telegram—expected you *long* ago . . ."

"Pulled in four hours late," I said. "Now I'm here, at the station, with exactly fifty minutes between trains. But if it's all right, I'd like to hop a cab and . . ."

"Of course it's all right! You come right along. I've been *so* eager to know you!"

266

Two minutes later I was in a taxi, riding out toward River Road. In a way this was a mission—a pledge I'd made to myself and to my wife. I *had* to see John Larcher and Irene. But there were other things to remember, too. "I've got to catch that nine o'clock they make up here," I said to the driver. "Can you pick me up in time?"

He nodded, and I settled back to find my breath. In the blackness the rain thrashed as hard as ever. A few houses showed candlelight, but most were in complete darkness. The driver said you couldn't buy a candle in Walford Junction for love or money.

The anticipation of seeing John again, of meeting his wife, of exploring the strange world in which these two lived, kept me tense. I had promised Babs, my own wife, a full report. Babs and I had been working in my paper's London office that time we got the news of the Larcher wedding almost a year ago. Since then we'd wondered a thousand times what kind of girl John had married. In his letters he always spoke of her as being "beautiful," "lovely," "gracious"—using the words the way other men use them, as though he could actually *see* her beauty and graciousness.

And that was what awed us, for John Larcher was blind.

He'd lost his sight during the war, when an ammo depot blew up under German strafing. And he hadn't met Irene until two years later, when he'd gone out to Kansas to buy his little weekly paper. So we knew he had never *seen* his wife. She was part of the eternal darkness that surrounded him. Yet he spoke happily and with confidence of her beauty. How could he know? . . .

"Here we are," the driver said. "I'll honk, quarter of nine."

When I ran up a path through the rain, John Larcher himself opened the house door. I stood there for just a moment with the beam from the taxi's headlights shining past me into the hall. Then I laughed a greeting.

We banged each other's shoulders and pumped hands in

sheer joy. We were like kids. He called me an old bum, and
I called him a son-of-a-gun, and for a while we were back in
the old days of the Paris *Herald* where the two of us had
spent seven years together. Then John shut the door, took
my coat, and hung it on a hook. He led me by the arm
through the darkness, quickly, so that I realized, with a pang,
how accustomed he was to walking in blackness. It was I who
was blind here, not he. He stopped me at a chair over which
I might have stumbled.

I couldn't see Irene when she came into the room, but I
heard her—heard her step, the rustle of her clothes, caught
a faint flower scent. Our fumbling hands found each other,
and she squeezed mine in welcome.

"I've looked forward so long to meeting you, George!" she
said. "You've no idea how often John's bragged about you
and Babs." She had a lovely voice, rich and friendly.

"Meeting you," I answered, "was the highlight I'd planned
for myself on this trip. John's letters have been pretty lyri-
cal."

She laughed—warmhearted laughter. I strained in the
darkness to see her, moving my head from side to side; but
I could make out only a blur.

"Those were the letters John wouldn't dictate to *me*," she
said. And then she added in apology, "I wish I could give you
a light, George. But I used up our last candle in the kitchen.
. . . John said you're a bourbon-and-soda man. There's one
on the end table to the right of this chair."

So we all sat down in darkness. I found my drink, and for
a while we talked of things that had to be said. I told them
how I was on my way to interview the parents of a potential
presidential candidate; how Babs was in New York, with a
few weeks more to wait for our baby. And all the time, peering into blackness, I kept wondering about Irene, wondering
how much I could see if I lit a match. I wanted a cigarette
and spoke of my desire as casually as I could. I fumbled and
found a pack in my left trouser pocket. Hopefully I asked

Irene if she'd like a cigarette. She refused pleasantly, and
though I strained and tried I couldn't see her face at all as
I lit my own cigarette. . . .

John told me about his paper. "It took all my back pay
and everything I could borrow," he said. "But now it's beginning to pay off. It's really Irene who runs it."

"Nonsense," she said with affectionate reproof. "You *are*
the paper, darling."

"She's my eyes," he said with a chuckle, "I couldn't run it
without eyes."

He didn't speak of his blindness as if it were tragic, and
neither did she. They seemed to accept it without bitterness,
as part of their life. I gathered that Irene had been working
for the *Walford Weekly Eagle* when he bought it, and she
had stayed on.

"Of course," she said with her soft laugh, "I fell in love
with my boss from the start."

From the way their voices blended it seemed to me she
must be sitting on the arm of John's chair. I bent forward,
almost squinting, but it didn't do any good.

She told me how they worked, how eager John was to keep
up with the happenings of the world. "We get half a dozen
big-city papers every day," she said, "and I read them all to
him. And, of course, he has the radio, too. We save the evenings for books and magazines. In the afternoons he does his
dictation, and I type most of it. You ought to read his edi-
torials, George—they're really *something*. He's made Walford Junction world-conscious. I feel prouder week by week."

We talked for a half hour, and as Irene went on, I was
keenly aware of her warmth, her friendliness, her deep affection for John. These things you could *hear*. Somehow I had
the impression of a generous woman; one who had a profound understanding of her husband. I liked that voice. I
liked its confidence and contentment, as though he were
warmed by her pride in him. . . .

The taxi sounded its horn outside long before I was ready. A quarter of nine . . .

We all got up. "You've simply got to come again, George," Irene said. "And soon. You and Babs and the baby. We'll have a play-pen ready. Any time you can . . ."

An hour later, on the train, I wrote Babs a letter. I set the words down quickly, letting them flow as they came. Without hesitation, almost without thinking, I had written, "Darling, I've just visited Irene and John, and I must tell you he didn't exaggerate a bit. I found her a lovely and gracious person . . ." I went on describing her vividly as a person with beauty and charm.

Suddenly I stopped. I realized I'd seen her only through her voice, and as John saw her—a presence in the darkness. Yet I knew that I, too, had *seen* her beauty.

50

LESLIE GORDON BARNARD

Four Men and a Box

WHAT PRICELESS WEALTH did these men carry
through the jungle in the box? Day after terrible day in the
green hell, they toiled on toward the coast. And their
reward? Mr. Barnard, a Canadian author with a fine sense
of the dramatic, has something unexpected to provide. It
is a climax, too, to remember as the last of these fifty short-
short stories from This Week.

THEY CAME FROM the primordial jungle, four gaunt speci-
mens of the human race, walking as men might walk in their
sleep, or before a taskmaster whose lash drives them on to the
limit of their endurance. Their beards were matted, their
skin full of sores, and the leeches had sucked their blood
day and night.

They hated each other with the hatred of men bound by a
duty, confined by the green walls of a jungle whose paths
led through hell and was as eternity. They hated still more,
as time went on, the thing they carried; but they bore it as
if it were an ark of the covenant and their God was a jealous
God.

"We got to get Markgraff's stuff through," they said. "He
was a good guy. We promised him."

Of the reward at the journey's end they said nothing; but
each man mumbled of it in his own mind, in his own way.

They had gone with Markgraff into his green hell because
he paid them well in advance. Now he was dead and they
were living. Death had struck him down—some swift tropical
disease had ended this geologic madness of his.

They would have understood the whole thing better if his

quest had been for gold. But Markgraff had said, smiling: "There are substances which science has found to be more precious than gold." At the end they thought Markgraff had failed, that all he'd found in the jungle was Death. But it seemed otherwise; the box he gave them to take back was heavy. He'd made it himself, roughly hewn, and with the secrecy of the scientist he'd packed and sealed it when he knew that he, himself, was doomed.

"It will take four of you to tote it—two at a time," Markgraff had told them.

"There are four of us," said Barry, the student.

"You'll have to spell each other," Markgraff directed. "I want every man to promise me that he'll stick with it until it's safely delivered. You'll find the address on top. What you have there, if you deliver it to my friend Professor MacDonald at the coast, is more precious than gold. You won't fail? I can assure you that you'll be rewarded."

They promised him because he was a dying man and they respected him. His personality had held them together when, a score of times, with the jungle's vast monotony eating into them, they might have quarreled fatally.

Then Markgraff had smiled at them, and died. He did it quietly, as he did all things—this elderly scientist, this man who'd bound them to him by ties of intangible strength. They buried him in the heart of the jungle, baring their heads, and Barry, the student, spoke brief, remembered words of committal. Even as the clods fell, the jungle loomed larger, more menacing. Each man felt a shrinking of his own stature, a terrible aloneness, a doubt of his fellows, a suspicion that, with Markgraff gone, it would be every man for himself.

They were a curious assortment: Barry, the spectacled student; McCready, the big Irish cook; Johnson, the down-and-out, the bum Markgraff had enticed out of a water-front tavern to follow him; and Jim Sykes, the sailor, who talked a lot about home but never went there.

Sykes had the compass and map, which, when they stopped to rest, he would get out and study. He put a stubby finger on it and said, "There's where we've got to get to." It looked easy—on the map . . .

The jungle deepened about them. They missed Markgraff, who no longer could encourage them with an optimism that was usually justified, who could find in an almost impenetrable tangle some logic for going forward. At first they talked with each other, the sound of their voices important to them. . . . Soon speech became only anathema against the weight they carried, toting Markgraff's box through the forest. . . . Then silence fell on them, and something worse than silence.

Longing for his water-front tavern as a parched soul in Inferno might yearn for water, Johnson began to find that sudden ways opened to him, on the right hand or the left, tempting him. McCready's face grew sullen and dark; he kept repeating, "I'm goin' my own way. I'm not traveling with this outfit any more. I guess I've got the guts to make it." And he would cast a brooding, speculative eye on the map to which Sykes, the sailor, clung.

As for Sykes, he developed a closed-in horror of this jungle, this high-walled man-trap. He wanted the sea. He demanded horizons. He mumbled about it in his sleep, and by day he cursed the death that lay where grotesque insects and deadly reptiles waited for the unwary. He spoke of his home, and how for years he'd meant to get back to the missus and kids— and now never would.

Barry, the student, said little, but there was a girl of whom he was thinking. He'd lie sleepless, tormented by insects, tormented by a face that at times, like the faces of those dear to us, refused at this distance to come clearly. To think of her was to think of a campus, green with spring and russet with autumn; of a sports field, and classrooms, and a library; of dances and moonlit walks, and a sweet, tearing moment of good-by.

Sometimes one or another of them would pray—call out in a way that the insensitive might think was cursing: He had made this fierce jungle, these incredible trees, these flowers, so large that they seemed to reduce man to a pigmy. But the mind cannot quarrel with Nature successfully; so it turns on its own kind. There had been bickerings and quarrels even when Markgraff was with them, but his personality, and his cause, which was their cause, had muted the quarrels.

Now, there was only Markgraff's box, growing heavier as their strength grew less. It was real—when everything else had become a mental haze. It held their bodies when their minds rebelled. It chained them when they would have split apart. Turn and turn about—this routine held them; two men alone would long since have abandoned the precious thing.

They hated it as a prisoner hates his chains, but they carried it as they'd promised Markgraff they would.

They watched each other, covertly, lest any come near the sacred thing except to lift and bear it another torturing mile.

Then came a day when—suddenly—as by a miracle—the walls of the forest opened.

"Glory!" Sykes cried. "We made it." He took out the map, and, putting his cracked lips to it, he kissed it.

"Yes," Johnson breathed, his eyes queer, and no quarrel now on his lips. He even slapped McCready, the cook, on the back and they laughed with strange hysterical laughter. . . .

When they lifted their load again, it seemed lighter, but only for a while. They were weak now, because safety was in sight, and their job all but done. But eventually the four of them bore it up a street, while natives and a few whites stared at them. All four men now were staggering with exhaustion.

All they asked was to deliver it, and have done.

And yet, when they asked for a Professor MacDonald and found him to be a withered man in a greasy white suit, there was a triumph in them for a moment rising above their personal emotions, the glory of a thing shared.

When they'd rested, Professor MacDonald gave them food, and they told him of Markgraff, of his death, and of their promise to him.

It was Johnson who, running his tongue thirstily across his lips, spoke of the reward.

The old man spread his hands in a gesture of inadequacy. "I have nothing," he said, "not a thing to reward you with except my thanks. Markgraff was my friend. He was a clever man. He was more than clever, he was a good man. You have kept faith with what he asked you. I can only thank you."

Derisively Johnson stared at him. "In the box," he said hoarsely. "In the box."

"The box," echoed Sykes eagerly.

"Now—you're talking," McCready said.

"Open it," they demanded. They put their joint strength to it, prying off layer after layer. McCready began to curse. "All that weight, all that damned carrying," he complained, and Johnson said, "Wood, and more damned wood. What kind of a joke is that?"

But Sykes said, "Something is there. I heard it rattle. I heard it when we walked. Look, you're through to it." They all drew close, their minds leaping, remembering the substances which science had unearthed and harnessed, beyond money and beyond price; they stared at the old man when he took the loose bits of rock in his hands, and let them drop. "Worthless," he said, puzzled, trying to feel his way into Markgraff's mind.

"Worthless!" said Sykes dully.

Then McCready, the cook, exploded. "I always thought that guy was nuts. Telling us what was in the box was worth more'n gold."

"No," Barry said quickly. "I remember his exact words. What he told us was 'What you have there, if you deliver it to my friend Professor MacDonald at the coast, is more precious than gold.' "

"So what?" shouted McCready, angry disappointment in his eyes.

"Yeah, so what?" echoed Jim Sykes, the sailor. "I could do with some ruddy gold for the missus and kids, and myself."

Johnson just ran his tongue thirstily along his dry lips.

Barry looked at them all: at McCready, the big Irish cook; at Sykes, the sailor, who might some day go home to his missus and kids; at Johnson, the water-front bum.

Then, he thought of a campus green with spring, and a girl who waited; he thought of the jungle from which they had come—the green hell in which many a man, wandering alone, was now only a heap of whitened bones; and he thought of the dogged resolution which had made four men fight through together to keep a promise, four men held together only by this common cause. This had been Markgraff's gift to them.

"He said we'd be rewarded," Johnson whined. "I heard him say it, myself. Now what do we get out of it?"

Barry turned on him, quickly. "Our lives," he said. "That's what we get—our lives—for what they are worth."

STEWART BEACH

How to Write a Short-Short Story

Even though you never intend to try your hand at fiction, we think this essay will increase your reading enjoyment of short-short stories. And if you are a mildly discouraged writer, it may clear up some of the reasons why your manuscripts come back with discouraging little slips which begin, "The Editors regret . . ." But read it and see. Good luck!

THE SIMPLEST WAY to think of a short-short is as a brief short story. In length it can be anything from, say, a thousand to two thousand words, as compared to the five or six thousand that an average full-length "short story" runs in today's magazines. Except for this matter of length, there is no separate pattern which marks the short-short as different in form from the short story. The structure is almost identical, and in the comments which follow I have made no attempt to differentiate between the two, except in making occasional specialized points. I have used the label "short-short," but most of the technique described applies equally to the short story.

What distinguishes a short-short chiefly from the full-length short story is first of all length and then the simplicity of its theme. To be successful it must deal with a strong emotional situation which can be developed without elaborate complication, flashback and exposition. It must be the kind of idea which can be roundly told in a thousand to two thousand words. But the bigger, the more novel or striking the idea, the greater the story's impact is bound to be. The short-short is small in size but it is at its exciting best when it reaches for the grandeur of human emotion.

One thing the short-short is *not* is the character sketch or piece of mood writing in which the author plays with people and emotions, exposes them to the reader's observation and judgment, but tells no story. Such literary pieces may be moving and beautiful, but it is not the writer's purpose to tell a story. Through his writing skill and insight into human nature, he is painting a dramatic picture in words.

He lifts the curtain on a situation involving one character or several, creating a mood out of what is said and done and thought within a certain space of time. When the piece is finished, the characters have moved from here to there. But there has been no ending to the situation which the author exposed when he lifted the curtain. The characters are left in suspension—wiser, perhaps, but no nearer a resolution of their problems.

With the author of the short-short, on the other hand, the story itself is the primary ingredient. It goes without saying that his narrative will have style, will be told skillfully with sure insight into the characters he portrays. But however great the beauty with which he tells his tale, he never permits the writing itself to impede the flow of the action. His story moves swiftly. He never lingers over a piece of lush description for its own sake. He never spins out a witty passage of dialogue beyond its dramatic usefulness to the development of the story.

It would be nonsense to suggest that there is a set of rules for writing a short-short in the sense that there are rules, say, for constructing a sonnet. Except that it must have plot, I know of no other rule for the short-short. But there is a structural pattern which every successful writer knows and follows. It is not a rigid pattern. Plenty of deviations will be found in any collection of short-shorts. But this basic method, growing out of the logic of experience, represents the way a short-short is constructed to get the utmost in dramatic satisfaction from the raw material of the original idea.

A great short story is a combination of inspiration, talent

and a sure knowledge of the craftsmanship which brings its idea to life. In a great story, the pattern is never apparent. The action flows over it effortlessly, and the characters move inside it with apparent freedom. But the pattern is there, nevertheless. It is the framework which keeps the story taut and irresistible. It is the writer's guide to what he is doing. Once he knows the pattern instinctively he may judge for himself when a departure is justified by the effect he wishes to achieve.

The pattern of the short-short is simply the natural way of telling any story—in conversation or on paper. Its basis is the classic beginning, middle and ending—the secret of good storytelling since Homer.

The beginning promises to tell what happened to a certain interesting individual at a point of high crisis in his life. He must be interesting, or no one will care what happened to him. The crisis must seem important, or the audience will be quickly bored. The beginning reveals the problem which this crisis has presented to the individual who now becomes the story's chief character. It shows what sort of fellow he is. It introduces at least the more important minor characters and provides the audience with all the preliminary facts needed to understand this original situation. And that is the end of the beginning.

The middle part of the story shows the chief character struggling to solve his problem through various courses of action. Each experience is a greater test of his determination. Finally, he sees that there is one course open which will solve his problem once and for all. He may not succeed but even if he fails he will have disposed of his problem by the very means of his defeat. He decides to risk everything on this move. This is the climax of the story and the end of the middle.

Now comes the ending, swift moving with the conclusive action which flows out of the chief character's decision. The reader learns the answer to all the questions which have bothered the chief character through the story. The problem is solved. Through the action in the ending it has simply ceased to exist.

This is the basic pattern of every successful short-short. It makes no difference whether it is a tender romance or a tough murder story. The method of construction is the same.

The logic of this is based deep in the writer-reader relation which takes place when a person looks at the first paragraphs of a story in a book or magazine. The writer announces that he has a tale to tell. The reader is receptive. But what catches the reader's attention is the reality of a person (the chief character) faced by a problem which he must solve. It is the prospect of this personal conflict, this struggle, which engages the reader's interest. However exciting or perilous the incidents through which his quest for solution leads the chief character, it is not these incidents themselves which hold the reader. It is watching a human being as he struggles through them. As the reader identifies himself vicariously with the chief character, he experiences himself some of the emotional drama the author has put into his story. It is as simple as that.

To produce a successful short-short, two qualities must be present in the writer. First, he must possess the developed talent of using words dramatically. This talent can be assisted by study, practice and, to a certain extent, instruction. But unless the talent is there to begin with—a sensitive imagination which can conceive a story, plus a sure ear for dialogue and the rhythm of dramatic narrative—no amount of study, practice or instruction will produce a writer. Good writing, like painting, sculpture, music, is an art which some find they possess and others search for in vain. Unless the talent appears fairly quickly under determined practice, an aspirant must conclude sadly that it is not part of him.

The second quality a writer must possess is a sound knowledge of how to use his talent, once he has discovered it. In the short-short, this means a sure understanding of construction, or the talent will never be developed to its ultimate effectiveness. Learning to build a short-short so that it catches fire quickly in the reader's mind and flows with absorbing movement to its conclusion is the technique, the art, of writing short fiction.

It has been my experience that people who have been reading short stories for years have never stopped to consider what makes the good ones tick. That is no great handicap to the enjoyment of anyone who simply reads stories. But it is instantly fatal to the person who tries to write them. So let's examine the fundamentals.

A short-short represents the struggle of a single individual to accomplish some purpose, to solve some problem, that is of supreme importance in his life. *Importance* is a vital ingredient. There must be an urgency about this individual's problem which the reader feels and believes in. Otherwise, the beginning will fail to catch his interest. He simply will not read the story.

A writer, immersed in his own narrative, is inclined to feel that any reader must share his own interest in the theme he is developing. And he is just as wrong as he can be. The immediate appeal of the chief character as a likable person, the nature and the importance of his problem, together with the style and skill with which the author presents them in his opening paragraphs, are the essentials which persuade the reader that here is something he likes and wants to hear more of. And they were also the qualities which made an editor feel when *he* began the story that this was a manuscript with promise.

To the fact that a story represents the struggle, or conflict, of one individual, add now that it is normally told through the eyes and other senses of this individual whom the writer has selected as the chief character. Throughout the story the point of view does not shift to any of the minor characters.

The logic of this is readily apparent, once it is understood that the story's interest rises out of the chief character and his problem. The story proposes to show this chief character in his struggle to solve a problem of vital importance in his life. The action will show him undergoing a succession of tests. Once the point of view is changed to another character— even though it is someone as close to him as his wife—the writer has begun to tell another story: the story of a different character. The original story line has been broken and another substituted for it. Interest drops while the reader adjusts his own approach to the story.

The unified point of view means that your reader sees all the action through the mind of the chief character. He sees everything the chief character sees; he knows the chief character's thoughts. He is always inside his mind, and in this way he identifies himself with the chief character's thoughts and actions. He understands why he thinks and acts as he does, even though he doesn't always agree with him. He always has *sympathy* for him.

The unified point of view most frequently produces the kind of story in which the reader is never conscious of the writing or of the writer. The story seems actually to be happening as he reads. The author uses the third person in his narration. He never injects himself into the story with editorial comments or asides. The reader is aware only of the characters and the action—never that this is a tale which is being told. To all intents and purposes, it could be a motion picture in words which requires no narrator. Most magazine fiction today follows this method.

But sometimes it may seem more effective to the author to write in the first person—to have a recognizable "I" tell the story. This requires no sacrifice of the unified point of view, and there are two principal methods by which it is done.

In the first, the narrator—the "I" of the story—simply becomes its chief character. The reader sees all the action through his eyes. And since the "I" is very much involved in the outcome of the story and plays a principal part in its development, the reader has, again, the feeling that the story is happening as he reads. The method of construction is exactly the same as with the impersonal third-person narration.

The second type of first-person narration is much more the armchair variety. The reader has the sense that a gifted storyteller is spinning out a tale. The author creates a fictional "I" to be the narrator, gives him personality and involves him personally in the events of the action, but usually as a sympathetic observer as much as a participant. The entire story is told as the narrator—the "I"—saw it unfold, but the crisis is usually a crisis in the life of others. The point of view is the narrator's. He describes characters and events as they came under his observation. He may guess at the motives of others, but the point of view does not shift from him to one of the other characters. The narrator, in other words, is still the chief character for purposes of the story's construction, even though he remains more of an observer than the person who actually motivates the action.

The simplest illustration of this unified point of view is the detective story in which the chief character is the detective himself—his problem, the solution of a crime. The reader follows the detective as he works on the case; he acquires the same information; he examines the clues. But if the point of view were shifted suddenly to the criminal the detective is seeking, the illusion of the chase would be lost. The reader would no longer be following the struggle of one man to solve a problem. The tension of the story would be broken.

Use of the unified point of view places certain responsibilities on the author. He must report faithfully everything the chief character knows which is relevant to the story. Conversely, he must never conceal anything the chief character knows for the purpose of contriving a surprise ending.

I remember a story once which concerned a spirited and rather puzzling conversation between a psychiatrist and a woman guest at a dinner party. The ending revealed that the woman was his estranged wife—and that was all! Why the writer should have thought there was great satisfaction for the reader in this discovery I shall never know. The entire conversation is a cheat, for the reader does not know the identity of the woman, though the chief character does. The reader can feel only that he has been deliberately fooled.

There is this further ingredient in the original conception of a story: The chief character should possess a *governing characteristic* which controls and complicates his struggle. Individuals react differently to situations, depending on the kind of people they are. The chief character is a very individual person, and his reactions are based on the fact that (for the purposes of this story) he has one governing characteristic. It is a simplification, a distillation, of the kind of man he is.

It may be that he is shy, which makes it incredibly difficult for him to approach a sophisticated creature he loves. It may be that he is chivalrous, which makes him blind to the crass motives of a man who is trying to cheat him. This characteristic will govern his acts throughout the story. In fact, it is almost the reason there *is* a story.

Once this governing characteristic is introduced, it follows that the chief character's decisions and actions are motivated by it throughout the story. If a man is generous, the climax of the story should turn on his generosity—or flow from the ironical fact that in this one instance when he was *not* generous he made a mistake—which shapes the ending of the story. In either case, his generosity is the motivation.

To sum up, these are the fundamentals of the short-short:

1. It shows the struggle of the chief character to solve a problem of vital importance in his life. His struggle to solve it means that he will be in conflict throughout the story.

2. A governing characteristic shapes his decisions and his actions at all times.

3. The point of view is always that of the chief character. The reader sees the action develop through the chief character's eyes and thoughts.

THE STORY IDEA: Once a man understands what a short-short is and how to go about constructing it, he is ready to search for a suitable theme or *story idea*. And in this, a writer is entirely on his own. No one can guide him in finding the dramatic circumstances from which a successful short-short is born. What will appeal to me as having all the ingredients of high drama may not appeal to *you*.

And that, I suppose, is where inspiration enters. There is a certain amount of inspiration in the genesis of every story idea. Something clicks in the writer's mind, and a story has been born. How good it will be when it is finished depends on the writer's talent, his technique and the quality of the idea itself. But the story is there now for the constructing.

What suggested the idea in the first place? That is not always easy to establish. Of course, any skilled writer can sit down at his typewriter and, out of his knowledge of essential ingredients, manufacture a story. But the chances are that it will never rise very far off the ground. No, there must be that breath of inspiration, that inner urging to produce something memorable.

It may be a snatch of overheard conversation, a rhythm of words that keeps repeating itself insistently till it possesses dramatic meaning, a lonely cottage on a headland overlooking the sea, the vivid impression of a face seen in a crowd. But it is *something* which mixes itself with other experiences stored up in the writer's mind and starts a story flowing.

Or it may be some real incident which the writer has seen or has read about in a newspaper, some situation or character in the town where the writer lives that suggests his story. Some writers keep extensive notebooks or card catalogues in which they store away bits of description, of characterization or incidents that some day might work themselves into a still unplanned story. Others depend on the inspiration of the moment. There is no best way to do it. For writers are individuals with governing characteristics, too.

Once, when I was sitting at home alone listening to Beethoven's *Sixth Symphony* on the record-player, an entire story came to me out of the music. It had nothing to do with Beethoven, though it did have a musical background. The characters, the plot, the whole structure of the story were complete in mind before the last record was finished. I wrote the story in less than a week.

Of course, I tried to induce fiction through music again, but the charm had gone. I shall never know how themes out of Beethoven could have inspired a totally unrelated theme in fiction.

DEVELOPING THE STORY IDEA: Story ideas rarely suggest themselves as completely as in the fortunate circumstance I have just described. Usually they are fragments—a character, a situation, even an ending for which the story itself must be found. Two things must happen now. First, the writer must draw up his cast of characters, select the chief character, the minor characters and develop in his mind the living, talking individuals they are to become. Second, he must begin to construct the plot.

CHOOSING THE CHIEF CHARACTER: When a writer starts working over the bare materials of a story idea, it is not always immediately apparent which character is to be the most important. But the test is quite simple. Since conflict must always be present, the person to whom the situation presents the greatest conflict inevitably becomes the chief character.

A standard romantic situation will serve as illustration. Let's go back to the shy young man who has fallen in love with a beautiful and sophisticated creature—object, matrimony. His problem is not only to capture her affections but

to force himself, because of his shyness (the governing characteristic) to take the necessary steps to attract her attention.
Throughout most of the story, presumably, the sophisticated
creature is to brush his efforts aside. There is no conflict for
her. But there is continuous conflict for the shy young man.
Therefore, he becomes the chief character.

This is a useful point to make, since the story might have
suggested itself first to the writer in the person of the girl.
If the writer had not analyzed his materials carefully, he
might have become bemused by her attitude of indifference
to the shy young man, not realizing that, however amusing
he might make her indifference, there was no conflict. The
result would be a static story.

For the girl to become the chief character in this situation,
there must be an entirely different motivation. She must
become the pursuer, reluctantly attracted at first, then piqued
because the young man pays her no attention, then determined that she will make him fall in love with her. In this
case, the story has been entirely turned around. Either approach might produce a pleasant enough light story. But
they are two entirely *different* stories.

THE PLOT: Once the writer has his chief character and
minor characters established he is ready to proceed with the
plot. The plot is the *plan* of a specific story, whereas the
pattern is the general structure which applies to all plotted
fiction. The plot is the original situation, plus the sequence
of scenes (and the action within each) by which a story moves.

The ideal way to construct a plot is to outline it on paper.
Divide it first into the three component parts of beginning,
middle and ending. Then subdivide it in terms of its scenes
and what happens in each. Each scene should represent a
step by the chief character toward the solution of his problem—a test of his determination. There should be no static
scenes in which people just talk without advancing the story's
development. Of course, people meet and talk in short-shorts,

but there should be a development in their relationship to each other within the scene itself. In fact, their relation should have altered in some way as a result of the encounter. To exaggerate in order to drive the point home, if two people meet in friendship, they should part in anger.

As the scenes progress, there should be a mounting tension in the tests the chief character meets, and a parallel mounting doubt in the reader's mind that he will solve his problem at all. In this process lie the mechanics of suspense.

SUSPENSE: Suspense is usually associated with stories of tense excitement—the secret agent, pursued by secret police through the darkened streets of some Iron Curtain town. And such stories quite definitely generate suspense. But the suspense is *within the reader*, not in the events themselves. Suspense is a feeling—of uncertainty, of anxiety. In fiction it is the reader's uncertainty, his active doubt that the chief character will come through the successive tests and solve his problem at last. The reader's anxiety is constantly raised as the tests become more and more trying. By this means the writer carries the absorbed reader eagerly to the story's end.

Of course, the stimulation of suspense is far easier in a story of secret agents than it is in a story of family life. But the mechanics are the same. It is almost more important to plot carefully in a quiet story than in one whose scenes explode with shots in the night. Secret agents have an exterior excitement of their own. In a quiet story, the writer must make sure that he is supplying the necessary ingredient of increasing emotional tension.

With this brief analysis of plot and its corollary, suspense, let's go back to the story pattern and consider its three basic parts, beginning, middle and ending, in a little more detail.

THE BEGINNING: Think of a play: When the first-act curtain rises, the playwright must make his audience acquainted as quickly and as naturally as possible with the situation and the actors. The speeches in the early minutes are all calculated to serve this purpose. They are exposition. Once the playwright has his exposition out of the way, the play moves forward with the audience in confident grasp of the situation.

The beginning of a short-short serves this same purpose. When he begins a story, the reader has no idea of its theme and characters. It is the author's task to inform him immediately so that he will be prepared to understand and enjoy the action that follows.

The writer should introduce the chief character first, so the reader's interest will focus on him immediately. He should dramatize his problem in the shortest possible space. He should display the governing characteristic, sketch in the crisis which the story is to portray in detail. Minor characters are introduced. (All the characters in a story with the exception of the chief character are minor characters. Even the sophisticated creature our shy young man was persuading to matrimony is a minor character, though the principal minor character in the story.) If there is need for flashback to explain the background, it should appear in the beginning, with any other exposition that is necessary. When the beginning is finished, everything should be cleared away so that the chief character can embark on the various tests by which he will solve his problem.

THE MIDDLE: The tests begin immediately. The chief character is determined now to force a solution to his problem. He tries again and again, with each test more severe than the last—till he sees the action he can take which is bound to dispose of the problem. It is crucial action. By taking it, he may lose all. Or he may solve the problem to his satisfaction. But it is the only action (he feels) which will solve this particular problem. He wavers. Then he decides that he must do it. He makes the climactic decision. So the middle part ends with the climax—on a high note of anticipation and anxiety (for the reader) over what may happen now.

The middle is usually the longest part of the story, though in a short-short it sometimes does not work out that way. (It always does in a full-length short story.) But a thorough plotting of the middle is one of the requirements of a successful short-short. One of the most frequent causes of failure I have observed in reading some thousands of short-short manuscripts is that they are often composed of an original situation (promising) but are completely lacking in a middle. The characters merely "run in place" for a page or two until the time comes for the author to explode his surprise ending.

Nothing loses interest quite as quickly as a short-short which isn't going anywhere except to a so-called surprise ending with "surprise, surprise" telegraphed so hard through a lifeless middle that the reader either throws the story aside in disgust or skips forward to the "surprise" he has been warned to expect.

A proper surprise comes when the reader is so absorbed in the action of a story that he is quite unprepared for the ending. It is a genuine surprise. But all too often the ineptness of the writer gives the impression that the characters, by their inaction, are just waiting in the wings for their "curtains-aside" surprise. The surprise ending is a wonderfully satisfying thing when it comes off. But I am sure it has spoiled more stories than it has helped.

THE ENDING: The ending begins as events flow from the chief character's climactic decision. Throughout the story he has forced the action. Everything that happened was caused by his own decisions. But the action which results from his climactic decision is often out of his own hands. He no longer controls it because he has deliberately taken a step whose outcome depends on the reaction of others. Nevertheless, the ending grows directly out of what he has done. It would not have happened without his decision and his action. So, in a sense, he *has* motivated it, though he cannot always govern what will happen. He has been driven to a point of desperation which required him to act. The ending is the result of that action.

One further point of great importance about the short-short becomes apparent in the ending. Now that the crisis has passed, some permanent change has taken place in the chief character because of the experience he has been through. His life has been altered. This change grows naturally out of the requirement that the crisis shall be an important one in itself. If nothing vital hangs on it, then the story, however briefly entertaining, seems trivial. It lacks the quality which produces a truly memorable story.

CHECK LIST FOR WRITERS

HERE ARE A number of points to consider when you have a story idea and begin to work it out. They have not seemed to fit easily into the general discussion and are noted separately here.

1. Don't write stories about dreary people in dreary situations, unless something in the very dreariness makes them interesting. As a test of this, would you tell your friends the story in conversation and expect them to be fascinated? There is a quite bogus literary feeling that drabness in itself is dramatic. Too often writers become bemused with such "literary" situations which require a "literary" response among readers to acquire any audience. A story based on such an idea has only the smallest chance of selling to any magazine of wide circulation.

2. Individualize every character quickly with some characteristic which lets your reader see him—and repeat it. He "rubs his nose thoughtfully"; she "laughs gaily"; he "speaks quickly and runs his words together." This device lets your reader see the people.

3. In writing dialogue, keep the attention of the reader focused on the people as they talk as well as on their words. Do not write solid dialogue. Break it up. Like this:

"Darling," he said eagerly, leaning across the table. "This new job is going to take us places."

She saw his eyes catch fire and turned away because they had kindled no spark in her. "That's what I was afraid of," she said quietly, and was aware of the hurt she had given.

4. Does your story contain a flashback? Then put it in when the character is naturally in repose. Do not have him pass his life in review as he is raising the garage door. Wait till he is seated in the living room looking into the fire.

5. Beware of writing a story based on some sequence of

events a good friend tells you. Memories are tricky things. Your good friend may quite honestly tell you something as having happened to a friend of his. But the fact may be that *he* got it second-hand from another friend who had read it in an old copy of a magazine and had forgotten the source. If you use it, you may be innocently guilty of plagiarism. Always make sure of the origin of your story ideas. The best insurance is that they were born within *you*.

6. If you decide to write a story inspired by some real occurrence, use the facts as basic materials and do not be encumbered by them. Change them completely in developing your story, if that makes the story better. There is no greater delusion than that a story based on truth is interesting. Fiction has a truth of its own. For some odd reason, to say that it is based on truth destroys the truth of the fiction.

7. To tell a short-short in the first person places special handicaps on a story. My own experience has been that first-person narration is best only when it is used to tell a "strange and wonderful" tale. It is never good in telling a routine one. It is at its most awkward in the romance, for the "I" of the story can hardly insist on himself as an attractive and irresistible person. I would reserve first-person narration for stories in which the narrator is telling, as a good story-teller might tell after dinner, an absorbing tale from far places. (I have always had an aversion to first-person stories told by a woman author when the narrator was a man, or vice versa. This is a personal thing, and I don't know whether it affects all readers in the same way.)

8. *Style*: The short-short lives with *style*. In this brief story, the excitement of the writing in the first few paragraphs is the difference between success and failure. Unless the reader's interest is immediately caught, he will not read on. The short-short *moves* with style, too. Without intruding as a conscious literary device, the style of the early paragraphs of a story will give it excitement or dull a reader's interest. The style should be brisk, fresh, interesting, without the

literary ornamentation which would ever make it appear self-conscious. Here, again, the writer is on his own. No one can teach him style. That is his affair. But without an ear for it, he will have a hard time making the short-short his daily bread.

9. *Mood*: Style is also important in setting the *mood* of a story. A tale of tense, dramatic action has a tightness in the writing which will accentuate the danger lurking in the scenes it describes. A romantic story, on the other hand, dances with an airiness which lights the mood of young lovers. To achieve these different moods in writing is as precise a study as the orchestration of a symphony. It is not only the characters and the action which the author must set down. He must set them down in the *mood* which displays them in their dramatic fullness. Once more, this is something the writer must play by ear. A teacher can tell him that he is out of tune—and where. But the writer himself must find the pitch.

10. *Humor*: Of all the types of fiction, humor is most difficult to define. But here style must go hand in hand with mood to create laughter. Think of the funniest story you know. It is really funny only in terms of a man who knows how to tell a funny story superbly. And he tells it superbly only because he loves humor and finds a good story irresistible. So, if you want to write humor, you must acquire that same sense of making a story irresistibly funny by the way it is told. Remember, it is not only the substance of the story itself that is funny. *It is the way it is told.*

In Conclusion: There is an old saying that writing is the only art in which there are no amateurs. And this is so true. You can have a great deal of satisfaction playing a piano for your own enjoyment. You can paint with no idea of selling a single canvas. But when you write stories, you must sell them or there is no satisfaction. The excitement goes out of it. The inspiration is dead.

Writing fiction rises out of the urge to communicate emotional, dramatic experiences, shaped from the author's imagination. But the urge develops only with discipline—and practice. Trial and error and further experiment provide the confidence with which a writer pursues his art to fulfillment.

The purpose of this essay has been to set down what the trial and error of thousands of writers (and tens of thousands of stories) have shown to be the logical pattern of story construction. I hope it may save new writers from losing heart through unrealized mistakes. But at its best it should provide the writer with a guide by which he can analyze stories critically and judge their merits. He will detect not only the mistakes of others. With a little detachment, he may find the structural flaws in his own.

GLOSSARY OF SPECIAL TERMS

Pattern. The general plan, or technique, by which short-shorts are constructed.

Plot. The plan and scene-sequence of a specific short-short.

Story Idea. The original conception or inspiration from which the writer will work his materials into a finished short-short.

Scene. The action which takes place in a single setting with a single set of characters. If different action begins with the entrance or exit of a character. Then a new scene begins.

Chief Character. The central figure in a short-short, through whose eyes and other senses the reader sees the story unfold.

Minor Character. Any of the other characters in a short-short, no matter how important to the action.

Governing Characteristic. The particular quality of the chief character which shapes his actions throughout a short-short.

Unified Point of View. The method of short-short construction by which all action is viewed through the eyes of a single character.

Problem. Dilemma faced by the chief character. Its solution provides the plot of the short-short.

Conflict. The constant struggle of the chief character to solve his problem which provides the driving force of the action.

Exposition. Explanatory information about characters and situation which the reader must know in order to understand the story.

Climactic Decision. The determination of the chief character to take a certain action which will solve his problem.

Suspense. The feeling of doubt generated in the reader that the chief character will succeed in his purpose. More apparent in stories of exciting action, but it is a part of every successful short-short.

Flashback. A scene of past action, relived dramatically and actively in the mind of the chief character.

Dialogue. Conversation between two or more characters.

LEE ROGOW

That Certain Flavor

The Editor's Analysis of "That Certain Flavor," by Lee Rogow. The numbers beside the text refer to similar numbers in the analysis which follows.

THE BEGINNING

1 Polly Kingsley had a kitchen range with an array of dials and controls like the instrument panel of a Lockheed Constellation. Polly Kingsley had a card index of tested recipes as big as a radio writer's gag file. Polly Kingsley had the assistant manager of Holschweig's butcher shop in thrall; no woman in Manhattan's middle Seventies ever got such cuts of meat, or had them weighed with the butcher's hands so scrupulously behind his back.

2 Polly Kingsley had all these things, and she also had a husband who had liked his mother's cooking.

3 Each evening Larry Kingsley would come home from the industrial designing office where he worked and kiss Polly very thoroughly and satisfactorily. Then he would go into the bathroom and wash his good-looking mug, making sounds in there as if he were wrestling an octopus. He would emerge from the bathroom with his face shining, seat himself at the dinner table, and look hopefully at the door of the kitchen.

In a few moments Polly would appear with his dinner, over which she had spent from one to three hours of her afternoon. Sometimes she would present Larry with lamb chops, broiled to the split-second of perfection on the Stove of Tomorrow. Sometimes the

3

feature would be stuffed peppers, oozing succulent rice and savory meat. Sometimes she devised salads, with mounds of tuna fish which somehow managed to be creamy and flaky at the same time.

One typical evening, in the eighth month of their marriage, Polly served her lord and master a stew, with big chunks of beef swimming in rich gravy, and golden carrot rings peeping hopefully from behind enormous mushrooms. She placed it on the table before her man and watched him, her hazel eyes serious and intent, her fresh skin flushed with cooking and concentration.

4

Larry spooned a generous portion onto his plate, speared a piece of beef, and lifted it to his mouth.

"How is it?" asked Polly.

"Pretty good," said Larry.

"Only pretty good?"

"I mean it's wonderful."

"How wonderful?"

"If you served it to a maharajah, he'd probably send you around a trunkful of rubies in the morning."

"Is that all?"

"Oh, darling, do we have to go through that again?"

"Yes," said Polly. "We have to go through that again."

"Look," said Larry, "you wouldn't respect me if I told lies, would you? I mean, it wouldn't be much of a marriage if a woman couldn't depend on her husband to be truthful in little things; would it? I mean, you want to respect me, don't you?"

"We can skip the acrobatics," said Polly. "You don't think the stew is as good as your mother's, do you?"

"Let me put it this way, dear heart," said Larry.

"It's good, extremely good. But Mother's things had a certain definite flavor that this lacks."

"I don't understand it," wailed Polly. "I buy the finest ingredients. I toil in the kitchen for hours. I have the latest equipment. What *could* that woman have done to food that I don't?"

"Search me," said Larry. "All I know is I haven't tasted food like hers since she died. Why don't we just skip it, dear? I like your cooking well enough. Cooks like Mother are a once-in-a-generation phenomenon, like Albert Einstein or Joe Louis."

"I won't forget it," said Polly. "I won't, I won't, I won't! I want to be the best thing for you that ever was. I can't stand it that anybody, even your sainted mother, should have done something better for you than I can."

"I'd be glad to say you've succeeded," said Larry, "but you want to be able to respect me, don't you?"

"Oh, eat your stew before it gets cold."

THE MIDDLE

And so it went for months. Polly spent more and more hours in the kitchen, basting, tasting, planning, experimenting with herbs and seasoning. Sometimes, as for example when a thunderstorm collapsed a soufflé, she cried tears of frustration, which would drop off her nose and sizzle into salty steam on the Stove of Tomorrow.

The food she produced would have tempted a strong-willed yogi to break a fast. Larry ate heartily, but he always insisted her productions lacked that certain definite flavor.

Polly grew morose. Once she even snapped at the assistant manager of Holschweig's meat market, who promptly overcharged her five cents a pound on a rib roast. Polly noticed, of course, but she was past caring.

6 {

When a woman's morale is at that low an ebb, what she needs more than anything else in the world is somebody to tell about it.

So when Polly met Min Frobisher coming out of the supermarket one afternoon, and Min said where had she been keeping herself, and Polly said she'd been working hard in the kitchen, and Min said she never thought Larry Kingsley was the sort of man who would make a household drudge of a woman, but you couldn't ever tell by appearances, could you, and Polly said it really wasn't Larry's fault, and Min said nonsense, Polly was just protecting him, and she wasn't due at the hairdresser's for forty-five minutes yet and why didn't they drop into the Town Lounge and have a cocktail and talk about it, and Polly said she wouldn't dare, she looked a perfect fright, and Min said not to be silly, she just wished a simple little daytime dress looked as well on her as it did on Polly, Polly said well, she really shouldn't, but seeing as how she saw Min so seldom, well, all right.

7 {

Polly Kingsley got home at twenty minutes after six with her hat on the side of her head, a box of spaghetti and a ten-cent can of tomato sauce under her arm, and a dangerous look in her eye. When she went into the bathroom to wash her face she noticed Larry's robe draped over the clothes hamper.

Wasn't that just like him, Polly thought. Min Frobisher was absolutely right. A woman was a fool to make a slave out of herself for a man who not only didn't appreciate it, but who figured ways to make extra work for her.

Polly was ferociously breaking the spaghetti into a pot of boiling water when Larry came in. "Hello, dear," said Larry. "I've been trying to get you on the phone all afternoon."

"I was out."

"Out where?"

"Just out. Would you like a minute-by-minute account of where I was?"

"Certainly not," said Larry, startled. He kissed her. Then he drew back and looked at her strangely.

"Cooking sherry," said Polly defiantly. "You have to taste it every so often to make sure it isn't going sour."

7 Polly slapped two settings down on the dinner table and went back into the kitchen. The flame under her saucepan had been up too high: the tomato sauce for the spaghetti had been scorched. Polly took a spoon and grimly scraped the burned mixture out of the pan and dumped it on the pale, stringy spaghetti. She kicked open the kitchen door and placed the platter on the table before her husband. Then she stood and watched him, her arms crossed.

THE ENDING

One word, she said to herself. Just let him speak one word. She'd put on her hat and go right over to Min Frobisher's. Min had a lawyer who had handled both her divorces and was simply wonderful on those things.

Larry twisted some of the spaghetti up on the fork and carried it to his mouth. Just let him say one word, said Polly to herself. One syllable, even.

8 Larry chewed silently for a moment. Then a strange expression came over his face.

"Polly!" he said. "Polly Kingsley!"

"Anything wrong?" she snarled.

"Wrong?" shouted Larry. "I don't know what you've done, genius girl, but this is *it*!"

"Hah?" said Polly.

"This spaghetti is just like Mother's!" said Larry.

8 {

"That flavor, it's all there!"

Polly blinked. Then she got her hat off the hall table, and went and put it in the closet. Then she went over and sat on her husband's lap and put her arms around his neck. She could fix herself a snack in the late afternoons, she decided, and burn Larry's food afterwards.

It would be a dirty trick to play on the Stove of Tomorrow, but it was little enough to do for the man she loved.

The Editor's Analysis of "That Certain Flavor"

THIS IS AN extremely light story but it is kept from seeming inconsequential because a very serious issue is involved—the permanence of a marriage. In another household, the situation which causes the crisis here might have produced only minor irritation. But because of the governing characteristic of Polly, the chief character, a problem arises between this wife and her husband which becomes a major conflict. This characteristic, of course, is Polly's pride in her superior cooking.

Both of these are essentially nice, pleasant people. In a light story, this is a necessary quality. The mood is one of fun, and if the reader doesn't like the characters he will hardly care what happens to them. Even when Polly's temper is tried to the utmost, she never commits an act or says angry words to her husband which would make a full reconciliation impossible. When the story ends with the solution of the problem, the reader can believe that Polly will have a full, happy life with her husband for the rest of her years.

Now for the detailed analysis. The numbers refer to numbered sections in the story.

1. Introduction of Polly, the chief character, with emphasis on the governing characteristic which is to motivate her actions throughout the story—her excellence as a cook and her preparation to delight her husband at every meal with such dishes as an epicure might dream of.

2. Statement of the story's theme and introduction of the problem which establishes the main conflict of the story. Polly encounters a complication in the very field where she had confidently expected to excel.

3. Introduction of the principal minor character, Larry, and a further development of Polly's excellence as a cook,

together with her pride in concocting delectable dishes for Larry's enjoyment. Notice that all the action is shown from Polly's point of view. When Larry enters, the focus never shifts to his eyes. The reader sees these scenes only as Polly sees them. He views Larry only through conversation and attitudes, aided by Polly's reactions.

4. A full development of the original situation, dramatically treated in a scene between Polly and Larry. All the exposition is taken care of in this scene. The reader knows what kind of people these are, as well as the conflict which has risen between them to cloud Polly's full satisfaction with her success as a wife. When Section 4 is finished, the reader is in possession of everything he needs to judge the future actions of the characters. So this becomes the end of the beginning. The question now is: How will Polly solve her problem?

5. The middle of the story opens with Polly striving determinedly to find a solution. She tries and tries, but each attempt ends in the same frustration till she is close to desperation. Finding that "certain definite flavor" Larry misses in her food has gone beyond being a simple challenge. It is now almost an obsession.

6. In this mood, she meets an old friend. Through their conversation she sees, for the first time, the need for putting an end to her frustration, whatever the cost. This marks a turn in the story, the beginning of the mood of determination which leads to her climactic act. Larry's attitude (under Min's prodding) has driven Polly to the point where, one way or the other, she is going to take action which will solve her problem with finality. Either Larry gives unqualified approval to the dishes she sets in front of him, or Polly intends to divorce him.

7. She goes home, not caring what Larry has for dinner. There is anger and contempt in her purchase of the box of spaghetti and ten-cent can of tomato sauce. There is tension and fury at Larry when he comes in (though Polly never

ceases to be an attractive person). Then comes the act which motivates the climax of the story. She burns the tomato sauce. Her climactic decision (the climax of the story) comes when she decides to give the dish to Larry even though, in her perfectionist mind, it has been ruined. Neither Polly nor the reader knows what will happen as a result of this action. Up to now, she has forced the action at every point. Now it is out of her hands. This is the end of the middle part of the story. The question now is: What will happen as the result of Polly's act?

8. The conclusion is swift. In Larry's delighted reaction to the burned tomato sauce, Polly learns what that certain definite flavor was which he had missed in his wife's cooking. Her frustration is over; the conflict which threatened her marriage has disappeared; the problem is solved. The story, therefore, is finished.

This is an almost perfect example of short-short construction. The story concentrates on a single, simple situation of vital importance to the chief character and on a problem which can be solved. Suspense is raised for the reader as he follows Polly through her various attempts to solve her problem. Because this is a light story, it is unnecessary to explore Polly's moods and emotions deeply. To go further than the author has would slow down the action and detract from the movement as well as—in all probability—give the story a sense of heaviness which would be out of place.

The writing is light, reflecting the mood of the story, but it is extremely skillful and filled with the sense of movement that gives it pace and crispness. There are no static scenes. The style is bright and rippling with just enough sense of being mannered to sustain the light-hearted mood.

About the Editor

STEWART BEACH, EXECUTIVE EDITOR of *This Week,* and in charge of selecting its fiction, has been an expert in the short story for many years. His real training began when he was an instructor in creative writing at New York University. Whatever profit students may have gained from his courses, he says he found his own teaching so persuasive that he became a successful short-story writer himself, and his fiction has appeared in most of the big magazines.

His most challenging association with short stories, Mr. Beach reports, is his present task of selecting them for *This Week,* the Sunday magazine which appears as part of thirty-three newspapers with a combined circulation of ten and a half million—the largest magazine audience in the world.

The roster of outstanding authors in this collection is proof that he has earned a reputation as the kind of creative and sympathetic editor who not only develops new talent but draws established writers to his magazine. With the exception of four years' Army service during World War II, in which he attained the rank of Colonel, Mr. Beach has spent his life as an editor and writer. He is the author of *Short Story Technique.*